Spanish C

SARAH MAY

Spanish City

❧❧

Chatto & Windus
LONDON

Published by Chatto & Windus 2002

2 4 6 8 10 9 7 5 3 1

Copyright © Sarah May 2002

First published in Great Britain in 2002 by
Chatto & Windus
Random House, 20 Vauxhall Bridge Road,
London SW1V 2SA

Random House Australia (Pty) Limited
20 Alfred Street, Milsons Point, Sydney,
New South Wales 2061, Australia

Random House New Zealand Limited
18 Poland Road, Glenfield,
Auckland 10, New Zealand

Random House South Africa (Pty) Limited
Endulini, 5A Jubilee Road, Parktown 2193, South Africa

Random House UK Limited Reg. No. 954009

A CIP catalogue record for this book is available from the British Library

ISBN 0 7011 7281 9

Papers used by Random House UK Limited are natural,
recyclable products made from wood grown in sustainable forests.
The manufacturing processes conform to the environmental
regulations of the country of origin.

Typeset in Bembo by SX Composing DTP, Rayleigh, Essex
Printed and bound in Great Britain by Mackays of Chatham PLC

To my father, and others, who have told me stories such as these

Acknowledgements

My thanks to Rebecca Carter at Chatto & Windus for her unflinching diligence, perseverance, powers of reason, and ability to judge.

My thanks, also, to Clare Alexander at Gillon Aitken Associates.

Contents

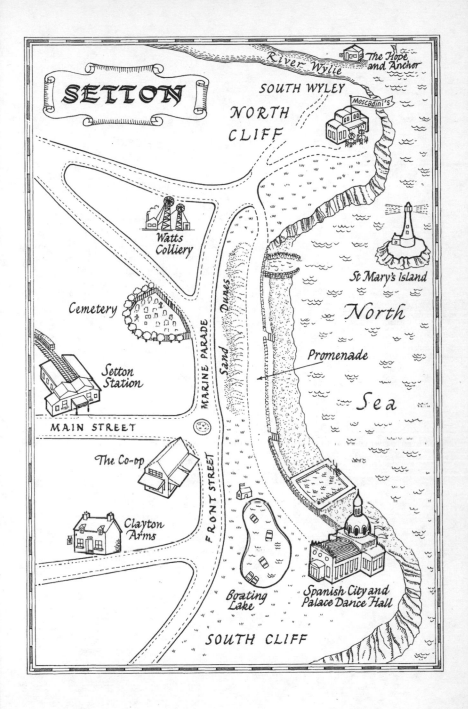

Amantes ut apes vitam mellitam exigent

Graffiti found on a wall in the House of Lovers, Pompeii

Prologue
Great Salt Lake, Utah,
Summer 1926

Mr Delaval and his only child's nursemaid were sitting opposite each other in a small blue boat in the middle of Utah. Every so often she would jerk suddenly as a brine fly bit her, something which set the boat rocking so badly that he had to grip its sides and stop rowing. Neither of them said anything. But he saw her eyes flickering, trying to detect the flies' approach, and after a while she even started to hit herself where they landed on her skin. She soon became so efficient at doing this that it wasn't long before he watched her inspect a small black smudge in her palm and mutter, 'Bastard' triumphantly. She looked intently at the water after she said this, trailing her hand in it with loose fingers and tight lips. In a matter of minutes she lifted her fingers out of the lake and put them into her mouth, giving them a quick curious suck. This made him glad, gladder than anything he could bring to mind right then.

'The lake water is eight and a half times saltier than sea water.'

She wiped her wet fingers across her dress and didn't say anything.

'You could fall asleep lying on your back in this water. That is to say, you wouldn't even need to will yourself not to drown.'

'I can swim, sir,' she said quietly, not looking at him, and emphasising the word 'can'.

He observed that he had offended her in some inexplicable way, and wanted to right matters. He pulled back hard on the oars and watched the spray from the lake pockmark her grey dress.

'Even if to drown was your intent, you wouldn't be able to. Not in these waters,' he said carefully.

She looked out over the sides of the boat and followed the lake's surface into the horizon. He had told her that there were salt flats to the west, which had once been the floor of a prehistoric lake, but she didn't understand these things, and couldn't tell, anyway, where the great lake ended and the desert began.

The air smelt rotten and there was no breeze, let alone a wind. It was stinking hot as well and although Mr Delaval had given her an outside thermometer reading earlier, she didn't need a number to tell her that her body was sweating out more salt water than she was floating in right then. Her hand went for the leather pouch round her waist, but he anticipated her, and in seconds was leaning forward, his cigarette case open, and the handles of the oars crushed against his belly.

She wanted to lie back and smoke his cigarette like she did her own on the beach at Setton on the odd Sunday afternoon she had off, but felt too ill at ease. In fact, she felt terrified. Terrified at finding herself alone in this boat with this man, surrounded by a landscape whose defining features had names she couldn't pronounce: the Oquirrh Mountains, Wasatch Range. Her hand shook as she accepted his light and then, when he went back to rowing and staring at the shore, she slipped her shoes off and swung her feet, still in their stockings, over the edge of the boat and into the water.

Mr Delaval had wished, when he picked her up from the Municipal Baths at Wasatch Springs, that she hadn't been wearing her uniform: the grey didn't suit her. He wondered if she had dressed in uniform on purpose. When she got into the car there was a yellowish rim around the top of her white collar, and the fabric under her arms and round her waist was dark grey.

He heard a slap as she hit at a brine fly on her neck, and turning towards her again saw that she was half lying, and that her legs were no longer in the boat, they were in the lake. Her shoes stood together, empty, at the bottom of the boat in a small pool of water. The leather would have salty tide marks when they dried, as would the leather of his boots. She had mannerisms instead of manners, he decided, watching as every now and then she lifted her eyes from the water to look at the sky, and the high dry ridges of the Oquirrh Mountains opposite them.

'You're not happy, Charleston,' he said at last.

She laughed sharply, and the cigarette fell out of her mouth. 'It's too big here.'

He took his hat off, laying it on the seat beside him, then rolled up his sleeves.

She watched the sleeves rise up the lower half of his arms, then turned towards the water again. The indistinct sounds of people enjoying themselves reached the small boat, but the bathing huts and striped canopies of the refreshment tents on the shore were just dots. Cheerful, and inconspicuous.

He wondered whether she wanted to be in the boat or not, and whether they could be seen from the shore. Not without binoculars, he guessed, and part of him hoped they could, all the same. Dropping the oar handles into his lap, he turned to look over his shoulder in the direction they were going.

'You can see it now,' he said, unable to hide the pleasure in his voice. The surprise, every time, at finding it still standing.

She looked up lazily from the surface of the lake. There ahead of them, standing on iron stilts so that it looked like a beast carrying its young on its back, was the pleasure palace known as the Spanish City.

Built at the water's edge so that it could be approached by land or water, as they were doing now, the Spanish City was walled, and had four towers, one on each corner. The iron pier stretching out into the lake was black, but the city on top was entirely white and moving slightly from side to side as if it were floating. There it was. That vast palace of pleasure he had alluded to, half spoken of, whose existence she had doubted. It was real.

'Do you want to get closer? We can get closer,' he said taking hold of the oars again.

She pulled her legs out of the water and put them back into the bottom of the boat, then picked up her shoes and held them in her lap. As Mr Delaval started to row again, more rhythmically now, she could hear the water against the side of the boat and the sound of screams, as well as music, coming from the Spanish City.

'The sounds we make when we lose consciousness, whether through pain or pleasure, are all the same.'

'There's dancing?' she said leaning forward, ignoring him.

He could hear the music as well, and looked at his watch, aware that he ought to be keeping time.

'All the time, any hour, day or night. The dance floor stretches as far as you can see in all directions.'

She held her shoes even more tightly, and at last a light wind from the Bonneville Salt Flats started to move across the water and over them, blowing salt into their eyes. There were even waves that began to rock the boat. Part of her wanted to stand up and announce her arrival in some way, but she stayed seated in the prow, clutching her sodden shoes whose laces were now stiff.

'Are we going there?' she said, anxious.

'If you want to,' he replied, watching her carefully again.

She didn't say anything, and he carried on rowing towards the floating palace until they started moving through the shadows cast over the water by the iron pier. Then they were close enough to see the name of the manufacturers welded into the structure's legs, and the date: 1893. The water went black as they sailed beneath the stilts supporting the city of pleasure, and they were in darkness.

4

The sounds that came to them were the booming of feet from the boards above, and dance music. She wondered if he had danced to that kind of music but couldn't quite see it somehow. Were they going dancing now? Then she saw the square of sunlight ahead, directly beneath the centre of the pier where it should have been darkest. As he rowed them into the sunlight she looked up and saw the sky crossed with what looked like miniature rail tracks.

He stopped rowing, only occasionally dipping one oar into the water so that the boat turned round in small circles.

'What is it?' she said, looking up hard at the construction, half expecting something to appear, or for it to fall.

He didn't answer immediately. 'It's somewhere people can come if they want to scream in public,' he said quietly, 'if they want to experience pleasure in public. Pleasure is about to experience a Golden Age.'

She thought about this for a while. It was as though he was talking about her rather than to her, and he still hadn't answered her question.

'What is it?' she said again.

One of the oars slipped out of his hand into the lake, but she didn't want to say anything. It stayed near the boat, moving backwards and forwards.

'A roller-coaster.'

'What do you do on a roller-coaster?'

'You ride it.'

She looked at the tracks again, but couldn't see where the pleasure lay.

'There used to be a switchback train here, like the one on Coney Island. A small gravity-powered train that rode in a wooden trough down a hill, then up the other side. Gravity,' he started then trailed off. 'Coney Island was created by a railway company who put a pleasure park at the end of their line to make sure that people would carry on travelling it. LaMarcus Thompson put the gravity switchback train there in 1884. The company charged five cents a ride, and made back its investment in one week.'

All this made him breathless, even though he wasn't rowing any more.

There seemed little point in his talk and she wasn't used to people speaking to her without reason. Usually they spoke to give orders. Here in this boat there was nothing to be done, and she didn't know what he expected her to do about what he was telling her. She supposed that the most she could do was to try and remember it.

'I'm here because a man called John Miller invented a device that holds the coaster train on to those tracks above us. This means more speed, more dips and dives. But mostly more speed. Things are going to be moving much faster from here on in. I wish I were John Miller. These are times for people with appetite.'

He leant forwards and looked at her after this.

It became clear that he thought she might have the answer. She didn't know what to say so looked down at the lake surface again. His words got her thinking all the same, about appetites, and she laid her hand neatly on her stomach, having always supposed that the only thing a body had an appetite for was food. This was all hers had the time and energy for at any rate. Anything else it occasionally strayed towards, she dismissed as nothing more than hankerings. She sat up and straightened her back.

'It isn't finished yet,' he added when she said nothing, then leant over the side of the boat and retrieved the lost oar from the water without even looking. 'You don't seem to have much to say.'

She watched his hands as they grasped the oars again, the veins on them fat and blue, moving.

'I'm hot.'

This wasn't what either of them had expected her to say, and she was as surprised as he was. It sounded, unintentionally, like a cry for help.

She ran her fingers around inside the cuffs of her sleeves and looked down at the dress she was wearing, becoming aware of herself in it for the first time.

'When will it be finished? The roller-coaster?' she said with difficulty.

'I don't know exactly – a year.'

This seemed to embarrass him.

They were no longer in the sunlight; the square had moved and was now at an angle so that shadows of the tracks above lay across the water. She didn't feel awe, Mr Delaval realised. Judging by her face she was experiencing nothing close to it; it was almost as though she was trying not to laugh. He was, admittedly, often reduced to laughter himself by the fragility of the structure, but still, awe was what he had expected her to feel. This new disquiet was broken by screams from behind them, and as he turned the boat around they saw the lake just beyond the western side of the pier full of the heads of swimmers.

'They've opened the waterslide for the afternoon,' he said, instinctively putting his hat back on.

The swimmers made their way back to the platform and walked up the curling iron stairs to the top of the pier in order to slide down again.

'I can row closer so that you can see them come off the bottom into the lake.'

She shook her head, then set the boat rocking as she pulled her shoes back on. They both watched for a while as the bodies in their wet black costumes and multicoloured caps hauled themselves out of the water on to the platform. The slap of their wet feet on the iron stairs could be heard as they ran back up to the top.

She sat rigid now with just her right foot tapping nervously on some rope coiled beneath the seat.

Mr Delaval sighed as he started to row again, only remembering as they passed out from under the pier, why he had brought her here. He needed to name his ride, to christen it, and had hoped she would be able to do that for him. He needed her to come up with something to prevent him naming it after her.

I

Hal Price walked into his windowless office at 7 o'clock that evening, dressed as a cat. He was always the cat, every Christmas without fail, the annual pantomime cat. He took off the costume, smelling it briefly. Despite the years that had passed, he was convinced sometimes that he could still smell her in it. The world smelt different then; women smelt different. He hung it on the wall behind him, next to his suit. It was a one-piece costume, which had remained unmodified since its inauguration in 1944: black with a white belly, twenty-five buttons up the back, a pink dickey-bow, and a hole cut out for the face. Which meant that he had to make up, something he had become so expert at that, before he made them laugh (which he also did, annually, without fail), every child was terrified.

He stood in his vest and underpants behind the desk, about to put his suit back on. The name on the door was Mr Price, used occasionally by some colleagues, and the uninitiated. Most of the staff called him 'Pricey' to his face, and although the children performed the usual linguistic feats with his name, executed with dexterity on toilet walls, etc., 'Pricey' was still the preferred formal and informal code of address with them as well.

The four or five Christmas cards he got every year made the lack more apparent than if he had received none at all. But he put them up anyway, reading the card manufacturers' poems, printed inside, out loud to himself.

At 7.10, he was still standing in his underwear and make-up, complete with whiskers, when Will and Victor, brothers, one a current, the other an ex-pupil, entered his office by force.

'Sit down,' the older boy said. Victor had been one of the most violent pupils in the history of the school. Both he and his brother were charges of the local children's home.

Hal sat down and felt for the roots of his whiskers, giving them a light tug, but they wouldn't come off.

Victor had an elaborate new tattoo around his neck, and smelt of grease. The lines in the palms of his hands were black with oil.

Will sat down on the Formica chair in front of Hal's desk, risking his brother's stare.

'Do you remember Irene Trench?' Victor leant forward and started to peer at Hal, but soon moved back when he couldn't find him beneath the intricate layers of kohl and false eyelashes.

'Gypo,' Will put in automatically.

Hal looked intently at Victor. 'Is she still alive?'

'I hope so. I spoke to her this morning.'

'How do you know Irene Trench?'

'I don't. I didn't until this morning.'

'And how does this concern me?'

'I can't tell you yet. Not in front of Will.'

Will didn't react to this in any way. He was used to his brother speaking for both of them.

'Will's sixteen today.'

'Are you, Will?' Hal said, turning to the younger boy. The left corner of his mouth, under the white grease paint, shook.

Will nodded, and couldn't help smiling.

'Does that mean anything to you?' Victor suddenly shouted.

Hal turned back to him, startled. He shook his head, helpless.

Victor sat on the edge of the desk and drew a gun out of his pocket, letting it rest along his thigh.

All three were staring at Pricey's full in-tray and the desk calendar that was turned methodically every day. The tail on the costume hanging on the wall swung slightly, and for a moment Will thought it was still attached to Pricey. He looked quickly at his brother and saw that he too was watching the tail's white tip move backwards and forwards. Then it stopped.

'Get dressed,' Victor said abruptly. 'You're driving us somewhere.'

Hal sighed as he took his suit down from its hanger, his small black painted nose twitching. The photograph on the wall, now exposed, was of the cat, arm in arm with a soldier. He put his socks on first, then his shirt.

'That you?' Victor said, staring at the picture.

'Someone I knew while I was in the army.' Hal kept his head bent.

This information made Victor want to tell him to shut up, and he would have done if it hadn't been for the fact that the shadows playing on Pricey's bent head made it look as though two small ears were growing out of the grey hair. Instead he kicked the wall of filing cabinets, and once they had an adequate number of dents, stopped, and began pulling them open. He was anticipating being able to throw armful after armful of paper around the office but his hands encountered something other than paper.

'Records,' he said to Hal who was tying the knot in his tie. 'These drawers are full of records. You, and music? Never would have guessed it, Pricey.'

Will got up to have a look for himself.

Hal could hear the gun rattling on top of the cabinets as the drawers were opened. He was dressed now and stood watching the younger brother, Will, his eyes never leaving him, not even when he felt the beginnings of a nose-bleed trickle down his upper lip and into his mouth.

Will, turning round, saw the blood and helped the old man

back into his chair. Victor punched his brother automatically in the stomach, angry that such gestures were in his nature.

'Where are we going?' Hal said at last.

'None of your business. We'll take your car and you just drive where I tell you to.'

'Who are we meeting, Victor?' Will asked.

This sudden question of his brother's was unanticipated.

'Ghosts,' Victor said after a while, staring straight at Hal, proud of his reply.

'Ghosts,' Will whispered.

'Do you believe in ghosts?' Hal asked him quickly.

Will shrugged, pretending to read the listings on the back of the Bobby Vee album he was holding. 'What's it to me?'

'What did Irene say to you?' Hal said, slowly, carefully.

Victor snatched the gun off the filing cabinet.

Will waited patiently, watching his brother's hand as it wavered, faltered, then disappeared with the gun into his jacket pocket.

'I know you now,' Victor hissed. 'Oh, I remember you all right, Pricey.'

All three of them were tall and they had to curl themselves up to fit into Hal's Mini. Their heads brushed against the vinyl that wasn't only yellow in places where foam was visible, but rusting as well where water had leaked through from the roof.

Will was still holding the Bobby Vee album, but this wasn't deliberate. Victor sat hunched over, the gun resting on the back of the driver's seat, the muzzle scraping Hal Price's spine where it ran down between his shoulder blades. It was an unnecessary pose, but nobody said anything. Every now and then Hal caught sight of his cat's face in the rear-view mirror.

They drove for a while then turned the corner on to Front Street, passing the boarded-up gates of the Spanish City Pleasure Park. The dome of The Palace Dance Hall, and the rusting white big dipper tracks of the park's signature ride, the Charleston coaster, were still standing. Spanish City gave Setton's skyline notoriety, although now from pleasures past only. In its heyday it had been Mecca by the sea.

'Spanish City,' Hal pointed out.

'Just head for the coastal road,' Victor grunted, but his eyes were already surreptitiously following the tracks of the Charleston coaster, following the route the carriages used to take. He knew every dip and turn, and his stomach remembered them as they passed the boundary walls that used to be white.

'Where do young people go on holiday these days?'

'Been to Ibiza and Majorca, haven't you?' Victor said, turning to Will. 'I took you there.'

'So far away,' Hal put in. 'In my day . . .'

Will let out a laugh.

Victor thumped his brother again and they were silent as, once over the roundabout, Front Street became Marine Parade, and Spanish City fell behind them. Nobody looked at the silhouette in the rear-view mirror where it was perfectly reflected.

A few snowflakes hit the windscreen. At least, they looked like snowflakes. They rarely got snow on the coast, although Hal remembered occasions in the past when it had coated the dunes, the roofs of the beach huts and even the beach itself.

The council had strung multicoloured lights from lamp to lamp along the promenade to replace the original electric lighting put there in 1924, but an indecent number of bulbs were dead. Hal could see them from his bedroom window. The houses on Marine Parade were built in the late thirties when the sea ceased to provide labour and Setton became the fully fledged resort it had aspired towards since the 1880s. By the 1950s, the last remaining fishermen had left and the pleasure-seekers moved in. The houses had only a strip of tarmac, a mini golf course, and the promenade between them and the sea. They were painted white and had a lot of glass on the front of them: windows, covered verandas. Some of them became hotels during the boom years; some of them still were and the signs hung there, even though there were no guests. The one on the end next to the cemetery, number 77, belonged to Hal, but he didn't even look at it as they drove past, out on to the headland.

Once the last streetlamp was left behind, the beam from the lighthouse could be seen more clearly and the Mini kept driving through it at four-minute intervals. In the distance were the six towers of the aluminium smelting plant, the tops of their chimneys lit red to warn low-flying aircraft. They could all hear the wind now.

'We're headed towards Moscadini's,' Hal said to himself.

'Shut up,' Victor said automatically, cold now, then added, 'We're meeting someone there.'

'Irene?'

'Just someone,' Victor repeated.

The road took them away from the cliffs and the lighthouse beam and started to run alongside the walls of Watts colliery whose conveyor belts and cranes looked as though they might start moving at any moment. This always struck Hal at night when the rust couldn't be seen. Or the weeds growing from the slag heaps. Watts colliery dominated North Cliff as much as Spanish City used to dominate South Cliff. The smell of sulphur was still in the air here. His father, Jamie Price, had worked at Watts, but it had been dormant for years, and now they were talking of turning it into a country park. When the council were able to find the money.

At the end of the boundary walls the road branched, and since the pit closure this junction had been known as Watts Corner. To the left it wound further inland until it joined the main road to Wyley. To the right it got smaller and rougher until it became a track leading down to South Wyley. Never anything more than a row of houses and a pub, all derelict now, South Wyley had once been a sailors' haunt when Wyley itself, across the estuary, was one of the largest ports in the north of England. A small ferry used to operate between Wyley and South Wyley to save people making their way over to the main road in order to cross the river. The pub in South Wyley, the Seven Stars, satisfied most of Wyley's bloodlust for decades, and made it easy for local natives to blame the foreigners that passed through for their hidden appetites.

Moscadini's was on the headland just after Camelot, the

caravan site, before the track plunged downwards into derelict South Wyley.

Hal switched the windscreen wipers on and Will jolted at the sound. It was definitely snowing now. There were a couple of stunted horses grazing on the wasteland opposite.

The darkness was making Victor nervous and more aggressive.

'I don't like horses,' Will said.

Hal shut the engine off and accepted the vigorous new jolt of the gun in his back.

'What you stopped for?' Victor demanded, looking through all the windows in the car.

Hal had started to cry.

'Your make-up's going to run,' Will said, irritated by these first signs of tears.

'Start the engine,' Victor shouted. The car was getting smaller by the second.

Hal was straining to hear the sea, but there was only the sound of dogs.

He switched the engine back on and the car turned right on to the track towards Moscadini's.

A hearse pulled up outside 77 Marine Parade, and parked. After placing his *Funeral Director on Business* card on the dashboard the driver got out. He was wearing a trilby hat with a feather in it, to keep his head warm, and to spruce up the more mundane anorak. He wore mittens rather than gloves; fat mittens made of sheepskin so that as he walked his arms hung heavily down his sides making his whole body look stiff. His shoes shone as he passed beneath the streetlights; he was a believer in shiny shoes.

It wasn't until he reached the front door that he realised there were no lights on inside the house. He went back to the front gate and checked the road; there was no sign of Harold's car either. The wind was roughing up the sea now and he could feel the spray spitting at his face. The lights on the tankers kept appearing and disappearing because of the waves.

He went back to the front door, turned his spare set of keys in the various locks and entered the house. He was early, but only by ten minutes. Eight o'clock was the time Raymond Clarke always arrived at his cousin's house on a Wednesday night. After all these years, Raymond still felt the need to keep an eye on his cousin, Harold. Sometimes they played dominoes. Harold often lost at dominoes as well as the other games they played, but he was a gracious loser. Something he, Raymond, who won far more often, wasn't.

He had always suspected that Harold might be a potential suicide, and the absence of electric light in the house tonight made him think for a moment that his private prophecy had come true. He shut the front door behind him and listened, having found, through countless years of experience, that dead bodies often make more noise than people. He sniffed the air briefly as well, but smelt none of the telltale signs.

He was fascinated by suicides, and had seen enough laid bare on the downstairs table at Clarke & Sons Funeral Services to write a history of them. Up until ten or so years ago, the kitchen and bedroom had been the most popular places for women to die, depending on whether they stuck their head in the oven or took an overdose. The number of women he had seen dead on all fours or sprawled on their backs was shocking. Men often chose the bedroom as well, only they tended to hang themselves or use a gun. A surprising number of men, usually from the middle classes up, chose to die at work. The motive tended to vary from person to person, but as a rule of thumb, women usually died because of men, and men because of women.

Harold had once said to him that when he passed away, people would be able to sum him up by saying that he was somebody who had never sought his fortune. Raymond didn't disagree. His wife, Daisy, however, who outwardly damned Harold at every given opportunity, secretly (Raymond suspected) thought he was rather magnificent. In fact, he was sure she did, although as far as he could see the world had never yielded Harold a single thing.

15

Wiping his feet on the mat he went into the kitchen, past the brass rubbings and framed photographs of roller-coasters with titles underneath such as *Tom Rabbit, Elemental, Hercules, Cyclone, Slammer, Primal Scream, Ultimate*. One of these claimed to be the world's biggest. He never could remember whether Harold had bought these from somebody or whether he had taken them himself. Raymond had no understanding of these pleasure machines. Harold had once told him that some of them reached a G force beyond that experienced by astronauts leaving Earth. He couldn't see, personally, why anybody would want to experience the sensation of leaving Earth behind.

In the kitchen, which still smelt of Harold's breakfast, he turned the lights on. Opening the cupboards he saw nothing but some tomato ketchup, HP Sauce, a selection of sachets of flavoured powder that became a meal when water was added, and some tins of fruit (all peaches) as well as a can of condensed milk. In the small larder there were a few scones left over from the batch Mrs Banks baked and brought round on Sunday. Nothing pleased Mrs Banks more than to feed lonely men. Even if they showed no apparent signs of hunger. The container for Harold's false teeth was open by the side of the sink, and Raymond half-expected to see his cousin's teeth in there.

He sighed then switched the kettle on for a cup of tea, and thought about phoning Sergeant Pearce. He used the last tea bag then started blowing on his tea to cool it down and ended up whistling a few bars of Glen Miller's 'In the Mood'. The shaving mirror on the windowsill above the sink was tilted so that he could see his face perfectly. There was an open packet next to the mirror and something plastic. He picked up a pair of cat's whiskers, then remembered that today was pantomime day, and shuddered. Harold must have been trying out a new brand. There were a few black fingerprints on the sill as well he noticed, now he had made the connection with the pantomime. He finished his tea and, taking one last look around the kitchen, picked his gloves up from the bench and pushed them into his pocket.

There was no sign of Harold in the lounge. He checked his watch against the clock on the mantelpiece: they were in sync; time wasn't the miscreant here. They had never missed a Wednesday night before, and over the years Harold had become a real creature of habit . . . had almost become Raymond, in fact. So where was Harold if he wasn't dead?

Raymond walked noisily through the downstairs rooms of the house and even checked the cupboard beneath the stairs, before running up them. It was the first time he had ever been upstairs in the house, and he felt a stab of guilt he hadn't felt downstairs.

Harold hadn't had the original windows in the house replaced with double-glazing, or the fireplaces taken out. In fact, apart from the orange streetlight outside that washed over the walls, it could have been the year the house was built.

He walked over to the window in the front bedroom and looked out, but there was still no sign of the Mini, only his hearse parked there. Then he sat down on the edge of the bed, checking first in case he was going to sit on anything or anyone, and stared into the triptych of mirrors above the dressing table opposite, wondering why he looked different (if only slightly) in each one.

On the bedside table there was a crocheted runner (he recognised Harold's mother's handiwork), a lamp, a clock and a photograph. This was the only photograph in the room, and must have been taken in the mid-fifties. Harold, him and Daisy were walking, arms linked, dressed to kill. They were going dancing, walking along the promenade towards The Palace with its chequered dance floor. He could see Spanish City, brand-new, in the background with the dome of The Palace rising up out of the middle of it. Setton used to be a renowned venue for all dance bands. They were striding out, laughing.

They used to love to go dancing. He looked at himself in the picture, lean with curly hair. He still had curls in his hair then. The window panels started rattling and he went over to look out of them again. In the distance, through the snow that was beginning to fall, he could just make out the dirty white outline of Spanish City. He looked at Harold's face in the photograph, which was still in his hand. Perhaps Daisy was right; perhaps there was something magnificent about Harold after all. Or at least there had been. He couldn't understand why Harold kept this photograph by his bedside, there were others surely more suitable, intimate and private. Raymond was touched.

He stood it on the windowsill so that he could see the promenade thirty years ago on a summer evening against the promenade now on a cold winter's night.

The wind was blowing a gale up on the headland. It made the lights inside Moscadini's flicker as though the wind had somehow got inside as well. Every year one or more caravans from the site got blown over the edge of the cliff because of high winds. Despite this the Camelot campsite wasn't modified in any way to combat nature and there was never any threat of closure. It was always presumed by the people of Setton that those taken over the edge weren't regulars or even holidaymakers, but life's stowaways, involved in illicit passions; people who were morally biodegradable. There were lights on in some of the caravans tonight.

Moscadini's had been started by, and was still run by, a Moscadini, of Scots-Italian descent. It opened the same year Spanish City was built. Up until then the building on the headland had been known as the Panama Café. So called because Panama Jack, who ran it, was once a diver involved in the construction of the Panama Canal. Others said he just jumped ship in Wyley and the name of the ship was HMS *Panama*. Either way, in 1955 the Panama Café became Moscadini's, and whatever it was during daylight hours, at night it became the last pit-stop, port of call, haunt of the pleasure-seekers from Spanish City. They came to fill the red booths, to dance, let blood, or play pinball, to smoke, eat ice-cream, pass the rest of the night, their pleasure spent or on the lookout for more. Until the first light of day, when they could give up and go home. Hal knew all this because he was once a pleasure-seeker, a primal screamer.

Moscadini's was the beginning and end of all pleasures. It was where most people whined for a first taste of childhood's most edible pleasure: the knickerbocker glory, precursor to far greater excess. Hardly anybody ever finished their first knickerbocker glory, and Moscadini was always on the lookout for those who did. They were the ones he knew he would have to keep his eye on.

Nobody knew why Moscadini, who had a string of successful ice-cream parlours to his name in Edinburgh, decided to start his last business venture on this desolate part of the north-east coast. Maybe the fact that it was by the sea was enough. Ice-cream was served at all hours and it never seemed to shut. Old Moscadini said it was as if he had gone to sleep one night only to wake up the following morning and find himself in Setton.

Danny the Deer, the small electronic ride, still stood outside, its metal change box struggling to keep up with currency reform. Hal stopped by the double doors; he hadn't crossed the threshold for sixteen years.

'Don't worry, Mr Price, it hasn't changed one bit. You won't notice the years,' Will said, considerately.

Victor pushed in front of him, opening the doors and scanning the premises professionally even though it was impossible to see who was sitting inside the booths.

Will was right. It hadn't changed a bit. The banquettes near the door were still red, with their razor slashes disgorging as much grey stuffing as they had always done. A collection of dusty cacti grew on each table and the vinyl floor still glowed with grease. The old juke-box in the right-hand corner was counterbalanced by a couple of one-arm bandits and a pinball machine in the left-hand corner. The counter was the same magnificent sweep of steel and glass supporting the plastic effigies of knickerbocker glories, banana splits and strawberry sundaes, stood in an illuminated row along the top. Exactly as he remembered them.

The centrepiece was the large chrome geyser and Horlicks machine. The geyser was steaming and he didn't recognise the girl at the counter although he presumed she was a Moscadini. She didn't smile at them, but her eyes lingered on Will with a certain audacity.

There were few Christmas decorations, apart from some metallic paper chains strung across the ceiling, and a blue tinsel tree, slowly melting in the geyser's steam. Windows ran the length of the right-hand side where the veranda was, facing out to sea. It was dark now and the only thing to be seen through the window was the four of them, reflected.

The back wall of Moscadini's wasn't a wall; it was a picturescape, like the backdrop for a stage, covering the entire surface and lit from behind by electric light bulbs. Moscadini himself had once told Hal the name of the place in the picture, but he had since forgotten it. The sea and sky were Technicolor blue and the electric light shining through the back of the picture really did look like sunlight. Even now, despite the rips in the plastic and the Sellotape repairs, you still wanted to put your hand through and come out on the other side.

The old stone buildings, trees and red flowers went right down to the water's edge: perfect and unreal. It was the sort of place you invented for yourself, and it had been a stroke of melancholic genius on the part of Moscadini. This was his Italy, as he remembered her. Hal would always sit in the booth near the door, as far away from the picture as possible, where it looked most like the view through a window. Moscadini's was the only place in the world where you had a vista of both the Mediterranean and the North Sea side by side.

The girl at the counter was staring at Hal, and for a moment he thought she might have a message for him, but she didn't speak.

'Can I get you anything?' she said at last.

'We could go for knickerbocker glories, but maybe just three teas?' Victor asked.

Hal nodded and turned to look at the door the wind was beginning to tease open, half-expecting somebody to walk through it.

Victor leaned heavily across the counter towards the girl,

laying his belly and arms on it so that he could make a show of staring at her breasts.

The doors were pushed inwards again with a slight wheeze.

The geyser spat boiling water over Victor's hands.

'Careful,' he yelled.

The girl looked bored. She pushed the three pots of tea towards them and splashed boiling water over his hands again.

'That's £1.50.'

'We're not bloody well paying after what you did.'

'What did I do?'

'Burnt me, that's what.'

'Look, here,' Hal said, getting his wallet out of his pocket.

'Put it away, we're not paying,' Victor hissed.

'She burnt him,' Will added.

The girl stood by the open till, staring at Hal.

'Pantomime today was it, Mr Price?'

'I thought I knew your face,' Hal managed, smiling.

'I left two years ago. Been working here ever since. Don't know how much longer it's going to stay open.' She tried to stand up a bit taller. 'I hated school. Worst years of my life,' she added, defensively. 'The cat again this year, were you?'

'I'm always the cat.'

'That's right,' she said more gently, as if she was worried she might have upset him by not remembering this, or that he might not believe she was who she claimed to be. 'You scared the shit out of me when I was little. Then after that you just got funnier and funnier. Nearly used to piss myself. I remember you as well,' she said brashly, staring at Will.

'You do?' He seemed pleased, but not particularly interested, still casting his eyes over the booths.

'He's my little brother,' Victor stressed, leaning towards her again as he picked up the pots of tea.

'What you doing here?'

'Waiting for somebody,' Will said importantly, glancing quickly at Victor, as if he had the power to conjure people up out of thin air. Whoever it was they were waiting for, wasn't there yet.

21

'What, all three of you?' It made little sense and the girl wasn't convinced, but accepted the situation anyway. 'Look, you haven't got that £1.50, have you?' she said at last, flicking her eyes up at Hal.

'What do you say?' Victor said softly.

The girl was trying to smile, but her face just wouldn't do it. She had done her eye make-up too heavily, Hal noted.

'Please?'

'No,' he said, still wheedling.

She thought. 'Sorry?'

'That's the one.' Victor stood up. 'But we're still not paying.'

The girl slammed the till shut and slammed herself back down on her stool.

'Sorry, I have to ask,' Hal said as he picked up the cups, and Will the milk. 'Are you a Moscadini?'

'I am not,' she said, outraged, and turned her back on them, staring into the window at her reflection there.

They sat in a booth near the pinball machine so that Victor could play and keep an eye on things at the same time. He checked the doors on to the veranda, giving them a hard shake despite the fact that the girl had already yelled, 'They're locked,' and Hal enjoyed watching Victor make these preparations in the belief that he had a prisoner whose only thought was of escape.

Hal and Will sat opposite each other, listening to Victor bang and yelp as he hit and missed at pinball. The boy looked over his shoulder a couple of times at the girl on the counter then realised Hal was watching him, and shrugged, 'Not up to much anyway.'

Hal smiled and drank his tea, watching the sun shining down on the Italian coast. He thought he heard the doors go once, but didn't turn round. It was 8 o'clock; he brought his hand down on the table.

'What?' Will said, jumping.

Victor hadn't heard, he was too busy thrashing the machine.

'Tonight's Wednesday, I forgot. Raymond,' he added, to himself.

'Well it's too late now. Victor won't be letting you go nowhere.'

'Can I telephone?'

'No. Don't ask Victor, it'll get him going. Later, maybe.'

Hal sighed, thinking of the gun weighing down the left-hand side of Victor's jacket.

Will looked uncomfortable, and moved his hand away, under the impression that Pricey had been about to take hold of it.

'What are we waiting for?' Hal whispered, suddenly frantic.

Will shook his head, angry that Pricey thought he could get an answer out of him, thought he was a soft touch.

'Victor knows,' he said, holding on to his cup, apprehensive for the first time.

Then before he knew it, Pricey had leant forward and taken hold of his hand.

'I'll tell you a story,' he said.

2

Hal never knew whether his father minded spending the war years covered in coal dust from head to toe, inside and out, whether he was secretly relieved or whether he yearned to wear a uniform.

Jamie Price was a tall man. He could have been taller still only he had never had the strength to grow by himself; he was a man who needed stretching. The war might have done that for him, then again it might not; he might have grown shorter. But he was never put to the test so he never found out.

Matters weren't helped by the fact that his wife did wear a uniform. Charlie Price worked for the Auxiliary Territorial Services packing artillery parts and ammunition for the aeroplanes. Once the packing was done she would despatch it to airstrips within a fifty-mile radius. In order to do this she rode a motorbike, and cut quite a figure riding around in uniform. Hal used to imagine that she went down very well where she made her deliveries.

But the thing that really put Jamie Price's back up wasn't the uniform, it was the fact that the RAF commandeered his motorbike, and not just for the War Effort, but on behalf of his wife. He was made to take off the sidecar and hand the bike over to the RAF paint workshops so that they in turn could hand it back to his wife in new regulation colours.

He was even expected to teach her how to ride it, and Hal

remembered the scene in the back street that ran behind their row of houses the day his father took his mother over every inch of metal on the bike. She had put her uniform on for the occasion, to remind them both of the formality and necessity of what was happening, and to prevent him from brooding too much. The motorbike sagged and twitched when she first got on and she had trouble getting her feet to touch the ground. There were quite a few people watching by then and she had a lot of leg on show, but his father was more worried about the bike.

The neighbours weren't sure what to make of Mrs Price sat astride her husband's bike, but they knew they had to make something of her. She sensed it too. She asked his father to switch the engine on for her, and sat there for a while as he watched each part of it fill with life, ignoring the crowd, and Hal knew that he wanted to throw her off it. He was standing in his trousers and vest, a vast lily-white man with skin that saw so little daylight that the sun touching him then just seemed to be bleaching his skin whiter still.

His mother started to laugh loudly so that she could be heard above the engine. Her laughter sounded raucous and a few people joined in. Then she signalled to his dad to turn the engine off, and had a smoke. Once she had the cigarette in her mouth she stretched her left leg out, stroked his father's upper arm and let rip a couple of exceptionally crude jokes. Charlie Price was renowned for swearing like a trooper. Hal couldn't remember what she said that afternoon, but everybody laughed. She knew she wasn't going to be afraid after that, she was going to make a success of the motorbike.

So she rode it slowly up the street, carefully turned round then rode back down again. There was cheering and applause, and people were watching her face intently, waiting for a laugh. She only had to pucker her mouth in a certain way and boggle her eyes and she got it. At one point she nearly veered off into the allotments, which made even his dad swear, but Hal could tell, watching, that she had done it on purpose to get a rise from the crowd. By the time they wheeled the bike back into the garage, most of the crowd had disappeared indoors for tea and only a handful of onlookers hung around the garage doors to talk and tease a bit more.

By the end of it all, his dad was smiling and even tapped her lightly on the backside as she left the garage. The motorbike and sidecar were never joined again after that although for a few months following the handover his dad did carry on tinkering with the sidecar.

His mother's performance out on the motorbike had been nothing more than antics. Antics were what she was good at, although she called it making a fool of herself. Hal never realised, until he discovered his own ability for antics, that they were more than this: she had a genuine talent for making people laugh. She once said that telling a joke was the best way of telling the truth and that there was no point making people cry, when you could make them laugh instead.

The Prices were considered good people. Which was why, Hal realised, everyone presumed he would follow suit and treated him accordingly, as a good boy. Nobody knew why there was only Hal. The Prices hadn't consciously stopped at one, but no others seemed to arrive. At a time when children were mouths to feed, the Prices were looked on with a certain amount of envy and rancour, but this rarely manifested itself into anything more threatening. They remained good people and carried on living in their upstairs flat at 53 Ellsworth Row, with none of the signs of improvement that might have antagonised people further. The residents of Ellsworth Row were lucky, their houses backed on to allotments. All the other miners' rows backed on to each other, which meant that everybody lived in a world of windows where there wasn't a corner left to crawl into. Every breath drawn was drawn in public and the only way to survive was conformity, never to take a step out of line.

Hal's father's allotment yielded more vegetables than one family could eat and he had always been generous with the overflow, especially during the General Strike and the more recent Jarrow Crusade. This wasn't forgotten. So the Prices were pretty much left alone with their good luck.

26

When Hal started school at five, it was discovered that he was clever, and his being clever was something Charlie Price had never thought about. It was one thing to have a 'smart lad', but it was quite another to have one who passed the 11+ and went to the grammar school.

It had always been presumed that he would become a miner like his father, and it became clear to Hal during Sunday afternoons spent in the garage with the motorbike (pre-RAF) that his father cherished the thought of sharing the walk to work with his son in years to come. Of his wife packing up bait boxes for both of them. There was continuity in this. However, as the years passed, everyone began to realise that this wouldn't be the case. This became particularly apparent on one of the annual visiting days when miners' families were taken down the pit shaft and given tours of their underground livelihood. As the cage descended Hal started screaming and the further down they went the more the screaming began to echo until it echoed so badly they had to take the cage back up to the surface. Jamie Price was mortified, and disgraced, but worst of all (and he never told anybody this), his heart was broken. For weeks afterwards when he descended the shaft he could still hear his son's screams.

Hal passing the 11+ left Charlie Price helpless in the face of fortune; she didn't know what having ambitions for one's children meant. In her own family of three sisters and two brothers success had meant reaching the age of ten and still finding yourself alive. The most she ever dreamed of for him was that he might not have to work underground. A mechanic or engineer in the mine workshops was a hierarchy she understood. Before he passed his 11+, before they realised the full implication of his passing the 11+, Jamie Price talked in quite concrete terms about sending him to one of the technical schools and training him specifically for that. Neither of them could fathom a life not lived in shifts.

They went to the school outfitters in Newcastle to buy Hal's grammar-school uniform, which was an almost impossible financial outlay for them, even with the vouchers supplied by the school. He remembered standing in the full regalia including hat, coat and scarf, at the back of the shop in front of the man who hadn't let them touch a thing, and his mother looking horrified.

'What the bloody hell do we do now?' she had said, helplessly.

The uniform scratched and itched, but he knew it meant an escape of sorts, although he couldn't work out from what because he was happy enough. Charlie Price kept staring at her son and started biting her nails in a nervous manner as if he were an orphan recently arrived on their doorstep or, worse, a changeling. He thought his parents might have arranged to have his photograph taken professionally at the photographer's on the sea front but all his father talked about was the bloody price of it all. 'He ends up passing the eleven plus and we end up paying for it.'

After that Hal would always try and be in the bedroom when his father came home from his shift, so that he wouldn't have to stand in his school uniform and confront him, covered in coal dust still, the whites of his eyes staring out as if they had nothing to do with the rest of him. Sometimes he would watch through a crack in the door as his father squatted in the tub in the front room and his mother helped scrub him down, with a vague feeling of unease that if he was caught watching he would be belted half to death. The washing was a ritual they should all have been present at, but he knew he was excluded even though nothing was ever said, and as a consequence it became shameful, something to bestow stolen glances on from behind shut doors. When his mother began working for the RAF she was excluded as well, and his father took to washing alone.

They carried on going to the Miners' Picnic every year, but Hal stopped entering the races; and for the first time the brass band, which had always sounded magnificent to him, sounded vulgar. He no longer cheered with the rest, and found the atmosphere of addictive loyalty impenetrable. From that moment on, the sound of brass bands haunted him.

There were boys from school he saw at the picnic. One of them was called Fred (not short for Frederick like everyone at school thought), and wore his school uniform to the picnic. Hal never did work out whether this was inflicted on him by his mother's pride or simply because he had nothing else to wear. The handful of boys recognised each other but didn't go so far as an acknowledgment. They never talked to one another at school either. They knew they were referred to as the Banner Boys after the banners carried at the Miners' Picnic, and hoped that by keeping themselves to themselves this collective term would become more difficult to justify. But even the meekest and mildest among them were treated by the masters as a potential threat to stability within the school. This was made worse for Hal by the fact that Watts pit, where Jamie Price worked, had a reputation for militancy.

Hal didn't have a single friend at school, but wasn't unhappy because he had never set out to enjoy himself, only to learn. This attitude made many of the masters suspicious towards him, but he decided that this didn't matter either because whether those who taught him liked or disliked him, at the end of the day they still had to teach him. He was bullied moderately by his peers and superiors, but saw quickly that, given his position, this was inevitable and unavoidable.

In the absence of any friendships he started to daydream about leaving Setton and what this would mean. The older he grew, the more far-fetched the daydreaming became, veering unimpeded towards the heroic. He dreamt frantically of a future in terms of either Allan Quatermaine or Zorro: exploration and personal gain versus the fight against injustice. The clothes he wore in his version of the future were covered in mud, blood, and always torn. He never once doubted that great things were in store for him.

So he got up and went to school every day, worked well into the night, got himself a Saturday job as a delivery boy for Gregson the baker, sometimes helped his cousin, Raymond, at Co-operative Funeral Services, and generally just bided his time. The only thing that made him shiver was his parents' company, and the way (when they were all in the flat together) they tiptoed around him, rarely speaking, even to one another. When he left the room he always expected them to burst into laughter from the strain of it.

On his fourteenth birthday he worked out how much it cost his mother to feed him per week and gave it to her out of his delivery money. It made her afraid, not grateful, as if she sensed it was a foretaste of things to come.

'I'm not taking money from a child,' she said, staring at his hands as if they were filthy, and needed washing. So he started to leave it in the toby-jug. He waited until his father wasn't around – usually Sundays, the only day he didn't work – because he knew, inherently, that it wouldn't do for both males in the house to be giving her money. It was never there by the evening.

After that she became much more physically affectionate with his father, in front of him. Something his father responded to with gestures as overt as hers until the room they were in started to smell of conspiracy and Hal began to feel like a eunuch taunted.

Then it all ended.

Six months before he was due to take his final exams, Fitts, the House Master, called him into his study. Outside was an impromptu waiting room with a couple of benches from the gymnasium. Somebody seemed to have turned up the volume of the ticking clock on the wall.

Hal usually saw Fitts on an annual basis to collect his report; was congratulated, told his parents would be pleased, and dismissed with minimum eye contact. That was the sum total of their shared history. Fitts was meant to be one of the meanest thrashers around, and thrashing, apparently, gave him a real rise, but Hal had never sensed this in his presence. Perhaps because he had never given Fitts reason to thrash him.

There were three other boys sitting on one of the benches, and he recognised them all as Banner Boys. They nodded surreptitiously to each other and stared down at their hands. A tea lady from the refectory walked in, knocked on Fitts' door and re-emerged a minute later bearing a tray with a silver teapot on it, two cups and saucers and a plate of crumbs. They watched her leave and a few moments after that a boy nicknamed Brutus walked out of the office. Brutus got on the same bus as Hal and had grown steadily fatter over the years. He stared briefly at Hal, back at the office door closing on Fitts, then he left. They heard him coughing in the corridor outside. After this the tea lady returned carrying the same tray only this time there was steam coming from the spout of the teapot and there were biscuits as well as crumbs on the plate.

The boy sitting next to Hal was called, and Hal watched him pat down his hair and pull his jacket straight before going in. There was something about Fitts more than any other master that said you stood a better chance with him if you spruced yourself up first. This boy had crumbs and a smile round his mouth when he came out; he didn't have Brutus's downtrodden look. The ceremony with the tea tray was repeated another two times before Hal was called in.

Fitts yawned as Hal sat down. The office was heavy with smoke and Fitts' fingers were a colour flesh was never intended to be. There was a chessboard on his desk, and three oars on the wall behind him. Hal never had been able to make the connection between these and Fitts. They looked like something he had inherited rather than achieved.

Fitts had a good office; at least Hal presumed it was good because it had a view over the playing fields where younger boys were playing rugby. In the distance, after row upon row of rooftops, he could see the sea and in the far left-hand corner of the window, the chimneys and one of the wheels at Watts pit. His father was there right now, underground. Perhaps he was under this ground, underneath this very office. Hal half expected the floor to split open at any moment and to see the light from his father's helmet shine up through the crack as he emerged beneath Fitts's desk bringing with him the blasts of a brass band. He drew back in his chair and tightened his grip on the armrests. Fitts was staring at him.

31

'Price? Harold Price?'

'Yes, sir.'

'Tea?'

'Yes, sir. Please,' he added quickly.

He watched Fitts pour the tea and couldn't stop himself from clanking the cup as he took it from him.

'Thank you, sir.'

The cup, saucer, tea and spoon were all precariously balanced and he began to see that the drinking of it was a feat to be accomplished. He held it awkwardly on his lap, watched by Fitts, who drank his without a single slurp.

'Biscuit?'

He was handed the plate and took one, hoping that he would be able to keep his tea upright in his lap with his left hand while he held the biscuit in his right.

'How is everything, Price?'

'Fine, sir.'

'Work? Exam preparation?'

'Everything's fine, sir.'

'Good. And you were pleased with your mock grades?'

'Very, sir.'

'You should be. We anticipate you doing as well, if not better, in the real things.'

Hal looked at the tea tray, then at the field outside. It was difficult to determine how the game was going; without sound the players all looked as though they were running about at random with no adherence to any rules.

'Are you going to eat your biscuit?' Fitts said at last.

Hal started.

'Of course, sir,' he said, taking a first bite.

He could feel the crumbs building up on his lips and at the corners of his mouth, but didn't dare take his left hand off the teacup to wipe them away. Instead he used his right hand even though it was still holding the remains of the biscuit.

'Not the back of your hand, Price,' Fitts said, looking disgusted.

Hal could barely swallow by this stage, but Fitts was soon

smiling again. This was something he had never seen Fitts's face do before. It made him afraid to think of Fitts outside the hours of 8.00 am to 4.00 p.m.

'Believe it or not, Price, I have taken it upon myself not only to guide you through life while here in school, but also in those initial messy stages when you pass through our gates for the last time.' They both turned towards the window, but the school gates weren't visible from the office.

It was obvious from Fitts's tone that this was a lie, and that somewhere or other along the line he had pulled a short straw. He wasn't even begrudging about it, it was worse than that, he was damning.

'I don't know if you have had any thoughts on this matter.'

Hal no longer knew whether he was expected to comment on these new responsibilities that Fitts had undertaken for his future. He felt that the master was about to transgress in some way.

'I've been thinking a lot, sir,' he said neutrally. Knowing from what he knew of Fitts that it was essential at this stage not to antagonise him.

'About your future?'

'Yes, sir,' Hal confirmed.

They were silent.

'And?' Fitts said, irritated.

'I was hoping for some advice on university.'

'University?' Fitts said slowly, smiling again now because all his suspicions had been confirmed.

Fitts, Hal realised, had anticipated this despite their only really having spoken to each other for the equivalent of one hour over the past five years.

'Ah, university,' Fitts repeated, more sombrely this time.

Up until this moment Hal had had the impression that he was hearing what every other boy who had passed through his office that morning had heard. But now he realised that he was the one Fitts had saved till last, and he didn't even have the stamina (because of the complication with the tea and biscuit) to brace himself.

'And what do your parents say about university?'

'They don't really, sir. That's why I was wanting to ask somebody like you.'

'Somebody who's been to university, you mean.'

'Well, sir . . .'

'And what got you thinking about university?'

Nothing in particular. Dim notions, conversations overheard, the fact that most of his peers were going, but most of all dim notions, the dim notion in particular that this was something you went through before you took your first step into the world, especially the first steps he was hoping to take.

'What were you specifically hoping to do in . . . in . . . life, that you feel university would be beneficial to?'

Hal's overriding sense of self-protection kept him silent. Zorro and Quatermaine should not be mentioned.

'Well?' Fitts insisted.

He was outraged by the boy, outraged that he spent every day of his life looking so quietly hangdog when really all the time he had enough dreams and aspirations to go round every boy in the school; twice over. It was always the law-abiders who had to be watched the most carefully.

'What do you want to be when you grow up?' he said, stressing each word.

'When I grow up?'

'Yes, when you grow up. If you grow up that is, nothing's certain.'

'You mean the war?'

'The war and the world at large. This big mean place we live in.' He smiled again, satisfied.

'I don't know,' Hal said at last.

'You don't know,' Fitts repeated, in disbelief. 'You mean there isn't a walk of life you can see yourself in?' He was almost jumping out of his seat with excitement now. He could give this boy the hammering of his life if he wanted to, and had a whole variety of strategies at his disposal that Hal could never hope to combat. There was nobody to stop him. There would be no retribution, only the aftertaste. 'You haven't the

34

slightest idea what you want to make of your life and yet you presume that some university out there will have the time to entertain the idea of you?' Fitts said, loudly.

Hal had to bite his tongue to stop himself from speaking, from showing Fitts the map of his dreams, which he had never shown anyone before.

'University is for people with ambitions.' He paused.

Hal nodded in agreement and understanding.

'Traditions,' Fitts added more quietly. 'I don't know whose time you're wasting most. Mine or yours.'

'That's not fair, sir.' Hal couldn't stop himself at this.

'Not fair?' Fitts said, imitating Hal's voice as closely as he could.

'I didn't ask to come.'

'Unfortunately arrogance is never in proportion to talent, Price.'

'I wasn't meaning to be arrogant.'

Fitts remained silent long enough for this explanation to sound like an apology.

'Frankly, Price, university would be a waste of time. Especially in light of the fact that you will be qualified when you walk through our gates, to start making money. To earn a living.'

Earning a living had never figured in Hal's dreams. Earning a living didn't have anything to do with freedom.

'So that you can clothe yourself, feed yourself and keep a roof over your head. Undoubtedly one day you will have others in your keep who will also require clothing, feeding and keeping warm.' This last part Fitts seemed to find even more distasteful than the first. 'Price,' he finished forcefully.

Hal couldn't work out who he was attacking, but wasn't able to avoid the fact that Fitts was to all intents and purposes speaking the truth. It sunk in now for the first time. He heard a couple of loud yelps from the field outside.

'Had you for a second contemplated who on earth was going to pay for your four-year jaunt at university?'

'No, sir,' he said, feeling the full impact of this oversight, which Fitts made quite clear was unforgivable. 'I thought there might be scholarships. Or assisted places,' he added lamely.

'Competition for those is very stiff. And they aren't just awarded for academic prowess. Character comes into it also. You have to prove that – ultimately – you will be of some credit to the university. Charity doesn't really exist, you see, Price.' Fitts's diagnosis of the meaning of life was becoming increasingly lurid and he could see the boy shrinking in the face of it. Reality, he decided, really was the best cure. The one thing he wanted to ensure, really ensure, was that the children who entered his office as children, didn't leave in that state. 'Fortunately for you, I have been doing some thinking. On your behalf. I've read through this.' He placed a dossier with Hal's name on it on the desk between them.

The tea lady knocked on the door and came in to collect the tray. She looked at the cup in Hal's lap and he was about to hand it over with relief when Fitts explained brusquely that he hadn't finished. The woman left, looking distrustful.

'What about teaching?' Fitts said, brightly.

'Teaching?' Hal couldn't help the way he said it.

'Yes, teaching. Training to become a teacher.'

Fitts was watching very carefully now and even reached out for a biscuit before remembering that the tea lady had taken them. 'Bloody woman,' he mumbled to himself.

Hal looked out of the window – the field was empty now – and briefly towards the door.

'The school has excellent connections with a teacher-training college in Newcastle and we've already put your name forward. They offer a very good bursary scheme for exceptionally gifted pupils. Like yourself. The teaching profession is increasingly keen to attract a high calibre of candidates. In fact I would even go so far as to suggest that your place is assured.'

Hal stared at him. He couldn't understand how it was that he had never noticed Fitts before when Fitts had been there all the time. How was he to know, how could he have known that all these years Fitts had had him nailed down from the start?

'I see,' he said carefully. Then, feeling that something else was more appropriate, 'Thank you, sir.'

'The school has issued this letter for your parents' information.'

Hal took hold of the envelope passed to him, addressed to Mr and Mrs Price.

'Thank you, sir,' he said again, nodding.

He smelt the carpet, furniture, windowpanes, wallpaper, wood of the doors, Fitts' shoes, suit, everything intensely for a moment, then he sank back into the chair, deflated. He knew from his five years at school, watching adults about him, the sort of adults he hadn't come across before, that their world was divided up among those who were successful and those who failed. Hal's world up until then, the world of children, was divided up among the weak and the strong. Despite the bullying, he had always contemplated himself in terms of strength. Now, for the first time, he was forced to acknowledge his weakness. Perhaps he had been a weak person all along, and weakness had as much depth as strength. The power drained out of him into the comfortable chair he was sitting on. And he knew that after this he would start every day of his life, not with breakfast, but with this conversation between Fitts and himself.

'Good,' Fitts said, still watching him.

Hal at last leant forward and put the teacup and half-eaten biscuit on the desk, so that his hands could concentrate on the letter. He was trying to think of something else to say when the fire alarm started up. They couldn't ignore the alarm these days because of George Tiverton, a capable eleven-year old pyromaniac (also a Banner Boy). Fitts, whose duties as air-raid warden had virtually ceased, was now fire warden.

It never occurred to Hal, sitting there listening to the alarm, that all he had to do was hand the letter back to Fitts, thank him for his trouble, assure him it wasn't necessary, and walk out of the office. So he just sat there as the siren wailed and the building shuddered with panic.

Fitts put his steel fire warden's helmet on, which suddenly made Hal want to laugh. It was the combination of tie and helmet. He coughed and hoped Fitts wouldn't notice the upturned corners of his mouth behind his hand.

'Come on, we have to leave the building immediately.' Fitts wasn't just repeating the standard drill, there was an urgency in his voice, and Hal was even more afraid of Fitts's motive for wanting to save him than he had been of anything so far. 'Go on, run. Run straight into the playground.'

Usually he was among the first in line, keen to save himself in light of his future importance to mankind, but Hal couldn't move.

Fitts grabbed the roll call and stuffed it into his pocket. The Lower School was already walking in formation across the playing fields.

'Move,' he hollered at Hal, who had to start coughing again.

The sight of Fitts as an angry fire warden was worse than the sight of him as just a fire warden.

'Right,' Fitts said, and unravelled the roll call, until he found the fifth form. He put the paper pointlessly down on the desk so that Hal could see his name, then placed a tick by it. 'Whatever happens, you were in line when you were meant to be,' he said bringing his face close to Hal's for the first time.

'Sir?'

'What?'

'Can I ask you something?' Hal didn't wait for an answer. 'Do you see everybody? Does everybody get to see you like this?'

Fitts walked round the desk. 'What do you think you are, Price? A free man?'

Hal instinctively shut his eyes and brought his hands up to his face, sure he was about to be hit. He could smell the adrenaline running through Fitts, but he didn't strike. Instead he moved away to the door.

'Are you coming?' he said more calmly.

Hal didn't say anything or even shake his head. He didn't want to turn round and look at Fitts even though it meant leaving his back exposed.

38

'You stupid little prick,' the master said quietly, then slammed the door shut after him. A few seconds later Hal could hear his whistle sounding down the corridors.

It was 3.00 p.m. Three stragglers from the last line of boys jogged past the window and the alarm petered out. Putting the letter in his blazer pocket, Hal left the office, went into the toilets next door, and had a pee.

The entire building was empty. He started to walk up the corridor, crossing the hallway in front of the headmaster and deputy headmaster's office, something they weren't usually allowed to do. He left by the nearest exit, which he was also forbidden use of and which so few feet passed over the carpet was barely worn. Then he carried on walking down by the music block he'd never seen the inside of, the tennis courts his feet had never trodden, and straight out through the school gates that Fitts had just elevated beyond their material existence.

Walking back to Ellsworth Row that night, he stopped at the small enclosure of green where the donkey was kept, opposite the front of their house. He stood up on the fence, something he hadn't done for years, and willed the animal over to him. His mother once made him believe that the way to get Dobbin's attention was to sing 'Amazing Grace', and she had left him standing there belting out the hymn at the top of his voice while she sat on the wall behind the hedge with tears of laughter running down her cheeks. He only went to see Dobbin after that to throw stones at him.

Their landlady's daughter, Daisy Downstairs, so called because she lived in the ground-floor flat, was sitting on the stairs that led up to his flat when he reached home. There was a comic beside her.

'Listen,' she said, smiling at him as he came through the door although she hadn't meant to, 'I can hear your mam.'

Hal could hear nothing.

Daisy leant over and pulled up her socks where they had collected round her ankles.

'She's been crying for ages.'

39

He stared at her.

'They're like lovers, your mam and dad. Even after all these years of marriage,' she carried on, sighing. 'Your dad never plods home like most men. We can hear him running up the stairs. Two at a time.'

Hal was shocked at how easily and inadvertently they had become part of Daisy's life. For a brief moment it reminded him of Fitts.

'Sometimes I come out into the hallway after he's gone up, and I swear I can smell flowers. He must bring her flowers all the time. After all these years of marriage,' she said again.

'He never brings her flowers,' Hal said, shortly. Then, relenting a little, 'He only picks them sometimes if we go out walking on Sundays.'

'Oh.'

He was now able to hear his mother's pacing for himself on the floorboards above.

'She's inconsolable,' Daisy said, nodding.

'Inconsolable?'

She carried on nodding. 'They had an argument.'

'So?'

'A man from the Union came round. Someone's been laid off up at Watts and he wanted to talk to your dad about strike action. Your mam sent him packing, and when your dad got home he went loopy. You should have heard them.' Daisy put her hand over her mouth and laughed sheepishly. 'Then he tried to make up to her.' She blushed and executed a few quick dance steps, sitting down again with a sigh. 'He wanted to take her to The Palace dancing, but she wouldn't go. Why do they never dance at The Palace? Their dancing upstairs drives mam mad.' Her eyes went suddenly bright. 'Maybe he's in so much torment that he's gone to kill himself.'

'Shut up,' Hal shouted.

'I think they're lovely together,' she muttered, by way of a reconciliation. 'That's all.'

He swung his satchel round on to his back and started to climb the stairs. He waited for Daisy to move her comic but she didn't,

40

she stood up instead, arching back slightly over the banisters.

'Your dad's gone to the Club to get drunk so Mother said I was to keep watch over Mrs Price. Like a guardian angel.' Daisy was smiling generously.

'Well, I'm here now so you can sod off.'

'I'm not very good at sodding off,' she said quickly, unoffended.

'That what your mother tells you?' he said, standing on her comic.

She nodded and brushed some muck off the back of her skirt.

He carried on walking up the stairs, but she grabbed hold of him.

Hal tried to pull his hand free, but Daisy only held on to it more tightly. Holding her hand was different from holding his mother's. Or his father's. It was like holding his own.

'. . . Mother said that Mrs Price dances beautifully. Even if the sound of them up there does drive her mad.'

His hand relaxed in her grip until she let go of it and disappeared through the door to her flat, shutting it gently behind her.

His mother was still in bed when he got upstairs. This had never happened before, and for the first time he no longer felt safe once the front door was shut. Inside the flat it felt just like the rest of the world. He put the letter from Fitts on the mantel against the jug his father's combs were kept in. The jug was cream and had fat blades of grass painted on it.

His mother stayed in bed underneath the covers. Sometimes he heard a low moaning sound as the lump on the mattress moved about and changed position, almost by the hour. But he took her tea, which she drank, and a sandwich that she ate. She didn't say anything to him and he didn't hear her cry properly once, just that persistent whimpering. He knew that this was the real face of tragedy, snotty-nosed, down-at-heel, and without glory, and wondered what had passed between them. At about 7 o'clock his mother came out of the bedroom dressed in her ATS uniform.

41

'I'm going to work,' she said.

'Do you think you should? Tonight?' he said, forcefully. It was their first exchange as equals.

She left without answering him and he saw her go into the garage. It was twenty minutes before the doors opened and she came out on the motorbike. He heard the door downstairs go and knew it was Ada Crombie, come out to have a good nose. She must have heard everything, especially Charlie Price walking down the stairs. Ada was likely to be daunted for days by the sight of his mother leaving on the motorbike. He knew she wasn't going to work; her pride made her lie to him. She had gone looking for Jamie because he hadn't come home.

Once she had gone he sat in the growing dark at the table by the window, his back to the letter on the mantelpiece, staring out at the allotments. Daisy was right, he had never seen his parents dressed up to go dancing. The couples walking up the back street on a Saturday night in their ballroom finery were like a parade; the sounds of the women's heels an overwhelming clatter, as they made their glittering exodus away from everyday life. Every Saturday for as long as Hal could remember, when the exodus began, before his father switched the radiogram on, Charlie sat with her face pressed up against the window watching them go.

At about 10 o'clock he was sure he saw a couple of young boys in balaclavas digging up vegetables from their patch. They walked back holding the stolen goods in their jumpers and he wondered how many times it had happened before. His father referred to them as the snaggy hunters when they came for the turnips in October. He had always admired and been afraid of the snaggy hunters. 'It's only a dare between boys, Hal,' his father had once said when they had watched them together through the garage window. Then even more warmly, 'Little buggers. I bet their mothers know.' He had sounded fonder then of those masked snaggy hunters than Hal had ever heard him sound of him.

He got up from the table and went over to the mantelpiece, watching himself in the mirror as he picked up Fitts's letter,

42

and turned it round and round in his hands. At 10.30, he heard the flush on the outside privy and opened the door to their flat, instinctively putting the letter back down. Daisy was sitting out on the stairs again, in her dressing gown, but with her shoes and socks still on.

'What are you doing?'

'My mam says I have to sit here and keep an ear on you.' She paused. 'And an eye. Your mam hasn't come home yet, that's why.'

He looked down at the crown of her head for a few moments where the hair parted and was tightly plaited, then sat down next to her. She smelt heavily of the privy, and there was dried egg yolk on the collar of her dressing gown.

'I'm joining up,' he said.

She looked closely at his face, surprised she hadn't detected this momentous news there when he came home earlier. But she didn't say anything.

'I'm joining up,' he repeated.

Daisy spat on her shoes and rubbed the spittle in until they didn't shine any more.

'They can't have called you up already.'

'I haven't given them a chance,' he said impressively.

'It's going to end soon,' she said grinning. 'Didn't anybody tell you that?'

He thought she might have taken hold of his hand again, but she had her chin on her knees and was too busy grasping her own ankles.

The door to the downstairs flat opened quietly and he saw Mrs Crombie watching them through the gap.

'It's none of your business anyway,' he said loudly, suddenly standing up.

As he did so his mother walked through the back door, still in her uniform and with her hair all loose. She was pulling his father by the hand, and both of them smelt of alcohol.

She took one look at Daisy and Hal sitting on the stairs, and another quick look at Ada Crombie, who had emerged fully into the hallway as soon as she heard the outer door open.

'He's joining up,' Ada said, grabbing triumphantly at anything that would break up the picture of drunken bliss that Charlie and Jamie Price made standing in the open doorway.

'He's what?' Charlie shouted, sobering up immediately.

'Joining up,' Hal said defensively, backing up the stairs.

'You little bastard,' she said making towards him, her arm raised.

Daisy leapt out of the way in time, but the comic she had left on the stairs earlier got trampled to bits; first by Hal, then by Charlie Price.

'I think you're beautiful,' Daisy said, gasping at this display of fury, the soles of her shoes sticking to the hallway lino, and not taking her eyes off Charlie.

Jamie Price, who hadn't yet moved from the doorway, turned and quietly shut the front door. He edged past Daisy with a quick, ''scuse me,' doffed his cap at Ada Crombie then, glancing up at the ceiling, made his way up the stairs.

'And people talk about me,' Ada said.

3

There were lots of jokes about Camp Eden, but most of them were in German. Camp Eden was a German POW camp in North Yorkshire. It was also, Hal discovered, a training camp where he spent weeks shooting at straw men dressed· as Germans. An airstrip was the only thing that separated the two. Perkins said that the Germans finally saw what they were up against when they realised that the English failed to see anything perverse in this.

Hal first saw Perkins two weeks before they were due to sail for France, standing up against the fence on the German side of the airstrip. Well, he wasn't standing so much as slouching, and Hal watched as he hunched over to light a cigarette thrust at him from the other side. After the cigarette was lit, he passed several packets of something through the fence. In return something was pushed back from the German side and Hal thought it looked like money, felt sure he caught a whiff of it on the wind. This transaction was quite an achievement given that last week a vicar had been arrested for trying to smuggle a box of apples into the camp. But then the vicar hadn't learnt that trade was permissible where acts of goodwill weren't.

Hal knew (even at a distance) that he was in the presence of someone who had either known many Fittses and overcome them all, or known none at all. And for a brief moment the late June sun was shining down, not on a narrow strip of concrete, but a vast desert where the trail of two horses crossing it side by side could be seen. Then it was gone. But the short man by the boundary fence wearing a greatcoat that was too big for him, and that it was too hot for, had played a trick on his eyes that only the North Sea used to be capable of.

He was halfway across the airstrip, heading towards Perkins, when he heard the words 'Guten Morgen' flung at him from behind the fence. He had never heard German spoken before, and froze to the spot. For one wild moment he thought that he was on the inside and not the outside of the camp fence. That he had been caught in the act of some gross transgression and that rapid gunfire was sure to streak across the tarmac any second now. Instead, the only thing that came streaking across the tarmac was the sound of footsteps followed, at close range, by laughter.

'He said "good morning", you stupid bugger,' Perkins said, hauling Hal up from the crouching position he had instinctively assumed.

A nation of baby snatchers and child-eaters, of bogeymen beyond your worst nightmares, Daisy Downstairs had whispered incessantly before his departure from Ellsworth Row. And it wasn't until that moment, exposed in the middle of no-man's-land, that he realised he must have believed her all along.

'Good morning; Guten Morgen,' Perkins said quietly.

Close up, his breath smelt of toffee, and although Hal wasn't sure whether German spoken with a sweet tooth made him less or more afraid, he readily shook hands and exchanged names. Convinced that with Perkins before him he was in the presence of a man of the world.

'You speak German?' Hal managed at last.

'I'm learning. From the krauts over the fence,' he said with a flick of his head. 'Never know, might come in useful. Never know . . .' he paused, glanced at Hal, then chanced it, 'which side of the fence we might find ourselves on. One day. Maybe.' He gave Hal a broad reassuring grin.

Things moved quickly and by that evening they were

46

revealing prize possessions. Hal's amounted to a couple of Dainty Dinah toffee bars that Perkins ate readily, while Perkins's were far more impressive. First he drew a shoe box out from under his bunk, lifting it on to his lap with a grunt.

Inside the shoe box was a collection of pamphlets from the Charles Atlas, 'Are You a Man or a Wimp?' Body-building series. The price on the back was in dollars.

'Yank gave me these,' he said, further proving his man-of-the-world status.

'Do they work?'

Perkins stared at him for a moment, then grinned.

'I'll let you off the hook for that. Just this once, mind, but in future, you've got to stop asking such bloody stupid questions. Look at me,' he finished, putting the lid brusquely back on the shoe box and sliding it under his bunk.

Next he drew an old ration tin out from underneath his pillow, tapping the lid before gently pulling it off in a way that made Hal hold his breath. Inside was another book.

'This is the best of them all,' Perkins said, putting the book confidentially into Hal's lap so that he was forced to pick it up: *How to Become a Millionaire*. The price on the back was also in dollars.

'There's a whole two chapters on the Rothschild family,' Perkins whispered, giving the front cover a brief stroke.

The rise of the Rothschild family, it transpired, obsessed him, and he said the word 'Rothschild' with gap-toothed excitement.

'I mean, I've got plans,' he confided to Hal. 'Shoes. I've got visions of shoes. One day I'm going to have a Shoe Emporium on the Strand. And that'll just be the first of many. I've got visions all right, but these people,' he said flinging the book open at a black and white portrait, 'they're worlds ahead of me. I want to make money, lots of money,' Perkins added, staring straight at him.

'The whole world wants to make money,' Hal felt he should agree.

'Those who don't make money spend their lives looking for

the other thing money can't buy. Not me,' he finished triumphantly, as though his worst fears were behind him. He sighed, then hurriedly shut the lid of the tin as if he regretted having shown his treasure.

'D'you know what I thought?' Hal said watching him respectfully.

'What?'

'When you first got that box of yours out do you know what I thought was in it?'

Perkins shook his head.

'A Bible. I thought you were about to tell me you were the unit's chaplain or something.'

Perkins shook his head again, without grinning. 'Well, you know what I thought when I first clapped eyes on you in plain clothes stepping off that bus with the rest of the new arrivals? I thought you had "conscientious objector" written all over you. And it turns out you're not even a conscript.'

Perkins never took leave from Camp Eden to join the others in York. 'What would I want to go on leave for? Women are a waste of time, Hal. You should make sure that any transactions between you and other human beings involve money; it's the only way to survive.'

After another month of being at war with straw men, they were sent to France together.

They had been told they were landing at Le Havre, Normandy, and sat on the ship across the Channel next to a group playing successively violent rounds of pontoon. In the end they came into port on the south-west coast of Brittany at Nantes, but as far as Hal was concerned Le Havre could have been Nantes and Nantes, Le Havre: he was in a foreign country. Virtually without the excuse of a war, given the success of the Allied invasion on 6 June.

When the ship docked they disembarked, but were kept waiting in the shadow of it for half a day because of a mess up with the papers. In the end, he and Perkins were sent on alone in the back of a field jeep, leaving the rest of the regiment behind, and it took Hal all the energy he had left not to grab hold of Perkins' hand. They were billeted on the coast near a town called Guérande, thirty miles north of Nantes, with a regiment of Welsh soldiers and a handful of sappers. The building, which overlooked the Atlantic, had been nicknamed the Rat Castle by its most recent inmates due to the increasing number of dead rats found on the premises. Dead rats were much more worrying than live rats, and nobody had yet discovered who or what was killing them. The Rat Castle had once been a Jesuit seminary and after that a children's holiday camp.

It tickled Perkins to find graffiti scratched into the walls of their dormitory: verses and pictures depicting the Jesuits as rats.

'There were rats here before us. This has always been the Rat Castle,' he claimed.

'So you speak French as well?' Hal said.

'I'm learning,' Perkins responded brightly. 'Never know. Might come in handy. Never know . . .'

'. . . what side of the fence we might find ourselves standing on,' Hal finished for him.

The walls in the dormitory were that particular shade of grey walls go when they forget what colour they were once painted. There were some murals still visible of lions, elephants and palm trees, half-heartedly painted to keep children's nightmares at bay. The Germans who were there before them had made comfortingly pornographic additions to the murals, and the Welshmen had carried on where the Germans left off. A couple of them made Hal laugh out loud the first time he saw them.

When they arrived at Guérande, Lieutenant Murford told them he didn't need any more soldiers, and Hal felt, from the way Murford squinted at them, that they might be asked to take their uniforms off altogether. Perkins started to fidget and look about him while Hal managed to stay still, despite the drops of sweat trickling into his nostrils.

'There hasn't been any fighting, proper fighting, down here for a month,' Lieutenant Murford said, looking more intently at Hal, 'which is why it's dangerous. Peace, now, in its infant stage merely means that the war continues or, rather, starts again outside the public sphere. A war of retribution between those who fought on the same side: known and rumoured collaborators, and known and rumoured non-collaborators. We're all treading on something very private here. Revenge,' he said with precision. 'And when we're not treading on something very private, we're bored.'

Perkins laughed.

'We're not here to be laughed at, you fucking dog's arse,' Murford said, bringing his cane down sharply into Perkins's right arm.

Hal could tell Perkins was biting his tongue; he was used to standing up for himself. Perkins looked down at the officer's shoes then straight ahead again.

Their arrival at the Rat Castle turned out to be a clerical error, but Murford kept hold of them and assigned them to the Entertainment Corps, which had been in the camp for a week, and was planning to perform a pantomime in another month's time.

There were a couple of other men like them at the Rat Castle, men who had missed or more precisely escaped the war. It reminded Hal of his Banner Boy status back at school. They all recognised each other for what they were and then stayed well clear. There wasn't even the slightest hint of camaraderie; they knew that their best chance of survival was to disperse, to dilute themselves.

At the time Hal never fully appreciated the real necessity of their doing this. Not until much later did he realise to what extent he, Perkins and those other boys were tolerated. Really tolerated. How much of an unbearable strain their presence was to the other men (many of whom had been wearing uniform since 1939) who knew that treading in their midst were those who had lost nothing.

This was why Lieutenant Murford had assigned them, with an insight still intact, to the Entertainment Corps. Where they would, ultimately, perform and be laughed at. This eased the pressure, and prevented anything untoward (which Murford knew his men to be more than capable of) from happening. Pressure and balance became Murford's sole preoccupations in this last year of the war.

A road separated the Rat Castle from the coastal path. On the other side of this road there was a beach called St Michael's Bay, and at the left-hand side of the beach there was a small swimming pool. Although the pool had long since been drained there was a wooden sign boasting that the water was RECHAUFFÉE. In the changing rooms at the side of the pool there were still a couple of swimming caps with rubber flora on them hanging from the pegs, as well as a pair of sandals on the rack below; the Germans had hardly touched the place. Major Stanton thought it was the closest thing to an amphitheatre he had ever come across.

The Entertainment Corps rehearsed at the pool every day from 8 o'clock until midday, then from 3 o'clock until 6, knocking off for the hottest three hours of the day because there was no shelter (apart from the changing rooms which soon became full of costumes and props). *Dick Whittington* was Major Stanton's idea and he had just completed a militarised version, which successfully transposed key elements of the original, making it more appropriate for the times they were in.

The main emphasis in Stanton's version was on the plague of rats, and he found the rats far more interesting than Dick himself, or Dick's rise to fortune. The hero's failure to brush against the dissolute elements of life (to which he must surely have had increasing access as his fortune grew), and his marriage to the merchant's daughter, he thought nauseating. And anyway, at the end of the day, Dick was only as good as his cat. So Private Roberts became Dick, chosen because he was certain to bring a lack of flair to the part. Then Stanton turned his full attention to Tiddles the cat, who, it was rumoured, was to be played by one of the nurses, while Lieutenant 'Libby' Libberton coached the rats.

51

The rats, being Welsh, were the chorus, dressed as German infantry with swastika armbands. These the men sewed themselves, and as they sewed Stanton could already hear the guaranteed boos, hisses and cheers he had engineered with such care in the script. Perkins was the only non-Welsh rat, following Hal's discovery that he suffered from stage fright. Stanton, who had perceived Hal as a liability capable of jeopardising the chorus as a whole, quickly and effectively demoted him to a behind-the-scenes position: make-up.

Libby composed a series of variations on well-known songs, bulging with indecencies that made the rats sing louder. He knew there would be a handful of nurses in the audience but most of them by now had seen what the insides of the majority of men looked like. After much deliberation, Libby decided to add a drop of sincerity by closing with a hymn he intended to write from scratch. 'To give those who want to cry the opportunity to,' he explained as justification. Stanton thought he was being unnecessarily heavy-handed but let him have his way, secretly hoping that when the time came the men might back out, or that the mood of the moment wouldn't allow for it.

Perkins made friends easily, especially here, because he had no interest in understanding others. As a consequence he abandoned Hal during the day in order to join the large group that went to the inland marshes behind the line of hills Guérande stood on, where crayfish and girls were to be found. Despite his urban upbringing, Perkins was an authority on how to turn anything living into something edible.

Hal never questioned Perkins' treatment of him; it seemed in keeping with the way others treated and had treated him. He knew anyway, even though nothing was ever said, that the few hours spent walking along the coastal path or sat on the sand in St Michael's Bay at night meant more to Perkins than all the crayfish in France.

St Michael's Bay hadn't been mined because it was so small and rock-infested that nothing amphibian could approach it from the sea. Perkins called it fucking paradise when they first clapped eyes on it, and was amazed, every time they went, to find themselves alone there.

Perkins was happy to stick to the boundaries Hal imposed on their night-time walks: the Napoleonic watch-tower to the south, and the recently vacated German bunker to the north. Whether this was because Perkins was afraid of the dark, Hal never discovered, and too much was at stake for him to ask.

Sometimes Hal swam. Perkins never swam, refusing even to paddle. But lying back in the sea, looking up at the stars, he often heard Perkins's voice reaching him out on the water as he practised the rats' songs from the pantomime. It reminded Hal of times at home when he had fallen asleep in the summer, and heard through the open window the sound of his dad's clear tenor voice practising the Watts Colliery Choir repertoire as he tinkered in the garage. Some nights Perkins would still be sitting on his rock singing when the waves brought Hal back to shore and he walked up the beach.

But one night, treading water out at sea, Hal saw him scramble off the rocks and stand at the water's edge, perfectly still. He could only think that Perkins had seen something on the headland above the bay, and Hal turned in panic, fighting against the current in order to reach the shore. Before he got there Perkins ran up the beach and disappeared into one of the caves at the back of the bay.

Hal crawled out of the water, ran for his uniform and struggled to get dressed, yelling, 'What is it? What is it?' He was still wet, and now covered in sand.

'There,' Perkins said, emerging from the mouth of the cave into the moonlight.

He wasn't pointing up at the cliff face behind them, but out at sea. Hal tried to remember every drill they had been taught for surprise attacks.

Perkins disappeared back into the mouth of the cave, but Hal couldn't move from where he was standing in the middle of the beach.

He shouted out to Perkins that nothing could happen on

a night like this with virtually a full moon in the sky. Then he saw what it was in the water that Perkins had seen: the head of a swimmer.

He was aware of Perkins somewhere behind him in the mouth of a cave, of the swimmer out there in the Atlantic, and of himself standing on the beach, but all he could hear was the wash of the waves on the shore. Perhaps it was *only* the head of a swimmer, and if it was a whole swimmer, body and everything, was it a dead one or a live one? After a while his immobility induced Perkins from his cave and he came to stand beside him on the beach.

'The swimmer's alive,' Hal said, watching the head's smooth progress shorewards.

'Swimmer?'

Hal watched for a few seconds more.

'A German?' Perkins said.

'A woman, I think.'

They both watched as the black head grew a face and the face, features. Then a woman staggered, without grace, out of the water. They heard her legs ploughing the current. She was as clumsy as a creature evolution had forgotten, one not used to walking on land, and the thought came to Hal that she might be wounded or in the process of dying. They could hear, distinctly, her breathlessness now, and the way her arms clawed at the shore pulled at something inside Hal.

'A woman,' he repeated.

'A German woman?' Perkins whispered.

Hal didn't say anything.

'Guten Abend,' Perkins's voice said clearly, into the night.

The woman stopped, her arms hanging down by her sides, the water still flowing around her ankles. She had time to turn back, to wherever it was she had come from, and Hal thought for a moment that they would hear her crashing back into the sea. But they didn't. Instead she threw her head back and it was laughter they heard.

For the first time since seeing her, Hal and Perkins looked at each other.

The laughter stopped.

'You had me for a moment then,' she called out to them, then disappeared behind the rocks Perkins had been singing on only minutes earlier. Still neither of them moved and eventually she reappeared in nurse's uniform, climbing over the rocks as clumsily as she had emerged from the sea. Her towel was curled under her arm.

'I haven't seen anybody here before,' she said as she reached them.

'I haven't seen you anywhere before,' Perkins said, staring at her.

'This place is always empty. Night or day. It's the only place big enough to take a bath,' she went on, ignoring him. 'At the beginning of the war the Resistance attacked a group of off-duty German soldiers in broad daylight here.' Her eyes briefly scanned the beach. 'It was a frenzied killing, and the massacre became known, even in terms of war, as a crime. They made a bonfire . . .'

'Does anyone else know about this?' Perkins cut in.

'It's not generally known, no. But that's because I just made it up. Here on the spot. I've had various notions, but that's the one that struck me just now. Of course, it may not be untrue.' She looked at both their faces, pushing her feet down into the sand.

Then she started to laugh again, and, watching her, Hal realised that she had no regard for tragedy and no intention of ever understanding it. Whether this was inherent or something the war had done to her, he didn't know. He had always held things very close and very tightly to him, but it was obvious that she had never held anything before. The laughter was both careless and calculated, and she had just proved that she did the same thing to words. She was an easy laugher, like his mother. But while his mother only ever laughed in response to other people's laughter, this girl seemed able to generate it from nothing. Hal had been taught to trust in laughter, to believe in it.

Then she stopped, suddenly, and if there hadn't been

echoes still in the air around them, he would never have guessed, looking at her face, that she had had her mouth wide open only seconds before.

'You work in the stable-block with the Germans? The ones left behind?' Perkins persisted. He hadn't once taken his eyes off her.

She nodded. 'I give morphine – when there is morphine – to anyone who asks. If somebody wants to die, I let him. If someone screams, I scream louder. I shoot anybody who can't be cured.'

Perkins laughed.

'What's funny?'

'Sorry, I . . .'

'So don't get ill,' she cut Perkins off, turning suddenly to Hal, who jumped.

Hal had seen the stables converted into a field hospital, and the beds with men lying on them and nothing to define them as Germans.

'I can speak German, you know.'

She said it in a whisper.

Hal jumped again.

'How's that then?'

'My mother's Dutch.'

'So you speak Dutch as well,' Hal said automatically.

'I could do. Or I could just be lying.'

He kept thinking he heard an accent in her voice. Not really regional, foreign maybe. At one point he was sure it was South African, but the next it sounded more like a German speaking English, like the ones he had heard at Camp Eden cutting deals with free men. But just as soon as he became convinced that this was what she sounded like, she lost all trace of any accent and spoke plain King's English. Better than either him or Perkins. Perfectly, in fact.

'The name's Stella. See you.'

She ran lightly off up the beach and Perkins turned to watch her while Hal remained looking out to sea. Then she disappeared over the cliff top.

They were on the coastal path with the Rat Castle in sight before Hal realised that he was walking barefoot, and that his boots were still standing on the beach.

It had become so hot during the day that they rehearsed at night rather than in the afternoon, when there wasn't a corner of the swimming pool not under direct sunlight. It wasn't until 8 p.m., when the rats finished singing their chorus for the tenth time, that they realised there was a woman among them. Nobody could actually see her, but the air between the men changed colour and all eyes turned to the corner where Stanton was standing. Even Hal sensed it from inside the changing room. When the rats stopped singing it wasn't just silent, it was silent with expectation. Hal went outside and, from his vantage point at the side of the pool, could see what it was that Stanton's huge bulk was concealing.

The strangest thing of all was that Stanton was laughing. Nobody had ever heard Stanton laugh before.

'The cat's here; the cat's here,' Libby said, running into the corner and pushing Stanton to one side

A cheer came up from the bottom of the pool as the men convinced themselves suddenly, unanimously, that this was what they had been waiting for. It was the girl from the beach: Stella.

Libby pranced up the pool with her on his arm. Watching her, Hal couldn't decide whether the shyness was affected or not. She hadn't seemed capable of shyness. Stanton shuffled behind, and if she had been wearing a train, he would have been carrying it. Stanton, like Perkins, had decided at some point in his life that he would not suffer women, and the men were trying to work out why she alone had been spared Stanton's damnation.

'Wait until she opens her mouth,' Libby put in, reading their minds.

She shook his arm, as good at mock-fury as she was at mock-shyness.

'We'll be needing that cat costume soon,' he said, glancing up at Hal.

Stella turned her head briefly towards Hal and nodded.

After that she shook hands formally with the entire cast, and the more hands she shook, the more rats there seemed to be until it occurred to Hal that the act of shaking hands was multiplying them, and he wanted to shout at her to stop.

Then she got to Perkins.

Hal never knew afterwards whether Perkins did what he did because of the others, because he knew that something of the sort was expected of him, or because he couldn't help himself. But when Stella extended her hand towards him, with no apparent sign of recognition, he leant over it and, very professionally, kissed it. Afterwards he stood up straight again without a trace of a smile. Which sent the men into hysterics. Genuine anger crossed Stella's face, but she soon managed a smile. There may even have been a laugh, Hal couldn't remember. But what he did remember clearly was that afterwards Perkins didn't dare turn to look at him.

Hal was sitting at the trestle table he and Lydia, an Australian nurse, had erected in the changing room, oiling the sewing machine she used to make costumes with, when he realised there was somebody standing in the doorway. It couldn't be Lydia, who had cycled into Guérande to see the major she was having a half-hearted affair with. He looked up. It was Stella.

'What are you in the play?'

'Nothing,' he said.

'Why's that?'

'I got stage fright. I tried for a while but I forgot my lines. All two of them,' he added, trying to bring up a laugh.

'Definitely?' She came and stood over him. 'You don't know for sure,' she said. Then added, irritated, 'Why are you so ready to condemn yourself?'

'I'm not.'

'And why are you so ready to believe Major Stanton?'

'He should know.'

'Well it was probably just an attack of nerves. Nothing

more. So stop puffing yourself up with such grand diagnoses. There isn't always one for everything you suffer.'

He watched her as she picked up a pot of rouge Lydia had been trying to make, and put it on her lips.

'I've worked with Major Stanton before. He's furious about his theatre.' She licked her lips and scowled. 'He got me posted up here on a pretext so that I could do his show.' She took a notebook out from under her arm and put it down on the table in front of him. 'The major said you had to help me learn my lines. I've got to be word perfect, see.'

Later Hal left the changing rooms, snapping the padlock shut behind him. As he jumped down from the wall on to the road, he fell into Perkins.

'What were you doing?' Perkins said, pulling him to his feet.

'In the changing rooms, locking up the props.'

'And where are you going now?'

'Back to the Rat Castle.'

Perkins nodded, pleased with this. There was dust on the seat of his trousers and Hal guessed he had been sitting out on the rocks reading *How to Become a Millionaire*, which was tucked under his arm.

'What are you doing now then?'

'I'm going swimming,' he said, grinning.

Perkins never smiled, he only grinned, and Hal had never seen his grin have less to do with joy than it did under the moonlight right then.

'Where?'

'The beach. The beach right here. The one with the sea next to it.'

'But you don't swim; you can't swim. Can you?' Hal said.

Perkins gave him a friendly thump on the arm that Hal felt bruise immediately.

'I heard rumours that there's a nurse comes down here every night about now,' he said. 'And I thought . . . she likes swimming, I can't swim . . . who knows, might get something going. On a night like this what kind of man wouldn't?'

He started to walk away towards the beach.

'You all right?' he called out to Hal.

'Tired,' Hal shouted back.

He hadn't expected Perkins to add anything further to this, but he did.

'So you don't mind my going swimming then?'

Hal stopped for a moment, but couldn't think of anything to say to this; at least nothing that would make him feel less lonely and Perkins less satisfied. Perkins's entire emotional world evolved around gain and loss, and Hal was no match for that. He watched him walk off down the road and disappear over the headland, out of sight.

Hal now spent most of his time in the company of Lydia who, it turned out, was the queen of ersatz make-up. The donations of lipstick and mascara they had collected from among the nurses weren't enough to paint the chorus of rats and Lydia was forced to improvise. Three different guinea pigs were sent in every day for her to experiment on.

Lydia leant very earnestly over her concoctions, which used flour and animal fat as their base. With her pot in her hand she had no trouble working in close proximity to men's faces. She had a nervous giggle and spoke quietly as though afraid everything she said might be interpreted as blasphemous. Once the men got used to the professional fondling they enjoyed the novelty of wearing a different face.

However much people strove to endow animals with human qualities, it was much easier to endow men with those of animals, Hal discovered. After much experimentation he and Lydia decided to go for the naturalistic approach. Something that invoked praise from Stanton, and although Hal tried to point out that it had been a joint effort, the major was staring over his moustache so exclusively at him, and Lydia was grinning so encouragingly, that he decided to forego any mention of her involvement. Hal and Lydia took more notice of each other following this minor egotistical omission on the part of Hal.

Rehearsals had moved to the stage erected at the end of the

Rat Castle's garden, but the cast still came to the swimming-pool changing rooms to be made up. They then had to make their way back up the coastal path past the ever-growing crowd of jeering and awe-stricken local children. Confused that the grown-ups had time to do this, and unsure as to whose benefit they were doing it for, the children continued to throw stones, sand, grass and flowers at the men dressed up as rats making their way to and from the Rat Castle.

It was Perkins who told them in perfect Cockney French that there was going to be a pantomime with singing and dancing. This was greeted by a chorus of obscenities shouted in such a way that not even Perkins was sure they had understood. After this the leader, who carried crutches around with him all the time, turned tail and fled, the rest of the crowd following, south towards Batz-sur-Mer.

'Poor buggers,' Perkins said, with genuine sympathy, then promptly forgot about them.

When Perkins came in to be made up, Hal stood to one side, presuming he would make straight for Lydia. But he didn't, he made straight for Hal, even squeezing his shoulder hard before sitting down.

'Any smudges?' Perkins said once he was done.

Lydia looked over at him, then quickly away.

Hal shook his head.

'Well, there better not be because I'm not even going to look in a mirror, Hal. That's how much I trust you.'

He cuffed him on the cheek, gently once, winked at Lydia, then left.

One afternoon Hal went to the changing rooms, only to find them empty. He hated being alone there because of the smell of wet children that still hung in the air, and was about to leave when a cat over five feet tall walked out of one of the cubicles and over to the mirror hanging above the line of benches. It rested its made-up face in its paws then laughed and looked straight at Hal.

The cat was black with a white belly and had what looked

like real claws. When the tail started to twitch it was impossible to discern whether a length of string ran from the tail to the right forepaw or not. Hal couldn't see any.

Then the cat sneezed. The dust was bad in the changing rooms because of the rotting plaster, and after the cat sneezed, Hal noticed a few strands of long hair poking through the back of the cat's head. It put a forepaw up against its mouth and nose as it sneezed a second time.

'Stella?' Hal said at last.

'I can't make my mind up,' she answered thoughtfully, staring at herself in the mirror again.

'About what?'

'About the accessory; the one defining accessory I think the costume needs.'

'It's perfect as it is,' he said quietly

'You think so?'

'Definitely.'

'No. It needs something else. Just a little something else so that the audience knows whether it's a boy cat or a girl cat.'

'Does it have to be either?' Hal said, confused. 'I never thought of it either way. The cat's just a cat.'

'Surely you can see that if the cat belongs to Dick, and the cat's female, then that gives me', she hesitated, '. . . much more room to swing my jokes in. Anyway who wants risqué when you can have filth?' She looked down at her tail then leant even further forward until her face was nearly pressing into the mirror.

'I think a pink dickey-bow. I don't know what made me think of that, but a pink dickey-bow is exactly what this cat needs. And maybe some lashes.'

Hal couldn't think of anything to say. He was sweating.

She muttered a few of her lines into the mirror, and he automatically corrected her. He knew her script by heart now.

'You're a dreamer, Hal Price.'

He wished he could let go and smile, or bring some element of charm to the moment.

'Perkins dreams.'

'Perkins plans,' she said sharply back. 'You dream.'

He started to walk towards the door.

'Did Perkins meet up with you that night?' he said at last, asking her the question that had remained unspeakable between him and Perkins.

'What night?' The back of the cat's head moved slightly, but she didn't turn round.

'I see.'

'If you want to know whether I went with him or not, the answer's yes. I couldn't think of any reason not to.' She at last turned round to face him. 'I once rode a roller-coaster with such a drop that when the carriages went over the top of the tracks, my body lost contact with the seat, and I was thrown into negative gravity. You need to lose your sense of gravity, Hal . . . exchange real time for air time.'

'I've never been on a roller-coaster,' he said. Then, with real anger, 'You know, I've never been on a roller-coaster.'

'It's pure sensation, that's all,' she said, sounding suddenly tired. As tired as the minister at the chapel he had occasionally been taken to, who had died young from the strain of trying to inspire awe in his congregation, from standing in tears Sunday after Sunday in front of a dry-eyed crowd as the organist played. 'Sensation can be pure, Hal.'

He left the changing rooms without another word, leaving her alone with the smell of wet children, and headed back in the direction of the Rat Castle. Before he reached the main gates he heard the chorus from over the wall, singing the song he hadn't been able to get out of his head and had been whistling for weeks now.

Lydia was standing by the gates, and it wasn't until he reached her that it occurred to him she was waiting for him. He glanced down at her hands half-thrust in the pockets of her uniform. There were black and white smudges from Stella's face all over the back of them.

'She looks . . . the part,' Lydia said at last, hesitantly.

They both knew that this wasn't what she had meant to say; she had meant to say, beautiful. And the word, unspoken,

nearly suffocated them. Thinking about it, Hal realised that he
didn't think of Stella as beautiful in the way Lydia meant, and
wanted to tell her this, but couldn't.

Before turning in at the gates, Lydia looked back over her
shoulder at the road Hal had just walked up.

'You shouldn't believe everything she says.'

'Shouldn't I?' Hal said, feeling suddenly cold, not towards
Stella, the liar, but towards Lydia for telling him this. 'How
long have you known her?'

'We've been together throughout the war. We made sure
we stayed together after we became friends. She once told me
she was an orphan.'

'She told me her mother was Dutch.'

'She told me that as well, the day after she told me she was
an orphan.'

Sensing that she was about to take hold of his hand and lay
claim to some shared emotion, behaving all in all like too
much of one of life's survivors, Hal strode on ahead towards
the stage, but he could hear her footsteps in the grass behind
him.

The sky was intermittently black the day of the dress rehearsal,
the first time it hadn't been blue since Hal arrived off the boat,
and he heard Murford mumbling something about how
unpredictable the Atlantic was. Because of the sky, Stanton
decided at the last minute to erect a canvas awning over the
stage and risked a demotion by dismembering four field tents
in order to accomplish this. They left the tent with the least
suggestive stains on it intact, to use as a dressing room. Once
people were in costume though, they had to be made up
outside. It was too stifling under canvas and Stanton was
agitated about the make-up running.

By the time Hal and Lydia had finished painting the face of
the twenty-fifth rat, Perkins, who was leaving it until the last
moment before getting into costume, had read out extracts
from most of *How to Become a Millionaire*. He had just finished
highlights from the chapter, 'How to Make this Century

Yours' when a man in major's uniform walked round the corner of the stage. His blond hair and the absence of any moustache made him look far too young to be a major, and for a moment Hal thought it was one of the Welsh boys in costume. But the way the men paused, respectfully, in whatever they were doing soon made Hal realise that the 'major' was an offstage major; the real thing.

Perkins hadn't noticed and carried on reading. It wasn't until the major's high-ranking shadow fell across the open book that he stopped. Perkins jumped to attention, but kept the book in his left hand.

'*How to Become a Millionaire,*' the major said, turning his head sideways and reading down the spine. 'May I?' He took the book from Perkins, ignoring the slight tug he had to make to get it out of his hands.

Perkins kept a close, jealous eye on his book as the major took his gloves off and leafed through it.

'This has been very avidly read,' he said, wiping the sweat off on his thigh. 'Anyone would think it was pornography.' He gave Lydia a quick look to excuse himself.

The men laughed readily, even Perkins.

'That's Major Delaval. Only seen him here once before,' Roberts whispered to Hal. 'They're talking of sending us down south,' he added, hoping that at the very least this would give Hal bad dreams. He considered being afraid a worthwhile and vital state to be in.

'Delaval?'

Hal was clenching a kohl pencil and three lipsticks in his hand and dug the pencil so forcefully into Dick Whittington's cheek that Roberts cried out.

'Will you be at the pantomime tomorrow night, sir?' someone shouted out bravely from the stage.

The major turned round.

'I'm not staying, I'm afraid.'

There was a low groan and he let this sink in for a few minutes before adding, 'I expect I'll get to see the beginning though.'

At this a couple of the rats on stage stamped and started to practise the odd bar from the chorus.

After a genial pause the major returned the book. Perkins grabbed it and tucked it into his lap.

The major made to leave, but stopped when he was level with the corner of the stage. He put his gloves on then pulled them slowly off again.

Hal moved forwards to see what it was that had stopped him in his tracks.

Stella was being helped to jump off the front of the stage by Stanton, who smiled and gave the pink dickey-bow a brief tug. Then she made towards the stable-block and German prisoners. The next minute Perkins pushed past Hal, following her into the dark among the trees.

The garden got busier and busier as the day went on. At 5 o'clock an old man from Guérande appeared and assembled his camera in the same way they had been taught to assemble machine guns at Camp Eden. His legs were so bowed that they made him look as though he had spent his entire childhood suffering from rickets. He made it clear that he understood English, but refused to speak any so his orders were slow in being understood even with Perkins translating. Only Stella managed to stand in the right place, but whether this was instinctive or because she also spoke French, Hal couldn't tell.

The photographer propped up a board against the legs of his camera. The board had his name on it and a row of medals, and underneath the medals there were photographs of couples getting married with all the men in uniform. It took him two hours to take three shaky photographs: one with all the rats sitting across the front of the stage and Private Roberts and Stella standing up behind them; then another in reverse with Stella and Roberts sitting on the front of the stage and the rats behind. One was meant to be taken just of Stella, but she pulled Private Roberts up beside her at the last minute. The photographer doffed his cap with grace at the cast after packing his camera away, and Murford, lurking at the side of the stage, was the only one who suspected him of irony.

Delaval, whom Hal had seen sporadically during the last run through of the pantomime earlier that afternoon, came to watch the photographs being taken. Nobody spoke to him, and he sat without moving throughout the two hours it took. Afterwards he got up, sat back down again, then got up and walked over to the stage. Hal thought he might speak to Stella, but he didn't. He spoke to the photographer instead.

Stella soon left, heading in the direction of the stable-block where she was relieving Lydia from duty for the next three hours. For a long time after she left, the major stood there without moving, only finally distracted by the arrival of Murford, who shuffled uncomfortably around the periphery of the makeshift theatre. They soon disappeared into the Rat Castle.

Even though the dress rehearsal didn't finish until 11 o'clock and there had been a lot of forgotten lines as well as unchecked verbal abuse, Hal could see Stanton felt it went well because he and Libby were affectionate with each other afterwards. Nobody minded rehearsing in moonlight for the last hour and the chorus was still singing as they made their way back to the Rat Castle.

Hal and a few others helped to store the costumes and props beneath the stage then walked up the garden back towards the Rat Castle themselves. He was by the old vestry, in the corridor leading from the mess hall, when Roberts ran past, shouting, 'Night, Price.'

Within seconds of Roberts passing, the door with the word SACRISTIE still painted on it opened.

Major Delaval stood there, the low light bouncing off his blond hair. There were two maps on the wall behind him.

'What did that man call you, Corporal?'

'Price, sir. My name, sir,' Hal said, without looking at him.

'And where are you from, Corporal?'

'Setton, sir.'

The moon disappeared behind clouds, and the corridor went dark as the major sighed.

'Doesn't the coast around here make you homesick?'

Hal at last looked up to find the major staring intently at him. He hadn't been sure earlier, but now at close quarters he knew, from pictures he had seen in the *Setton Echo*, that this was John Delaval's son. Just before the outbreak of war there had been something in the papers about him trying to import a rainbow pleasure-wheel from America, which travelled at speeds of up to 40 m.p.h.

'What do you think it means, you and I being here?'

Hal shook his head, unsure what Delaval meant. He thought he heard the sound of children laughing stealthily on the other side of the window behind him.

'Goodnight, sir.'

'Goodnight, Corporal.'

Hal could feel the major's eyes on him as he walked slowly up the corridor, trailing his hand along the wall in order to feel his way in the dark. He had just reached the foot of the staircase when the major called out, 'Are you in the pantomime, Corporal?'

'No, sir.'

The darkness quickly swallowed his words and he didn't know whether the major could hear or not. He could just make him out, standing in the foggy patch of light outside the vestry. But after a few seconds the major's voice came back to him.

'Oh,' he said, sounding genuinely disappointed, 'I thought you might have been.'

The next day they put out all the chairs they could find from the mess hall in front of the stage, but there were only enough to seat the high-ranking officers. The rest of the audience would have to sit cross-legged on the grass as they had once done at school.

Hal stayed in the make-up tent for most of the afternoon. He was busy tidying the used rags covered in white, red and black greasepaint into a pile when he heard a shot. He could tell from the silence, which was sudden and alert, that everyone was holding their breath. No other shots followed this one. He watched the shadows of the trees move across the canvas of the tent, and waited, still holding the rags in his hand. Rapid gunfire could easily become background noise, but there was something definitive and crucial about a single shot. Sounding out with the clarity it did. The shadows of the trees kept on moving across the canvas as the sun made progress, but he no longer connected this movement with the passing of time. After a while he heard the sound of people outside again, singing even, and the stamping of feet on the boards of the stage. When Lydia appeared in the tent doorway, he was still stood in the same spot, holding the used rags. Stanton walked in immediately behind her, ducking his head to accommodate the flap.

'Hal,' Lydia said, turning to look quickly at Stanton, then back at him, opening her arms expansively. She smiled and let them drop back down by her sides.

Hal dropped the rags at the same time.

Stanton smiled encouragingly and then turned his attention to the details of the make-up tent.

Lydia opened her mouth to speak, but before she had time to, Stanton strode purposefully over to Hal, put his hands on his shoulders and pushed him down on to the stool.

'You're going to play the cat,' he said slowly as if trying to hypnotise him. Then gave his shoulders a brief congratulatory squeeze.

'Me?' Hal said, looking up into his face.

'Yes. You,' Stanton said, trying to convince himself more than Hal.

'Where's Stella?' he said in a sudden panic, trying to stand up. But Stanton pushed him firmly back down on to the stool.

'You're word-perfect, I heard.'

'You are, Hal,' Lydia put in.

'Well, yes, I've . . .'

Stanton reeled back, clutching at himself. 'I can't believe it, I can't believe it, to get this far . . .' he kept saying, over and over again.

69

'Major, sir. Major, it's all right.' Lydia gently prised his arms apart from where he had wrapped them around himself.

'Yes,' he said. 'Of course.' Then he rushed back over to Hal and clamped his hands on his shoulders again.

Hal thought he was going to speak, but he didn't, he just stood up and left the tent, saying 'Dress him' to Lydia, as he passed.

'Where is she?'

Lydia shook her head and moved towards him.

'Where is she?'

'I don't know.'

'What's happened?'

'Something. I don't know.'

Hal thought about the single gunshot; the time spent standing still all afternoon; the shadows of the trees moving across the canvas.

'Is she alive?'

Lydia kept her head down and didn't reply.

'I can't do this.'

'You saw Stanton. You have to.'

Hal stood up, unsure whether Lydia was actually going to try and undress him. She shrugged, turning her back on him, and started to push the costumes on the rail to one side, in search of the cat.

Hal found Stanton after the show behind the stage, staring heavenwards, close to tears.

'Word-perfect,' Stanton said. 'Perfect.'

It wasn't until Hal had been standing there for some time that he realised Stanton was speaking to him.

'And the costume fitted,' Hal said. This suddenly seemed to him the most important thing because not one of them, Stanton, Lydia, or himself, had doubted for a moment that it wouldn't.

'I never thought of you,' Stanton carried on, the memory of Hal more vivid than the real Hal standing in front of him, 'and yet you were there all the time. You were perfect; you've got a gift, *the* gift.' He didn't specify further.

When Hal got back to the make-up tent it was empty. He heard later that most of the rats stayed in costume after the show came down, and were lynched by inebriated fellow Welshmen, confused by the swastika armbands.

Someone had laid his uniform out neatly on the trestle table. Lydia, he guessed, and was touched at the sight of it. His ears were full of the boos and hisses of the pantomime audience, and he was relieved to step out of the cat's costume.

Once he had his uniform back on, he picked the cat costume up and shook it out, lifting it briefly to his nose. He looked over his shoulder to make sure he was alone, then folded it up and put it inside an empty tool bag before leaving the tent.

Outside in the garden everyone was making more noise than they had been earlier during the pantomime. Some of the men had started to take the set down but given up halfway through. A couple of local children in clogs were banging their way backwards and forwards across the boards.

He saw Lydia standing near the bank of chairs. Perkins, still in costume, was talking to her, his hands round the top of her right arm. She was trying to pull herself away, but Hal could tell from the angle of Perkins's head that his grip was stronger than her will. Whatever it was he had wanted out of her, he couldn't have got it because he soon stalked off.

'Lydia.'

She looked less terrified once Perkins had left, but wasn't completely at ease. Hal pretended he hadn't seen, but the fabric of her sleeve was heavily creased where Perkins's hand had held her.

'You were a natural, Hal,' she said.

She had made herself up with the left-over grease paint, and her lips shone. He could smell alcohol on her and had to resist the urge to cause her pain. For knowing what she knew and deciding not to share it with him. But he somehow managed to carry on smiling as gently and ineffectually as he could.

'Where've you been?' she asked, and before he had time to answer, repeated, 'You're a natural, Hal.'

There was a low rumble and everybody around them started to panic as the children running about on the stage began to scream. Hal stood watching them, unable to understand for a moment. Then he felt the rain on his face. The storm, which had been building up since yesterday, was at last breaking.

'It's raining,' Lydia said, impatient at having to point out the obvious.

He started to walk towards the house without saying anything, but at the last moment, just before he was about to mount the steps, she tugged his arm and said 'No' so loudly he stopped.

'Why?'

Then it was her turn to walk away, up the drive and through the main gates. It was the most purposeful thing she had ever done. Hal only paused a moment before following her.

He thought they would turn right, towards St Michael's Bay, but they didn't, they turned left instead, following the road that led to the old Napoleonic watch-tower. She didn't once make any gesture or say anything to show that she minded the rain. The watch-tower was in sight when a field jeep passed them on the road. Hal was sure he saw Stella inside it, wearing a hat and rubbing her hand backwards and forwards across her mouth. He saw her even through the rain; it was definitely her. She turned to look at him, her fingertips pressed against the glass.

It wasn't until the jeep disappeared from sight that he broke, pointlessly, into a run.

He heard Lydia behind him, trying to keep up, calling out his name. The air around them was full of the smell of gasoline.

'She's gone,' he said simply as they reached the door of the watch-tower.

'Gone where? She hasn't gone anywhere.'

'That was her. In the jeep.'

'I didn't see her,' Lydia said, but without looking at him.

Instead she took a small key out of her pocket and unlocked the new padlock on the door. She waited until he was inside then shut the door behind them.

'Will she mind us being here?' he said looking about him with curiosity.

'How did you know it was her place?' Lydia was irritated, but managed to giggle anyway. 'I've been here lots before; she just doesn't know, that's all,' she said, trying to establish some sort of complicity.

So this was where Stella came. With Perkins? Maybe. The remains of an upper floor jutted out from the walls above his head, and there was the beginning of a small spiral staircase, which now led nowhere. The floor was covered in birds' droppings and he could hear wings moving in the rafters above although it was too dark up there to see anything. Apart from a puddle that was forming quite near the door there weren't any other leaks.

Lydia kept trying to stand close to him, but he always moved away in time. In the end she went and sat down on a small pile of regulation blankets near an old trestle table that looked as though it was once the property of a local bar. There were lovers' initials carved into the wall, from this century and the one before. The last pair had commemorated each other here in 1939. There was nothing after that. He started to look more closely, for traces of Stella. He was sure she wouldn't have come here and not left her mark.

'She doesn't keep much stuff here,' he said.

She came and stood behind him, and he thought he felt her hand on his back.

'She comes to think here, that's all,' Lydia answered quickly. 'And sometimes to sleep.'

'She might surprise us now. What are we going to say if she walks in on us now?' he said loudly, turning round suddenly and taking hold of her roughly by the arms.

'We're not doing anything.'

'But that's not the point. The point is you're not even supposed to be here at all, are you?'

'No,' she tried to shout back. 'Anyway, she can't,' she said, the same terrified look in her eyes as he had seen when Perkins was with her earlier.

'Why not?' Hal let her go and went to sit down on the blankets. 'I saw her in the jeep,' he insisted.

Lydia didn't say anything, and by the time she came to join him she was smiling again. There was nothing in the tower apart from the blankets and the table.

'There used to be a whole string of these towers down this coast. Do you want something to drink?'

He looked at her and nodded. Lydia was going to be one of those people who would always have to pay in some way for other people's company. With some effort she lifted up the windowsill, which was loose, and pulled out a bottle of clear liquid from the hollow underneath. She looked sheepishly at him then sat back down on the blankets, only pausing a moment before lifting the bottle to her lips, coughing and passing it to him.

She would probably drink like that for the rest of her life he thought; always pretending it was the first time. He drank a lot before handing it back to her. She put the bottle in her lap and held it against her chest. They were silent and could hear the rain on the roof and outside.

She was excited now, not taking her eyes off him.

Then he hugged her, suddenly, with more warmth than he had meant to, and after that they sat holding hands. He wished she wouldn't keep laughing, but took hold of her again anyway, pulling her even more tightly against him this time. They were still as wet as if they had just crawled out of the sea. He could have left if he had wanted to, but he didn't. He wanted to see what it was she was waiting for. A heart transplant maybe.

'What's that round your neck?' he said, leaning forward and pulling the chain away from the wet skin it had stuck to.

'It's my St Christopher's chain.'

'What's that then?'

'St Christopher is the patron saint of travellers.'

'Have you travelled a lot?'

'With the war: Greece, Turkey,' she said apologetically.

'Who gave you the necklace?'

'My dad. He didn't want me to come.'

'Here? To France?'

'He said it was too far away, too dangerous. He's English,' she added pointlessly.

'Do they miss you? I suppose they do,' he finished quickly for her, and took another mouthful from the bottle. 'You're white. I thought Australians were meant to be brown. All that sun.'

She kicked off her shoes, curling her legs up under her, and carried on waiting. She wasn't going to give up that easily.

He found himself almost beginning to like her. Or to tolerate her at least.

'I used to dream of Australia. And other places.'

She didn't answer.

'I heard that there weren't enough white people to populate Australia, to populate paradise. That's what it's meant to be, isn't it? Paradise? What's out there that makes people want to leave?'

'My dad's English,' she mumbled.

'You said.' He paused. 'And what is it in the air that makes Australians speak English the way they do? I hate the way you sound.'

At that she moved suddenly back into the middle of the blanket, scraping her damp arse across it, and pushing her feet forcefully back into their shoes.

'Well, you're hardly speaking the King's English, are you.'

She was right.

After this he knew she was going to cling on, if not to him, then to her night. It wasn't long before she was kneeling in front of him on the edge of the blanket, still waiting, and suddenly feeling brave enough, despite what had happened, to try a laugh. It was as if her mother once told her that you could always trust an Englishman, and she had believed her.

'What are you most afraid of, in the whole world?' she said at last.

Hal only needed to think about it for a few seconds, it was always there, pressing against him.

'Cousin Raymond. Becoming Cousin Raymond. He's an undertaker.'

She couldn't stop laughing at that, and nearly fell forward, face first, into the blanket by his boots.

'And the stupid thing is, Raymond's a happy man.'

'I can imagine Cousin Raymond,' she said.

And the way she said it made him think for a moment that she really did know Raymond, that she knew he was the kind of man who kept life at arm's length.

'Well don't, you've got no right to.'

Then he reached forward, took hold of the St Christopher's chain again, and pulled her towards him. She smelt different now; of the rain, which had soaked into her skin, and of grass from the wet blades, which had stuck to her legs when they had run through the garden. The sea spray had tangled her hair making it thick and crisp. When she held his face in her hands he could smell the dust of the canvas, the musty aroma of rot and, above all this, her sense of betrayal.

She was unlacing his boots clumsily because they were so wet. He twitched when she touched his ankles and calves because she did it so lightly it tickled him. The undressing of men was something she did perfunctorily, and every time she sped up he saw her consciously trying to slow down, to find her old ability to anticipate the best rather than the worst.

Her face was too close for him to see her clearly, and she had lost the lethargy that had made it easy for him to be rude earlier. He let her experience and desire dominate the moment, and as soon as he let go, she started to speed up, unable to dispel the sense of urgency the war had made inherent, and surprised at his lack of will after his anger before. After undoing her dress, she eased her breasts out of her bra so that he could hold them. He sat up on his elbows to suck her nipples, which tasted slightly antiseptic. She had pulled her

76

skirt up and her thighs fell over his, much bigger and softer. When she brushed her forehead against his, he could feel the perspiration there, and elsewhere, on himself too. The rain was almost deafening and was steadier than their breathing.

Then it came; a sudden desire for her, making her immediately more powerful, more substantial than she had been all evening as she pushed him into her, laying her ambitions bare. And the moment came when he did forget her name. Then it was over.

He must have fallen asleep because when he woke up he heard the rain insistent, loud, and the girl was speaking to him. His shirt was pushed up above his nipples still and there was a pink mark just below one of them, better formed than a lipstick print, where she had bitten him.

Lydia was furtively doing the buttons on her dress up again, and her face was full of a hysterical sort of hope.

Afterwards, when he thought about making love to her in the watch-tower, this was the part he remembered most clearly: her kneeling on the blanket doing up the buttons on her dress. Once all the buttons were done up, she remained kneeling, fiddling with the St Christopher's chain to make sure it was still there.

'Stella's gone,' she said.

She had nothing to lose now, and having nothing to lose was as good as winning.

'I know. I saw her in the jeep.'

'Stella's gone,' she said again, ignoring him.

He couldn't stand hearing her say it again. It was impossible now to disbelieve her. She didn't say anything more so he sat up and grabbed hold of both her wrists with one of his hands, and hit her across the face with the other. It was the first time he had ever successfully hit anybody.

She started to cry, and moved away from him down to the end of the blanket.

'They've taken her away,' she sobbed.

'Who has?' Then, when she shook her head, he yelled, 'Just shut your mouth.'

He didn't know whether he wanted her to stop speaking or crying. His foot went out for her and he didn't dislike the sensation of it against her belly.

By the time she found her feet again she was as angry as she was scared.

'I thought you were all right. I thought you might be all right.' Her hand was on her stomach now.

She got up and walked towards the door.

He heard the sole of her sandal rubbing the dirt on the floor backwards and forwards. Any minute now she was going to leave.

'What did Perkins want with you?'

She sniffed loudly. 'To know where Stella is.'

'Do you know where she is?'

He wasn't surprised when she didn't answer, and got up with only his damp shirt still on, tripped over his boots and stumbled towards her

'Do you know where she's gone?' he said, taking hold of her again. Her arms felt familiar in his hands.

She shrugged her arms free of his grip with real anger.

Then she left, and he didn't try to stop her. He listened to her departure, to the sound of her shoes running up the road, and, as the wind brought it round in waves, of crying. But these didn't last for long.

When he left the watch-tower he didn't bother to put the padlock back on, or even to shut the door, which was left swinging in the aftermath of the storm.

4

It was snowing when Hal got out at the station, and the streets of Setton smelt not only of sulphur as usual, but of snow as well. Winter was a good time of year for homecomings, he decided.

He walked slowly down Main Street. It was all still there: the chemist, cycle shop, drapers, Presbyterian church, and opposite it the Spiritualist church. It was difficult to see sky in places because of Union Jacks, but the carnival itself was long since over and the flags were stiff with frostbite. Post-war administrative chaos had its grip on the town as telegrams arrived to say that sons expected home any day were in fact dead, and children answered the door only to find their dead father standing on the doorstep. Proof of life and proof of death were no longer definitive, and the living and the dead wandered freely between both worlds. Nations and not men win wars, Hal thought watching the weather-beaten Union Jacks, while its people are left to face this transgression of a universal law alone. He looked among the faces of the shoppers, but didn't see any he recognised. Feeling suddenly nervous and conspicuous, he cut across the links down on to the promenade.

He stopped when he reached the Clock House Café. This was where he always used to stand on the railings and look out to sea. When it was the sea that is, which it wasn't always.

Sometimes it was the Sahara desert or a Mexican plain whose dust his bullwhip licked. But now he was taller and the only thing he could see through the waves of barbed wire curling up over the railings were the pill-boxes and tank traps, and the sea was just the sea.

He peered through the windows of the café, half-expecting to see a young couple canoodling over spilt sugar. Or Frank leaning on his elbows, his gut on the counter. But it was boarded up for winter. He carried on until he reached the open-air swimming pool where there was snow at least a foot deep on each of the diving platforms. Then he turned right towards The Palace.

At the end of the last century The Palace had been known as The Empress Ballroom. The dance floor was made of Canadian maplewood and there was room on it for 2,000 dancers. After Queen Victoria's death (although this wasn't officially given as a reason), The Empress Ballroom became known simply as The Palace. The Canadian maplewood, which had inadvertently caused many accidents, was stripped, and black and white floor tiles laid instead. Hal had had his eyes on the dome of The Palace all the way along the promenade. It was the only place in Setton where something other than real life seemed possible. Behind The Palace was the open-air concert platform where musicians, pierrots and other entertainers performed. Up until the end of the war the annual sight of men in drag on the concert platform during high season had filled his nightmares.

He passed the rusting pylons of the Great Aerial Flight. This used to turn without a single squeak, and as it built up speed the small wooden boats suspended from wires would move outwards and upwards, pulled by a centrifugal force. He always had to ride it alone because his father was too heavy and his mother suffered from vertigo. There were only two boats left now, hanging lopsided from their wires.

The small scenic railway had a padlock over the doors the carriages used to shuttle through. The billboard, painted in 1912 and propped up inside the kiosk, still promised to take riders to the Antarctic where they would follow in Scott's footsteps. It was the only ride in the Pleasure Grounds that didn't look derelict.

The snow was thick here and a single set of footprints marked someone's passage from the Pleasure Grounds to The Palace. Hal followed them and was soon standing in the covered walkway that ran around the entire building, which was windswept whatever the weather, whatever the time of year. Geordie, boiler and repair man, as well as cloakroom attendant, in season, was outside sweeping up rubbish; sweeping so gracefully that he looked as though he was dancing with the broom. When Geordie used to work at Watts he had been responsible for organising two of the biggest strikes the pit had ever known. Jamie Price had never gone on strike, and was one of the few to break up the total closure, suffering years of abuse and threats because of it. Geordie knew that Jamie Price got up an hour earlier than usual when the strikes were on so that he could walk the three miles to Watts through thigh-deep snow when the buses were down, not only to get to work, but to get to work on time. Because of this, Geordie always made a point of showing respect, an enemy's respect, to Jamie Price's son. Often, depending on how much he had drunk, an uncomfortable amount.

'All right, Harold?' Geordie said, standing up straight and pulling the broom towards him, letting him know that he'd seen Hal before Hal had seen him.

Hal nodded and managed to smile.

'Haven't seen you here for ages.' Geordie nodded at the uniform, a gentle jibe. 'Want a look inside? Come to give a penny to the monkeys?' he added, knowingly.

Hal nodded again and he walked past him to the entrance of the dance hall.

'Good to see you back in one piece, son,' Geordie called out after him.

Hal stood on the threshold fighting back the tears. 'Son' was nothing more than a colloquialism but Geordie was the first person in Setton he had spoken to since getting off the train and he had become, he realised, more susceptible to words like 'son'. For a second he felt almost heroic, then he walked through the doors into the foyer of The Palace, nicknamed the Penny Arcade because when it was first built none of the amusements cost more than a penny to play.

When his grandad was still alive Hal used to belong to him for two hours every Sunday afternoon, and every Sunday afternoon they came to the Penny Arcade so that Hal could watch the wise monkeys play in their glass case. The wise monkeys stood at the foot of the stairs leading up to the Dance Hall, and were a Victorian taxidermist's masterpiece. All five of them wore waistcoats and fez hats, and each one played a different musical instrument. While he watched the wise monkeys play his grandad would put pennies in a couple of the quieter machines and then went to visit his friend Barry Smallwood. Barry Smallwood was curator of the North of England's largest model railway, housed in a room of its own as a sideshow to the Penny Arcade. Hal had hated Barry, not only because of his false leg and the fact that he would never let him touch anything, but because he wore the same uniform as a real train driver when he didn't drive real trains. Then Barry died, and his grandad died shortly after, which didn't surprise anyone because he never did have much of an appetite for life once his wife died. Hal only came to the Penny Arcade a couple of times after that.

The reason they used to come Sunday afternoons was because this was the only time the huge velvet curtains that separated the Dance Hall from the Penny Arcade were shut. The Arcade had always been full of children on Sundays.

Now it was empty, and the only thing Hal heard was old-fashioned music playing. When he looked for where the music was coming from he saw that the curtains ahead of him at the top of the stairs, held back by cords as fat as a giant's arteries, were open. It was the first time in his life that he had ever seen them open, and an unbelievable amount of light was shining through.

When he got to the wise monkeys at the foot of the stairs, he stood for a long time with his hands pressed against the glass case, looking intently for any signs of change. He had no idea, until that moment, how much he needed them not to have changed. They hadn't. The one holding cymbals that used to terrify him still had its unearthly grin. He searched around in his pocket, drawing out a handful of foreign change, and managed to find a penny. After a brief whirr and smooth clatter, the monkeys started up.

A penny's worth of their mechanical chatter brought back all of his pre-war life. He checked a sob and turned to see if anyone had heard. But Geordie was still outside and there was nobody manning the change kiosk. The monkeys reached the end of their piece, and the chattering finished before their bodies settled fully back into place. Hal turned to the foot of the stairs leading up to the Dance Hall where there was a board with the words TEA DANCE written on it as well as a time: 3 o'clock–5 o'clock.

A man started singing along to the band's music in a high-pitched voice, and as Hal drew closer he could hear the clatter of tables and chairs, and old people's laughter.

Halfway up the steps he saw the glass dome, which could be seen from all over Setton. Inside it looked even higher, and because of the dark green lichen creeping up around the rim it felt like being underground, the glass dome the only thing reaching the world above. He had heard people talk about the chequered dance floor at The Palace and how dancing on it fast after drinking you no longer knew whether you were dancing on floor, ceiling or wall as all sensation of gravity was lost.

Even without setting foot on the dance floor he began to feel disorientated. He had never expected it to stretch as far as it did, as far as the eye could see. Like the prairies the world news man talked about on the wireless. He had never expected all those things everybody said about The Palace to be true. Even at 4.30 in the afternoon, in the throes of a tea dance, and after coming through the other end of a world war. He felt elation and absolute depression at the same time.

There were hardly any people dancing and those that were looked very old to him. The couples were clutching on to each other, and some of the old men looked as though they were crying. Possibly from the strain of dancing to music they used to dance to with agile bodies. He could tell from the way their mouths moved that some of them were singing along to the music. The old women as they passed smelt powdery and flowery in the way old women do on special occasions.

The dancers were moving closer and closer to him and he thought he saw his grandparents, wearing their favourite clothes. His grandmother's dress, the one with small blue polka dots on, brushed his shaking legs and his grandad nodded at him as he led his wife proudly on. Hal's eyes followed them as they completed the circle and came dancing towards him again. But before it was their turn to reach him another younger couple passed. The woman he recognised as his Aunt Rose, Raymond's mother. He didn't recognise the man she was dancing with, and despite her high heels he was much more smartly dressed than she was. Aunt Rose couldn't take her eyes off him. They were both enjoying the tea dance, tepid as it was, as much as any of the old folk there. Until she passed him Hal had forgotten what she looked like. Aunt Rose wasn't talked about because she did something quite extra-ordinary: she walked into the sea and was never seen again.

All the dancers in The Palace were close and distant relatives, now dead. He felt suddenly terrified of seeing his parents there, but there was no sign of them. As they all circled round a second time they started waving to him. His hands went out for the velvet curtains as the air grew colder and colder and, keeping his eyes shut, he turned around until he was facing the Penny Arcade with his back to the dance floor. But the hairs on his arms and the back of his neck were up as he listened to the shoes of the dancers moving across the floor, keeping time with music that grew slower and slower.

He ran back down the stairs, his greatcoat trailing behind him. Geordie was in the cloakroom, rubbing something off the front of his waistcoat and didn't look up as Hal passed.

84

He went outside where the wind from the walkway filled his ears and left no room for the music from the tea dance, then made his way back across the links on to Front Street, no longer looking to recognise the faces he passed.

Just before Macey's corner shop, he passed a group of miners making their way home, leaving speckled trails of black in the snow. He looked, but his father wasn't among them. They left a heavy smell of sulphur in the air behind them, mingled with cigarette smoke. Which reminded him, he smoked now, and had wanted to turn up on his doorstep with a cigarette jammed between his lips, the end glowing against his greatcoat. So he went into Macey's.

Macey smiled warmly and knowingly at him, but still only said, 'How's things then, Hal?' Despite him standing there in uniform and despite it being the first time he had bought anything there other than rhubarb and custard sweets or Dainty Dinah toffee bars. Macey stood at the window and watched him leave, waving. He had spoken slowly and carefully to him, Hal noted, as if he suspected he might no longer understand English.

He started to count the numbers on the houses now; he was nearly there. There weren't many people about, and some houses he passed had no smoke coming from their chimneys. Sometimes he saw the odd face, either very old or very young, pressed against a window. He saw Mrs Marshal's face at number 41, and guessed, from the anxious eyes, that the war hadn't helped her achieve the blissful state of widowhood she had hoped for. Mr Marshal was no doubt due home any day now. Before Hal had left, Mrs Hayes, who kept the wool shop, had said that sod's law meant Mr Marshal would probably be the only one out of all of them to come home. The women on Ellsworth Row were great believers in sod's law. Mrs Marshal smiled and gave a small wave as Hal passed, and he almost blew her a kiss.

He was ecstatic and terrified now, and had to remember to keep trudging. Trudging, as opposed to just plain walking, made a more permanent impression on the minds of those watching. The back of his greatcoat fanned out over the snow behind him, like the train of a robe, and the snow became so packed under the soles of his boots he could hear it squeaking.

He wanted to reach 53 Ellsworth Row before it got properly dark. The whole of England had lit up and although he had got used to it again elsewhere, he didn't want to see the streetlamps on again in the streets of Setton. It would make him think of other times when he had walked home under lamplight, before the war, when he had been a hero in a chrysalis.

He turned right down the lane that led into the back street running behind Ellsworth Row. It wasn't so quiet here. There were children playing, and the snow was thick enough over the allotments to allow them to use these as extra hunting grounds. They ran about, involved in the intricate rules and regulations of their made-up games, without getting cold. The sight of the returning soldier in his greatcoat made them even more excitable and they ran up to him, tugging and asking for trophies, souvenirs, bones even. One small boy he recognised as the youngest of the Annegan brothers asked him for what he had seen.

Hal smiled good-humouredly, but nervously; he didn't have a way with children, didn't know how to answer their questions. After a few more minutes of tolerated tugging and pocket-searching, they scarpered off across the frozen allotments and their laughter, which came cracking back across the snow towards him, wasn't kind.

The backs of the houses were much blacker than the fronts; he had forgotten this. Against the snow they looked blacker still. He passed their garage. The doors looked a little looser on their hinges and two of the windowpanes were smashed. He didn't look in, and stood instead by the coal hatch, lighting one of the cigarettes he had bought from Macey's. He stood there smoking, and intermittently wiping his running nose. A door slammed on somebody's outside privy; his cigarette shook in his hand.

He edged round the side of the coal hatch, and was relieved

86

to see that the lights downstairs at number 53 weren't on. The last person he wanted to see sitting on the stairs right then was Daisy. There were lights on upstairs and the dim sound of music and laughter reached him. In the end he stubbed the cigarette out before going indoors, not wanting to look arrogant. He walked up the path, keeping his eyes on his boots and not daring to look up again.

He pushed open the door of the privy as he passed. The usual stack of printed matter was in there to use for wiping yourself after, but they didn't look like *Beanos*. The hallway downstairs was as spotless as it had ever been, and he half-thought of taking his heavy boots off, but decided in the end that it was his right now to keep them on if he chose. His father always did and Mrs Crombie never shouted at him. He even stamped the snow off and watched as it turned quickly to water. That would give Daisy something to think about.

Despite the cold in the hallway he could still smell cigarette smoke. He could smell perfume as well, but it wasn't his mother's. The loud banging of footsteps crossed the floorboards upstairs.

The staircase, he was sure, was narrower and he had to turn sideways to walk up it. The walls were still greasy from Mrs Crombie's frying, and he could smell lard on his fingers. Once he was at the top of the stairs the music became more distinct and he made out the sounds of a big band. He turned the knob, which didn't look as though it had been polished for a while, and opened the door.

There they were. His mother's legs were bare, and on the small drying frame to the left of the fire all her most intimate items of clothing were steaming. This surprised Hal; she had always been very particular about what she dried in the front room.

More to the point, they were dancing. Every piece of furniture in the flat rattled as the moves got flashier and flashier, and his father, in a new jumper, let out a whoop as he went crashing into the drying frame. Hal stood on the threshold, his head bowed, waiting for them to notice him.

More outraged than if he had found them dead. They didn't know whether he was dead or alive, and yet here they were, still able to dance.

'Oh my God, Hal,' his mother said, suddenly seeing him, and burst out laughing.

She danced over, spinning out of his father's arms. Jamie Price executed a few waspish moves of his own in an improvised solo while keeping his eyes on his feet. The tune on the wireless stopped and a new one started as Jamie looked up at Hal and gave a sheepish smile.

'You're home,' Charlie said.

She put her hands on the tops of Hal's arms, feeling him out. Then she kissed him nervously on the cheek and stood back to take him in from head to toe. Her forehead was glistening with sweat and she was wearing a perfume he hadn't smelt on her before.

After that he picked up his kit bag and walked in.

Jamie Price managed to step forward and knock Hal's hat affectionately off his head.

The nearer the fire Hal got, the more the steam rose off him and he looked down helplessly as the water collected on the rug. The room was tiny, and he wondered how on earth they had all spent so much time in it together.

'Must have been Providence who sent you today,' Charlie said picking up a box of cigarettes from the mantelpiece and lighting one. Behind the jug that held his father's combs, Hal saw the letter, now greasy and discoloured, addressed to Mr and Mrs Price from Fitts, propped up there, unopened still.

'Why's that then?'

'We've got a fire. Don't get one as often as we should because of the fuel shortages.'

She rattled the cigarettes slightly, looked at him again then offered him one.

'Take your coat off; it makes it look as if there's two of you.'

He took it off, but didn't know where to put it. In the end she hung it for him over the hat-stand, shut the door then came back to the fire.

It was while she was at the hat-stand that Hal noticed the man sitting at the table with the button box in front of him. He was the thinnest man he had ever seen.

The man stood up once he saw Hal had seen him, and held his arms out, suddenly frail, until Charlie noticed him and went to stand by him.

Jamie spat into the fire, but didn't look at Hal. He just started whistling to the tune on the wireless and tapping his right foot in time to the music.

Hal noticed some makeshift crutches in the corner by the table.

'He doesn't need those any more,' she said defensively, following Hal's eyes.

Hal looked at the man, but he wouldn't look back at him.

'You do remember Tom, don't you? Uncle Tom?' she said nervously.

'Uncle Tom?'

'Last time you saw him you were probably about this high,' she said measuring the air with her hand. Tom watched carefully and copied her. 'So maybe you don't remember.'

'I remember you,' Tom said suddenly, pointing at Hal. His voice was strange, like a deafening whisper.

'Tom was in the war. Like you. Then he was made a POW by the Japanese in Burma,' she said taking hold of his hand quickly. 'And now he's come home. To live here,' she looked at Hal, 'with us.'

Hal looked at his father, but Jamie still wouldn't look at him. He quickly saw that Tom had brought as much of the war as they could bear into the house. He was too late; they had already celebrated one homecoming, and it wasn't his.

Hal stared out at the allotments for a while, but it was nearly dark, and there were no longer any children playing. He went to shut the curtains and his dad gave his shoulder a squeeze as he passed.

Tom left the room and Hal heard the springs on his old bed creaking. Charlie came and sat opposite him at the table.

'Tom can sleep on the sofa. I can ask him. It's just, he's so long, it would be bloody uncomfortable for him.'

He didn't say anything, so she took hold of his hand and held it so that he could feel the metal of her rings. They had, he realised, been dreading his homecoming because of Tom. It made him remember something she had once said to him: that a death's always followed by a birth. There's always someone to step into someone else's place if they don't need it any more. Things never stay empty for long.

'I'm going outside.'

'It's cold,' she said, but neither of them stopped him.

He left her sitting at the table in the dark room, with the impression that she wanted to talk to him about something important; happiness, he was sure. He sat down on a step halfway down the stairs, but it didn't seem to accommodate him like it used to. And this was how Daisy found him when she pushed the back door open.

Hal watched the shadow of the bent head at the door, and was unprepared for the red that filled the hallway when the young woman entered. It was someone the same height as his father; it was Daisy in a hat, and when she took it off, on seeing him, there were no braids underneath, but large rolling curls. Her lips were red as well, and she stayed near the door, unsure whether to come closer or not. Despite the lips, and the curls, the thing that overwhelmed Hal, almost to the exclusion of everything else, was the red. The red coat, and the red dress. He had never seen anything so heroic, and it made him gasp.

'Where've you been?' he said at last, asking her the question she should have asked him.

'Out,' she answered, clutching her handbag against her breast, and taking in his uniform at the same time.

Speaking gave her the courage to walk to her front door. Her shoes made a tall steady sound across the floor, which meant that her footsteps no longer sounded as though she was about to break into a run.

'Are they not dancing?' she said, looking up at the ceiling.

'They were.'

90

'They dance all the time. To every song that comes on.' She paused, and opened the door to her flat. 'It drives us mad.'

Hal stood up, and walked down the stairs towards her. The red was no less close up.

'Will you come in for a cup of tea?'

5

Perkins's mouth was hanging open, but he couldn't help himself. Having passed through a heavy set of doors in the shop front, he had found himself standing in a small dark reception room where the carpet was so soft that when you walked it felt as though you weren't wearing any shoes. There was a man in a suit behind the desk, paid exclusively to smile when customers walked in, then pull the heavy curtain by the desk to one side. He had nodded at Perkins, but hadn't held the curtain for quite long enough so that it fell back into place too soon, knocking off his hat. Perkins had picked it up, rammed it back on and snarled at the curtain. Then checked himself, and put his best foot forward in order to walk down the narrow panelled corridor and under the small stone arch in front of him.

It was after passing under this, and finding himself in a cathedral made of iron and glass, that his mouth fell open. He instinctively took off his hat, covering his heart with it. In sheer size and magnitude, Victorian, yes. But the shoes, row upon row of them, showed a commercial savagery that was very of the moment. They stretched as far as the eye could see; just as he had prophesied they would. This was, truly, a wonder of the modern world. Perkins felt the awe a commercial man should feel; he was home. The rush surrounded him: the voices of eager, hysterical and browbeaten assistants, women's wails of disappointment, the clatter of lids being taken on and off, on and off, to reveal more and more shoes . . . tills ringing. Here was somewhere you could come and not be alone; here was life.

He knew that the slightest whiff of neglect would be the death of the place. But they, the customers, had no inkling of this. It was made of iron, it was huge, it was here to stay. They believed in it. He walked slowly down the aisle between the first few banks of shoes. It was all he had imagined, dreamt. Down to every last button on every assistant's jacket. The only thing he would have changed was the carpet, which he would have preferred to have been red. But he saw, looking down, that the blue of the aisle was far better. Red would have been too gaudy, the work of a huckster. But then this wasn't anything he had to worry about because this emporium belonged to Williamson, not him, and Williamson had got it right.

It looked like a busy time of day. Or maybe it was always like this, from the moment the front doors opened until the moment they shut. People were walking up the aisle in their droves, not a single one without a bag in their hand. Perkins found himself smiling at them in an idiotic way. He was watching a people mastered, only he wasn't the master. The sun was shining through the glass, making the nylon on the women's legs shine; the smell of shoe leather and money filled the air.

He turned suddenly on his heels and walked back the way he had come; from now on he wouldn't have to imagine, only remember. As he passed through the velvet curtain into reception he kept his hand over his hat, and rushed to open the shop door himself without giving the man behind the desk time to make it clear that he wasn't going to open it for him. He hurried out, keeping his head down until he reached Leicester Square.

Crossing road after road back to the Strand, he was in no fit state to avoid traffic so the traffic had to do its best to avoid him. There were shouts and cursing, but he didn't hear. These sorts of things never left dents in Perkins.

93

In Williamson's shoe emporium he had come face to face with the giant of his heart's desire. One that had been inside him since childhood. He had stared his giant squarely in the face only to find that it wasn't his after all; it was Williamson's. The only moment of real feeling had been one of anger when his hat was knocked off and he had to bend to pick it up. The memory of that anger came back to him clearly now, standing outside number 12 the Strand where he felt the flush of it again.

A. Perkins Shoes. He sighed. This is what the wooden letters across the shop front would have spelt, if the 'S' in 'Shoes' hadn't fallen off. The sunshine was bright and Mr Andrews had pulled down the yellow blinds to stop it from fading the stock in the window. The dusty outdated stock. He thought of the acres of glass at Williamson's and the brash display of shoes directly under it, and laughed out loud. Williamson, the bastard, would sell those before the sun faded them.

He was still laughing loudly when he pushed open the shop door and set the bell jangling. Mr Andrews, who had been poring over a newspaper at the cash desk, twiddling a pencil up his nose, started. He had an alcoholic's nose, but was in fact a teetotaller. He didn't even tipple. Fate was cruel. He wore a green cardigan, washed out of shape. Perkins had asked him again and again to exchange it for a suit jacket and each time Andrew nodded and said 'yes, of course, sir', but the next day Andrews would turn up still wearing the cardigan. He would just shrug and say that his arthritis was bad, and the cardigan was the only thing that kept him warm. This was Andrews's very polite way of saying that the premises were entirely unheated. Yes, he could see his breath again today standing inside the shop.

Perkins liked the 'sir', spoken without irony. It was one of the reasons Andrews had been kept on for as long as he had. That and the fact that he didn't mind occasionally not getting paid. Andrews had been a POW in the war and Perkins had the distinct impression that *A. Perkins Shoes* had in many ways saved Mr Andrews's life. Perkins had got rid of the other man,

Sedleigh, his assistant manager, because his snide comments and burning ambition were getting him down. He had half-expected to see Sedleigh today at Williamson's.

Andrews was smiling benignly at him as he hung his coat and hat up, then, with a shudder, put the coat back on.

Perkins glanced in his window, which was nothing more than a jumble of wire racks. A shoe had fallen off and was lying on its side. He went to pick it up but couldn't be bothered. Without knowing how it had happened, he had somehow slipped behind the times. He had always thought of himself as cutting edge, especially in the commercial world, but looking at the button-down slippers in the window of his shop, he suffered another bout of laughter.

The back wall of the shop was false and made entirely of hardboard with holes punched into it. There were more wire racks hung up here with shoes and slippers on them. He went to the corner and undid several brass hooks, then slowly pulled open the hardboard wall to reveal the real back wall of the shop, still covered in its turn-of-the-century wallpaper. There was a door in the wall. Mr Andrews moved out from behind the counter and hovered near the front door. He liked to do this when Perkins opened up the back wall of the shop and disappeared through the door.

Perkins heard Andrews closing the wall behind him as he descended the narrow staircase into the basement. There was a bell, operated by pressing a concealed button on the desk, and linked to the cash desk upstairs. He pressed that when he wanted Andrews to open up the wall. It had cost a fortune to have it installed.

The Missing Persons Bureau had been up and running for three months. Their first client, a friend of Mr Andrews, had wanted to track down his estranged son. The son had been found in Bangor of all places. Perkins had a gift for this, a natural talent, and his reputation spread through far-reaching surreptitious channels. He had few scruples and was happy to look for people who didn't want to be found. Andrews, to Perkins's surprise, proved to have as few scruples as him and made a far better assistant to the bureau than he had ever made to the shoe shop upstairs.

He shuffled the cards in the Bakelite desk calendar so that they showed the right date, Tuesday 14 February 1950. 'Valentine's Day,' he said aloud, then laughed again. The walls were bare apart from an old dartboard and a map of England. The only furniture other than his desk and countless boxes of shoes was a battered green leather sofa. All these things he had found here when he started to rent both floors. He was in debt and had borrowed bad money, but things were on the up. There were three books on his desk: a telephone directory, *Who's Who*, and *How to Become a Millionaire*. The map of England on the wall behind him had pins in it.

Somewhere above he heard the shop door ring. There was silence then the sound of footsteps, slow, ponderous. The next minute he heard the back wall of the shop being pulled out, and the door at the top of the stairs opening.

'Somebody to see you, sir,' Mr Andrews called.

Andrews didn't come down, and had given no prior warning, which meant that he trusted the stranger, that he had listened to his request and known that it would interest Perkins.

It became suddenly much lighter in the basement as sunlight from above poured briefly down the stairs. Then the door was shut and it was back to its usual badly lit gloom. The stranger on the stairs, who brought with him the smell of sandalwood, hesitated, then plodded down, looking about him in confusion.

Perkins recognised him immediately, in a way that left no room for doubt. Even the dull light in the basement managed to illuminate the stranger's blond hair and the toes of his highly polished shoes. Perkins's heart, he was amazed to feel, was actually beating faster, and he had to stop himself from extending his hand and saying, 'Major Delaval.'

Delaval took his gloves off, put them back on, then took them off again. Perkins saw him hesitate over whether to say 'Mr' before Perkins and, after a moment's deliberation, said, 'It's Perkins, isn't it?'

Perkins nodded. The name meant nothing to Delaval. He was jumpy, like everybody who came down to see him. For most of them it was their first brush with the darker side of life. Delaval looked as tormented as the rest when he looked up into Perkins's eyes. As though he had been forced to seek salvation from his most bitter enemy. He was about to speak, peering more intently as his eyes became accustomed to the dark. Perkins drew himself up, and bore the scrutiny with patience.

Delaval had, inherently, the build and bearing of a military man. But he had lost weight, his face was sallow and no longer reckless, and it was strange seeing him in civilian clothes. Delaval didn't apologise for the scrutiny.

'Do I know you?' was all he said.

Perkins waited a moment longer.

'Do you?' he said to him.

'Do I?' Delaval returned, gathering his coat about him in case he needed to make a run for it.

Perkins took *How to Become a Millionaire* out of his small pile and pushed it across the desk to Delaval. 'France. Nineteen forty-four,' he said.

Delaval continued to stare, then his face broke. 'The Rat Castle. Yes.'

Perkins knew, as well as if Delaval had said the name out loud, who it was he had come looking for. Had known, in fact, as soon as he recognised that it was Delaval standing on the stairs. Reason never made its way into the Rat Castle, but rumour did.

'Dick Whittington.' Delaval carried on with his telegram of memories. 'You were reading this just before I . . .' Delaval took him in again then shook his head. 'I don't think this will . . .'

'Work?'

'Yes.' Delaval thought about it. 'I hadn't expected to know', he gave a slight laugh, 'the private investigator.'

'That isn't quite what I am. All that I am,' Perkins corrected him.

'Yes, but . . . I don't think it will work.'

'Everybody who has crossed my threshold has found what they came looking for. One way or another,' Perkins said.

Delaval grunted.

'Maybe you've already heard that?'

'Yes, Mr Andrews' ('Mr' Andrews, Perkins noted) 'explained on the telephone. But your name, I didn't recognise the name.'

'Why should you?' Perkins said pleasantly.

This seemed to work as, with a sigh of exasperation, Delaval sat down, taking his hat off and putting it on the desk between them. He leant forward, the sleeve of his coat obscuring the Bakelite calendar, but soon sat back in his chair. The pose had been too intimate.

'You left the Rat Castle suddenly, I remember.'

'You remember my leaving?' Delaval said, surprised.

Perkins shrugged in order to play the memory down.

'They sent me south,' Delaval said. 'Then after the war I went to Utah. My family has holdings in a pleasure park there. On Great Salt Lake,' he added. 'But that's dead and buried now. Then after Utah, finally, we returned to England.'

'We?'

'She didn't want to come to England. She was with me all the time in France, all the time in the States, but she didn't want to come to England, she said.'

'Major,' Perkins insisted. 'Who is she?'

He felt Delaval retreating.

Delaval looked as though he felt he had already said too much. Getting up out of his chair he went behind the desk to look at the map of England. Perkins had to swivel round to keep an eye on him. 'I need a name,' he hissed.

Delaval turned round suddenly.

'Stella Armstrong,' he said with a nervous laugh.

Perkins sat back in his chair and closed his eyes. 'Armstrong,' he repeated. He had never known the second part of her name.

'You remember her?' Delaval said uneasily.

98

Perkins instinctively shook his head.

'But the pantomime . . . she was meant to play the cat in the pantomime,' Delaval persisted.

Perkins shrugged, as if to suggest that they were both too old to talk about pantomimes.

'I took her south with me,' Delaval carried on, relenting, 'and after the war, to Utah.'

They were both silent.

'And where's Stella now, Major?'

Delaval shook his head, oblivious to the fact that Perkins kept addressing him as 'major'.

'She escaped. That's was she calls it.'

'It's happened before?'

'Yes, but she always comes back after a few days. It's been a month since I last saw her.'

'And I'm to presume that you and Miss Armstrong', Perkins said carefully, 'aren't married?'

Delaval dropped the pin he was holding and bent to pick it up.

'In the past when she's escaped, have you had to go looking for her or . . .'

'She has always returned of her own accord.' Delaval put a pin at the bottom of the map. 'That's where she disappeared: the Metropolis Hotel, Brighton. It overlooked the pier. The sea as well, of course. But it was the pier she was interested in. That's why we went to Utah. In France she made me tell her about all the pleasure grounds and amusement parks I'd been to in America. Over and over again. She was obsessed with my descriptions of roller-coasters. The one in Utah was designed by my father . . .' Delaval put another pin halfway up the map. 'But I'm no engineer.'

'What was the name of the place in Utah?'

'The Spanish City.'

For the first time since entering the basement Delaval realised that Perkins was writing all this down. He watched the man's bent head and the slow deliberate hand movements of somebody who had learned to write late in life. He remembered the boy now quite clearly; this man was nothing more than a neglected version of that boy, and he had given himself entirely to him without even realising it. The rest of his life lay between these four walls, in this grubby basement.

'The Spanish City was about to be demolished when we got there. At first they wouldn't even let us on to the pier it was so dangerous, so I told her that we'd go south and ride other coasters: Jack Rabbit, Slammer, Thunder. But it was the Charleston she wanted to ride. You've no idea how much persuading it took to get them to let us ride it. I told her it was a death trap, and that it might cost us our lives. This . . . of course . . . made her desire to ride it even greater. Here.' He turned away from the map and drew something carefully out of an inside pocket. 'Photographs,' he said, dropping them on to the desk.

Perkins laid them out and Delaval watched his hands spread over them.

'They were taken . . . everything you need to know is written on the back. Date. Place.'

Perkins didn't turn them over.

'I never did get one of her smiling,' Delaval said, glancing briefly over Perkins's shoulder, then away again.

Perkins put a lot at risk when he asked the next question, but he knew he had to. 'Are you sure you want to try and find her?'

Delaval gave him a strange anguished look. 'I need to find her.' The words fell unevenly out of his mouth.

Perkins sighed with relief.

'As I said to Mr Andrews, I pay well.'

'How well?'

Delaval picked his hat up and put it on his head, then picked up the copy of *How to Become a Millionaire*, holding it against his chest.

Perkins automatically stood up.

'I phoned earlier to see you. Your Mr Andrews told me you were out. Then, eventually, he told me you were at Williamson's Shoe Emporium.'

Perkins never blushed. Instead a grey pallor spread across his face.

'You've almost given up, haven't you. But not quite.' Delaval gently put the book into Perkins's outstretched hand. 'Never give up. You don't know what's round the corner.' Delaval met his gaze head-on. They had stripped each other down to the bone. For Perkins, money was the heart of the matter. But this didn't repel Delaval, it made him suddenly pleased. Happy almost.

'Now you need to tell me everything,' Perkins said.

'Everything?'

'Everything, no matter how small.' He pressed the button underneath the desk and they headed for the stairs. 'Come back tomorrow, Major,' he said, opening the door at the top. 'That should give you time to think of everything.'

The false wall was still shut. Through the holes they saw Andrews shuffle across the shop floor then undo the catches. The wall swung begrudgingly open making the shoes on their racks rattle.

'New shoes?' Perkins said lightly then sniggered.

Delaval cast his eye round the shop then shook his head. He didn't smile.

'I will find her,' Perkins said. But Delaval had left. He turned desperately to Andrews, suddenly wanting more than anything right then for him to explain why all this had happened. Now, in the middle of this other life he had built for himself, when he least expected it.

6

Ada Crombie was lying on her back with her eyes closed and her toes pointing upwards. Her dress was short-sleeved, her arms were folded, and her hands were wearing white gloves. The only flaw was the laces on her shoes, which weren't quite long enough to tie in a bow due to the fact that her feet were bloated. There was also a slight lipstick smudge on the thumb of one of the white gloves. Other than this, Mrs Crombie was still Mrs Crombie, despite being dead.

Raymond Clarke stood in the corner of the room, wiping his hands on a cloth.

'You've done a good job,' Daisy said enthusiastically, as she circled the coffin. She wasn't looking at so much as inspecting her mother, and although she held a handkerchief, she showed no sign of needing to use it. Her hands were wearing the same white gloves as her mother's. The gloves probably were her mother's. She leant forward, and for a moment Hal thought Daisy was going to kiss her, but realised as her nostrils flared that she was smelling her. Then she rubbed her hands over the satin inside the coffin and stood back, satisfied. 'A really good job, Raymond,' she said.

Raymond came out of the corner.

'She looks grand, doesn't she?'

Hal thought Mrs Crombie looked uncomfortable about the fact that she wasn't wearing a hat, but he didn't say anything.

When he was younger he used to help Raymond in the Parlour on Saturdays. He hadn't liked it then, and liked it even less now. The Parlour often fell into sudden darkness when the electricity went down, which it did regularly. This was something Hal never got used to, whereas Raymond was able to sit waiting patiently for it to come back on, even with his hand still on the face of the corpse he was preparing.

The Co-operative Funeral Services was beneath the Co-op Department Store, which stood on a corner, linking the bottom of Main Street to the end of Front Street. Raymond had started work there in 1933. He spent most of his time alone, and the only other person he ever saw on a regular basis, who still had a pulse, was Mr Chappel, the appointed agent, who spent vast amounts on petrol travelling around the north-east in his Austin, looking for commercially viable locations in which to establish new branches of the firm.

Raymond never had much to say, and was his most talkative with the monumental stonemason who dealt with headstones. Raymond had a profound belief in the power of inscriptions, and ensured that those carved on headstones he was responsible for would make mourners even out of those who had never known, let alone loved, the deceased.

Sudden deaths, through either accident or intent, were often taken straight to Raymond at the Parlour before anyone else was involved. People had few inhibitions about telling him the true circumstances of a death so that as the years passed, he could have become a real chronicler of the times. By the time Mrs Crombie passed away, there weren't so many being laid out on his Parlour table that he could name. Nowadays more strangers were dying and being brought to him.

In the evenings and at the weekends he worked at the Setton Voluntary Lifeboat Brigade, which operated from South Cliff.

The Parlour never felt like a basement; it was more like a room high up in a building, perpetually shuttered. The air was very dry, and this was the reason behind Raymond's preference for artificial flowers. Relatives did sometimes request real ones, but the smell (especially of the lilies) was not only overpowering, but also offensive. The carpet was green and the pile quite deep, which lent an element of luxury to the room that bore traces of a real parlour with its coat-stand, as well as the highly polished hat- and umbrella-stand. Raymond still hadn't found a way of concealing the lingering smell of wet umbrellas. The oil he used in his hair to keep it wavy, as well as his cigarette smoke, could also be smelt.

Brown and orange tiles ran round the lower half of the room, and above them painted tiles, depicting a highly glazed Creation. The sign on the door, at street level, said Co-operative Funeral Services, and the lettering was gold leaf. Mr Chappel thought that the gold leaf made people put their trust in them. There used to be a small window display of artificial flowers with a green velvet curtain behind it, but the cleaner always forgot about them and Raymond found the dusty flowers distasteful so the monumental stonemason made a headstone for them with the firm's name engraved on it. This was Mr Chappel's idea and was even more distasteful than the artificial flowers with their dusty silk petals and sun-bleached plastic stalks, but Chappel had a commercial instinct it was beyond Raymond's power to wrestle with.

Raymond was brought up by his father, and had been, ever since the age of fifteen, the breadwinner. William Clarke wasn't only unemployed, he was unemployable. This was because of his two dogs, Betsy and Flyer, greyhounds he took on the bus with him down to Wallsend where he raced them at the track on Thursday and Friday nights. He drank the money he earned and called it a 'clean way of living'. Occasionally he queued with the other men to see Lucille, the girl who stripped at the Clayton Arms on Friday afternoons. There were other rumours Raymond had heard concerning his father and the stripper, Lucille, but he had so far found no substantial evidence, and managed to keep them at arm's length.

Daisy picked up a needle and thread from Raymond's desk

and started sewing up one of the buttonholes on the front of Mrs Crombie's dress, the one over her cleavage that kept coming undone, making the front of the dress gape unpleasantly.

'Are you coming to the funeral?' she said to Hal.

'Of course.'

Mrs Crombie had been part of his life for as long as he could remember. Number 53 Ellsworth Row still smelt of her frying even though she no longer wielded her frying pan there. And when his mother and father danced they still anticipated the bang of her broom coming up through the floorboards.

'It'll swell the numbers from three to four, if you can.'

'I've already said yes.'

'I can get Dad to come,' Raymond put in.

'I don't want him to, he'll only bring the dogs. The vicar won't want those in his church.'

Hal looked at Raymond, unable to tell whether Raymond was offended by this or if he saw her point.

She pulled a pair of tweezers out of her handbag and set to work on Mrs Crombie's eyebrows.

'What are you doing now?' Hal said, disturbed by this last detail.

Daisy stood back and sighed, 'Trying to make her look beautiful. She never was.' She moved in with the tweezers again, pulling so hard that Mrs Crombie's left eye started to open.

'Just leave her,' Raymond said.

'Are you coming dancing tonight or not?' she asked Hal, ignoring Raymond.

'I'll stay here. With your mother,' Raymond said, pointedly.

'The funeral's not until tomorrow.' Daisy, unlike most people, didn't falter under the weight of Raymond's judgments. But she gave the tweezers up and moved away from the coffin to fiddle with the flower display by the door. 'Well, I'm going dancing,' she finished, taking her scarf out of her handbag and starting to tie it under her chin. The scarf had a pheasant print on it and Hal couldn't decide whether it suited her or not.

They left the Parlour together, Hal grabbing at Daisy's departure as an excuse to leave. He couldn't stand the sight of Mrs Crombie laid out any longer. At the end of the day, the English, he decided, had a secular approach to death. Something that would explain their ability to become embarrassed on the corpse's behalf, that it should find itself in a different condition to everybody else in the room.

As the door at the top of the stairs opened, Raymond heard the noise of the shop-floor staff from the Co-op above. One unified mass clocking off and making their way out of the building's back entrance, home. Daisy and Hal disappeared into it.

There had been a time, a few years back, when everyone thought she and Harold were going to marry. Then the moment passed. And Daisy continued to wear red. No marriage proposal from any other quarter seemed to be forthcoming either, but then Ada Crombie had at one time in her life been Setton's only prostitute. These thoughts, as well as the sight of Daisy in her red dress and pheasant scarf walking up the stairs, threatened Raymond's sense of stability in a way he couldn't fathom.

He walked over to Mrs Crombie and gently shut the left eye Daisy had pulled open with the tweezers.

Hal stood in front of the fireplace so that he could see himself in the mirror. Pushing a few of his mother's hairpins, and some firelighters to one side, he got a partially clear view of his face, the dusty blue velvet bow tie he was wearing, and the top of his black jacket. The bow tie was an affectation, and the age of ridicule wasn't far away, but he had dared himself to wear it anyway. He was going dancing, and as long as he kept a low profile before and after, he knew that among the dancers themselves he was in tolerant company.

While Raymond was burying the last of their grandparents' generation, Hal was busy with the next. At school, standing in front of a class of children, he often ran out of things to say and didn't know what to do about the fact that his lessons were essentially boring. The children didn't torment him like they did the other teachers because they couldn't make their minds up about him. Relative youth and the fact that Mr Price had been spotted dancing at The Palace during high season stood in the way of any verdict being reached. He hadn't defined, clearly, whose side he was on.

When Hal had first joined Setton Secondary Modern in 1949 to teach geography he had encountered a handful of teachers who had not only survived, but who were visionaries. Then there were those who didn't survive: there were teachers who drank on the job, slept on the job, and who discovered vast reserves of brute force within themselves. Hal soon realised that he was, and would remain, a survivor, but one without a vision. He was either pleased with the children or annoyed with them, but he never came close to loving them. The children had the ability to make monsters out of them all. So that no adult knew for definite, at any given moment, whether they belonged to the abused or the abuser. This confusion generated some spectacular behavioural patterns.

Mr Collins, headmaster of Setton Secondary Modern, finally caught on to the 1948 Employment and Training Act in 1952, and appointed Hal Youth Employment Advisor. There was no extra pay involved and he was expected to sacrifice a great deal of his spare time in order to teach children the value of plying a trade. It did mean, however, that he was given an ex-broom cupboard that he could pass off as an office, even though it took Weevil, the caretaker, who disliked Hal immensely, a good two months to remove all his brooms and ladders. Hal just about managed to fit an old desk into the space although he had to crawl underneath it in order to reach the chair behind.

Apart from a couple of shabby accidents on the part of Weevil during the inaugural week (such as spilt bleach on the chair and 3-in-1 oil over the desk), the broom cupboard soon became colloquially known as Youth Employment Services. Despite repeated requests, Hal was only in the end supplied with relevant forms for Watts colliery, the Co-operative Society, Welwyn Electrics, the aluminium smelting plant and the new power station in Wyley. After really putting his foot down he was given additional forms for the secretarial college, several shipping companies at Wyley docks and the Wilkinson razor factory.

This was the weaponry he had at his disposal to combat the desires of teenage boys and girls who asked, with straight faces, for information on how to become film stars, racing drivers, bass guitarists, night club singers, and who had no intention of ever wearing overalls to work. So there he was, responsible every year for the futures of 150 children after having in some inexplicable way forfeited his own. And the thing that stunned him most when these boys and girls entered his windowless office, now painted blue but still stinking of bleach, with its one bookshelf, humming light, and wastepaper basket that was always empty, was that they genuinely believed he had the means to ease them into their dreams. For the duration of the fifteen to twenty-minute interview they treated him more as an oracle than a teacher. And this was because he lied to them; he never told them the truth. Mr Collins was aware that Hal wasn't expounding the doctrine of honest toil, but left him alone in his broom cupboard while he pursued the handful of girls that blossomed into pageant queens during their final year at school.

Hal, in fact, had no doctrine other than not to laugh in their faces. Some didn't turn up to their appointments at all; some came to tell him they were starting at Watts after Easter. The only single moment of real joy he had had was a letter, now framed on his office wall, from a boy called David, whom he had given a lot of help to with his application form for the Royal College of Art. The letter, written from the RCA, said that he often thought of Mr Price, that he always would. There was even an invitation to a private view, which he nearly went to, but in the end couldn't summon up the courage. London was a long way away.

Without taking his eyes off the mirror he picked up the clothes brush, shook it for any dead moths that might have fallen among the bristles, then gave his jacket a quick brush. He liked to dress up, especially during high season when he knew the evening would end in dancing. Tonight, as well as the bow tie, he wore cufflinks and a tie pin that had his initials on. A gift, surprisingly, from his dad, who had Harrison order them specially. Round his waist was a fat black belt with a gold-coloured buckle the size of a fist on it. He knew he was prone to looking not just faded, but ridiculous as well. Not entirely convinced that tonight was no exception, he took his hands out of his pockets and turned away from the mirror.

Strings of electric lights not yet lit stretched along the length of the promenade from the cemetery right down to South Cliff where The Palace Dance Hall stood. There wasn't a bulb missing along the way or a paving stone cracked. The railings on the promenade were painted turquoise, and just before the dunes started, beds had been planted with flowers whose colours looked just as good under electric light as they did under sunlight.

The holiday camp up by the lighthouse on North Cliff was full, which meant that the promenade, at this time of night, was also full. It was high season, and Setton's everyday self was hidden; for the next few months it was somewhere people escaped to rather than from, and they paid money to do it. The mines, aluminium smelting plant, and other industries were forgotten in the seasonal appetite for pleasure. Hal, along with thousands of others, became a pleasure-seeker. With high season came the illusion, which lasted for two months of every year, that he was a free man.

He was wearing his dance shoes and could see the setting sun reflected in the shiny black toes as well as being able to feel the promenade itself through the thin soles. He was strolling with his hands in his pockets, hoping that he might look disaffected or at least louche, but it was difficult to pull off with his hair being as highly waxed as it was. This look was plainly more achievable in younger men. Still, he hadn't given up all hope.

The promenade had been built in stages, and had taken from 1879 until 1922 to complete, as the town above it grew from fishing village to pleasure resort. The base of the lamps along the promenade had thick sea serpents curled around them. These same sea serpents formed the legs on all the benches along the sea front. The benches not occupied by dazed young mothers were being sat on by louche young men (the real thing), by girls wearing ferocious sunglasses; by all sorts, out and about, with or without a reason. It was that time of the evening when it was just beginning to get dark and when the air smelt not only of the day past, but of the night to come as well.

At low tide, the beach that ran below the promenade offered itself to those couples who chose not to or were unable to observe the usual courtship ritual; it was also available for chance encounters. Hal had a beach hut he paid annual rent on further along towards North Cliff where there were still tank traps and a pill-box. He once opened it up for a couple he particularly disliked the look of. The boy had a twisted mouth and baggy jacket pockets; the girl had a huge forehead and the back of her dress caught up in her underpants. He opened the hut up for them because he hoped to become a deciding factor in two people's lives, to have the pleasure of engineering a real moment. He wanted to hang around in the dunes behind the hut and see the outcome of his gesture, even though his behaviour could too easily have been mis-interpreted, but the boy turned the offer down anyway, tugging the girl behind him.

Uncle Tom, who still lived with them, was employed as a gardener for the council, and responsible for the upkeep of all flowerbeds and lawns along the promenade. Hal had little to say to him in private and his long neurotic figure, still prone to outbursts of screaming, was the last thing he wanted to see or communicate with in public. Fortunately Tom stayed away from the promenade at night and was as terrified of The

Palace, or any reference to it, as he was of Burma. Nearly.

A couple of boys walked past laughing and looking over their shoulders, their suit jackets flapping excitedly in the breeze blowing up off the sea. One of them was gap-toothed and the other was holding what looked like a girl's yellow sweater in his hands. He had it bundled up tightly and kept staring at it in disbelief. Hal thought he recognised them, possibly from one of his classes at school, but they didn't look his way, and he wouldn't have wanted to recognise them if they had. The boy holding the yellow sweater wore his suit well, Hal noted, as they half-walked, half-scampered back up the promenade. As they passed him again their laughter wasn't warm; it was the laughter of children no longer interested in being children. Sometimes he recognised faces from school at The Palace, but it was never referred to by him or them. He danced as well as they did, often better, even though the music they danced to was becoming increasingly 'their' music. He had got away with it so far because he wasn't married; there was no wife he left at home in order to come dancing. But he was at that dangerous crossroads when the fact that he wasn't married would turn from being a help to a hindrance.

Night was closing in now, and it wouldn't be long before the lights were switched on. He liked to watch people's faces the moment this happened. All of a sudden, once the lights were on, there weren't so many children around, just puddles of ice-cream where last minute treats had been dropped and melted colourfully into the pavement. It was high tide. The mobile piers, wheeled down on to the beaches every July and used by pleasure boats, were now half-submerged. A group of boys were diving off the end into deep water.

There were still a couple of donkeys being rounded up down on the sand. The donkey man in his filthy anorak kept yelling at the beasts as they blundered through sandcastles made earlier. It was still the same bowlegged donkey man Hal remembered from Donkey Derby days when he was younger.

Frank was closing the doors of the Clock House Café and winding up the canopy for the night. The scraping of metal chairs over the terrace could be heard as he stacked them into piles to save them getting covered in seagull droppings. Frank gave Hal a quick smiling nod, as if vanquishing his side of an earlier argument. Hal waved back enthusiastically and had to straighten his suit afterwards. Then he heard the strains of music from The Palace. The Clock House was usually the first place he picked them up from. It was verging on 9 o'clock.

The open-air pool and the boating lake lay still and empty. When The Palace chucked everyone out in the early hours of Saturday morning the over-excited and desperate would fall into boats inadequately moored at the edge of the lake, and paddle across to the island where, among statues of Alice and her Wonderland acquaintances, they pursued ideals of happiness. Hal went in a boat once, and the thought of himself slumped drunkenly in the prow still amazed him. He was left in the bottom of the boat, his long legs caught under the seats, as the girl and boy who had paddled him to Wonderland went stumbling around the island, half-looking for privacy. Only the girl returned and she rowed them back to the boathouse alone, treading all over him in her broken sandals, not realising that he was still there.

The open-air swimming pool at South Cliff only became a swimming pool when the tide retreated, leaving it full of seawater. There was an Olympic-height diving board at one end of the pool, which had proved fateful to a large number of late-night escapades, but hadn't yet been closed off.

For some reason, diving from the highest platform was the one thing that didn't give his Uncle Tom the shakes. The days he had off gardening in the summer, he came to dive. People would queue along the sides of the pool to watch the skinny man, who still wore knitted trunks, leap off into the air, arms outstretched, making no splash. Often there was applause as he climbed shaking out of the water and made his way towards the changing cubicle with not so much as a backward glance.

The music from The Palace was now clearly audible, as were the screams. The screams were a mystery, and could only be heard at a distance. Once you set foot inside The Palace you never heard anyone screaming, there was just the din of music and human voices. Hal had never worked out why; it was just one of those things.

The promenade lights went on, and as soon as they did the sky and sea seemed suddenly much darker. Once the lights went on, it became night, and he felt ready to partake in the great forgetting that was Friday night. He was walking faster now, ready for that first drink, the one that would make him believe he didn't know what the evening held in store for him. The Palace was half-Roman amphitheatre, half-Norman castle, made of pioneering ferro-concrete. Sturdy square walls formed its outer shell; inside it was more delicate and confused: circular with stone pillars. The pillars formed a misshapen terrace that circled the dance floor. The ceiling above it was made of glass, and this glass dome let in a strange hallowed light. Hal entered.

Shaking hands with Geordie, he passed into the Penny Arcade, kept open for dancers with itchy fingers as well as itchy feet. Geordie reckoned the cloakroom wasn't what it used to be. These days people danced in what they arrived in, rarely shedding any layers, and the women didn't even wear shawls any more. Changing times made Geordie more of a security guard than a cloakroom attendant, but he still wore his original uniform, the one that made him look like a cinema usher.

There was only a handful of people playing the penny slot machines. Depending on his mood, Hal still sometimes played the wise monkeys, but not tonight. He passed through the curtains into the main dance hall, walking straight up the marble steps on to the balcony. The old fever was on Hal, the same fever that hit everyone who crossed the threshold, and made them forget two things instantaneously: family and the fear of starvation, yesterday and tomorrow. Suddenly he stretched no further than his own fingers and toes.

The dance floor was full and eager, and the heat of the day had been trapped under the glass dome, which amplified the sound of thousands of feet. The sound used to be that of steps danced in unison; these days things were more discordant. He recognised a lot of Setton faces who had come because, being high season, there was a high probability of spending the night dancing with a stranger, and strangers brought hope. Hal knew from experience that the boys preferred tripper girls, and the girls preferred boys from the holiday camp or, if they were feeling really lucky, those with a bit more class, staying in hotels. The boys claimed to be looking for a quick fix, the girls a summer fix. In everyday life they might be overworked, underpaid, unemployed, abused, or abusers, but here they came to dance despite the everyday. They weren't interested in democracy, just in establishing a new order more in their favour.

Hal walked along the balcony to the bar, the Tropicana, and ordered a straight vodka. The Palace was one of the few places in Setton where it was all right to order something other than beer. He liked the idea of himself drinking vodka, although the taste of it made him queasy after a while. The barman, Fast Eddie (so called because he could sling a drink across the bar without spilling a drop), didn't have much to say in the way of banter, and had been there since most people's parents' generation. Possibly the generation before. His hair was silver, and his face, whatever the weather, whatever the music, morose. So it was with some surprise that Hal saw Eddie smiling as he waited to order his vodka.

He was smiling at the man in front of Hal, the man sitting on the barstool with his hands held quietly together in front of him. Eddie was shaking his head at something the man on the stool had just said while the man watched intently as Eddie poured different coloured liquids into the shaker. It was the first time Hal had seen the shaker being used at the Tropicana. The bar was quite a mess with slops from bottles usually kept on glass shelves up on the wall behind. Bottles people no longer thought of as anything other than part of a display. The man on the stool was listening to Eddie's running excuses about the limited means he had to work with, without responding. At last the shaker was opened and a thick brown liquid that looked a lot like chocolate ice-cream was poured into a short fat glass. Eddie had even given the glass an extra wipe with his towel before filling it. He started to look around for something to put on top.

'Lime?' the man said, helpfully.

Eddie's cheeks went red as he looked around for the lime he knew he didn't have. The man gestured with his hands that it didn't matter, but Eddie had had the little joy he felt knocked out of him by his unexpected failure at this late stage. He put the incomplete drink on to a tray and pushed it towards the man who left the stool with a brisk nod after filling the empty tray with some notes from his pocket.

Hal knew even without seeing his face that he had never been to The Palace before. He walked slowly; the way people who went there alone walked. When Hal ordered his vodka, Eddie was still watching, aggrieved, as the man disappeared, and Hal didn't want to point out to him that the spillage from the various bottles was beginning to drip over the edge of the bar in multicoloured streaks.

Hal stood against the balustrade looking out over the dancers who obscured the black and white floor, trying to see if Daisy was already there or not, but there didn't seem to be anything red on the horizon. He recognised a girl he had been with one night in his beach hut, two years ago. She was married now, to Rob Gregson the baker's son. Hal and Daisy would sometimes watch the dance floor and place light-hearted bets on the pairings that might or might not take place. He liked it up on the balcony more than on the dance floor itself these days, but stayed away from the dark corners where the carpet smelt of beer and piss. The corners were where a lot of underage drinkers went and where a new kind of violence he didn't understand was breeding. Occasionally people would get cut up in the corners. Girls stayed at the tables on the edge of the balcony where they were caught safely in the light from the dance floor.

The dancing was much faster these days, and there was a lot more sweating done in public, but The Palace seemed to take this evolutionary process in its stride. The council no longer had the power to insist on the soft-soled dance shoes that Hal still wore out of habit. They put all their efforts these days into barring the sailors who docked at South Wyley. For some reason the Norwegians were the only ones allowed in. There were no Norwegians in tonight though. He couldn't see Daisy either, but he could see the man from the bar. He was threading his way slowly towards the stage at the far end of the dance floor.

Hal felt a sharp pinch on his arm, which nearly made him drop his drink, and turned round to see Daisy standing there with Melita and Tinker Trench behind her. Melita and Tinker appealed to Daisy's apocalyptic vision of romance, and she talked about them in the same way she used to talk about his parents. She had appointed herself guardian angel of the romance that was Melita and Tinker. An interest that wouldn't last; it never did with Daisy.

He watched as she moved off towards the Tropicana but didn't attempt to join her, unable to bear the high-pitched false southern accent she put on when ordering a drink. She said Eddie understood her better when she did this, and gave her more for her money. Wearing polka dots and with a Babycham in her hand, Daisy lost a lot of her daytime edges. She had a capacity for getting tipsy quickly, something Hal had never expected of her until they started to come dancing. He had only ever seen her vomit through drink once in the past ten years, which was to say that she had a curiosity for alcohol without pinning all her hopes on it.

'How long have you been here?' Tinker said.

'Not long.'

Tinker's suit always looked cleaner and newer than Hal's, even though they both only had the statutory two. And he smoked like a woman, slowly not greedily, holding his cigarette between the two fingers, never dropping the ash on the floor unless it was unavoidable. The waves in his hair caught the light as he leant out over the balustrade to look at the dance floor. He worked with Daisy at the dairy counter in the Co-op.

Melita had arrived on the shores of Setton a decade previously as a Polish refugee. Everyone thought that Melita, who had integrity, would be the last person to succumb to Tinker's veneer-like charm, but maybe she just believed in it, and in turn made him believe in it himself. Melita once rode a bicycle past the corner Tinker was hanging around on (he hung around on a lot of corners); when he saw her he shouted out, 'Hail fair maiden on thy chariot,' and she stopped. Things went on from there.

'Where's Raymond?'

'With my mother,' Daisy said.

'Oh.' Melita frowned. Raymond made her nervous.

'I thought your mother was dead,' Tinker put in.

'She is. That's why he's keeping her company.'

Hal followed the course of her drink as she raised it slowly to her mouth, her eyes on the dancers.

'It's busy. And loud,' Tinker said touching his ear, then drawing back and smiling at Hal.

Raymond also had this habit of following everything he said with a gesture, as if he was afraid of being misunderstood. He didn't do it so much any more. Raymond was a force to be reckoned with at The Palace. However dingy he looked at work, he always shone when he came out dancing. Despite his preternatural shyness, he was a very good dancer.

They all sat down at a nearby table, Hal tapping his tobacco tin in time to the music. Daisy had taken up smoking because it gave her something to do in company when she ran out of things to say. At one time she also did it in the hope that it would disguise the greasy aura of her mother's cooking. Nauseous amounts of perfume were applied for the same reason. Hal couldn't help noticing that, like 53 Ellsworth Row, Daisy still smelt of Mrs Crombie's frying.

Daisy was out of sorts tonight because of Melita's new dress. She drank her Babycham in minutes, then sat back chewing her lip as Tinker escorted Melita lightly on to the dance floor, paying a lot of attention to the way his hands hovered over shoulder-blades and buttocks.

117

'I thought I'd be married before Mam died,' she said suddenly.

This was something they had never talked about before, it was too potent, too unmentionable.

'I wanted her to see me married before dying. Not the church or the dress, but afterwards. What I really wanted was for her to see me make a good go of it, for her to have to cross my threshold, and come visiting me in my house,' she said suddenly, then looked down. 'I don't want to be like her, Hal.'

Hal instinctively took hold of her hand, more to stop her talking than anything else. The sudden gesture made her wince with surprise, but she let her hand rest in his without pressure for a few minutes, before sliding it back across the table and into her lap.

'People'll think I'm here with you if you do that. Then they won't ask me to dance,' she said looking around nervously.

Hal was about to ask her himself when Bill Noble, who also worked with her on the dairy counter at the Co-op, walked smiling up to the table with an outstretched hand.

'D'you want to?'

'All right,' she said, but sounded tired, and pushed her shiny red clutch bag across the table to Hal. 'D'you mind?'

He took hold of it, resisting the temptation, as always, to open it. This wasn't made any easier by the knowledge that Daisy probably wouldn't mind if he did.

When he looked at the dance floor again, Daisy was no longer with Bill Noble, now visible on the balcony opposite talking to Les, who did up cars and raced them at Kielder Forest. She was nowhere to be seen at all, in fact. He had drunk enough to feel like dancing himself so he went in search of Daisy.

He tried to walk round the perimeter of the floor, still clutching her bag, but there were too many dancers. Even walking round the edge as he was, he had his feet trodden on and could feel, through his trousers, the brushing of skirts against his legs. Sometimes an elbow caught him or he was whipped across the face by hair that had come loose. If he stayed standing for too long, things fell at his feet: earrings, a watch, ribbons, a pair of broken spectacles even. In the end he was forced to dance on the spot, keeping Daisy's clutch bag pressed tightly to his side, making the most of the breaks between songs, when people stood poised, to move as fast as he could through them. But she was nowhere.

He had almost reached the centre and there was still no sign of her. He was worried about her, something that hadn't happened before. The buffeting of the dancers no longer made him laugh, it was affecting his sense of balance. Some people no longer smelt as good as others, and he was rapidly losing sight of the rest of the evening. Then he was jolted so badly that he fell into the back of the girl who had been dancing up his left-hand side. She fell into the boy in front of her, and Hal recognised one of the boys from the pier, who didn't look upset at finding the girl in his arms.

'You drunk, Pricey?' the boy said, looking at the clutch bag, and Hal saw that he wasn't just gap-toothed; a lot of his front teeth were actually missing. His freckles stretched over a broken nose.

It offended Hal, being addressed as Pricey here of all places, so he turned his back on him to end anything that might start, and found himself facing the back of the man from the bar. He was shorter than Hal had thought, and was moving his hips backwards and forwards efficiently to the music, dancing with a strange sense of proprietorship as if he was the manager of the place. The woman he was dancing with was Daisy, who was smiling, but looked scared. Judging by the funny colour of her hands, he was holding them very tightly.

Hal tried to get her attention, but his jacket was pulled from behind. It was the boy again, and he was now convinced he had given careers advice to him only last term.

'Mr Price,' the boy said as Hal turned round. 'You pushed Liz here.' He tried to put his arm round the girl, and although she let it rest there, her shoulders were rigid. She wasn't looking at either of them. 'You pushed Liz.'

Hal could see the arse of the man from the bar moving in time to the music from the corner of his eye and, sporadically, he could smell Daisy. The boy from school, whose name he dimly remembered as being Jerry, was smiling at him. If he had given him careers advice at the end of last term, he would have left school by now. Leavers were dangerous. Especially ones like Jerry who had laboured and suffered.

'Sorry, Liz,' Hal said, genuinely, but still distracted.

'It's Elizabeth,' she corrected him.

'Elizabeth,' he repeated, inclining his head towards her.

'And Liz fell into me,' Jerry carried on, almost panting now.

'It's Elizabeth,' she said again, impatiently manoeuvring herself away.

He soon had his arm around her again.

'Liz could have pushed me right over. But it wouldn't really have been her fault; it would have been yours. See, if you're too drunk to stand up straight on the dance floor, you shouldn't be here. In my opinion.'

They had more space around them now. People had heard the talking, even above the music, and seen the way they were standing and not moving.

'Get off,' the girl said at last, throwing his arm off her, but he only took hold again, pulling it tightly round her neck. She carried on whining.

'Don't get fussy, Liz,' he chided her, knocking her lightly on the crown of her head with his knuckles.

Hal tried to remember Jerry running up the pier with his friend, suits flapping, carrying the yellow jumper; he looked a lot older now.

'So there I was, dancing with Liz.'

'I wasn't dancing with you,' she managed to say.

'Shut up,' he cut in, dusting her head with his knuckles again.

Hal could no longer see Daisy or the man from the bar.

'So there I was, dancing with Liz, and who should butt in, but you, as if I was some kid having to sit there listening to you yap on, then getting reminded I wasn't paying enough attention. I'm a working man now.'

Hal didn't doubt it, and was unable to see, given that he hadn't disagreed so far with a word Jerry was saying, how he was going to stop him from talking himself into a frenzy.

'Good. Very good.'

'It's more than bloody good.'

The boy let go of Liz and stood in front of her, but she didn't hang around. Hal saw her soon after on the balcony, a friend bent over her with a handkerchief. Hal and Jerry reached a standstill. Jerry, used to baiting and provoking men, was confused at Hal's good humour, while Hal was wondering how to bring the conversation to a close.

Some of the dancers close by had stopped, forming a circle of onlookers around them. Hal didn't dare turn round to look for Daisy now in case it antagonised the boy.

'Are you going to say sorry or not,' Jerry said, caught between lunatic illogic and a genuine sense of injustice.

Hal, relieved to find that there were guidelines to follow, managed to apologise without difficulty, and was turning slowly away from Jerry towards the crowd, when he was pulled back by his sleeve.

'Is that all it takes then at the end of the day, a few nicely spoken words?'

Confused, Hal apologised again, but this only seemed to make Jerry angrier.

Hal was now being shaken by him and trying at the same time to hold on to Daisy's clutch bag.

'Are you listening?'

'Of course,' Hal said, automatically.

'We'll make it look as if you are, then.'

Hal didn't know how to do this, so just stared at Jerry instead, hoping that the boy would feel he was paying him enough attention. Jerry was in the grip of past injustices, as well as his own nature, which made no night out complete without at least a taste of violence.

Hal could still hear the sound of people dancing, a sound that filled the air and rose up to the glass dome. But the circle of those not dancing was growing. Now people were waiting. Hal had never stood in the centre of a circle before. He also realised, the more he looked at Jerry, that he hated the boy. Absolutely hated him. He tried to conjure up some warmth towards him, if only to disguise the hatred, but it was too late, Jerry had already seen.

Jerry's hatred of him, which wasn't a thing of the moment, but long-standing, vibrant and impersonal, had made them equals. Suddenly things didn't seem so lopsided any more.

The first thump was light and caught Hal just above his kidneys. But it was the shove, the shove that sent him stumbling backwards that made him angry. Once he got his balance back, he ran forwards, his arms outstretched, and gave Jerry the hardest push he could. Jerry didn't fall, he just executed a strange jump, which left him standing upright, intact, just a few feet away. Hours earlier they had passed each other, oblivious, on the pier, Hal walking towards an evening out, and Jerry chasing girls. Now they were here facing each other, at war. There were a few more rudimentary shoves, then the shoving stopped and they started to pace around each other instinctively in time to the music, which was still playing. When they stopped pacing their arms were no longer by their sides; they were raised and making fists. Although Hal had never done this before, it didn't feel like the first time.

After they had taken a few trial punches at each other's chests and arms, Jerry suddenly closed in on him, pummelling Hal's right arm with his fist, so consistently and efficiently that it soon hung dangling by his side, a dead arm. Jerry gave it a final thump near the shoulder and with a scream Hal fell to the floor, at last relinquishing his grip on Daisy's clutch bag.

It was the closest he had ever been to the dance floor, and he watched Jerry's feet, walking towards him and walking away over and over again. Every now and then as he slowly swung his head, Daisy's red shoes crossed his line of vision. Her shoes were the only things that stood out in this new world of legs and feet. Hers, and Jerry's, which were shuffling and stamping, and every time Jerry stamped, Hal jerked in anticipation. Thinking, this is it, this is the one that will bring blood.

As he managed, slowly, to get into an upright position, Jerry began bouncing and displaying various other signs that his movements were a result of professional training. An unbearable weakness descended on Hal just as suddenly as the anger had, which made him want to walk away, but he knew he couldn't leave this unfinished. Unfinished business was dangerous, it made enemies, and he had enough of his perceptive powers left to see that it was better if he continued and lost. A misjudged kick was delivered to his thigh. He saw the shining shoe make contact with him. Wobbling on the spot, he waited for the sharpness of the pain to subside into a throb.

Now he was really suffering and could tell from the lethal way Jerry was bouncing that he was about to move in again. The boy's shirt was sticking to the sweat on his chest. Hal wasn't just breathing heavily any more either, he could hear himself, he was grunting from the pain. The grunting made it sound as though he was talking to himself and this made Jerry let out a short excited laugh as though insanity was even better than blood.

Then it came, full-throttle, the fear, the really putrid fear, and he knew he was ready to do anything to save his own skin. After only a few knocks and bruises, relatively speaking, that would heal and that wouldn't even alter his appearance, he was already at the beck and call of this fear. He straightened up; Jerry was coming for him again.

Jerry slammed his arm straight into the middle of Hal, who had the wind knocked out of him but nothing else. Now it was Jerry's turn to fall screaming to the floor, clutching a bloody right fist, his face twisted as he watched the drops of blood start to fall.

Hal looked down slowly at his stomach, even more terrified of not feeling any pain than he had been of feeling it. He had heard stories of men who had been cut in fights and realised, minutes later, that the better part of their intestines were lying at their feet. But looking down he saw that he was intact and, undoing his suit jacket slightly, the reason for his heroism: the large belt with the clasp buckle. A last-minute accessory he nearly hadn't worn. The belt might have saved his life, and, if not his life, none the less had saved him. He glanced down at it again, then hurriedly did his suit jacket up.

Jerry was biting on his wounded knuckle with the outrage of someone who has been unexpectedly tricked. Looking at him, Hal could see that he was still hating, that he wasn't afraid. They hadn't exchanged a single word since the fight began and Jerry had an appetite for this Hal couldn't hope to match.

A woman called out his name; it must have been Daisy. Her voice made Jerry look about him, still chewing on his knuckles.

Then he suddenly came for Hal, and Hal, who hadn't had time to brace himself, tripped over his own feet in the confusion, and landed on his back unaided. He knew what was going to happen next; Jerry was going to sit astride him and start – with his one remaining good fist – on his face. He was going to lose his face unless he got back to his feet.

Jerry fell on to him, but before he had time to pin Hal down, Hal managed to get on top of him and started punching the boy wherever he could until there were people other than Jerry screaming, from the circle around them. The more he hit, the more energy he had. Jerry's face was spreading across the floor, as though it was rubber and some-body had taken hold of the ears, pulling them in opposite directions so that the face grew wider and wider. The more Hal hit it, the wider it grew until Jerry's face covered the entire dance floor, becoming the dance floor, and everybody there was walking over a part of Jerry's face, their shoes making no sound as they got stuck in the soft flesh.

He sat back, breathing heavily, and the circle around them broke as Geordie fell on to them both. The next minute he was holding Hal under the arms trying to haul him back to his feet. Hal could feel the hard gold braiding on Geordie's epaulettes digging into the back of his head, and the bristle on his chin rubbing against his cheek as Geordie braced himself to pick up Hal's weight in his arms.

'Off him. Off him, for Christ's sake,' he was wheezing.

Hal didn't know how to get off the body beneath him and was waiting for Geordie to lift him off. Geordie's knuckles interlaced across his chest, getting whiter and whiter as he lifted him off Jerry, inch by inch, until he was hanging high enough, in theory, to find his own feet.

His legs were shaking and, suspended in the air from Geordie's arms, he was suddenly, ridiculously, afraid of standing on Jerry and hurting him. He was finding his feet gingerly and his heels were slipping because the floor was wet. Then Jerry disappeared from under him, slowly and smoothly.

'That's it,' Geordie was saying, short of breath, but softly, sounding more like a doctor than a security guard. 'That's it, pull the bugger clear.'

It occurred to Hal that Geordie wasn't just speaking to him, and Jerry's body wasn't moving of its own accord, it was being pulled. There was a man pulling Jerry, and the legs were pinstriped and his shoes were even shinier than Geordie's. Cigarette ash fell on to the floor. Once Jerry's body was safely away, curled up and moaning, Geordie let go of Hal roughly.

'Stupid buggers,' he was muttering, straightening his uniform.

'He isn't dead then?'

'Course not.'

'He was just a boy,' Hal said. 'Just a boy.' This suddenly became the most critical thing of all. He sat still, his dead arm cradled in his lap. He saw Daisy's red shoes and smelt her perfume again as she knelt behind him for a few moments, her hands lightly stroking his back.

'Why did you do it, Hal?' she said, but her voice wasn't entirely disapproving. It sounded as warm and curious towards him as it had when she used to be in love with the idea of his parents. 'You all right?'

He nodded, and she stood up again, looking at her clutch bag, which she had retrieved from the floor.

She moved away without waiting for his answer and he heard her asking Geordie to keep an eye on him.

Daisy was the first person to leave the scene of the fight and only seconds after she had, the circle that had formed round the fighters broke up and the dance hall was echoing to the sound of people moving their feet again. At some stage the music must have stopped because he heard it starting up again now.

'Need to get the floor cleaned,' Geordie was saying.

'Here,' someone said, and the pinstriped trousers moved back into view.

'Thanks.' Geordie bent down with the handkerchief he had been given, to wipe up the blood. 'Nice hankie, shame,' he said, as he let it drop.

The hankie was shiny and had the sights of London printed on it. *A souvenir from London* it said. Geordie returned it to its owner who folded it back into a neat triangle, despite the blood, before tucking it into his pocket. The lining on the inside of his pocket flap was torn.

'Hal, I heard.'

Tinker Trench's voice came from somewhere above him. He saw Melita's legs twitching. Trouble always made her feel nervous.

'I'm fine.'

'Good, good.'

He could see from the angle of Melita's legs that she was tugging Tinker's arm.

'I'll be around if you need me.' He waited a moment more. 'Do you need me?' he said at last, despite Melita's tugging.

'I'm fine,' Hal repeated, no longer sure why he was lying.

They left, and he looked up to see who had helped Geordie break up the fight, who had stopped him from doing whatever it was he had been intent on doing only minutes before.

It was the man from the bar, the one who had ordered the fancy drink; the one who had been dancing with Daisy; the one wearing pinstripes.

'Thank you,' Hal said squinting up at him.

'Pleasure,' he said with a Cockney drawl.

It was Perkins.

Hal knew they were heading up the North Cliff road towards Watts because every four minutes the inside of the car was illuminated by the lighthouse beam. The car smelt heavily of oil and leather. Lying on the back seat, he was being jostled by several bottles of a poison that killed cockroaches instantly.

'Can't be too careful. My big fear they are,' Perkins said from the front, having no qualms about revealing this.

They stopped, and Hal could feel a strong wind as Perkins opened the back door and slid him carefully into an upright position. The car was parked in front of a small caravan, and was rocking from side to side because of the number of dogs rubbing themselves against it. The metal body, like the upholstery inside, was still hot from the day's heat. The dogs weren't barking, they were just nosing their way around the two men in silence.

They were at the tinkers' camp on top of the headland. Apart from the dogs there were no other signs of life. Hal thought he saw the outline of a horse grazing to the left, and the ground around them had the uneven look of a rubbish dump. Crossing between the car and the caravan, he fell in a puddle. His dead arm affected his balance and he had difficulty mounting the upturned orange bucket that served as a doorstep to the caravan.

The door shuddered when Perkins opened it even though he did it as carefully as he could, with a smile on his face that made Hal think there was a surprise inside for him. In a few seconds the remains of a meal had been scraped off the work surface and thrown outside to the dogs, generating such avid saliva that both Perkins's and Hal's faces were caught by a light spattering of it. At the same time, the contents of a large teapot were poured over the pile of scraps.

'Piss,' Perkins said, as the unavoidable smell wafted up. 'Suddenly got afraid of the dark.'

He lit a small kerosene lamp and stood it on the tiny work

surface, which was already bubbled and burnt from previous encounters with the lamp.

It was as he suspected. Perkins looked like somebody who smelt the way he did should look. At The Palace all the perfume and other scents of the pleasure-seekers had masqueraded as his true smell, which was why, sat at the bar, Hal's eyes had deceived him and he had thought Perkins was dressed in a new suit. Perkins had looked expensive. Now, in the light of the kerosene lamp, he saw that the suit was more brown than black, it was frayed everywhere it was possible for an old suit to be frayed, and the pinstripes on it only made the whole effect shabbier. What also became obvious, looking at the knees and shoulders, was that the suit wasn't even Perkins's suit. It had been a well-made suit; and in its current state it should have made the wearer look like a man down on his luck. On Perkins it looked stolen. His tie was a faded blue with black swirls on it and couldn't have been less of a match for the suit if he'd tried. His shoes, however, fitted, and still shone. Here in this caravan, Perkins looked like an animal that had been removed from its natural habitat. He was living like this either because of or for someone else.

The two men stood facing each other across two feet of lino, and ten years.

'Why are you here?' Hal asked.

'Came looking for you, didn't I?' Perkins said easily.

Hal knew he wasn't necessarily meant to believe this.

'Sit down,' Perkins said nodding towards the sofa at the far end of the caravan, watching him as he did. 'How's your arm?'

'I don't know. It hurts,' Hal said rubbing it.

'Want something to drink?'

Perkins started opening and shutting cupboards.

The sofa doubled as Perkins's bed and was covered in dogs' hairs. There were several large stains on it as well as a loose bundle of stinking sheets in the corner. Curtains with pink roses on were drawn across the windows and these looked as though they had never been opened. Hanging from the ceiling was a lop-sided five-tier chandelier whose half-melted candles seemed to be the cause of the upset balance.

Perkins sat down next to Hal on the sofa, handing him a glass of whisky. Every now and then the caravan rocked slightly and the dogs outside yapped as the wind blew.

'Did you know him?'

'Who?'

'That boy whose face you broke tonight.'

'I've never done that before. Never felt like doing anything like it.'

'I know,' Perkins said, soothingly.

'I did know him. His name was Jerry Dickson; I used to teach him geography.'

'You're a teacher then,' Perkins said, nodding, and it occurred to Hal that he already knew this, already knew all of this.

'I don't know why I did that to him. I never even gave him a second thought while I was teaching him. It was because of you,' Hal said, 'because I spent the evening following you.'

'Well if that's your excuse, I spent most of the evening following you. I followed you up the promenade, into The Palace. Then I overtook you so that I was at the Tropicana before you arrived.'

'How did you know I'd go to the Tropicana?'

'Doorman I tipped.'

'Geordie?'

'Geordie. He said that's what you always did, soon as you walked in there. Whether you were with Daisy and your cousin Raymond . . . or by yourself. The Tropicana was always your first port of call. I was waiting for you.'

There were a couple of the same bottles of cockroach killer on the floor here that there had been in the car and Perkins started to roll one absent-mindedly with his foot.

'What happened to the shoes?' Hal asked, watching Perkins's foot as the light from the lamp caught the polished toe.

'Died a death.'

'But there was a shoe emporium?'

'There was. In London, on the Strand. Right opposite the Savoy. And shoes . . . boxes and boxes of them, stretching as far as the eye could see. A prairie of shoes it was.'

'Really?' Hal couldn't help saying.

'Really. A prairie, it was that big,' he said, with a deadly earnestness.

'And it just grew and grew, did it? As you used to always say it would?'

'No, it didn't,' Perkins carried on, lightly again now. 'It got smaller and smaller. Then it died a death, commercially speaking.' He finished with a grin.

Perkins had changed his philosophy and Hal couldn't determine what the new one was, only that there was one. Perkins wasn't the sort of man to live without a philosophy. He was no longer polished, he was the opposite, in fact: tarnished. But, even in his greasy suit, Perkins was as much Perkins as the sweet-smelling, wide-talking cockney he had known in France. Perkins was proof that, over a space of ten years, a man could become the opposite of what he had been and still remain himself. Only now he had no need to assume the airs and graces of a man of the world; he was the real thing.

'What you thinking?' Perkins said watching him.

'I was wondering where you've got that copy of *How to Become a Millionaire* hidden.'

They laughed together at that, but Hal couldn't hide his surprise when Perkins got up, rattled open a drawer of what sounded like knives, and drew out the book.

'Is that your copy? The same copy?'

Perkins looked at it intently. 'Course it is,' he said, shoving it back into the drawer.

'So tell me more about the shoes,' Hal asked, as if the copy of *How to Become a Millionaire*, produced for his benefit, gave him the right to do this.

Perkins started to laugh.

'What's so funny?'

'You asking me about shoes.'

'There was a shoe emporium, wasn't there?'

'Of sorts, for a while. Until nineteen fifty. Then I converted to another sort of business.'

Hal glanced briefly at Perkins's neck, remembering the way he had said 'converted'. He half-expected to see a cross hanging there. Perkins could have become a believer; it wasn't impossible.

'I set up a bureau for missing persons. Below the shoe shop.'

'Emporium,' Hal reminded him. Then added, in disbelief, 'A missing person's bureau?'

'Of course. Don't know why I didn't think of it sooner. A very natural line of business for an orphan. Very wholesome work,' Perkins said, but it sounded as though he was using the word 'wholesome' for the first time. 'Got to travel lots. See all sorts of foreign places.'

Hal stared for a while at the flickering lamp, then at the dismal battered interior of the caravan.

'Did you always find the people meant to be missing?'

'Always,' Perkins said sharply. 'And I got to see all sorts of foreign places. Like I said.' He poured himself a third glass of whisky. 'Went to Utah once. There's a pleasure palace there, built out on to the lake. Great Salt Lake.' Perkins had moved right to the edge of the sofa. 'You wouldn't believe a place like that existed, Hal. You have to see it with your own eyes, your own . . .' he jabbed viciously at his eyes, 'eyes,' he repeated. 'The people who went there weren't just pleasure-seekers, they were pilgrims of pleasure. A huge dance hall, one of the longest water slides in the world, and one of the fastest roller-coasters. Not that I saw any of it . . . all over years before I got there. I'm just going off hearsay, you understand. But I saw other places . . . with my own eyes. Have you ever been on a roller-coaster?'

Hal shook his head.

'Well, you just have to see places like that with your own two eyes.'

Perkins finished his whisky.

'I've missed you. So much,' Hal said blankly. He hadn't meant to say that.

Perkins gave a sharp laugh, but didn't disbelieve him.

Hal's mind raced back to the day of the pantomime: the old photographer; the storm; Delaval.

He was about to speak when the door opened and a woman wearing a suit jacket identical to Perkins's, right down to the state it was in, entered the caravan. He couldn't see her clearly in the light from the lamp, but the details he wasn't sure of he filled in from memory because he already knew her. It was Irene, Tinker Trench's aunt; a fortune-teller. A dog entered the caravan with her, its back bald and mottled with disease, and straggled over to Hal.

'I know you,' she said, looking at Hal.

'I'm a friend of Tinker's. Your nephew.'

'A friend?'

He nodded, but she didn't look particularly impressed by this information.

'You came to see me once. Can't remember if Tinker was with you or not. Brought a tall red girl to see me.'

Her eyes scanned the minuscule units that comprised the kitchen.

'What d'you want?' Perkins said.

'Nothing,' she said hastily, taking the two steps it took to cross from kitchen to sofa. 'These,' she added contradicting herself and picking up the bundle of sheets.

'Don't cook and wash at the same time. Those sheets come back stinking of your stinking stews.'

'It's not stew, it's goulash,' she shouted, with as much delicacy as she could.

'It's bad enough eating your stew,' Perkins said, ignoring her, 'I don't want to sleep in it as well.'

She waited at the door, the sheets in her arms.

'Is he staying the night?'

'I expect so,' Perkins answered for Hal.

'He needs cleaning up. He's bloody.'

'Don't worry, it's not his blood.'

Hal was filled with revulsion at himself when he heard Perkins say this.

'I could clean him up.'

'All right,' Perkins said, as if he quite liked the idea.

Irene looked even more pleased with herself and, dropping the sheets by the caravan door, left, only to return a few moments later with a pan of scalding water and a hip flask of something which, once unstoppered, didn't smell unlike witch-hazel.

There were several large explosions outside as the woman knelt down in front of Hal.

'Kids with bangers,' Perkins mumbled, watching Irene.

Hal hated undressing in front of people and removed his shirt, when asked, with difficulty. He sat stiffly on the edge of the sofa while Perkins explained the fight in minute and accurately recalled detail and Irene applied what turned out to be a sort of paste to the relevant parts of his body. It was a perfect reconstruction of events, with Hal flinching in anticipation of her applications as he had done Jerry's blows earlier. By the time Perkins reached the end of the story, Hal's pain, along with any memories or traces of it, had completely vanished.

'I can wash the shirt.'

'It's all right,' Hal said, rushing to get it back on.

'But the blood?'

'It's all right,' he said, pushing her arms out of the way to get the buttons done up. 'Thank you,' he managed to add.

'I can do his fortune as well,' she said to Perkins.

'Not now. Another time maybe.'

Then she left, gathering her clothes about her as she walked to the door, afraid of making her already filthy clothes dirty. The dogs didn't start up again when she left.

Hal kept tentatively touching his body, half-expecting the pain to return, but it didn't.

'Fucking gypos,' Perkins put in from the corner of the sofa. 'Filthy fucking gypos.'

'What sent you to Utah?' Hal said, watching him.

Perkins looked down at his shoes. He was wearing a black and gold signet ring on his right hand, which was shaking.

'You lied when you said you always found the people you went looking for. You didn't find whoever it was you went looking for in Utah, did you?'

'You always were quick, Hal. Quick as lightning,' he said, his glass raised, looking down the length of it directly at him. 'No, I didn't find Stella in Utah.'

'You were looking for Stella?' Hal stared at him.

'What?' Perkins shouted.

It was the only time Hal ever heard him raise his voice.

'Don't you believe me? Look at me.'

Hal took in the brown pinstripes again. Honesty took the shine out of Perkins and made him as ugly as tears would have done.

'I still haven't found Stella, and when I do . . . it's a dead end. I was asked to find her; this isn't even my quest. She'll hate me for that. You don't know her, but . . .'

'No, I don't,' Hal said.

Perkins started to rummage inside his jacket, pulling out a scrap of newspaper and handing it to Hal.

It was a picture of The Palace, taken from the promenade. NORTH-EAST RESORT DESTINED FOR NEW PLEASURE PARK, the headline said. Hal read halfway down the small print.

'Delaval. It was Delaval who sent you looking for Stella.'

'He's going to rebuild the Spanish City here in Setton. Roller-coaster and all.'

'But nobody's seen him for years.'

'Don't you see? He's baiting her.'

'Why would she come?'

'She's a pleasure pilgrim. After the war she went anywhere pleasure was to be found in public. All the pleasure parks; all the rides.'

Hal heard again the careless unprovoked laughter. 'Is Delaval here now, in Setton?'

'He might not actually be here now,' Perkins relented. 'We broke off contact after fifty-two . . . but he soon will be.'

'How long have you been here?'

'A month. I was in South Wyley. In a room above the

snooker hall at the Seven Stars. Then I found this place.'

Perkins picked up the empty whisky bottle and tapped the last few drops into his glass, tipping his head right back in order to taste them. This deliberate but small movement, which betrayed a desperation he hadn't meant to show, made the whole caravan shake.

'When I got here I suddenly remembered you. I remembered you came from Setton. The same place Delaval came from. Strange.'

'I don't know Delaval.'

'And for a moment, one mad moment,' Perkins carried on, ignoring him, 'I thought, maybe Spanish City won't be the bait after all. Maybe . . .' Perkins got to his feet with no trace of unsteadiness and took Hal awkwardly underneath the arms, pulling him along the sofa into a horizontal position as though he were an invalid.

'If she comes here and I find her before he does, I'll get what he promised me. It's not too late.'

Perkins tucked a cushion under Hal's head.

'I'll sleep on the floor,' he said, without ceremony.

And Hal watched, already half-asleep, as Perkins got another blanket down and lay on the floor, his feet touching the sofa and his head by the door. It occurred to Hal that Perkins had made this arrangement because he was afraid Hal would try to leave in the night, and that being afraid of people leaving in the night was something Perkins had grown used to.

Hal shut his eyes.

'When did you last feel joy? Real joy?' Perkins said quietly.

Hal lay still, unsure whether this was a provocation on the part of Perkins, to ascertain whether or not he was sleeping. He didn't answer.

7

In a small smoke-filled room in the town hall, a scale model of South Cliff and its pleasures had become the plaything of four fully grown men.

When Delaval had walked into the offices of Setton District Council with a blueprint rolled up under his arm, some of the more elderly councillors had thought it was a plan for the dreaded pier Delaval's grandfather, old Jack Delaval, managed to get an Act of Parliament passed for in 1908. It wasn't; it was a plan for a city of pleasure, to be built around the existing Palace Dance Hall. Setton District Council hadn't been without a Delaval at its helm before, and they had, all of them, been staring at the door every day for as long as they could remember, waiting for it to open and for young Delaval to walk through bringing with him something that would make their world bigger again.

So, although initially the councillors shouted him down, their outrage was for form's sake, motions that had to be gone through. In reality, their arms were open from the moment the plans were spied crushed beneath Delaval's armpit. He had come home, and he hadn't come empty-handed. Despite the fact, mumbled older councillors who had known him in his youth before the war, he had aged badly.

Over the following months Setton's skyline was mauled to bits in the name of pleasure. Percy, the District Council's chief architect, had never been so busy. Work on South Cliff coincided with the continued demolition of the old miners' rows under the reconstruction scheme so that new council estates could be built. Only Ellsworth Row and a few others still stood. The two new estates were called Isabella and Ferdinand after the streets they replaced although nobody could remember how on earth two miners' rows came to be called after a Spanish king and queen. High-rises had been ruled out in favour of semi-detached houses with gardens and wash-houses. Those who had already been re-housed couldn't believe their luck and felt a surge of patriotism they hadn't felt since running water was put into the rows.

Percy, who had been involved in RIBA's Rebuilding Britain exhibition of 1943, could deal with the new council estates because they adhered to the policy of betterment for the people of Britain, a vision he had shared with others. He was used to designing buildings that matched in height, shape and colour other buildings around them – the new Setton public library was an ideal example of this. Spanish City, however, took nothing but itself into account.

The enterprise provoked Marston, MP, to mutter phrases such as 'We'll be opening the floodgates', which were as irrelevant as they were ominous because he was never able to identify who they would be opening the floodgates to. Marston had, in his youth, been convicted of an unspeakable crime whose taint had never left him. Letting go in public was an inconceivable idea to Marston for whom pleasure lay in a well-kept bed of wallflowers.

The obvious commercial viability, as well as Delaval's determination and young councillor John Munro's idealism and way with words, got the Central Planning Committee to approve the proposal. As Delaval pointed out, Delaval Pleasure Grounds Co. still owned both The Palace and the land it stood on. He could have hired a firm of architects and a private construction company. But he wanted the soul and spirit of Spanish City to be municipal.

Only weeks after an artist's impression of Spanish City

appeared in the *Setton Echo*, the number of hotel licences applied for doubled, and the demand for commercial properties increased as people sensed a bandwagon worth jumping on the back of. The council started to draw up plans for a caravan site, Camelot, and the branch line from Newcastle to Setton increased its services dramatically so that during the summer months there would be six trains an hour arriving at peak times.

Delaval referred to Spanish City at meetings as 'an achievement Setton should be proud of'; John Munro said it was 'a gift to the people', while Marston didn't hesitate in prophesying that it would be 'an unmitigated disaster'.

Behind closed doors, often after hours, Delaval and Alderman, the borough engineer, met to discuss the Charleston coaster. Alderman had worked in Utah with Delaval's father and other American engineers from the Philadelphia Toboggan Company, builders of the original Charleston coaster in 1926, and could list the coaster's every nut and bolt blindfolded.

'The tallest drop we can have is 157 feet, as on the original, and the steepest drop not more than 53 degrees. But if we can get the speed up to 89 m.p.h. that drop will feel like 1,157 feet,' Delaval said.

'Ed Morgan gave Disney's Matterhorn tubular steel and nylon wheels. We should work on that,' Alderman put in.

'The Charleston's being re-built exactly to plan. To my father's blueprint with a few modifications to bring it up to speed. When he designed this they didn't have the materials or engineers who were up to it. He was ahead of himself; too far ahead of himself. We've only just caught up with him.'

'They stopped riding it in Utah.' Alderman was a brilliant engineer, but a relentless pessimist.

'It flooded,' Delaval said, defensively. 'This Charleston's different. And of course they'll stop riding it here as well eventually.' Delaval's voice rose. 'But first they have to start riding it. These are times for people with appetite, gentlemen.'

Delaval drove back to Ellison Court with the blinds pulled down over the windows. The house had been built by the Ellison family in 1760. By 1870 there was only a niece left and the house was being leased out during the summer months. The niece was said to have been mad, and despite the hoards of physicians who came, prescribed, then left, the only person to recognise that she was going mad from celibacy was one Jack Delaval, son of a local farmer with barely a cow to his name. His fee turned out to be larger than that of any of the queuing physicians, and when the last of the Ellisons died of joy in 1879, Jack Delaval promptly moved into Ellison Court and made a fortune out of illegally selling land to developers that he was, in effect, a squatter on.

Landowning gentry were a thing of the past, a declaration he made well before the First World War. Like the declarations of many meteoric risers, his became prophecies. By 1887 Delaval was chairman of Delaval Pleasure Grounds Co., presiding over a boom town. The Duke of Northumberland had made an attempt to bring proceedings against Jack Delaval, but instead ended up buying a row of houses on the sea front for his friends to stay in, having savoured the delights of the resort himself. After this Setton, as it were, opened up.

Delaval watched the blueprints for Spanish City roll around on the seat next to him, and remembered the first time he went to Utah, in August 1926, when he was only twelve years old. For a whole week his father promised to row him out to Spanish City on Great Salt Lake, but when the day came he was left behind with the old nanny who smelt of stale urine and dead beetles. He remembered clearly standing outside the municipal baths where the nursemaid, Charleston, had taught him to swim underwater, watching the car containing his father and Charleston disappear towards the lake. He and the stinking old nanny were left standing alone in the shadow of scandal. The strain of disbelief was too much for her and she collapsed in the street. Delaval managed to find his way back to the hotel and his mother, who sensed the impending scandal as soon as he appeared alone.

These memories came back to him with all the fury of things repressed. The Utah incident came just three months after the incident with the dogs.

He could hear the rain now, patting gently on the car windows. This year was the first time he had been back to Ellison Court since his father committed suicide, but it didn't feel as strange living there as he thought it might.

The incident with the dogs occurred during the General Strike when members of the Setton District Constabulary were posted around the house because of his mother's fear of riot. He used to creep down at night to listen to the constables talking on their watch, and remembered one night passing along the passage that led from the kitchens to the stables when he heard the sound of the dogs whining in pain. The sound came from a small room leading off the passage, and his first thought was that rioters had already got into the house and were silencing the three Great Danes. He made his way towards the room the whines were coming from.

The smell was indescribable as he entered and the walls were covered in food. Some larger pieces of meat from what had been a stew had already dropped to the floor while some of the smaller vegetables and the gravy were still sliding down the walls. There were shards of china on the threshold that he stepped over, unheeding, and broke into even smaller segments.

Delaval remembered that one of the dogs, Duchess, was lying wheezing in the straw, her belly cut open in so many places that it made her fur look like a blanket that had been thrown over her rather than some inherent part of her. Some of Duchess's belly was obscured by old Prospero's head. At first, Delaval thought he was trying to lick at her wounds, but the nuzzling was unsteady and made the back of his head twitch frantically. His face was already inside her belly, trying for a better grip on her entrails in order to pull them out of her stomach and on to the straw where he could feed more easily.

The third dog, Beowulf, was licking whatever he could from the walls. There were no rioters. What Delaval saw instead was his nursemaid, Charleston, kicking Beowulf repeatedly as he carried on licking the walls.

She saw him standing in the doorway but she didn't drop the knife she was holding or do anything to account for the blood, which wasn't only on her uniform, but her hands and face as well.

He could hear the dogs whimpering, and Charleston saying clearly, 'All of this is bloody disgusting.'

It was the first time he had ever heard a woman swear. Then she told him that the dogs got fed more in one sitting than her entire family in one week. He would never forget her outrage; a real moral outrage, the sort that doesn't understand consequences.

Then she told him to go and find her some cigarettes.

He ran from the room, through the bottom of the house, which was empty, until he fell into his father's study, screaming, 'She's killed the dogs, she's killed the dogs.'

Delaval could hear himself saying this in his child's voice, and drinking the whisky his father gave him until he was able, comprehensively, to describe the room downstairs where he had left Charleston. His father's eyes stayed very bright as he talked, and his face never once showed any sign of anger. When he got to the part where Charleston had asked him to find cigarettes, his father couldn't stop laughing. Delaval had never seen him laugh like that before, certainly not with his mother, not even with friends, and he never saw him laugh like that again. It was triumph and joy rolled into one, as if he'd just won a bet or been proved right. He was overcome by the majesty of a sixteen-year-old girl who had had the will and the strength to destroy an animal twice her size. Now, older, and having laughed once in the same way himself, Delaval was able to make a direct connection between the laugh and his father's suicide. That laugh, which he turned out to have inherited, made him more his father's son than anything else.

He heard gravel under the wheels of the car as they turned into the drive of Ellison Court.

John Delaval had been a humanist, like his father Jack Delaval, in love with the human race for being exactly what it was, and not what it might be.

8

The summer of 1955 began with a record-breaking storm, and ended up (even before the close of the season) being christened the 'Golden Year'. Because of Spanish City.

'Oh dear, rain,' Mr Chappel said, as Raymond accompanied him to the top of the stairs.

Mr Chappel put his hat on slowly with one hand, pushing it back slightly so that it didn't come too far down over his forehead. He was influenced by the Westerns he saw at the picture house, but there was no harm in that, he did his job well, and the most people could do was laugh at him.

Raymond took a peek at the outside world. 'Do you want me to get an umbrella from downstairs?'

Chappel thought about it while pulling on his lightweight summer gloves. 'No, it's all right. I've got my hat,' he said, tapping it. 'Now, have I got everything I came with?' He patted his torso and stared briefly at a group of older children who had come out of the rock shop opposite, making a lot of noise. One of them had bought a large candy dummy and was swinging it from a length of ribbon. 'Right then, I'll be on my way.'

Raymond waited, but Chappel showed no sign of moving. The air temperature had dropped a lot since the morning; it was even getting towards being cold.

'Oh, that's what I was going to say . . . The Palace. Now I

know I'm in no position to dictate how you spend your leisure hours, but perhaps it would be better if not so many of them were spent at The Palace?'

Raymond looked at him, confused. Usually he was able to anticipate Chappel's attacks, but he had never expected one from this quarter.

'I mean an undertaker frequenting a palace of pleasure.'

'Mr Chappel, it's hardly . . .'

'There's no need to get defensive, Raymond. All I'm trying to say, and lightly mind, is that it might be hard for people to take a dancing undertaker seriously. Given your age . . . the effects on business of you dancing would only ever be indirect, but still we could save ourselves the trouble if you didn't dance so often.'

Raymond looked down at his feet.

'Now why did it have to go and rain,' Chappel mumbled, then walked off down the street.

Raymond heard the sound of the children's train as it trundled up the promenade.

He liked this time of day, especially on Fridays, when the week was drawing to a close, and the footsteps of the Co-op counter staff could be heard above. Daisy would be up there, fitting the lid over the butter barrel and cleaning the scoop. Sometimes he thought he could hear her footsteps in particular, above the others.

The shop bell rang to warn customers that there were only five minutes to go before closing. Daisy would be starting to undo the buttons on her overalls ready to hang them up on their peg for Saturday morning. This was the way of things, he thought, satisfied, and if things were going to change they would do so of their own accord.

Tonight was Friday night and he was going dancing, despite (but not in spite of) what Chappel said. Chappel had good reason to say what he said, and Raymond couldn't blame him for it, but the dancing was something he couldn't moderate let alone stop. He would have to find time during Chappel's next visit to reassure him discreetly. He wondered how Chappel had found out about him at The Palace, but didn't dwell on it for long. His attention was soon drawn to the beginning of an inscription he had been working on before Chappel's unexpected arrival: the tombstone of a child. He was about to phone the stone-mason and try to catch him before he knocked off for the night when the telephone rang. It was Poul, the Dutchman from the watch-house.

'Raymond? We were put on alert just five minutes ago.' Poul paused, overwhelmed by the gravity of the situation, and the presentiment he was nursing right then, sat up in the tower of the watch-house looking out to sea. 'You seen the weather?'

'Not from down here I haven't. It was coming on to rain before.'

'Well now we've got gale-force winds at sea. It's going to get worse, that's what the shipping office said. Have you not even heard the thunder?' he said finally, in disbelief.

'Not a scrap,' Raymond affirmed, looking towards the stairs.

'We need you over here, Raymond. There's a boat called *Nancy* in trouble. You know, Arthur's pleasure boat, the one that runs between North Cliff and South Cliff. It left North Cliff over half an hour ago, and just radioed to say that the storm came on it so suddenly that they're frightened of being carried over to St Mary's Island.

Raymond was already putting on his hat.

'That's bad news,' he confirmed.

'Bad news,' Poul repeated.

'I'll be right there.'

He turned out the lights and climbed the stairs to street level. The first thing he heard as he opened the door was the sea, which was bellowing. Outside it had gone very dark, and the streetlamps weren't yet lit. Mrs Thompson opposite was fighting with the striped awning of her rock shop while trying to beat her skirts down to a decent level. He could hear her cursing. The other shops along Front Street were all shut up, and there was nobody around. Within seconds of setting foot outside his face was wet with rain and sea spray.

The wind kept changing direction which made riding his bicycle difficult. Sometimes it was behind him and he was hurled along so fast that his feet couldn't keep up with the pedals. Then it was in front of him, and he had to dismount to stop cycling on the spot.

Inside the fish market, which was empty, crates were being thrown across the floor by the wind and the iron girders were creaking. Huge grey waves were coming up over the railings on the promenade, drowning the promenade itself and reaching as far as the dunes before retreating back through the railings to try again. The wall of the open-air swimming pool was completely submerged, and only the top tiers of the diving platform could be seen, rearing pointlessly up out of the sea.

The wind was so loud now it made him feel light-headed and dizzy. At one point, just after the Clock House Café, it pulled the bicycle from under him, so he left it against the scaffolding still surrounding The Palace. He could hear the penny machines chattering, the wind was shaking the walls so hard. It was screaming through the covered walkway as well. He took a handkerchief out of his mackintosh pocket to wipe his face with, and his hand wasn't just wet and raw-looking, it was shaking.

He walked the rest of the way, one hand in his pocket trying to keep his mackintosh pulled round him, and the other pushing his hat down on his head in an attempt not be stripped by the storm. He had forgotten to say anything to Daisy, to tell her they wouldn't be going dancing tonight, and now it was too late.

He passed the boating lake where the moored boats were smashing against each other then crossed the crazy golf course, jumping over an abandoned ball still knocking around hole number 9. After this he cut up through the Italian Gardens. The flowerbeds were already battered, and even the statues looked only slightly less torn.

When he reached the far end of the gardens at the top of South Cliff, he could make out the light from the watch-house. The blood pounding in his ears from his exertions was almost as loud as the wind. Looking back down the cliff he could just about make out the glass dome of The Palace as well as the huge crane and other far stranger structures for the city of pleasure they were building there. He shuddered and turned away. The furthest he could see out to sea was the top of the diving board. Other than this there was nothing. His face was still being stung by spray, even this far up the cliff. There was no sign of Arthur's pleasure boat.

Arthur looked to see how many children there were on board. If there were only a few he would let them take the wheel for a bit, maybe even let them wear his hat with its trimmings and all. They loved that, even though it was so big they had to tip their heads back to see anything from under it. That afternoon there were only two: a surly bugger called Robert, who had been on board every day that week with his mother, already wearing his own captain's hat, and a scrappy kid who didn't stop scratching, and had come alone. He paid for his ticket with the exact money, which, Arthur saw, cleared him out completely. A giggling young couple he would have to keep his eye on took the bench at the back of the boat. He would leave them be as long as no one else sat there.

Robert, Robert's mother and the other boy sat at the front of the boat just beneath the Union Jack, which was flapping nicely. Robert, in the captain's hat, was staring at the other boy because he didn't want him sharing their bench at the front. His mother, Mrs West, was staring as well. The boy turned his back on them, kneeling to look out over the side. He'd have to keep his eye on him as well, Arthur thought. Robert started to complain loudly about the smell of the boat, then he wouldn't stop screaming when a seagull landed right beside him.

They were about to leave the small harbour at North Cliff when a young woman jumped confidently on board and walked straight into the cabin.

'Where are you going?'

'Small circular tour.'

147

'Small circular tour where?' she said, smiling.

'Down to South Cliff. Out to sea. Well, just a little bit, and then back to harbour. Four shillings for an adult, two shillings for a child.'

'There's only me.'

'Four shillings for an adult.'

This made her laugh, even though he was in earnest. She handed him the money, deliberated over which end of the boat to sit at, then, seeing the couple who were already canoodling at the back, joined the children at the front. She was wearing a man's coat and sat with her hands in her pockets, staring out to sea.

The flag started blowing in the other direction and Arthur consulted his watch, which he pulled from his pocket. He was addicted to the details nautical life depended on, especially the time. The boat was called *Nancy*, after his brother's wife, which at the time had further complicated an already complicated situation. It was foolish, but he couldn't help himself. Nancy had never set foot aboard her maritime counterpart, but he didn't doubt the day would come. At least calling the boat after her gave him an excuse for saying her name out loud, in public.

'How many whales will we see?' Robert shouted, pulling on his mother's arm.

'I'm not sure,' she said, distracted, rubbing her lips together.

'You said we'd see whales today.'

'And did I say we wouldn't?'

The boy sighed. 'And maybe sea monsters. The monsters out there,' he carried on, pointing at the horizon.

The Union Jack started blowing straight now.

'We certainly won't see whales,' the scrappy boy said with assurance.

Mrs West started at his well-spoken voice; she had him all marked down, and this wasn't it; this wasn't it at all.

'We're too far south to sight a whale, especially at this time of year,' he said seriously. 'All we would need to do, though, is head north.' He looked at them all, even the woman sitting

148

behind him, and at the captain through the cabin windows. 'But I don't think any of us are dressed for it. So we shan't see whales today.' Then he turned away from them, sighing contentedly as he leant over the side of the boat again.

Mrs West looked outraged and turned to her son to gauge the devastating effects of this information.

The young woman leant forward and tapped the scrappy boy on the shoulder.

'Have you ever seen a whale?' she whispered hoarsely.

'Never,' he answered.

'I have,' she said solemnly.

He rested his head on his arms to stare at her more comfortably.

'We won't see any whales today,' he repeated to himself.

Arthur rang the big brass bell and started the engines up.

The boy grinned at the woman behind him, and she smiled back.

Mrs West tried to squeeze her son's hand, but he tugged it away.

Arthur steered them through the harbour walls and out to sea. Gulls landed on the prow of the boat then flew off again. The sea was ruffled and spray kept hitting the woman's hands and face.

Every now and then Robert would stand in front of the Union Jack at the prow of the ship and salute Arthur in his cabin. If Arthur wasn't in the middle of rolling himself a cigarette, he always saluted back. Sometimes the boy would walk up to the cabin and shout at him to take that filthy thing out of his mouth while he was on duty, which he did, dropping it on the floor and pretending to stamp on it. It cost him a lot of wheezing to pick it up again once Robert went back to his seat.

'A round-trip ticket costs two shillings,' the small boy said quietly to the woman behind him, 'for a child.'

She didn't hear at first, she had her head right in the wind, so the boy had to repeat himself. Then she turned to face him slowly, miles away.

'That's right,' she said gently. 'My round–trip ticket cost me four shillings. Because I'm an adult,' she added.

The boy looked down at the water.

'Where did you get the money for your ticket from?' he asked her.

'My pocket.'

'Where did you get it from before your pocket?'

'I don't know,' she said, and the fact that she was frowning as she said this gave him a certain hope. 'Where did you get your money from?'

'My pocket,' he said defensively.

'And before that?'

He hesitated before saying, 'I stole it,' whispering the words, which sounded brave and defeated all at the same time.

The woman thought about this for a while, letting her hair blow right across her face, then getting cross and tucking it down the back of her collar. 'That's all right.'

'Do you really think so?'

She nodded.

He got a handkerchief out of his pocket and blew his nose as quietly as he could, folding it back up and tucking it guiltily into his pocket again.

'Will you pay it back?'

'I don't think I can,' he said. Then, after making a few calculations, 'It will take a very long time,' he carried on defensively. 'I've watched the boats every summer and tomorrow we're leaving Setton for ever. Today was my last chance,' he said, still whispering so that Mrs West had trouble hearing every word. 'My last chance ever.'

'Wouldn't anybody give you the money?'

He shook his head, 'Not for the boats, no.'

'Why not?'

He shrugged, genuinely unable to understand the reasons he had been given.

'It's all right,' she said again. 'It really is.'

She would have touched him somewhere, his hand at least, but had the impression it would frighten him. 'It's more than

150

all right, it's good in fact, very good, to want to travel on the boat as much as you do.' She was automatically whispering as well.

They had both instinctively moved further away from the side of the boat as the sea started to wash over. There was also the distant sound of thunder.

'The first thing I did when I got off the train was walk down to the sea. And the first thing I wanted to do when I got to the sea was sail in one of these boats,' she said, tucking her hair back down inside her collar again.

She thought, from what she had seen of the boats, that they should have started to turn towards South Cliff by now, but they were still heading out to sea.

The other boy and his mother were no longer out on deck.

'Are you cold?'

'Yes, I am,' he said submissively.

'We should sit together then, further up the boat, because I'm cold too.'

So they moved to the bench against the front of the cabin, which was equidistant from port and starboard and gave the impression that the sides of the small boat were a more substantial barrier against the sea.

'There we go,' she said, pleased, as they settled closely against each other, her arm around his small body. His knees were badly bruised and his hair was in need of a wash.

'Wouldn't make much of an explorer,' he said tearfully. 'I came away so badly prepared.'

'That's not your fault, you probably just didn't have access to the right equipment,' she said, looking down at his knees again.

'That's right,' he acknowledged, and clasped his hands together.

The front of the boat was rising and falling now, no longer able to tell the difference between sky and sea. When it fell it banged and spat water all over the bench they had been sitting on. Her hair was full of sea-water and the boy had pulled the collar of his jacket up. They weren't whispering any more. They had to raise their voices to be heard.

'This your school blazer?'

'My school's by the sea,' he shouted, nodding.

'Do you watch the boats at school as well?'

'I do, but I can't get close. The sea's out of bounds.'

'That's a bit tough.'

'Only for me.'

'That's even tougher.'

'I tried to go swimming.'

'So that's why the sea's out of bounds. That was your punishment, was it?'

He didn't say anything.

She had her arm wrapped tightly round him, but his body was still trying to keep its distance in spite of the cold.

There was a row of dark undulating shapes on the horizon, and at first she thought it was land, and that they were now heading back to the shore. It wasn't until the boy in her arms started and said, 'Look,' that she saw the land for what it was: an advancing bank of cloud, so black and sure of itself that she had mistaken it for the coast of England.

The next moment they completely lost sight of the front of the boat as it plunged into the sea. In front and to either side a wall of water hung poised as though the boat was in a glass tank. Then the walls came crashing down and they were under water, still sitting on their bench, still looking about them for the view and clutching their tickets. As the *Nancy* rose, sea-water flowed down either side of her and she was making all sorts of noises that betrayed the cost of her struggles.

The boy's mouth was open, but he wasn't making any sound; he was sitting rigid, petrified, his hands holding on to the bench. Behind them the brass bell was ringing.

'Come on,' she said, trying to pull the boy to his feet as the boat started its descent again, leaving the sky behind. 'Come on,' she screamed, but he wouldn't move, and her stomach shot up to her mouth, the last bit of the descent was so rapid. It was too late and the boat plunged into the sea, the water pouring over the sides again. She was knocked off her feet and sent down to the prow, sliding on her belly between rows of benches on which the sun had shone less than twenty minutes earlier.

Just as she thought she was going to be sucked out over the edge, downwards, she managed to clutch the flagpole and the boat juddered, starting to rise again. Above her she saw the boy still sitting rigid on the bench, looking back down at her. As the boat rose the water drained away, and what didn't fell back down the deck against the boy on the bench and the cabin behind him, and she fell with it.

The brass bell was still ringing, and the salt water she had swallowed was burning the back of her throat. She hurt all over, and was angry because of the pain, blaming the only thing in sight: the boy. When she slid to a halt by his feet she put as much effort into hitting him as she did trying to get him to stand on his feet. But he was used to being hit, so used to being hit that her hysterical thumping didn't make any difference, not petrified as he was, in the face of something more unreasonable and more bloody-minded than anything he had encountered in his life so far.

As the boat peaked, she managed to prise his hands off the bench, dragging him towards the cabin. She pulled hard on the door, opening it just wide enough, despite the force pulling it shut on the other side, to push the boy and herself through.

They fell through the door and she heard a woman screaming, 'The water, the water,' and a man telling her to shut up.

Mrs West and Robert were crouching on the floor, staring at the woman and boy with horror because of the amount of sea-water that they brought in with them. They were looking at them as if they had more in common with the storm outside than other human beings.

As the woman shook her head a few drops flew from her sodden hair on to Mrs West's face. She started screaming and clawing at her face, then the captain's arm.

'You let the water in; look, you let the water in.'

'Shut up for Christ's sake,' he yelled, forcing her back as the boat began to rise. 'I should have had you in sooner,' he said, turning to the other woman with difficulty. 'I should have done, but I never saw this coming.' He looked at them both. 'How's the boy?'

'Not good,' she said, upset at the way she had hit him, and understanding what it was that made others lash out at him too, in the same way. The boy hardly seemed to notice her now; he had eyes only for the captain and the water.

'I tried to get you in sooner, but you didn't hear me.'

'Oh God,' Mrs West screamed as they peaked then plunged.

'This came from nowhere. Nowhere. Just came straight at us from the side. I got no signals on my radio, nothing. Nobody knew about this. Nobody could have known about this,' he ranted. And his ranting wasn't an excuse or an apology, he was begging for their forgiveness.

'Nowhere, nothing, nobody,' the boy repeated, thoughtful despite the water all around them, and the fact that he was petrified.

Robert, in his captain's hat, looked at the other boy, more terrified of him even than the storm outside. Robert's knees were bleeding and he couldn't remember how he had hurt them.

Arthur frowned when he saw the blood smeared over the white iron pipes.

'The lovers,' he said suddenly, turning to look through the window at the back of the cabin.

'What do you mean?' Mrs West said, hysterically.

'There were lovers to stern,' he mumbled, tugging persistently at the wheel, the only one to keep his balance while the rest of them were thrown about inside the cabin. 'Two of them, to stern. Thought they might be trouble when they got on board,' he said, staring at Mrs West, then straight at the other woman who showed far fewer signs of hysteria. 'Kissing and things. Carrying on,' he said, giving the two children a quick protective stare. 'But they were all right. I

154

forgot about them lovebirds. If they're not in here now, they'll have gone over.'

The woman tried to find the small boy's hand and, when she did, she took hold of it, tiny and wet as it was, pushing it, along with her own, into her coat pocket. The boy shuffled closer.

'Never seen anything like this,' Arthur said again as the boat rose. 'Look at *Nancy*, isn't she bearing it. I've radioed for help, I have done that,' he said, glancing at the children again, 'but I've never seen anything like it,' he finished, turning his back on them all. 'Nothing so back-handed, not in all my years.'

'How long will it last?' the woman asked. Arthur didn't answer. 'What are the chances of them finding us?'

'Will you shut up,' Mrs West screeched, 'just shut up.'

Robert was staring at his mother in horror.

The small boy tugged on the woman's arm. 'They'll find us if we're meant to be found,' he said in her ear reassuringly, so that Mrs West couldn't hear, 'that's what I'm telling myself.'

'Good idea,' she managed to say, before they were all flung forward on to the floor again where they remained huddled, their hands together still in her coat pocket.

'Do you remember when I said that the sea at school was out of bounds to me,' he said into her ear as the boat rose.

She nodded and pressed her head further towards his mouth.

'Stop them,' Mrs West started to shout, pulling at the captain's arm. 'Stop them.'

The captain tried to shake her off without taking his hands from the wheel.

'Because I went swimming when I wasn't supposed to.'

'That's right,' the woman said to the child, remembering what he had said to her earlier.

'That's not what made them angry at school.'

'Stop them,' Mrs West screamed again and again, pulling at both the captain's arms from behind, as if she had suddenly got it into her head that all their lives depended on the woman and child stopping their jabbering.

'What made them angry was my going swimming in the sea when I didn't know how to.'

'You can't swim?' the woman said, surprised.

The boy shook his head.

'So what were you doing?'

'I went into the sea to do myself harm,' he confessed, in the same voice that he had confessed to stealing his boat fare.

She looked at him in wonder and horror, and was just leaning forward to take hold of his hand when Mrs West's body was flung over their heads, and fell clattering into a corner.

Then a roaring filled the cabin and it wasn't the storm outside, it was Arthur, the boat's captain, who had taken his hands off the wheel and raised them above his head, enabling him to roar his loudest. From the back he looked as though he had decided to face up to rather than run from some beast. Now no longer interested in his mother, and with curiosity winning over fear, which had been pure and constant in Robert since the storm started, he stood up to get a look at the beast himself, being careful to stay behind Arthur.

As the wall of water broke this time he saw, coming through it to meet them, black rocks one on top of the other, and found himself instinctively pointing towards them.

Only the small boy saw, and he got to his feet, using both hands to pull himself upright, following the line of the pointed finger.

'Look,' he said excitedly to the woman who was still crouched on the floor, 'rocks.' He was almost hysterical with relief that a decision had at last been made, even if it wasn't in their favour; someone somewhere had made a decision on their behalf. 'The rocks,' he said again, transfixed as the whitest parts of the waves crashed through the crevices between them.

'Land? You can see land?' the woman said, looking at the two boys standing up, and the mother, crumpled in the corner, who hadn't moved.

'No, no,' the boy said impatiently, 'rocks, look.'

Robert remembered every coloured plate from every

seafaring book he had at home, from pirates to the history of the British navy, every picture of every shipwreck, famous or otherwise, and thought about how he would look at the sailors in those pictures. Now he was one of them, and he wondered who was watching him, ready to turn the page.

'Here we go,' the boy said triumphantly as the glass of the cabin windows shattered and a wave carried them straight on to the rocks where the *Nancy* groaned slowly then broke into pieces, every man for himself, all love between them lost.

Irene was crouching over a bowl of water on the floor of Perkins's caravan when she heard the car arrive. Between opening the door and shutting it he brought in most of the storm, and the chandelier shook.

'Perkins?' she said, sitting up and wrapping her wet hair in a towel.

'What are you doing?' he asked.

She sighed and got to her feet. 'I came to dye my hair. Can't stand the smell it leaves behind in my caravan, and didn't think you'd mind so much.'

He pushed past her and rifled through the kitchen cupboards, putting his hand up to his face because of the smell of ammonia from the dye. He'd been drunk again the night before, and mislaid the photographs Delaval had given him.

'You live like a pig,' she said, watching him. 'Why won't you let me clean up after you?'

'I live like a pig because I choose to.'

It took a while for the wind inside the caravan to blow itself out, and even when it had, Irene's earrings didn't stop moving.

'You put them inside your book,' she said, holding up *How to Become a Millionaire*, its shape distorted because of the brown envelope wedged inside.

'Why didn't you say so,' he yelled, grabbing her elbows. Then, more quietly, 'Tell me if she's here in Setton. Use the cards.'

'We've tried them before,' Irene cut in.

'I know, but I want you to try again, d'you hear?'

'Getting your fortune read will cost you,' she warned. 'Besides, I can't. Not in this storm.'

'I need to know where she is,' he said with difficulty.

Her hand brushed against the deep pocket in her skirt where the cards were and she sighed. Perkins, still close to her, smelt stale. His breath was in her face.

'I have seen something,' she relented, at last.

'What have you seen?' he said, laying his hands on her again in such a way that she thought he was going to force her down through the caravan floor into the earth below. Her hair, which was still wet, stuck to the sides of her face and a brown streak made its way across her chin then down on to her throat. When he let go, she opened the caravan door, and they were surrounded by the booms, thuds and screeches that signified the destruction of countless man-made things.

'She's over there.' Irene pointed straight ahead.

'Where?'

'There,' she repeated, keeping her finger pointing steadily straight ahead.

'What? Over there? Over the cliff?' he said, frantically, starting to walk towards the headland.

She watched him for a moment as the wind pushed and pulled him around, then shouted, 'The sea, she's out at sea in a boat.'

He turned round and stared at her in disbelief.

'Is that what you saw?' he yelled.

'It's what I saw,' she shouted back, 'but I don't know what the outcome will be. We'll just have to wait and see, like everyone else.'

Without saying another word or even looking in her direction, he threw himself back into the car, got it started after three attempts, and left.

Irene put her hand to her hair and stood for a moment trying to remember what it was she had been in the middle of before the interruption.

Raymond had never seen anybody come back from the dead before. He had heard people praying and begging but nothing ever came of it. This woman, however, whom he had only just laid out and whom nobody had asked for, was beginning to open her eyes.

He put his face over hers until he could feel her breath. Then he ran up the steps from the Parlour, eager for another witness to what he was instantly referring to as a miracle.

'Poul,' he shouted breathlessly as he reached the top of the stairs.

The car was still parked there and Poul was getting into it, oblivious now to the storm raging around them. It was shoddy, nothing but special effects; they had both been at the heart of the matter and seen it at its worse.

'What is it? Do you need my help?'

Raymond stopped, breathing heavily. It had occurred to him, as soon as he called out, that the last thing he wanted to do was share his miracle. He felt suddenly covetous of it.

'No, don't worry, it's nothing,' he said, managing to sound tired without difficulty.

'You sure?'

'Sure.'

Poul got back into the car then wound the window down.

'You need me to call in on you tomorrow?'

'No, I'll be fine, you get along home.'

Raymond waited on the threshold of the Parlour while Poul watched him for a few moments then drove reluctantly away. He locked the door. This interruption had given the woman the chance to die again, but when he got back downstairs she was alive still. He frowned, more afraid of her now. Why had she been sent? Even half dead there was something in her face he recognised; an intimation of chaos. He pushed his face closer to feel her breath on it again. Laid out on his table she didn't look beautiful, it was far worse than that; she felt beautiful.

As her irregular breathing continued, his premonition that she had been sent to do him harm, to do all of them harm, strengthened. He continued to move his face over hers, and once his mouth brushed accidentally against her lips. When he stood up to straighten his aching back, she stopped breathing. He held his own breath, to see what the outcome of this would be. Suddenly her entire body juddered as she coughed and choked, her hands around her throat as though she were trying to strangle herself. She let go of the North Sea and lay with it spilling unevenly out of either side of her mouth and nostrils.

Raymond stood watching and wiped his mouth.

'Where's my coat?' she croaked at last.

It was her white dress that had saved her. Even though, as the boat approached, they had kept losing sight of her as the waves submerged the rocks, clawing their way up the lighthouse itself then retreating. As the lifeboat got closer and the waves continued their assault, Raymond was sure that the next time the water retreated, the figure in the white dress would no longer be there. But she didn't disappear. She stayed on the rocks long enough for Raymond to jump over the side of the lifeboat attached to a rope and make his way through the sea and over the rocks to her. He had thought, during that first second when he laid eyes on her, that the sea had at last relinquished his mother. After all these years.

'Where's my coat?' she screamed again, then, more accusingly, 'where's my coat?'

She lay as still as she could, not wanting to overbalance the Parlour table she was convinced was floating. As she looked to either side she thought she saw the boy's blazer float past and a woman's high-heeled shoe.

'Help,' she said at last. 'Help me.' She hadn't been able to say this as the boat went down, but she said it now.

'My throat hurts.' She was trying not to cry.

'It will do; it's the sea that does it.'

'There was sea-water inside me?' she said with revulsion.

'Gallons,' Raymond confirmed, unflinching where simple facts were concerned.

She let her eyes wander around the room and everything in

it, especially the matchstick model of HMS *Victory* above Raymond's desk. Then she looked at him.

'You're an undertaker?'

Raymond nodded, not wanting to look at her too closely now her eyes were open.

'So you thought I was dead?'

'You *were* dead.'

She put a lot of effort into sitting up.

'I found you on the rocks. Do you remember the rocks?' he said.

'The only thing I can remember is sea,' she started to moan.

'You drowned on the rocks.'

'So you brought me here because I was dead?'

'You were dead. Trust me.'

'And now?'

'And now you're not,' Raymond said sharply, too distressed himself to offer any consolation.

She lay down again.

'Where's everybody else?'

'You're the only survivor. We didn't find anybody else.'

'You found nothing?'

'Not a single trace.' Then he added, 'Apart from a boy's school blazer and a woman's shoe. Black with a high heel.'

'I know. I saw those things just now. They floated right past me here.'

Raymond didn't contradict her. 'Are you cold?' he said suddenly, unused to being vigilant about physical comfort in the Parlour.

She didn't answer, turning her head away.

'You found nobody else?' she asked again.

'Nobody. Apart from you.'

'There was a boy. A little boy?' she insisted.

'Nobody.'

'But he was right by my side, he had his hand in my pocket.'

'Instinct would have made you discard anything heavy, anything that might have prevented you from floating.'

'So I discarded the boy?' she said slowly, afraid.

'You discarded the coat.'

'But his hand was in the coat pocket.'

Raymond didn't know what to say as she turned this over in her mind.

'Have you phoned anybody? The hospital?'

'I will do,' he said, automatically getting up.

'Don't,' she shook her head. 'I'm a nurse. I don't need the hospital, and I don't want anybody knowing . . .'

They both started as the phone rang, and despite what she had just said, he picked it up.

'Ray,' Sergeant Pearce's voice said.

'What is it?'

'Busy are you?'

'Not at all.'

'I've just heard that Arthur's boat went down. It's a crying bloody shame.'

'It is,' Raymond agreed.

He and Sergeant Pearce had known each other since they were knee-high and had a good professional understanding.

'Are you all right?'

'Tired.'

There was a pause.

'Poul said there were no survivors. I was just phoning to double-check, before I put pen to paper,' Sergeant Pearce said. 'So you haven't got anything for me?'

Raymond gave himself a second to decide.

'Not that I'm aware of,' he said. He heard the buttons on Sergeant Pearce's uniform rubbing along his desk at the station.

'Is your dad going to the dogs' (the sergeant paused to laugh at his oldest, most frequently repeated joke) 'next Friday?'

'Probably.'

'Tell him I'll see him there.'

'I will do.'

When Raymond came off the phone, the woman was sitting up inspecting her arms and legs.

'That was Sergeant Pearce down at the station.'

She didn't say anything.

Raymond sighed. 'Wanting to know if there were any survivors from Arthur Selman's pleasure boat.'

'What did you say to him?' she asked, so quietly that he could barely hear her.

'I said not as far as I was aware of,' he said, not taking his eyes off her bent head. 'Who are you?'

There was a knocking at the door.

'Please don't answer it,' she whispered.

The knocking stopped then started again.

Raymond went to the bottom of the stairs, and when he turned round she looked more forlorn and incapable of a struggle than anyone he had ever seen, including his father. He climbed to the top of the stairs.

There was a man standing outside, his face pressed against the glass door. Raymond recognised the black jacket of Hal's dancing suit, even though the collar was turned up against the storm. Hal looked mauled, not his usual trim self. He could see Hal far better than Hal could see him because of the streetlights. But Hal was pressed tight enough against the glass to make out Raymond's eyes, and they stood like that for a long time, Hal against the door and Raymond a shadow at the top of the stairs, staring at each other. Hal mouthed something and Raymond thought he heard him say Daisy's name. His stomach tightened, but not enough to make him want to open the door. A car passed by. After a while, and without making any further gestures, Hal walked away, hunched against the storm, which was still raging. The sign for Mrs Thompson's rock shop opposite was being dragged up and down Front Street, as was the boy and dog collection box for the Royal Society for the Blind.

Hal decided to go dancing despite the weather. The promenade was empty and every minute or so the sea came up through the railings reaching as far as Uncle Tom's flowerbeds. Even on top of the dunes he couldn't tell the difference between sea spray and rain. Sand was clinging heavily to the soles of his dance shoes, and the wind was so harsh that it was difficult to walk in a straight line.

The Palace was in sight now, but it looked grey. The scaffolding was still up, but a passageway had been made so that dancers could get through on a Friday and Saturday night. The rain was getting heavier and was running off his nose, but The Palace was closer than home so he pressed on towards it with no thought of pleasure any more, only shelter. His trousers were stuck along the front of his legs from thigh to ankle and, by the time he reached the covered walkway, he was trying hard not to breathe in water.

Geordie wasn't in the cloakroom and the curtains behind his desk were shut. Water was running off Hal on to the carpet where he stood. There was music playing, but it sounded as though the band was rehearsing rather than performing, and there was no sign of any dancers. It was as if everybody apart from him had known that there would be a storm that night.

Hal started as the wise monkeys suddenly began to play their tin-can tune and the band's music fell into the background. Somebody had put a penny in the machine and given the wise monkeys an unexpected lease of life on this empty storm-ridden night. He moved forwards slightly and saw Daisy standing in front of the machine, in red as usual, her hands and face pressed against the glass. She was wearing a see-through plastic mackintosh over the dress and a matching cap over her hair, which she had probably had set and blow-dried that afternoon. The plastic covering made her hair look grey when it caught the light.

Despite the mechanical chattering of the monkeys and the distance between them, he still heard her sigh. The monkeys stopped as suddenly as they had started, the ancient mechanism still agile. She put another penny in the slot and this time the same tune made the hairs on the back of Hal's neck stand up. He wondered if Daisy had seen him come in; she wasn't showing any signs of it. She was waiting for Raymond, and laughed quietly to herself as the monkeys carried on playing for her. He watched for a few minutes more then silently turned and followed his sandy footprints out of The Palace back into the night and the storm, leaving her alone.

Once she heard him turn and leave, she stopped laughing. She wasn't laughing anyway, she was crying, but this soon petered out. He was gone, his sandy footprints the only sign of his ever having been there at all.

Hal cut across the crazy golf course Raymond had cut across hours before. Setton was deserted, and the only sign of life he encountered was in the Clayton Arms. His suit was so waterlogged by this time that he felt as though he was wearing double the amount of layers he actually was. He would never be able to wear his dance shoes again they were so wrecked. The Royal Society for the Blind collection box came crashing down the street towards him and he let it pass without trying to stop the blind boy and his dog.

The Co-op had been turned black by the rain, and the rack of shoes in the window had fallen over as if blown by the wind. Hal knocked on the door of Funeral Services then pressed his face against it. At first he thought there were no lights on, then he noticed the dull glow coming from the bottom of the stairs. He banged again, and the green velvet curtains in the window shook slightly. After a few moments Raymond stepped into the light at the bottom of the stairs, disappearing into darkness as he climbed them, then coming into an uneasy light again just by the door.

'Daisy's at The Palace,' Hal mouthed carefully against the glass. 'She's waiting for you.'

They carried on staring at each other, but neither of them moved and he suddenly knew that Raymond wasn't going to open the door. One of them had to break away and Hal, standing outside in the wind and the rain, was the first.

'It's me, Hal,' he shouted, giving it one last try, then walked away. He didn't go far, just to the window with the toppled shoe display where he waited to see if the door would open now that he was out of sight, but it didn't. So he walked back to the Clayton Arms, hoping to find Perkins, but ended up stood next to Tinker Trench who was drinking himself into a coma and oblivious to the steam rising off Hal's suit.

There had been no lights on in the watch-house when Perkins drove on to the headland and parked on the grass outside the gate. But he had knocked persistently and after a while a tall shaggy man opened the door, a kerosene lamp in his hand. 'The electric's down,' he said sullenly, the poor light an excuse for his delay in answering the door. 'The electric's completely down.'

'Can I come in?' Perkins asked.

The inside of the watch-house smelt like the inside of a ship. The figureheads of lost ships were dotted in every corner, against walls, and up the stairs. Through the open doorway to the left, Perkins saw a dummy wearing an ancient diving suit and the end of a snooker table, the cues resting on the side from a game interrupted. There was a lot of water on the wooden floor inside the hallway, and a row of glistening yellow macs were hanging from the hooks beside the door.

'The storm's still bad,' Poul said, watching proudly as the man's eyes swept over everything that was precious to him.

'You're not English,' Perkins noted.

'Can I help you?' Poul said, lowering the lamp.

'I hope so.'

The door, which hadn't been shut properly, blew in forcefully against Perkins's back and sent him falling into Poul who held the lamp steadily and waited for the other man to straighten himself without offering any assistance.

'The men down at the quayside said you were called out tonight?'

'We were earlier.'

'They said there was only one boat out at sea and that was Arthur Selman's pleasure boat,' Perkins stated.

'That's right.'

'You went after it?'

'We went after her, yes.'

Perkins caught the smell of cigarette smoke coming from the other room. 'I think that someone I know', Perkins said with difficulty, 'was on that boat when it fell into trouble.'

'You *think*?' Then, after a pause, 'It fell into more than trouble,' the Dutchman said with feeling, but for the boat rather than the man. 'There's nothing left of it,' he finished, unable to repress the accusing tone that was slipping into his voice. He had learnt, through experience, not to trust strangers who arrived in the middle of the night.

'What about the people on board?'

The floorboards in the other rooms creaked as somebody walked over them and the light passed uneasily over the figureheads in the hallway.

'Never seen a sea like tonight's,' Poul said, taking in the man's flimsy suit again, and the way he kept trying to slick his hair back. 'We were lucky to get back ourselves.'

Perkins waited, the draught from under the door pressing hard against the back of his legs and his nostrils full of wet wool from where he had fallen against the other man's chest.

'We only found one person, but she was not a survivor,' Poul said, with precision.

'Was she young or old?'

'Oh, she was young.'

'But she wasn't a survivor?'

'She was wearing white,' Poul said, absently.

'White?'

Poul nodded. 'Raymond Clarke, the undertaker, took her.' He glanced again, saw the terrified look in the other man's eyes, and tried to make his tone more tender. 'The police will have to trace her.'

They listened as the watch-house creaked, echoing the aftermath of the storm outside.

'Raymond Clarke, you said.'

'That's right.'

Perkins stared at him. 'Thank you,' he said, pulling the door to the watch-house shut fast behind him.

Perkins stood outside Co-operative Funeral Services and banged on the door. Raymond Clarke climbed the stairs as wearily as he had done towards Hal the first time, unable, despite the woman's pleas, to let this call from the outside world go unanswered.

This time it wasn't Hal.

Perkins stopped banging when he realised Raymond was going to open the door.

'Raymond?'

Raymond nodded.

'Your friend . . . the Dutchman?'

'He's a Dutchman, yes.'

'Up at the watch-house . . . he said you went out after Arthur Selman's pleasure boat?'

'We were too late,' Raymond said. 'How do you know about Arthur's boat?'

'They told me at the quayside.'

'It's Perkins, isn't it?'

Perkins tried to smile but couldn't, extending his hand instead. 'I've seen you with Hal at The Palace. Dancing. That's right, dancing. You're a very good dancer,' he said suddenly to Raymond. He meant to flatter, but it sounded more like an accusation. He slid his hand over his hair from his forehead, over the crown and down to the nape of his neck. 'The Dutchman said there were no survivors.' Perkins waited for Raymond to endorse this, but he didn't. 'It's just that I knew somebody on that boat. Stella Armstrong?'

Raymond continued to stare at Perkins, then turned and walked carefully back down the stairs, gripping hard on to the banister. He heard the other man behind him, close on his heels.

The woman's eyes flickered as she took in Perkins standing in the doorway. He made no attempt to cross to the table.

'She was dead,' Raymond stated flatly. He was angry; there were rules of conduct they should stick to; that were there to help them through situations such as these. Situations that were awkward, intolerable, and that required, emotionally speaking, superhuman effort. But the woman who had come back from the dead was sitting motionless on the Parlour table, and Perkins stood motionless in the Parlour doorway. Neither of them looked capable of remembering let alone following any rules of conduct.

Raymond sat down at his desk, disgusted, and turned his back on them. His back remained turned as Perkins picked her up and carried her up the stairs, shutting the door at the top behind him. There were no sounds of struggle or resistance on the woman's part. In the distance he heard a car engine start up and disappear into the night.

Once they had left, the storm dropped suddenly. The Parlour smelt of the sea; it had never smelt of the sea before. He had been right, he thought, looking about him, to go into the line of business he had. Death wasn't to be trusted, which was why he made such a good job of burying them under the ground. His eyes rested for a moment on the table, which was still wet, but now empty.

He glanced briefly at the plans sent to him that morning from the council offices for the construction of a new crematorium. It would be Setton's first, he thought, as a tremor passed through his bowels. And they wanted his opinion on the efficiency of this particular form of waste disposal or gateway to heaven, depending on which way you looked at it. He sighed, regaining some scraps of the contentment he had felt earlier before the storm, before the woman, and before Perkins, then turned out the lights.

Stella lay along the back seat of the car, the streetlights they passed under illuminating her white dress. She picked up a bottle of insecticide from the floor, read the label then dropped it. 'Jesus Christ,' Perkins heard her mutter under her breath. 'Where are we going?'

'I don't know.' He didn't have the ability to let all traces of warmth out of his voice the way she did. This didn't sound as stone cold as he had meant it to.

He looked suddenly helpless in the light being thrown

around the inside of the car. Taking one hand off the steering wheel, he tucked a clump of stray hair back behind his ear.

'I saw you once. In Utah. You were so close.' She sounded tired, not triumphant about this. 'I even followed you for a while.'

The rest of her sentence got lost in a series of hacking coughs, and for a moment he thought she might be sick.

He slowed down.

'Caught in the act of trying to find me. I knew as soon as I saw you that it was him who'd sent you. Delaval.'

'He didn't choose me; it just happened.'

Another cough rattled through her.

'I knew it was him. You'd never have it in you to set yourself on my trail. Anyway, I thought it was going to be shoes. You used to say that shoes were going to make your fortune.' She pressed her hand on her chest then managed a laugh.

'It might still be shoes,' Perkins yelled, slamming the brakes on.

He heard her body absorb the shock of the car stopping suddenly.

'Why? How much did he promise to pay you if you found me?'

'It might still be shoes,' he repeated, looking out of the window to see where they were.

'It might,' she conceded. 'He's here in Setton, isn't he?'

Perkins didn't say anything.

They were at the end of the cemetery wall where they either took the road to the left, which led to Wyley and passed Ellison Court, or carried on straight up to North Cliff.

She was watching him; he heard her hair brushing against the leather seat as she turned her head.

'Are we going to him now?'

Perkins dropped his head on to the steering wheel and shut his eyes. 'We could go away,' he said. 'Far away.'

She lay still. 'How much did he promise to pay you if you found me?' she said again.

Perkins put the car into gear and turned left.

'He knows you. Delaval knows you . . . he knew you'd come because of Spanish City.'

'Is that why you think I'm here?'

'You are here. He was right,' Perkins said.

He thought he could see the sparse lights of Ellison Court ahead.

'Why don't you go?' she said, trying to sit up. 'Just go. Tomorrow. Anywhere. Back to London . . . anywhere. Don't you want your share of life?'

'I want you to stay,' he said suddenly, stopping the car again.

'I'm not your life. You know that.'

9

The walls of Spanish City were bright white, which, until it got properly dark and the lights went on, looked strange against the Setton night. Over the entrance there was a huge bull's head whose horns, gazed at from below, made an unholy silhouette against the sky, and the blue ticket booths had plastic orange trees growing outside them. People felt (even those who had never set foot off English soil) that they were entering a foreign country. On top of the pillar to the right of the bull's head there was the dancing figure of a girl, and on the pillar to the left the dancing figure of a boy. Both were cast in bronze, no expense spared.

There were no vacancies in any of the hotels or boarding houses. The town was full to capacity: the dunes were full, the promenade was full, the beach was full, the sea was full. Word had spread that something strange and exotic was rising up out of guttural Setton. Every available surface in the town had been covered by posters bearing the picture of a man lying on his back, his cap over his face, claiming that I FORGOT ALL ABOUT WORK AT SETTON.

Trying to walk down Main Street, Hal couldn't remember ever having seen as much traffic, motorised and human, on the streets of Setton, all travelling in the same direction. He kept looking among the crowd for Perkins, whom he hadn't seen since the night of the storm, but there was no sign of him. As the crowd turned on to Front Street the lights of Spanish City went on, and an almighty cheer rose. With the lights on, everything else, including the sea, went black.

Inside Spanish City there was barely room to breathe. At one point Hal heard a bang and thought that they were closing the gates, but it was only the fireworks. It felt, for a moment, as if there wasn't a living soul in England left outside the walls of Spanish City. He felt panic, and tried to smile when Tinker turned to him, his face transfixed, but ended up guiltily pushing his hands into his pockets. An infidel walking in the midst of all these pilgrims. Nothing would ever be the same again. The Palace would no longer be a place people came to dance in, and dancing would no longer be enough to lighten their loads. Only last season, you would have been able to hear the chattering of the machines in the Penny Arcade from here, Hal thought, and the dance band's music. Tonight, from the direction of The Palace, there was nothing but silence.

Hal, Daisy, Tinker and Melita joined the hoards queuing for the Charleston. Standing on the roller-coaster's loading platform, they had a good view of the whole of Spanish City. The rubbish bins were moulded to look like matadors, and there were side shows to rival those in Blackpool or Brighton any day. The council's euphoria had overridden their earlier planning refusal and a big wheel had been constructed. All that could be seen of the dodgems were electric sparks because of the number of people crowding around. The waltzer was halted again and again so that bleach could be borrowed from the lady at the change kiosk in order to sponge down the vomit.

Daisy let out a scream each time spray from the water chute hit everybody standing on the loading platform. She couldn't remember the last time she had been so excited. Probably not since her mother had died, that moment when she knew Ada Crombie was never going to open her eyes again. Ada Crombie was dead. She had wanted to say it loud and clear for all the world to hear. Ada Crombie was dead, taking a whole load of history nobody wanted with her. Tonight Daisy wasn't wearing red, she was wearing blue. In fact, the only ounce of red on her was the clutch bag she was holding. Hal noticed, but chose to say nothing.

Raymond, who was Daisy's chaperon, had chosen not to ride the coaster. It didn't take Hal long to pick out Raymond's face in the crowd because it was upturned, looking directly at them, and his expression was the same as it always was. Which, if you didn't know Raymond, produced the odd effect of making his face look expressionless.

He waved at them, but only Hal saw. Daisy was looking at the Charleston tracks stretching up into the night sky, biting her lip and clutching her bag. It was warm but there was a strong wind, and hair, no matter how heavily it had been slicked down, was blowing in all directions. One girl turned her head in the wrong direction so quickly that she lost her false eyelashes, which stuck to Hal's shirt. She soon pulled them viciously off him. Hal recognised a girl from school, Mandy Watkins, whose heels kept getting stuck in the gaps in the platform, they were so thin and narrow. Every now and then she spat pointedly through the gaps. The last time he had seen her was in the careers office at school with a can of yellow lighter fluid between them. She had fidgeted in her seat, her thin eyes unable to focus, her clothes covered in grass stains from where she had been found, staggering across the school playing-fields. He had ended up giving her can back to her, and telling her to grow up as fast as she could. Tonight she had a bag of chocolate drops in her hand.

The Charleston formed the south wall of Spanish City, and you had to tip your head right back to take in all of it. It looked fragile, and the structure rattled. Nine small cars, once filled with riders, made a 159-foot plunge, went up a hill, down another, along a piece of immaculately conceived dog track, followed by a camel's hump, leading to the penultimate thrill of the ride: the slammer. As the cars made an almost-vertical drop, the riders were left temporarily suspended in sky. Those who had experienced this sensation of negative gravity called it 'air time'.

The ultimate sensation of the ride had been sheer genius on the part of old Delaval. A low-slung steel beam was hung over the last continuous stretch of track. Cars went hurtling towards this overhead obstruction, which was on a level with the riders' necks, at a speed of 66 m.p.h., giving people an unforgettable sensation of imminent decapitation. At the last possible moment, the track dipped suddenly at a fifty-nine-degree angle, speeding riders away from their brush with death. This device was known as the *fine del capo*. Tinker whistled with admiration as the roller-coaster, filled for its virgin ride with notables from the town council and other general VIPs, screamed to a halt at the far end of the loading platform.

The councillors emerged, white faced, from the cars. Some of them stumbled, temporarily outside gravity's grip. The photographers from *Setton Echo* took their pictures before they had time to pose or to find their dignity. The crowd began to cheer and jostle. Smiles now broke out on Munro's and all the councillors' faces, even Marston's. Extra-large Teddy McKay was nearly pushed over the edge of the loading platform, but soon regained his balance, gasping and coughing at the sheer size of the evening. He, like everyone else there, had never believed that anything other than a revolution could generate crowds like this.

As he tried to tuck his tie back into his trouser belt, somewhere on the far side of his gut, he knew that this was the biggest thing Setton was likely to see. This year, 1955, was going to make history. People would speak of it as the Golden Year. He dusted himself down and turned to small weedy Councillor Jenkins. 'Golden, absolutely golden.' He tried the line out. Then continued in his booming voice, 'A golden moment, in a golden year.'

He let it hang for a moment then turned to the cameras, broad, beaming. But he saw out of the corner of his eye, despite the glare, Jenkins turn to Somerville when he thought he was out of earshot, and repeat word for word what he had just heard. As Jenkins turned to face the cameras he saw

Somerville turn to the mayor and whisper in his ear McKay's words. The mayor gave Somerville's shoulder a squeeze to get him out of the way then stood in front of the reporters. He had already prepared a speech, but this was the opening he had been looking for; a sweeping one that would blot out the tragedy of Arthur Selman's pleasure boat. He began (in a voice that already anticipated newsprint), 'Ladies, gentlemen . . . a golden moment in a golden year.'

McKay stood and wiped the sweat off his face then, turning quickly to check that no one was looking, waddled to the back of the huge queue stretching along the loading platform and beyond. He stood there with his neck craned, looking up at the tracks, their fragile structure plain for all to see.

The man who emerged from the fourth car was Delaval. Hal was too far away to see whether he had changed or not, but he was the only rider who didn't stumble; who emerged on to the loading platform smiling. Hal tried to move instinctively towards him, but was hemmed in by the mass of bodies on the platform. Then the queue shunted forwards and Delaval disappeared with the rest of the councillors.

Sitting in the tiny car, with Daisy in front and Tinker and Melita behind, Hal saw Raymond wave again. He had moved so that he could get a view of the loading platform. This time Daisy saw and waved back. Hal tried to swallow his fear, but as the cars made their false start (part of the ride designed to induce screams and laughter), he felt a panic he hadn't felt since the war rising up inside him.

As they pulled away from the platform Daisy turned to look at Hal, catching him off guard. Then he heard the mechanical chattering of the safety dogs beneath the car, not unlike the mechanical chattering of the wise monkeys in the Penny Arcade, only the tone was deeper. They started to climb, and as they reached the top of the first hill a small voice beside him said, 'Don't worry, Mr Price.' It was Mandy Watkins, her filthy hands grasping the bar across their stomachs.

They were reaching the crest of the hill, and all of Setton was below them. He raised himself out of his seat, instinctively wanting to disembark, but was pushed back down by one of Mandy Watkins's tiny hands. They shot downwards; his body had never experienced anything like it. His line of vision was repeatedly shaken, and closing his eyes didn't help. He was screaming continuously and couldn't have stopped if he'd tried. All he had to do was let go, and if he let go he might even feel pleasure, but he couldn't; he didn't know what the outcome would be. Every muscle in his body, all his muscles, were getting tighter and tighter and he didn't think his stomach could stand another drop. The next minute he was no longer just screaming, he was hyperventilating, and blacked out at the 60 m.p.h. approach to the overhanging projection, missing the climax of the ride: the *fine del capo*.

Tom had put the last roller in Charlie Price's hair and she was free to pick up the paper and finish the crossword. She would always read the clues out loud then throw a temper if anyone answered them. After tapping the end of her pencil on the paper and staring into space for a good ten minutes she got up and had a look out of the back window. Jamie was on all fours in front of the fireplace, trying to clean out the grate.

There was no breeze coming through the open window, and the air was stifling. She got claustrophobic in the heat, even though they only ever got it bad for four to six weeks of the year. There was a handful of children running about the allotments, which were looking more and more like a wasteland now that so many of them were going to seed. People didn't seem to have the time to grow their own food these days. She could hear the children screaming as they played in an old water barrel.

Closer to hand she heard the laugh of a drunken woman as Frankie, the new tenant downstairs, led her up the garden path. Frankie worked in the engine shop at Watts and had a son, apparently, but nobody had ever seen hide nor hair of him. The mother wasn't meant to be English. Frankie wasn't a drinker, but he always picked women who were, probably so that they wouldn't remember his face afterwards.

Mrs Marshal walked warily up the road towards Mrs Williams at number 61. After more than three decades of spectacular domestic violence, Mrs Marshal now spent Friday and Saturday nights at number 61 so that Mr Marshal came back from his drinking to an empty flat. The empty flat sometimes incited Mr Marshal to knock up the inhabitants of number 61 in the dead of the night, and then the whole of Ellsworth Row had to listen to his atrocities for up to half an hour. After which he would fall over on the spot and cry himself to sleep, usually in the back yard of number 61. One night he'd fall asleep and never wake up, and the sooner the better Charlie thought to herself as she watched Mrs Marshal scurry along, her hands at her throat.

It was almost dark now. Mrs Marshal disappeared from sight into the back yard of number 61, and Frankie's girl stopped singing. They started making other noises, and she was about to slam the window shut when, above the couple downstairs and the children round the water barrel, she heard the first screams from South Cliff, carried on the wind.

The screams came rushing into the flat, passing close enough to make her hair stand on end. Tom came and sat at the table, putting his button box in front of him. He opened it quietly.

'Hear that?' Jamie Price said standing up. His eyes looked bright as he said it and he was staring straight at her, wiping his hands on the cloth. 'We should go and see it. Live a little.'

'You know I don't want to see it.'

'Everyone in Setton will have seen it apart from you. Hal will have seen it; he's gone tonight.'

'So?'

He dropped the rag on the armchair near the fire and came and stood close to her. They both watched as Tom began to sort the buttons from the tin into colours; this was a nightly task he imposed on himself.

'You've always wanted to go on a roller-coaster.'

'Have I?' she challenged him.

'I'd love to take you.'

He came and stood closer still. Close enough to bend and kiss the back of her neck.

'Jamie.' She hit him away. 'We'll put the wireless on and have a dance.'

'Oh come on, Charlie love. Let your hair down. You know you love to let your hair down. Make fools of ourselves.'

Her hands instinctively went for the rollers Tom had just put in her hair.

'Oh well,' Jamie said, making his way to the front door.

'Where are you going?' she asked.

'The garage,' he said, defeated.

She watched out of the window. A few minutes later the light in the garage went on.

'Bloody, bloody stupid name for a roller-coaster,' she muttered to herself.

They were a good mile from the sea front, but even with all the windows shut the screams from the brand-new gleaming white Spanish City were all she could hear now there were no more children round the water barrel, and Frankie had reached whatever climax he had been seeking to reach. The screams were going to continue late into the night, late enough for her to have to lie in bed with Jamie beside her, listening to them. And when she thought about this it was as if all the goodness in her life had drained away and she was left with nothing she could make sense of.

Hal came to as the cars arrived back at the loading platform. His chest felt constricted and his head was lolling dangerously forwards. The pressure on his chest was caused by Mandy Watkins's arm holding him back in his seat. As the cars slowed down he pulled her arm away from his chest. It wasn't only filthy it was sticky and her fingers were covered in hundreds and thousands. He pushed the safety bar away from him and fell out of the car.

'Now was that heaven or was that heaven,' Tinker hissed into his ear as he helped him to his feet, his face red with jubilation.

People were getting out of the other cars with their hands around their throats. He left Mandy in the car without another word and followed Tinker and Daisy. Everyone was experiencing the sort of adrenaline rush only people who left Setton or dealt in the darker side of life there experienced. He wondered if this was what being Perkins felt like, and how long it would last.

'We should go dancing now,' Daisy said.

'I don't think I'm up to it,' Hal mumbled.

Tinker and Melita were already trying to make their way into The Palace.

When they reached Raymond he was watching riders stumble down the steps of the waltzer. One giggling girl fell flat on her face.

'Can we ride again?' Daisy said, to no one in particular.

'The queues are too long,' Raymond pronounced. Then added, 'It looked fun,' but his tone was so ominous that they thought, for a second, he might have the power to dismantle the roller-coaster, bit by bit.

Daisy didn't rise to the bait.

'We should go dancing,' she said.

Raymond looked down at his shoes, which were immaculately polished as usual, then smiled at her.

'Of course we should.' He patted Daisy on the back.

Up until the night of the storm, Hal had always figured, however dimly, on Daisy's horizon. After that, she had found herself standing on the horizon with no other soul in sight. Fighting the rising panic, the panic that nobody but the ghost of her mother lived on the horizon, she dug in her heels and waited. Then gradually, from a direction she had never anticipated, a slow figure came plodding determinedly into sight. Raymond Clarke, the undertaker. She hadn't felt joy. But she had sense enough to feel hope. She clung on, and started to move about the dairy counter at the Co-op with a certain amount of confidence. Just for good measure, she stopped wearing red. As far as she was concerned, intimate relations were something that had to be planned, plotted and schemed. From now on she had no intention of leaving anything to either instinct or chance.

She watched the waltzer start up again.

'What happened up there?' she said to Hal, looking irritated rather than concerned.

'I don't know. I just went.'

'Went where?'

'I just went,' he repeated stupidly. 'Blacked out' sounded too attention-grabbing.

'You missed the ssshhhh.' Raymond took his hand out of his pocket and made a slicing motion with it across his neck. Then he laughed and, putting his arm in Daisy's, started walking towards The Palace.

Hal was the only one who saw Daisy take a last glance at the Charleston. He watched them go, vaguely aware that he was meant to be heading in that direction himself, then turned to look at the waltzer again. There was a small blond man standing talking to the operator of the ride. Delaval.

The lanky Teddy boy operating the waltzer listened to Delaval's story with a stupid grin on his face. He waited until Delaval had finished and then started the ride. Once it had reached a terrifying speed he proceeded to walk around the wooden ramp and spin the cars, especially ones with girls in, eliciting deafening screams.

'Have you seen anyone of that description?' Delaval shouted. 'Have you seen her?'

'Yeah, I have,' the Teddy boy yelled, straightening out his jacket. Then he made another round of the undulating ramp, a cigarette clenched between his teeth. He grinned at the occupants of car number 9 as he gave them an almighty spin. Without thinking, Delaval set off himself on the undulating ramp into the middle of the screams, somehow keeping his balance by jumping from hump to hump as the ramp rose up. There was a look (for a split-second) of genuine admiration on the Teddy boy's face.

'Where?' Delaval hollered.

Out of the corner of his eye he saw something solid flash past and his hands instinctively went out for it. Too late, it was no longer there. He started to lose balance, but just about managed to stand up straight again, in a very shabby way, because the waltzer was starting to slow down. The Teddy boy looked disappointed at this missed opportunity for one-upmanship, then started to perform some kind of improvised dance. Delaval hung on to every tap of his boot as though it were Morse code. The waltzer eventually stopped. With a grandiose shuffle, the Teddy boy's gyrations came to an end, and he stood looking at Delaval, a stupid grin on his face once more.

Delaval was about to make one last lunge for him when suddenly people started piling out of the cars and this wave of people hit the wave of people making their way on to the waltzer. The sheer volume of bodies forced Delaval off so that he completely lost sight of the Teddy boy and, after a while, the waltzer as well. Someone dug him in the ribs and he felt like crying. Then he realised what the boy had been trying to tell him.

He had seen Stella, and when he saw her she was dancing.

Hal watched Delaval make his way towards The Palace. It wasn't hard to follow his blond head. Ever since the fight Geordie had started to tip Hal a mock-salute, and tonight was no exception. It was usually a bad time to play the machines; all the buttons were greasy from fingers that had just finished eating fish and chips. But tonight the Penny Arcade was empty. Everybody was outside. It was strange passing the tuppence drop, the one-arm bandits and the lucky dips, their lights flashing, but the machinery still. Nobody was playing the wise monkeys either, not that anybody apart from Hal did any more.

The music coming through the velvet curtains sounded far away, and when he reached the top of the stairs the dance floor was as eerily devoid of dancers as the Penny Arcade had been of gamblers. He walked along the balcony to the Tropicana.

Fast Eddie looked surprised to see Hal, like he had sold him up the river to a pack of cannibals and had never expected to see him again. A few dancers made their way round the floor to slow music played by musicians who had lost heart. The atmosphere was elegiac and there was no sign of Delaval.

Raymond, easily the best dancer there, had already taken to the floor with Daisy. Tonight, among the trash, they looked absurdly professional, glamorous even. Hal could see from Daisy's face that she was in exultation. He was about to go down on to the dance floor himself when he heard Tinker's voice from the corner behind him.

'It was like heaven up there. Can you believe it?'

Tinker paused, but he got no reply.

The pillars along the balcony were covered in tiny mirror tiles so that he could see Tinker and Perkins reflected hundreds of times over. He had been so busy thinking about Delaval, he had forgotten Perkins, who was staring straight past him, not taking in a word of Tinker's monologue. There was a pair of women's shoes on the table.

Hal's hand went out for the pillar and he didn't notice the badly placed mirrors cutting into his fingers.

'Where've you been?' he said, but the words came out so quietly he wasn't sure whether he had actually spoken them or not.

Hal followed Perkins's gaze, letting his eyes sweep across the dance floor. He heard the band stepping up its tempo, and saw Daisy standing alone. Then he spotted Raymond, who was dancing faster and more beautifully by the second, so that a space had been cleared respectfully around him. Hal could hear the screams of the woman he was dancing with, interspersed with quick excited laughs from Raymond. Hal had never heard his cousin laugh like that before.

The woman's dress was shiny and white, and as she moved there was a lot of net from under her skirt on show. She was dancing barefoot, one moment stamping hard on the floor, and the next barely touching it with her toes. Hal looked back at Perkins, and realised at the same time that the shoes on the table belonged to her; they were Stella's shoes.

As the music reached its climax Raymond pulled Stella ferociously towards him. When it stopped, he let go of her just as ferociously, walking rapidly off the dance floor while neatly patting at his forehead with a handkerchief. Within seconds he was by Daisy's side.

Stella remained on the dance floor looking about her, lost. Hal watched as she became self-conscious and started to pull slightly at her dress. She looked more familiar to him right then than anybody he knew.

People stared as she made her way over to the stairs because of the way she had been dancing with Raymond, and because of her bare feet.

Perkins tried to wipe the sweat from his face as she walked along the balcony towards Raymond. She smiled kindly at Daisy, who didn't smile back.

'He's a good dancer,' she said.

'I know.'

'He saved my life.'

'By dancing?'

'No. At sea.'

'This is the girl you saved?' Daisy said, turning to Raymond.

Raymond nodded, but didn't look at either of them. He made no attempt to clutch at the heroism offered him; he wanted nothing more to do with her. He took hold of Daisy's hand and led her back on to the dance floor.

Hal watched him with renewed awe, barely aware of Perkins, who had stood up, holding the pair of shoes in his arms.

Stella stared at Hal, but didn't say anything. Like Perkins, she had changed completely, and yet she was still the same woman she had been.

Perkins emerged fully into the light. He held the shoes out to her, but she didn't move; she just looked at them as if they had betrayed her.

'Put them on,' he said.

'The heels are about to fall off. Besides, they hurt my feet.'

But she took the shoes anyway and put them on, standing unevenly. Hal watched them both without a word.

'You remember Hal, don't you Stella? Corporal Harold Price? The Rat Castle?' Perkins started to cough, and beckoned in Hal's general direction with the hand that wasn't in front of his mouth catching phlegm.

She paused only a moment then they shook hands. Why had they done that? It was the first time they had ever touched, and he didn't even feel her hand. She wobbled in the shoes and tried to smile.

'It's been a long time,' she said.

'It has been a long time,' Hal said, more slowly. 'Eleven years. First Perkins, then you.' A steady stream of blood was making its way across his wrist and down into the sleeve of his jacket. He turned to Perkins. 'Can I borrow your handkerchief?'

Perkins pulled it straight out of his pocket, and both he and Stella watched as Hal spat on his wrist and attempted to clean up the streak of blood.

'It's a long time,' it was Perkins's turn to acknowledge.

They all looked out over the dance floor and Hal saw Stella's eyes on Raymond.

'I saw you dancing with him,' Perkins said.

'That man saved my life,' she said, ignoring him. 'The night of the storm. A lot of people died that night. A small boy died,' she said, turning her head away, 'and I didn't.'

Hal could hear the storm again as she said this, and saw himself stood outside the Parlour in the middle of it banging on the door and looking in at Raymond. She had been on the other side of that door.

Stella went and stood against the balustrade. 'I like it here. I like dancing.'

'He took you to the Parlour? He never said anything to me.' Hal looked at Raymond again, trying to fathom this.

'Raymond saved me and Perkins found me,' Stella yawned. 'Of all the places, where I least expected him. Perkins found me here.'

'He said you would come to Setton.'

Hal had never seen hope on Perkins's face before. Dogged determination and other qualities the gutter gave rise to, but not that most glorious of ones: hope. It made him look ridiculously childlike, and Perkins was one of those people who had never been a child. A man of the world, yes, but never a child.

'Get me a drink,' Stella said to Hal, her eyes on the dance floor again.

'Delaval's here,' he said suddenly.

Perkins became frantic, his eyes flicking all over the place. 'Where?'

'Get me a drink, Hal,' Stella repeated.

'You knew he'd come . . .' Hal heard Perkins saying as he made for the Tropicana.

'Make it doubles,' Daisy was saying as he approached the bar, turning her small red clutch bag round and round in her hands.

As Eddie pushed two drinks towards her she let out a short loud laugh of triumph.

'Guess what?' she said to Hal.

'What?'

'He's proposed.'

'Who?'

'Raymond.'

'Who to?'

Daisy couldn't stop laughing; Hal hadn't been so funny in ages. She even gave his knee a brief squeeze.

'To me. Raymond has proposed to me, and now we're getting married,' she said, taking real delight in the logic of life at that moment.

'Thank God,' Hal said, without hearing himself or even realising that he had said anything at all.

Raymond was sitting with his back to them looking out over the dance floor.

Hal held three fingers up at Eddie and within seconds Eddie pushed three vodkas across the bar. Hal drank one immediately and started to make off with the other two.

'And?' Daisy said, anxiously.

'And . . .' Hal fought desperately to remember what was required of him. 'And . . . congratulations.'

'I thought those were for us,' she said as Hal disappeared with the drinks.

'Later,' he called back over his shoulder.

When he got back to the corner there was only Tinker left sitting in the chair he had been sitting in when Hal first arrived, bent up double with laughter, his forehead on the table and his right hand banging on it in time to his laughter.

Hal placed the two glasses carefully on the table, staring straight into the corner where Perkins had been sat earlier. He looked out across the dance floor, which was getting fuller as the evening wore on. Then he saw Delaval, standing on the balcony opposite, staring straight at him. He suddenly tasted blood on his lips and when he looked down there was a splat of blood on the toe of his shoe. His nose was bleeding. He grabbed the handkerchief Perkins had given him to wipe his wrist with off the table. Perkins must have left it behind when he saw Delaval.

By the time Hal finally managed to stem the flow, Delaval was no longer there.

Tinker hadn't let up laughing for a second, and Hal had to refrain from smashing his head across the table. Within five minutes he was outside, still wiping his nose with Perkins's handkerchief. He couldn't see a thing because of a heavy sea fog that had moved in, and started blindly pushing his way into the crowd. Not even the Charleston could be seen. And the screams, which could still be heard, sounded much further away. As though the boundaries of Spanish City had suddenly grown, he thought in panic. What if he never found his way out? What if this was it, for the rest of for ever? Fog and screams.

He carried on walking, blundering heedlessly into people. Then he saw Delaval, staggering out of the Hall of Mirrors in front of a barrage of laughing teenagers.

They both saw Stella and Perkins at the same moment.

Only yards away, heading east. It was Stella dragging Perkins, her mouth and whole face as wide as if she had just stopped laughing. Then they disappeared into the fog. Delaval ran straight past Hal after them.

There was only one ride in the eastern part of Spanish City and that was the Vortex, a drum that rotated at speed and pasted riders against its sides. Hal watched the back of Delaval as he climbed up to the spectators' gallery. The staircase was shaking because the ride had already started. Hal glanced down at the pile of shoes at the entrance to the ride. Stella's were there, with their broken heels. He crouched down and picked one of them up, but when he turned round to see if anyone was watching, he saw the heavily made-up face of the woman in the Vortex kiosk, shaking her head at him through the grating in a tired way. He dropped the shoe.

There were more people up in the spectators' gallery, pushing to see down into the drum, than there were inside the drum. Delaval was leaning further over the railing than he should, and Hal hung back. After a few minutes Delaval started to push through the people crowding round the railings and veered off down the stairs.

Hal waited a second more then shoved his way to the railing and looked over. Stella and Perkins weren't in the Vortex. Nauseous, he tried to reach the stairs and would have fallen over if there hadn't been so many people to prop him up. The pair of shoes had been a decoy. Wherever Stella was, she was now barefoot.

He wouldn't have caught sight of Delaval again if it hadn't been for his blond hair. He followed him to the main entrance. Delaval paused beneath the bull's head then turned right towards South Cliff, leaving the white walls of Spanish City behind.

It wasn't until Hal started smelling roses, heavy in the night air, that he realised he was among the statues and flower beds of the Italian Gardens. He stopped for a moment and heard a cheer, an almighty cheer, as the coaster cars made their descent. Then there was silence. The fog was so thick up in the gardens that he could barely see a foot in front of him. If it had been clear, the view of Spanish City from up here would have been panoramic. He thought he could hear footsteps, but these turned out to be nothing more than the rustlings of nocturnal animals. It was so dark that he ended up stumbling into the bench Delaval was sitting on before he realised it. The ground behind the bench levelled out, which meant that they were nearly at the top of the cliff.

'Major?'

'Who is it?'

'Harold Price.' He moved forward so that Delaval could see him more clearly.

'Harold Price,' Delaval muttered. 'France. You were in France.'

The fog curled strangely around him, making him look grey.

Hal sat down slowly beside him.

'I've been following you,' he said. 'You lost them.'

'I sent Perkins to look for her. After two years and not a single lead, we agreed to call things off. I knew that even if he found her she'd never forgive me for offering somebody money in exchange for her. I knew that . . . did you see her tonight? I saw her dance. I've never seen her dance before. I should have taken her dancing.'

'Why didn't Stella play the cat?' Hal said suddenly, without knowing whether he expected him to answer or not.

Delaval shifted his weight again.

'You remember that?'

Hal didn't answer.

'I hadn't intended to stay for that pantomime. Then I did – because of her. That afternoon I heard a shot. A single shot, which sounded as though it came from some stable blocks where wounded Germans were being kept.

'When I got there I walked straight past a private called Cresswell, sitting at his post. Stella was holding a revolver in her hand, a revolver that was pointing restlessly towards a German prisoner, who still looked alive. I assumed that she had in all probability shot at him and missed. The arm holding the revolver was shaking, which meant that she was likely to try again, or turn the gun and shoot herself. Alternatively (and not to be ruled out), she might have turned and shot the interloper, i.e. myself. I quickly judged the distance between us to see if it was short enough to lunge across and tumble her to the floor, hopefully knocking the offending article out of her hand in the process. But before I got a chance to put this plan into action, she turned to me and said, "Please help me." She only said it once.' Delaval's hands were resting, palms upwards, on his leg.

'Within seconds I was holding her in my arms. It wasn't until then that I realised it was Private Cresswell she had tried to shoot. Private Cresswell, whom I had walked straight past slumped over his chair, was not asleep as I had presumed, but wounded. He was wounded, and not dead, because she missed. There was a comic on the table in front of him: *Dick Turpin Rides Again*. I remember that affecting me more than anything. I don't know why. Do you?'

Hal shook his head.

'Oh,' Delaval said, sounding disappointed. 'There was a glass of water by Stella's feet put there by Cresswell; a glass of water that the German POW with no legs, Matthias, had been crying out for. And Cresswell had put it there, where Matthias could see it but not reach it. She shot at him because, in spite of everything she had seen during the war, the burden of this single act of cruelty was more than she could bear the weight of. I knew then that I was going to save her.'

'So she tried to kill a man.' Hal shook his head, trying to dredge up from somewhere inside him his faculty to judge.

Delaval watched these thoughts cross his face. 'You look a lot like your mother,' he said, suddenly.

'My mother?'

'She was my nursemaid.' Delaval paused to give Hal time to confirm this, but he didn't. 'You don't know this? We once spent three months in Utah, near Great Salt Lake, where my father was doing some work for the Philadelphia Toboggan

Co. The PTC, as they were known, built – still build – roller-coasters. He helped design a coaster for the Spanish City Pleasure Palace on Great Salt Lake. My mother and I went with him. An unusual arrangement for the times, but my mother was susceptible to tragedy, and hated being alone. Your mother also came.'

'My mother's never left England.'

'She went to Utah with my family in the summer of nineteen twenty-six. I remember this very particularly', he said, 'because it was her and not me my father took out in the boat with him to see the Spanish City. She didn't believe such a place existed and it gave my father a joy he couldn't explain to furnish proof with wonder and awe. It caused a scandal.'

They were both silent, no longer able to decide who should be speaking and who should be listening.

'My father's passion', Delaval said, pronouncing the right word with difficulty, 'was never reciprocated. Your mother thought it unnatural and had no appetite for tragedy. He died later of a broken heart.'

Hal felt Delaval looking at him.

'The roller-coaster he designed for the Spanish City on Great Salt Lake was just a preliminary. He spent the following years of his life working on a blueprint for what he called the ultimate pleasure machine, one that would change people's lives, even if only during the few minutes it took to ride it. The design used every innovation known to roller-coaster engineers, and the concept as a whole was beyond revolutionary; it was visionary. He finished the blueprint just before he died. You rode his roller-coaster tonight.'

Delaval paused. 'Unlike my father, I had no intention of dying from anything as human as a broken heart. Until I decided to save Stella.

'Maybe legacies such as these are inherited. Or maybe not. Suicidal tendencies are meant to be, aren't they? I always used to think that salvation led to freedom. But it doesn't. These are times for people with appetite. That was his maxim. Times for people with appetite.'

Hal stood up, suddenly wanting to get as far away from Delaval as he could.

Then, as if forgetting something he had meant to say much sooner, Delaval said, 'Did you know your mother was named after a dance?'

'Her name's Charlie. What kind of a dance is that?'

'Charlie is only an abbreviation.'

'An abbreviation of what?'

'Charleston. Your mother's name is Charleston.'

Hal ran back into the fog and down through the Italian Gardens to Spanish City. The gates were still open, but the crowds had gone. Apart from the operators of a few rides, the pleasure grounds were deserted. The Palace was closing, but Raymond's bike was propped up in the walkway where he must have left it in order to walk Daisy home. Without a moment's hesitation, Hal took hold of the handlebars and started to push it through the empty Spanish City.

He cycled furiously, despite the fog, and was soon on Marine Parade heading up towards the coastal road and the tinkers' camp. When he got there Perkins's caravan was empty so he cycled back on to the headland at North Cliff. After a while a lit building on the edge of the headland came into view.

The effect of the illuminated Moscadini's wasn't as dazzling as it should have been because of the fog, but it was still a light in the dark. Looking about him, Hal realised that the headland was a dense mass of bodies all moving in the same direction. As the doors swung open and people entered Moscadini's two by two, blasts of music reached him. Leaving the bicycle outside, Hal followed the crowd through the doors.

Moscadini's was full, not of miners, shop girls and factory workers, but pleasure seekers. Every booth was taken and he had to push his way through the dancers to get to the chrome counter. The juke-box was belching out tune after tune and a man who could only have been Moscadini himself was mixing liquor and ice-cream and creating the sodas and floats he would later become famous for. Drunk by pleasure-seekers in order to prolong the illusion that they had all the time in the world ahead of them. Increasingly indecent cheering was coming from a booth by the side of the counter, but Moscadini showed no sign of breaking it up.

People either ordered what the person in front had ordered, or waited for Moscadini to weigh them up from behind the geyser and push a soda or float across the counter towards them. They soon realised he had perfect pitch and was able to assess needs and desires with unsettling accuracy, despite his glass eye. In between mixing drinks, Moscadini would thrust his face in the geyser's steam; this was the only thing that stopped his eye from weeping. The liquor, as he liked to call it, was kept under the counter and nobody ever saw the bottles it was poured from.

Hal, finding himself in the queue by the counter, cast a frantic look around, but it was too crowded to spot either Perkins or Stella. Before he knew it, he had a soda float in his hand. He drank out of panic with his eyes shut, and afterwards couldn't remember having paid for it. Then he made his way over to the far side of the room where there was a strange light that could have been daylight coming from the wall. As he got closer he made out a huge picture, lit from behind, covering the entire wall. There were a lot of people at that end of the room, but this didn't stop Hal from experiencing the effect Moscadini had anticipated, which was that of looking out of a window on to the Mediterranean Sea. He started to put his hand out, but stopped. Whether this was because people were watching or because he wanted to continue suffering the illusion, he didn't know.

'Not bad, is it?' a voice said at his right elbow.

He stared down at the matted black head belonging to Mandy Watkins. For an instant both of them were bathed in the sunlight of the Italian coast, something that didn't alter a hair of Mandy Watkins's head, but made Hal afterwards behave in an improbable way.

'Do you think places like that really exist, Mr Price?' she said, as they gazed out over the Italian coast.

'Of course they do,' he replied, irritated by her lack of faith. He thought about telling her to stop calling him Mr Price, but in the end didn't.

She got something out of her pocket as he said this and put it in her mouth.

'You were scared stiff tonight,' she said, her mouth full of chocolate.

'When?'

'On the coaster.'

'Was I?'

She nodded and tried smiling at him, but she didn't have a great deal of teeth left and those she did have were uneven.

'It made me laugh. It was the best thing, that roller-coaster,' she said, forcing more chocolate into her mouth. 'You were screaming.'

'I wasn't.'

Mandy Watkins shrugged. 'You were. Screaming your head off.' She wiped her nose.

'I'm going,' he finished.

She must have gulped the rest of her soda float back then followed him out of Moscadini's because by the time he picked up Raymond's bike she was sitting outside on Danny the Deer, one of the children's rides. He stared at her for a moment, then sighed. 'Come on then,' he said and helped her down from the plastic deer. It was colder than it had been earlier and he felt Mandy pulling her cardigan tightly around herself. He could have offered her his jacket, but didn't. They set off across the headland with her walking beside him as they pushed the bike, leaving Moscadini's behind. The grass was so long in parts that her feet and legs, which were very white and as scuffed as her shoes, got lost in it. He could hear her shivering, but sometimes it sounded like the beginnings of laughter and he had to keep checking; he couldn't stand the thought that she might be laughing at him.

'Don't you have a car?' Mandy said after a while.

'Is that why you followed me out?'

'No, I just thought you had one, that's all.'

He didn't say anything, vaguely worried that he had failed to impress this stinking child in a way he might have done.

'Were you hoping for a lift home?'

She shook her head and started to chew her nails.

They finally reached his beach hut with a good few hours to spare before dawn. He had known he was heading there as soon as they started walking. Once inside the hut, he felt suddenly nervous and had trouble lighting the small lamp that made the air smell funny when it flickered into life. Not because of the kerosene, but because of the dead moths that were set on fire. He hadn't been in the hut for ages and the canvas on the two deckchairs was damp with mould. It almost felt as if the hut belonged to somebody else, and he had just managed to pick the lock.

Mandy stood in the corner and, having finished her supply of chocolate, fell to sucking her fingers. There were chocolate stains on her cardigan sleeves where she had wiped her mouth.

'This yours?' she said quietly.

'It is. I don't have a car, I have a beach hut.'

'You can't go anywhere in a beach hut, though.'

He sat down on his dad's old decorating stool and shook the sand out of his shoes.

'Why aren't you married, Mr Price?' she asked suddenly. She kept slipping her foot in and out of her shoe and scraping the heel across the wooden floor. 'You were good to me, Mr Price. I'll never forget you.'

He wanted to be forgotten, and opened his mouth to say something cruel about love, but then stopped. Instead he walked over and kissed her. She tasted of chocolate and Moscadini's soda still. Part of him knew he should stop, but the other part felt that she was so broken anyway that any blow he dealt wouldn't make a blind bit of difference.

'Are you going to mess with me, Mr Price?' she whispered as he drew back.

He stared at her, his hands firmly gripping her arms still. She didn't flinch as she said it or show any other signs of life.

'I was going to mess with you, yes,' he said, dropping his hands.

He could hear her starting to breathe again as he sank back on to the stool. After a while she came and stood very close to him and he didn't know what had possessed him for the last few hours or how they had ended up at the hut in the early hours of the morning for all the world to see.

He took hold of one of her hands as he had found himself doing earlier.

'Expect one day I'll get washed up somewhere and they'll find me and take me to your cousin, Raymond Clarke.'

She sounded almost cheerful as she said this, and pulled her hand as gently as she could out of his grasp. After she had left he turned off the lamp and sat staring out of the open door until his eyes became accustomed to the dark and he could make out the dunes. There was no sign of her out there, all he had left was the taste of her.

Then his eye caught sight of something tangled in one of the door hinges, blowing stiffly in the wind. A piece of white net from an underskirt.

IO

Jamie Price stood on his workbench, humming 'My Love Is Like a Red Red Rose', and shifted a couple of planks in the garage ceiling to one side. After a few minutes his hands lit on the small suitcase they had been feeling for. Sitting back at his workbench he opened the case and took out an old black suit. It was the suit he had been married in and he had only worn it a handful of times since. The black cloth had faded with age rather than wear, but every time he got it out he had the same tickle in his stomach as the day he wore it for the first time.

He remembered walking to Nag's Farm before dawn and picking up William and Rose Clarke as well as a pony and trap, then driving a mile north of Setton to where Charlie was waiting just outside Wyley, standing in a ditch in her wedding dress so that she wouldn't be seen from the road. This was in case her dad realised she was gone and came to look for her. Rose couldn't stop her nervous laughing as Jamie pulled Charlie up beside him and they made their way to the small parish of Kirby whose vicar knew Charlie.

It was the day of her eighteenth birthday and as far as he was concerned there wasn't a day to lose. He didn't like churches, but went inside for her sake. Reverend Moore made a fuss of them and, after leading the service with a severity that the congregation of four didn't warrant, he let out a few deep smiles that made Jamie Price think that he and Charlie had somehow saved the old man's soul.

'That's it?' Jamie said afterwards.

'All done and dusted,' the old vicar said through his smile.

'There's nothing anybody can do? Nothing at all?'

'Nothing,' the old man assured him, his eyes straying over to where Charlie Price stood sniffing at her flowers.

'That's that then,' Jamie said.

He looked over at Charlie in her dress, which she and Rose had patched together. He knew that this wasn't what she had pictured at all, empty pews, field flowers, no proper gown, no photographer. But then she had probably never pictured herself standing in a ditch getting her feet soaked by dew while she waited for the sun to come up and him to arrive.

All four had a wedding breakfast in the apple orchard on the other side of the graveyard. They ate tongue sandwiches and drank beer. Jamie was halfway through his first bottle, his head tilted back, when the Reverend Moore came and tapped his shoulder. The vicar was smiling still, but his eyes moved uneasily.

'Could I have a word with you in church?' he had said.

Charlie tried to hold on to him, but Jamie tugged himself free.

'Don't worry, Charlie,' the Reverend Moore said. 'I promise he won't come to any harm.'

William Clarke chuckled softly while Rose tried to hide a bottle of beer behind her back. Rose wasn't a brave woman, and had only come because William had told her she was coming.

The Reverend Moore opened the church door, and it shut quietly behind them. When Jamie turned round the Reverend Moore had gone.

There was another man at the far end of the aisle standing in front of the altar.

'You,' Jamie said, recognising him immediately. Then added, instinctively, 'Sir,' as the other man's eyes turned on him.

They made no attempt to walk towards each other. Jamie had heard all the rumours doing the rounds about him and Charlie. Now Charlie Price.

'All's done?' Mr Delaval said, his hand stroking the altar rail. Jamie nodded. 'You're too late.'

'Oh, I was never given the chance to be too late,' he said, looking at Jamie with something close to tenderness.

'She's pregnant,' Jamie blundered. Then added crudely, unnecessarily, 'A shotgun wedding.' For some reason, hearing himself say this made his anger rise. Almost uncontrollably, and he started stalking slowly down the aisle towards Mr Delaval. He pulled up short halfway down. 'What have you come here to tell me?'

The more he spoke the more he could hear his accent, which made the words that came out clump across the air between them. He had never hated the sound of his own voice before but he did now. 'Is it mine?' he asked hoarsely.

'Of course,' the other man said, watching him in disbelief. 'Anything else would be impossible.'

But Jamie's anger wouldn't die down, and Mr Delaval's declaration, rather than reassuring him, made him start to respect the other man much less. He felt suddenly that he could squash him if he chose to. Jamie walked right up to him, panting in his face.

'She's a good woman,' he said, but it sounded cold, forced.

'Oh, it's not her "goodness".' Mr Delaval waved his hands to one side, irritated that Jamie should have got it so wrong. 'It's her appetite, the one she doesn't know she has.' He sounded tired, suddenly losing heart in his mission. 'I came because I wanted to see her. Before. But don't worry, I won't try to now.'

'You won't? It wouldn't make much difference. She won't want to see you.'

'She told you that?'

'I just know. I know her.'

Jamie felt Delaval withdrawing, the perverse intimacy or whatever it was that had existed briefly between them was broken. And Jamie felt small again, afraid of this important man, this local dignitary.

'Will you tell her you've seen me?'

'Never,' Jamie said quickly, while he still had the courage. 'You can leave now.'

'You don't want her to see me?' Mr Delaval said, turning quickly to him.

Jamie shrugged but stood firm, blocking the aisle to the main door of the church. Delaval stared at him a moment longer then made his way to a side door.

'Will you tell her one thing?'

Jamie didn't respond.

'I want you to tell her that she mustn't ever forget the things I've shown her. She doesn't have to think about them much, or hold them dear to her. She just mustn't forget them.' He had his hand on the door now. 'Tell Charleston that, will you?'

The door closed.

'Charleston?' Jamie said, starting forward.

But there was no reply. The door was shut. He went back to the apple orchard where they were finishing the picnic and he took hold of the beer William held out to him as he approached. Then he extended a hand to Charlie, pulled her up out of the grass and said, 'Come on, Mrs Price.' After that they got back into the cart, and paid a state visit to Charlie's parents.

He couldn't wipe the smile off his face, which didn't ease her father's temper. Her mother had recently suffered a stroke and didn't contribute much. Charlie wanted to stay a bit and help get her mother undressed for bed, but Jamie gave her hand a squeeze to let her know that he wasn't having any of it.

In light of the gold bands both elopers were wearing, the best tea set was produced, and everybody got through several pots of tea without alluding once to Charlie being Mrs Price. Her father sucked his pipe, satisfied himself with a few stolen glances at his daughter, then spent the remainder of the time talking about his vegetables with William. Rose was too tight to talk to anyone.

They all knew that it would be the last time Charlie would sit down and take tea with them. Mr Clarke asked no questions about where they'd be living or how they were for money. As far as he was concerned Charlie had made her own bed and now she could lie in it.

Jamie felt like a thief sitting with his swag bag full, taking tea with the family he had just robbed. There was remorse of sorts, but it couldn't have happened in any other way, and it had to happen. He knew that Mr Clarke loved Charlie more than anyone else in that room. His eyes lit on her, even now through the pipe smoke, in the way a man's eyes light on hope. He had expected great things of her because he had not only given her life, but given her *his* life, to make out of it what he hadn't been able to. All his talk of vegetables, Jamie suddenly saw, hid what had once been dangerous ambitions. He thought of Delaval in the church, and knew with as much certainty as if he had been told point-blank, that it was Charlie's father and not her mother who had named her.

Mrs Clarke's eyes were rolling in Charlie's direction. Charlie watched as she summoned what muscular control she had left in order to help down the food she was busy chewing in her mouth. Tom was nowhere to be seen. He would hardly dare show his face about the house now that Charlie was gone. She was the only one who had stood in the way of the beatings Mr Clarke gave his son, the beatings of a man frustrated at having spawned something less than perfect

Forty-five minutes were all anybody could endure and after this the Prices made their excuses to leave. Standing in the front porch, Mr Clarke asked his daughter for the key to the house, and the door shut on the first eighteen years of her life. Then they got back into the trap, which had to be returned to Nag's Farm that same evening.

Jamie waited for a series of coughs to rattle through him at these memories, then cut open the lining of the suit jacket laid out on the bench in front of him. Within a few minutes he had transferred a hundred pound notes from a bag in the old motorbike sidecar into the lining of the jacket. One hundred pounds, meticulously saved to feed his wife when he was gone, which wouldn't be very long now. They couldn't say when exactly, but it wouldn't be long. Cancer found its way into the lungs of most miners and there was no reason for him to be an exception. He was satisfied with his lot and had had a good run. It took him ages to thread a needle in order to sew the lining back up, but in the end he managed.

As he folded the suit away back into the case, he heard the screams from the new roller-coaster they had built over on South Cliff. The Charleston. He brushed aside any further memories of the church at Kirby, and half of him felt it was music to his ears. He would have liked to have ridden it with Charlie, especially now time was running out. He took one last look up at the ceiling then switched out the garage light.

II

The cancer finally got the better of Jamie Price, and he passed away in the summer of 1958, after a night of unbearable heat. Hal only found out about his dad's cancer when the doctor started to pay home visits at the beginning of what he termed 'the final decline'.

Jamie Price didn't take kindly to being bedridden. Charlie braced herself for the worst mood yet, worse than the one they had all suffered when war broke out and he didn't go to fight, losing his bike instead. She put on a clean apron, which she tied extra tight around her waist, and banged about the flat with even more assertiveness than usual. But the explosion never came, only a helplessness he had never before shown signs of possessing.

During his last weeks he lost what was left of his hair. The sight of him terrified Hal because he knew now that time was running out, and this still didn't give him the strength he needed to cross the threshold of his father's room. When he sat at the table eating and staring out of the window, he knew his father's eyes were watching him through the open door, waiting.

Charlie spent every second of his waking moments by his side, her hand in his. On the Monday morning of the final week he started a mumbling monologue, telling his wife all the things he had ever meant to tell her, and repeating other things he had told her before. It was as if he were emptying himself into her so that after he was gone she wouldn't be alone. He wanted what was left of him to last her for the rest of her life.

She didn't say a word, she just sat and listened as forty-odd years of human history, their history, echoed round the tiny room. He even told her the things that had come before her, before he laid eyes on her: his apprenticeship years, school years, childhood, because he didn't know how much she might need when he was gone. He talked about how wet with dew her shoes were when he lifted her out of the ditch and took her to get married. At one point he was so confused by the pain, and so full of all that he had to say to her still, that he forgot where he was, and asked her to marry him again.

During his last night, they were both in agony. At dawn Hal went outside and sat in the allotments where he could keep the house in sight without having to hear what went on inside it. Everyone on Ellsworth Row knew it was nearly the end because they watched Hal very carefully as he picked his way over to the old chair on the Prices' plot. Nobody ventured out on to the allotments while he was there. Most of the Row had already been in to pay their last respects, and although Jamie was in agony, they had all stayed just long enough for him to make them laugh. Even on his death bed he hadn't lost his touch. Their laughter, their share in him, irritated Charlie, but she kept her mouth shut.

All the while Hal sat outside in the allotment, playing Jacks or just throwing stones at the birds, waiting for his dad to die. Every now and then, when the sun was at the right angle, he would catch glimpses of his mother's face at the window and, even though he couldn't see her features, he knew for sure that she was in a fury with him.

Then it occurred to him, as he tried to stone bird after bird, that he wasn't waiting for his father to die, he was waiting to find the courage to talk. That's what it was, and as soon as he realised this it hit him like nothing else in his life had and he went running back across the allotments towards the house.

He needed to know that his father knew his mother's real name, and what it meant to love a woman in the way he had done. He wanted to know that whatever had happened before or after, he had been born of love.

He ran through the hallway, which still after all these years smelt of Mrs Crombie's frying, past Frankie who stood smoking expectantly in the doorway waiting for it to be over (because not even he had the audacity to bring women back to the flat now and the week of abstinence was telling), up the stairs and into the flat. And he knew as soon as he set foot in it, without a word being said, that it was too late. It was all too late.

Charlie lifted the kettle from the stove and put it on the stand, one hand on her back. She didn't turn round.

'We see them into this world and we seem them out,' she sighed, exhausted.

Then, when she got no reply, she turned to face him.

'Men, Hal. We see them into the world and we see them out.'

She finished making the pot of tea slowly and meticulously, then sat down and looked out of the window at the spot where he had been sitting, her hands pressed against her mouth. After a moment she got up and drew the curtains, and the flat went dark.

Hal stared at her wedding ring, then went as far as the bedroom door and looked in. His father had always been a tall man, and lying down he still looked tall. Even as Hal himself had grown, his father remained a step ahead, always taller, always wider. More substantial. That's what he had wanted to say to him, 'There's more to you than there is to me.' Death hadn't robbed him of this. Hal couldn't touch him.

'Shall I tell Raymond?' he asked, watching her pour another cup of tea then sit gasping over her cigarette.

'You won't need to. People will see them drawn curtains and the whole bleeding world will know within the hour. They'll know up at Watts and Raymond will be here before you get to him. Oh, they'll all know.'

She drank all the tea in the pot then made herself a cup of

chicory. You could get coffee in the shops again now, but her taste-buds had become accustomed to chicory during the war and she couldn't kick the habit, preferring the substitute to the real thing. She struck Hal suddenly as an exile, somebody who had woken up to find herself in a foreign country and wasn't only unable to go home, but wasn't even sure if home existed any more. He would have consoled her, but didn't know if she wanted him there or not. He had never consoled anybody before, not even himself. Her face was turned towards the window out of habit even though the curtains were drawn. A woman's voice came screeching up through the floorboards as Frankie tried to remove an unexpected visitor from the premises.

'Did he know?' Hal said suddenly.

'Know what?'

'Your name, and that there's a roller-coaster called Charleston on South Cliff.'

'You're never to call me by that name, ever. D'you hear? Shut your mouth.'

He remembered that voice from his childhood when he had misbehaved. It was the voice that preceded the fury, and it was unforgiving. 'It's not your story, Hal,' she added. 'So don't you even begin to think it's yours for the telling.'

'Delaval told me.'

'Then he's a sick man, like his father.'

Charlie was breathing heavily, but didn't bat an eyelid.

'A man died because of you. You were the cause of a man's death.'

'Against my will,' she yelled.

'Charleston. You never said a word to me all these years?'

'I never wanted to see the world, Hal. Seeing the world's a dangerous thing. You end up getting a new pair of eyes that don't belong to the rest of you.' She sighed. 'I always thought, make sure your clothes are clean and your shoes shine and then you'll be all right, they'll stay off your back because the world comes down heavy on the likes of us. Even if we so much as take a step sideways, or don't look sharp. But you

206

know, in the end, you've got to go your own way. People forget, life goes on, whole lives pass.' She dragged Tom's button box across the table towards her and absent-mindedly started to sort through them.

'Now get out of my sight,' she said quietly to him. 'I'm mourning.'

Hal stood banging at the caravan door so hard the whole thing began to rock, but there was still no answer. Through the scratched window he could make out an unmade bed and the sight of it made him feel sick. He sat down on the bucket outside the door in order to get his bearings back and after a while Tinker's aunt, Irene, appeared.

'Harold Price?'

He looked up.

'Was that you moving the caravan?' She tutted and hauled him to his feet. 'Come over and have a quick cup of something.'

'It's all right,' he said, shaking his head.

'Come on,' she insisted, already pulling him firmly in the direction of her caravan. 'It'll make you feel better.'

He gave her a quick look. Impossible; she already knew.

Irene had re-upholstered her sofa in velveteen. All the cushions were velveteen and the curtains as well. It gave the place a lugubrious atmosphere, and there was a smell like incense hanging heavy in the air. Smoke was coming from behind the beaded curtain in the corner, and Perkins's chandelier dangled from the ceiling.

'You know something?' she said, handing him a glass. 'Your mother came to see me the day before she eloped with your father and asked me what she should do. I told her she was going to marry Jamie Price and become Charlie Price.'

Hal stared at her and took a sip of the drink. It tasted the same as the ones at Moscadini's.

'So they married because you told them to?'

'No, they married because they were meant to.'

Irene poured herself a glass of the same stuff, putting the

207

bottle back in the cupboard before he had time to look at it. She drank it in one go and stood watching him. There was a vase of wild flowers on the bench behind her, and she was wearing some sort of daisy chain around her neck.

'They would have one child.'

'Me,' Hal said, feeling a sudden surge of joy.

'You.'

'And . . .'

'It was so,' she finished with a smack of her lips.

He stood up and handed her his empty glass, making the chandelier swing in the process.

'Stella's not home,' she said, looking intently at him. 'She's at Moscadini's. You watch how you go now,' she called after him as he left the caravan. Her windows had the same scratches on them that Perkins's did, as if at one time a hoard of wild animals had tried to get in. But she could see through them well enough.

Moscadini's was empty when Hal walked in, apart from Stella, sat with her right shoulder nudging against the Mediterranean Sea. She must have ordered a knickerbocker glory because Moscadini brought it over to the table at the same time as Hal walked in. He paused on the threshold for a moment, knowing that now before she saw him he could still leave. Then she turned and looked straight at him.

'Hal?'

She started to eat the ice-cream, pushing the cherry to one side.

'My father's dead,' he said as soon as he sat down.

She finished sucking on her mouthful of ice-cream, then looked up at him.

'When did he die?'

Hal realised, horrified, that he didn't know exactly when he had died. He hadn't even asked his mother this.

'I'm sorry, Hal,' she pronounced at last when he didn't answer. But she sounded weary, as if she was tired of obituaries.

She stroked the top of his hands briefly.

'Don't sit brooding on whatever it was you never got to say.'

'How do you know?' he said.

'It's what people do.'

She licked all traces of ice-cream away from her mouth. The spoon clattered into the empty glass and they heard Moscadini wheezing from behind the counter. Stella couldn't sit still.

'How's your mother?'

'Angry,' he said, thinking of her sitting hunched over her cigarette at the table. 'Devastated.'

Stella nodded her head in agreement with this analysis. 'Some people love more than others. Some don't love at all,' she finished.

And because he didn't have the courage right then to ask her if she was happy or not, he said suddenly, 'I'm not happy, Stella. I haven't managed to make myself happy.'

'Is that what you wanted to tell your father?'

Hal didn't answer.

'Was it me you came to see?' She drew back after saying this and he felt her legs against him. She drew back so much that for a moment he thought she had disappeared into Moscadini's Italian backdrop.

He thought of his mother as he had left her, and how the real secrets of a person's life lay in the details. Intangible things that could never be catalogued and certainly never be explained. Real life was lived in details.

'This is the first time we've been alone together in', she paused only a second, 'fourteen years. Since the war,' she added, in an attempt to sound less specific. 'I once did something and asked for Delaval's help. I needed his help very badly. Only he didn't just help me, he decided to save me.'

'I know. He told me your story.'

'Then you know that his father did exactly the same thing to your mother.'

'You know about her?'

Stella nodded. 'Like her, I didn't need saving.'

209

She got up from the table.

'I'm really sorry about your father. I would have liked to meet him.'

He followed her out of Moscadini's, and up the gravel path on to the headland. He no longer had any idea whether she wanted him to follow her or not, or where they were going.

She turned round suddenly, putting her hands over his face. 'What do you see?' she said, taking them away again.

Her breath smelt of ice-cream still.

'You,' Hal said.

'Just open your eyes.'

'I don't believe in tragedy.'

'Then you don't believe in life. We only get one, Hal. One.' She held up a finger then walked away.

Raymond took care of everything, and the day of Jamie Price's funeral, the Methodist church was full; not a single space left on a single pew. The remains of Watts Colliery Choir stood at the front, sheet music in their hands ready. Almost all of the congregation were miners, which gave the Reverend Tooth a limitless range of metaphors for his service. And Hal saw, looking at the pews fuller than they had been for years, that those who came to mourn hadn't come to mourn Jamie Price alone but the passing of a generation, an era. They were the last of their kind, and the world they had known was disappearing faster than they were. The old men were closing rank.

Charlie Price wore her glad rags, the dress that she wore to other people's weddings, and that had been modified over the years in order to suit the times as well as her fluctuating figure. Had she once been proud of herself in this? She felt dusty, no matter how much of her Yardley Rose she rolled across her wrists.

Throughout the entire service, Tom sat staring at the stained-glass windows. Charlie didn't cry once; there were things it wasn't safe to show in public, and grief, especially overwhelming grief, was one of them. At the end of the day you couldn't trust anyone. All the letters they had ever written to each other were tied in an old scarf and sealed in the coffin with him. All those words, written and spoken.

That last night he had been at great pains to mumble something about his wedding suit, and it was this she had insisted on dressing him in for the funeral. She hadn't realised until he lay there, washed in his underwear, how terrified she had been of it not fitting, but it fitted all right, not an inch too big or an inch too small.

The Reverend Tooth's breath stank as he shook hands with mourners after the service. He used both hands when it was Charlie's turn, as if he thought the additional pressure might induce her to tears. When Hal turned to look back through the open door the Reverend Tooth was walking down the aisle of the empty church, already in the process of disrobing.

'He used to be at the chapel,' his mother said to him, and this was the reason for the colloquial service, which she had found offensive.

Jamie Price was put in the hearse and Charlie, Hal and Raymond went in front in the other car. Raymond knew the driver well but, given his personal involvement in this funeral, didn't try and start up a conversation. Being the amateur mourners they were, Hal was glad Raymond was there to guide them.

'Wait, we're one person short,' Charlie said after a couple of minutes.

'It's all right,' Raymond said, 'Jamie's following in the car behind.'

Charlie looked round and Hal saw her lips counting them.

'Of course,' she said.

'It's quite usual,' Raymond explained. 'Often happens at the first family meal after a funeral. An extra place is laid by mistake, or somebody thinks a chair's missing when they all sit down at table. You still make allowances for the deceased, keep their space in life open, as if you're waiting for someone who's late. Very normal. Unavoidable, actually.'

Charlie took hold of Hal's hand, her thin fingers giving the leather glove a vibrancy and elegance.

It was the longest length of time he had spent in his mother's company for years, Hal thought watching her.

'How's your father, Raymond?' she asked, without looking at him.

'Same as usual.'

'And the children?'

'Fine. Fine.'

The Clarkes now had a girl and boy child.

'Daisy looks well,' she said automatically, and straightened the front of her coat, arranging it so that it fell over her legs and knees properly, then sat back to enjoy the ride.

He could tell that she liked the way people stopped and stared at them as they drove through Setton. She kept her head straight, only glancing sideways in order to register the impression they made.

The crematorium was the only building on the hillside. It was brand new and had been the subject of an article in the *Setton Echo* only weeks before. The main building was round with eight cement spines arching over glass panels. It looked like something belonging to the Ministry of Defence, and when they arrived black smoke was trailing from the brick chimney next to it. There was no sign of human life.

Daisy, William Clarke, Uncle Tom, and two very old friends of Jamie's arrived soon after and they stood close to Raymond by the entrance. Hal presumed, because of the black smoke coming out of the chimney, that they were waiting for a previous service to finish.

After a while there was still no sign of the previous mourners so they walked into an entrance hall through double doors where there was nothing but a table and a display of artificial flowers, not unlike the ones in the Parlour. Hal expected to see the Reverend Tooth again, or his crematorium counterpart at least, someone whose business was more exclusively to do with death. A short old man in a suit, that's what he expected. But there was no one to greet them; the entrance hall was as devoid of human presence as the forecourt outside.

Raymond led the way into the chapel itself, the one that had got its picture in the papers. Despite its being circular, inside it was laid out according to the rules of a rectangle. There were two banks of pews made of orange-coloured wood facing a wall of blue velvet curtains, in front of which lay Jamie Price. Only half of his coffin was visible, the other half was already inside a hatch, partly obscured again by miniature blue velvet curtains, which fell in folds over the coffin.

The carpet absorbed any sounds their bodies betrayed them into making. They were the only people, including Jamie Price, in the chapel. Their entrance was accompanied by music from an electronic organ, but again there were no signs of either organ or organist. They filed into the pew at the front, gladly following Raymond's lead. Charlie was fiddling with the netting on her hat, less sure of herself, trying to angle it so that it didn't interfere with her lipstick.

There were sheets laid out on their pew, with a prayer and a hymn typed on each. Hal looked at Raymond questioningly, but even Raymond looked confused and shook his head, disclaiming any responsibility for them. Charlie was staring fixedly ahead, trying not to look at the half of Jamie's coffin still on view, every now and then unable to resist the urge to turn round and look over her shoulder for the chaperone they all felt must surely be on his way. Then the organ music stopped and there was silence.

When it started again Raymond stood up and began singing the only hymn printed on their sheet. They all followed suit, stumbling uneasily and weakly through the hymn none of them knew, sitting down again when the organ music stopped.

Some black smoke from the chimney blew past the window as the wind changed direction, then a voice from nowhere started reading the prayer on their sheets and they mumbled along with it. There were no giveaway signs as far as the source of the voice was concerned, and Hal realised, concerned, that his mother was trying not to laugh. The

feathers on her hat were vibrating and he didn't hear her say
'Amen'.

After the prayer there was silence again until they heard a
motor start up from somewhere near the front of the chapel
and the end of Jamie's coffin began to judder and slide away.
Charlie had one moment of uncontrollable panic when she
nearly changed her mind and thought it just possible he might
still be alive, but she stood motionless, breathing deeply, and
let it go. So he went up in flames, and when he was gone there
was nothing for anyone to stick their nose into, nothing left of
their story, apart from what was left of her.

After a while Raymond stood up, taking hold of Daisy's
elbow and gesturing to Hal, who was sitting at the end of
the pew, to lead the way. They walked slowly back up
the aisle.

The entrance hall was still empty, as was the forecourt
outside, where their car was parked, waiting. The driver
jumped out with an eager smile on his face as if to insinuate
that there were still more treats in store.

'Your dad's only the fifth person to be cremated here,' he
said to Hal.

Raymond led Charlie and Hal over to the green door in the
wall, which had 'Garden of Rest' written on it. The sky
overhead was darker than elsewhere because of the black
smoke still rising from the chimney. They waited and waited,
but nobody asked why. The lights inside the crematorium
went off.

'Nice music,' Charlie said and opened the clasp of her
handbag. A minute later Hal saw her put a humbug in her
mouth. 'That's how I'd like to go,' she said thoughtfully to
herself. 'What about you, Hal?'

'Mother.'

'Well you'll have to think about it one day. I thought that
was lovely. Strange, but lovely,' she said, dropping the sweet
wrapper and unused handkerchief back into her handbag.
'Don't people have some marvellous ideas these days?'

Raymond disappeared behind the green door. 'Just a few

more minutes,' he said when he reappeared, shutting the door quickly behind him.

Charlie walked further off down the forecourt to where there was a tree and, standing under it, lit a cigarette, as if all the country about them belonged to her and she had no idea what to do with it. The air, once she was gone, was full of the creamy smell she always left behind her when she dressed up for a special occasion. It was the smell of her best beige coat, hat, stockings, black patent leather shoes, powder, lipstick, perfume and her own expectations. Most of all her own expectations. And the way she walked; he had forgotten that. So many people when they walked did so as though they were walking away from something; she was always walking towards something.

Hal joined her beneath the tree.

'I hope to God there's someone there when he gets to the other side,' she said, laughing. Then she dropped her stub impatiently on to the ground and looked back across the forecourt towards Raymond and Daisy, only glancing briefly at the black smoke filling the sky from the chimney.

'Don't know what she sees in him,' she said brusquely then went and climbed into the car. That last comment had been said for his sake, Hal realised. She had been vouchsafing her loyalty to him, in this and other matters neither of them yet knew about.

It was Raymond who took the urn containing Jamie Price when it was passed through the green door. The door opened and shut without Hal catching a glimpse of anybody. Then they all got back into the hearse. The driver was still placidly smiling and Charlie Price smoked all the way into Setton, flicking her cigarette ash out of the window and, every few seconds, glancing at the urn on Raymond's lap.

'Do they have the same size pots for everyone?' she said at last.

Both Raymond and Hal stared at her, but neither of them said anything.

'Sorry,' she said irritably. 'I've just never seen the likes of it before, that's all. I mean that someone so big could fit into

215

something so small. It's amazing, isn't it? What they can do these days. Looks like that pot holds nothing more than a handful of dust. When it's my time, I wouldn't mind going the same way myself,' she finished. 'Wouldn't mind at all.'

Charlie waited until it got dark, which was late that night because it was midsummer, then made a bonfire on their allotment out of everything belonging to her husband. People heard the crackle of the fire and pushed their heads out from behind curtains. At first they thought the Prices' allotment was on fire, then they saw two figures standing there.

What on earth was Mrs Price up to now? Some of them thought she was burning her dead husband then remembered that that had happened at the crematorium earlier. Well, whatever it was, she was up to something, always was. They began to recall the strange things they had heard about the Delaval family and her. Now that their throats were no longer warm with the laughter Jamie Price used to provoke, a lot of them decided that Mrs Price was an odd woman, always had been. And that boy of hers, Hal, he wasn't much better, never had been.

'Might have wanted to keep something of his,' Hal said as the pyre caught light. 'His comb, maybe.' He pushed his head closer and there was a whistle of air from the first rush of flames.

'Stand back, you daft bugger,' Charlie said, watching the flames with satisfaction. 'You don't need anything of his. This is the best way, believe me. This way I won't come across a jumper or a pair of socks. I won't pick up a jug and find his comb in there, or be dusting the mantelpiece and have to keep moving his baccy box. I couldn't live the rest of my life like that, Hal, always gasping, you know, gulping back the tears. D'you remember your Aunt Rose? She always used to say there's only one of you. Well, there was only one Jamie Price – there won't be another.' She paused. 'There's only one of you as well, Hal. You're unique, you are. You're a wonder. We're all wonders, every one of us.'

When the fire really took hold she started to pace, beating a track round it in case anything tried to escape the flames. Hal dragged the old wooden chair in which he had awaited his father's death close enough to the fire for it to warm him. She was much more vigilant about this home-made bonfire than she had been about Jamie himself at the crematorium.

'Hug me or something, Hal,' she said, turning to him slowly.

He stared at her, then opened his arms wide, a gesture he often used to signify confusion. But she interpreted it quite differently, sinking with relief on to his lap, and resting her head on his shoulder.

The bouquet of flowers from the Watts Colliery Choir had barely wilted, and the box of Midnight Symphony chocolates from the Masons had only just been opened when Setton began pronouncing its sentence on Charlie Price. It was just little things at first. She knew, as a widow, that she would have to find another widow if she wanted to go drinking at the Working Men's Club, in order to make her appearance there half-decent, but she couldn't find anyone to go with. The first few Fridays nobody felt up to it, then after three Fridays in a row she began to get the message. People stopped knocking at the door, and it went quiet in Macey's when she walked in. It had happened, although nobody knew why; Setton had chosen Charlie Price to bear the burden of its sins.

It was as if they had made a connection between her and Spanish City, associating her in some underhand way with chaos, which is essentially what Spanish City was to them. But nobody could say for sure.

People left Hal alone because they hadn't yet worked out the most effective line of attack. They dealt with Tom admirably: nobody said or did anything until one day a child called out, 'Burma Tom,' loud and clear. And the moment the words were spoken everyone knew that Tom had just been christened. The name sent Daisy and Raymond's son, John, into hysterics every time he used it, which he did frequently, to the extent that they had to stop visiting the Prices.

Setton was relieved when in 1959 Ellsworth Row was finally demolished and the inhabitants dispersed and relocated. Even Dobbin's tiny paddock went, and Dobbin himself was sent to the knacker's yard, although Charlie told Hal he'd gone to the man who kept the donkeys on the promenade. An absurd lie given both their ages. The Prices and Uncle Tom moved to a two-bedroom council house on King Alfred's Road. Number 18.

Inside it felt like a palace, and outside there was a garden at the front and back where Tom planted plastic roses and plastic tulips. Hal had wanted to rip them up when he came home from work, but after a particularly harsh exchange of words with his mother, he let them be. The curtains from Ellsworth Row were put in the outhouse and Charlie covered all the windows in the house with new nets from the Co-op. She also bought herself an electric washing machine, leaving the old mangle to rot on their allotment so that the runner beans soon covered this incriminating evidence of hard labour.

She spent a lot more time sitting down these days, surveying her domestic landscape, and discovering her new love of electrical appliances. The old stove that had to be blacked every week was replaced with a modern gas oven. She had running hot water and a whisk for cakes she could plug in at the wall. The modern world she decided, despite everything, was a good place to live. The word 'marvellous' crept into her vocabulary with increasing frequency until it became virtually her only adjective. She marvelled at the things men made, at how much easier her life had become, released from the toil and trouble of early years. 'These', she said, parading past her machines with a look of admiration on her face, 'will give me another ten years of life at least.'

Charlie was given a slight reprieve by Setton the day the first curry house, the Taj Mahal, opened by the railway station. At the same time Macey's was also bought by the Indians, or

'indjuns' as they were referred to. The new owners wisely
kept the word MACEY'S running across the top of the shop,
and on its first day under new ownership Macey's saw more
customers than it used to see in a month, buying bits and
pieces as a pretext to get a look at the indjuns. The population
wavered only a moment before the general consensus was
passed. 'People talk about them indjuns,' they said to one
another, 'but they're very polite. Considering.' So sentence
was passed on the Taj Mahal and its related business ventures.
The momentary reprieve was over, and rumours regarding the
Prices got worse and worse until it got to the stage where
every mishap from injury to accident, disaster to catastrophe,
had its source, according to local legend, on King Alfred's
Road.

Hal saw Raymond once a week. During the winter they
went to the Clayton Arms. They had to go on Saturdays so
that Daisy wouldn't think Raymond had gone to see the
ancient Lucille strip, and this Daisy was no longer the Daisy
who sat in pigtails and a dirty dressing gown on the stairs of 53
Ellsworth Row, or red Daisy who used to dance at The
Palace. This was Mrs Clarke. But then Raymond wouldn't
have gone on Fridays anyway, he was too afraid of bumping
into his dad.

When the season started, Raymond and Hal occasionally
went to The Palace. They didn't have bands any more; the
music belted out of a couple of loudspeakers up on the stage
There were no crowds, no dancers; it wasn't a place to get
lost in any more. Where had all the people gone? They
weren't outside in Spanish City, and even at the height of
the season the Charleston only pulled the younger ones in
these days.

Raymond and Hal were sitting dressed up like they used to
when they came to dance, only now they just sat there, a
couple of old-timers.

'Haven't recognised a single soul since I buried Geordie,
and that was March.'

Hal looked out over the dance floor. That night there were

a couple of girls drifting around the fringes, their hair hanging over their faces, and a few boys in groups jerking as if in the throes of epilepsy. It would have been difficult to convince a deaf person that girls and boys were dancing to the same music. Gone was the unified sound of thousands of feet shod in silver and gold, and shining black leather.

Hal glanced at Raymond's shoes, which he could still see his face in. They shone beautifully, and these shiny shoes that made people trust in Raymond had always been the thing, Hal realised looking at them, which had made him distrust him. This realisation came as something of a shock and he had to look away. He tried to drum his fingers on the table in time to the music, but couldn't follow it.

'Why have you never said anything to me about what happened the night of the storm? You never talk about what happened to Stella that night,' he said suddenly. He thought about saying more . . . how he felt when he discovered that the people moving in next door were Perkins and Stella, who got rapidly shunted up the re-housing list because of Stella's pregnancy, and the fact that the tinkers' site was at last being demolished in order to expand Camelot caravan park. That the walls of his house were so thin that he could hear everything happening next door. He thought about telling Raymond how Charlie, watching Stella with her arms full pushing through the front gate of number 16, had said, 'It's a wonder, isn't it, that being pregnant, one of the most natural things in the world, can become one of the most unnatural if it happens in the wrong order. And at her age too. They'll make mincemeat of her now.'

He had never said anything to Charlie about Stella, but there was an unspoken sympathy between the two women from the start. Only that evening, before coming out, he had left Charlie in a deckchair against the back wall of the house where the last of the day's sun fell. She had her shoes and stockings off, and a small white matinée jacket on her knitting needles, resting in her lap while she dozed with one eye shut.

Charlie had felt pity for Stella as well as relief that she would no longer be the road's only scapegoat. The larger Stella grew and the more apparent her fallen state became, the more intolerable the staring and whispering became. She was forced to become housebound, giving lists of necessities to Charlie to get for her.

Hal heard them through the walls at night, and he heard them at other times as well, shouting. The shouting was mostly Perkins. And among all the unbearable pain and agony being able to hear them provoked, he couldn't help feeling that he had been sent to watch over them. By the time Irene was evicted from North Cliff and moved her caravan into Perkins's back garden, where it stayed, despite persistent complaints to the council, he was sure that this was the case. That Irene was a guardian angel as well, and that the two of them were needed because of what was coming.

'They'll be closing the pit soon. Been a pit there since 1673, there has.' Raymond drained the contents of his glass.

Hal turned and watched Raymond's Adam's apple slide gracefully up and down his throat.

He made no sign of having heard Hal.

Hal said nothing else; he didn't have the courage to ask the same question twice.

Raymond stood up, one hand over his left breast smoothing his suit while the other hand patted his hair down so that he was ready to face the world. 'Well,' he said, 'must be getting home. Oh, and we should make next week a Wednesday rather than a Saturday night. They're making Saturday nights Lonely Hearts nights, and that's just not us, not us at all, is it, Harold?'

He watched Raymond leave, his hands hanging neatly down by his sides. His head didn't turn to the left or the right as the soles of his shoes tapped lightly down the marble stairs and he passed through the red velvet curtains out of the Dance Hall and into the Penny Arcade.

That was it, all these years they had been coming here as young men and now old, he had never seen it: Raymond was afraid of The Palace. He came here still, not to partake of it, but to keep watch over it. But now the dance floor was nearly empty, and he had seen it through almost to the end. What was there left for Raymond to be afraid of?

12

Hal didn't have the heart, in his broom cupboard, to tell the children who came to see him the truth. To show them what would happen to them when they stopped being children. So he decided to introduce career talks for school leavers, open to those taking and not taking exams at the end of the Easter term, and to be held in the assembly hall. These were voluntary, which meant that no other teachers turned up.

The speakers were procured through various official and unofficial means, and the paltry line up for the Careers Talks inaugural year in 1959 consisted of: Tom Mattheson, mechanic and owner of Mattheson's Garage and Scrap Yard; Mr Geldon, line supervisor at the Wilkinson factory, and Perkins, assistant in the shoe department at the Co-op. In the event, Mr Geldon never made it, choosing to spend the afternoon he had been granted leave to attend the Careers Talks at the Clayton Arms. This left two speakers.

Hal had tried to pull curtains over the windows running down either side of the hall in order to limit potential distractions, but the orange fabric was rotting from condensation. The sunlight beat bright tracks into the hall, across the heads of the children and the scuffed parquet flooring, illuminating vast chasms of dust.

Hal was wondering what had possessed him to put the chairs up on stage, and whether he shouldn't move both

Perkins and Mattheson down on to the floor in front of the audience, when Tom Mattheson got to his feet to speak first, standing in silence for the first five minutes, apparently stunned. Then he took off his hat and asked individual members of the audience he recognised if they were all right. 'All right, Patterson? All right, Stone?' winding up these acknowledgments by nodding at Hal.

Mattheson stank of the cars he laboured under every day; there was even something thick and brown streaked through his beard. Eventually he moved to the front of the stage, hat in hand. 'Right lads,' he said. 'I'm looking for greasers.'

The children looked at Hal, then stared back at Mattheson.

'Would you like to explain a bit about your garage, Mr Mattheson? The running of it?' Hal tried.

Mattheson walked heavily over to the side of the stage where Hal was lurking nervously, but didn't lower his voice. 'Everyone knows where the frigging garage is, I need greasers. I need greasers,' he yelled again, walking back into the middle of the stage. 'Any of you young lads will do. No pay, but board and lodgings free of charge. I don't hit.' He was stern, as if telling the truth to a sea of eager faces. Then he smiled, like a man whose joke has just been laughed at, and added, 'I started as a greaser myself,' pausing impressively to let this sink in, and give them time to work out for themselves just how much he had amounted to in life. He nodded at Perkins then stomped down the steps and out of the hall.

A girl called Dora raised a hand.

'Yes?'

'Can we ask questions, sir?' she called out.

'Of course you can, but not until Mr Perkins has finished his talk.'

'Why can't we ask them now?'

'Later.'

He looked up at Perkins, and was about to invite him to start his talk when Weevil walked pompously into the hall, his hands in his overall pockets. 'Mr Collins wants to see you,' he shouted to Hal from the back of the hall. He waited long enough for the effect of this announcement to ripple its way through the children gathered there, then added, 'Now.'

'As you can see, we're right in the middle . . .'

'Mr Collins said "now"!'

Weevil wouldn't leave, he carried on standing sententiously at the back of the hall.

Hal gave in.

'Mr Perkins from the shoe department at the Co-op has kindly come to join us today, but we will have to postpone his talk for now. If, however . . .' he paused and glanced at Perkins, 'anyone has any questions they would like to ask Mr Perkins, please come to the front. Otherwise thank you everyone for coming today,' he said, but it did nothing to break the silence. 'You can go now.'

No one moved.

'You can go,' he said, again trying to channel some authority into his voice.

They got to their feet, feeling more comfortable as the chairs made their familiar scraping sound across the floor. People paired up, and bodies started to jostle one another as they pushed and shoved, then straggled their way out of the hall, not unlike the way they had entered it.

Only Dora, with her ambitious French pleat, made her way towards the stage. She stood there, swinging shyly from side to side, staring first at Hal, then Perkins.

For a short moment, the presence of Dora between them made Hal feel closer to Perkins than he had for years. While the moment lasted, intensely close, close enough to take him in his arms almost. Standing there as he was in his new but cheap suit and dirty shirt. Not a trace, as far as Hal could see, of his former glamour. A glamour Hal had always presumed would pave the way to glory.

'Dora?' he said warmly to the girl.

'I was wondering', she said slowly, 'if I might ask something.'

'Of course.'

'You work in the shoe department, right?' Her tone had become suddenly aggressive.

Perkins nodded.

'Well, I've seen this pair of shoes I really want, only I don't want to get them if the sale's about to start. I know you're not supposed to say. But when's the sale starting?'

Mr Collins, the headmaster, had the same regulation curtains that were hung up at all the windows throughout the school, only his looked new. As did the three grey filing cabinets, the desk and two chairs. There was a coatstand in the corner of the room, but the only things hanging from it were Mr Collins's cap and gown, and a substantial cane, which, Hal knew, had seen a lot of action over the years.

On the wall there were two posters of the human body: man and woman. These were anatomical drawings from the British Medical Association and made the inside of the body look a lot more colourful and interesting than the outside. The bookshelves in the right-hand corner were full of rigorously ordered annals and directories as well as a pair of scales, presented to Mr Collins by some society Hal had never known Setton possessed.

On the desk there was a plastercast model of the human head intersected with black lines and Latin, mapping the human brain. The only other things in the room were some posters of the Austrian Tyrol, discoloured by the sun. Mr Collins sat smiling at him, his hands held together on the desk in front of him. He wore a lot of rings with strange symbols on them. Hal knew instinctively that this meeting didn't have anything to do with the Careers Talks.

'So, Mr Price,' Collins began. Then remembered that this was a private audience, there was no classroom of children behind them. 'Harold,' he added with some misgiving.

'Mr Collins?' Hal prompted.

'Hum,' he replied, stuck for words and got up out of his seat to stand by the window.

The office smelt of school. Of human life trying to find its way in unnatural circumstances.

Mr Collins made them coffee on his small gas stove and remained silent.

'Chocolate?' he said at last as he handed Hal his cup of coffee.

Hal shook his head and watched as Collins pulled open the top desk drawer, took out a chocolate bar and put the whole thing in his mouth. Chewing, he sat pensively on the corner of the desk near the plaster head and drew a letter out of his breast pocket. Hal froze; for a moment he thought it was Fitts's letter, somehow fallen out of his childhood and into the hands of Mr Collins.

'Mandy Watkins is dead,' he said, trying to keep the chocolate in his mouth, and having to wipe the saliva from his chin. 'You remember Mandy Watkins?'

Hal nodded as Collins waved the letter threateningly at him. Was he trying to implicate him in some way?

'When?'

'Day before yesterday,' Collins replied, running his thumb and forefinger around the perimeter of the letter. 'She hanged herself,' he finished accusingly, as if Hal should have been there to save her. 'Her mother finally woke from her alcohol-induced coma around midday and went upstairs to find her daughter dangling from the landing ceiling. She walked right into her, so to speak, on her way to the bathroom. According to Sergeant Pearce. Otherwise, God knows when she would have found her. The house was a pigsty and the mother a gibbering wreck unable to remember her daughter's name. According to Sergeant Pearce. Who felt he could be candid with me over such matters,' Mr Collins added, *sotto voce*.

Hal took all this in without comment. Then, realising that something more appropriate was required, said, 'It's a tragedy,' and sighed. The words and his sigh were fake, but he did genuinely believe it was a tragedy. He could see Mandy Watkins very clearly crouched in his beach hut and felt his cheeks go red at the memory. 'It's a tragedy,' he repeated, then paused. 'But I don't quite understand what business it is of mine.'

Mr Collins detected Hal's panic and slowly straightened the creases in his beige trousers.

'The letter she wrote, her suicide note, is addressed to you,' he said, tapping it against his nose. Then he dropped it in Hal's lap.

Hal turned the letter over and saw his name, although the writing was so bad it was barely legible.

'It's been opened,' he said, looking up.

'Of course it's been opened,' Collins said, raising his voice in warning. 'It's evidence from the scene of a crime.'

'But she hanged herself; she committed suicide.'

'Suicide's a crime, Mr Price,' he spat back at him. Then stared at the letter in his hand expectantly.

But Hal didn't open it.

'I'm afraid', Collins said heavily, 'that Sergeant Pearce from the station is here to ask you a few questions.'

'Why?'

'Just routine,' he said, opening the office door to admit Sergeant Pearce. 'The letter was addressed to you.'

Sergeant Pearce walked into the office with his hat under his arm, shook hands with Mr Collins and nodded briskly at Hal. He brought, ever so faintly, the sweet sugary smell of hundreds and thousands with him. Mr Collins went and sat back down behind his desk, leaving Sergeant Pearce to circle Hal in a grave manner.

'Crying shame,' he muttered. 'Not that her life amounted to much, with a mother like that.'

Hal stared at him.

'How's your mother, Harold?' He broke off suddenly.

'Fine.'

'This is a tragedy,' Collins reminded them both, using Hal's words.

'It certainly is. One that could no doubt have been avoided.' Sergeant Pearce started to sigh, then halfway through his sigh suddenly said to Hal, 'When did you last see Mandy Watkins?'

'I can't remember.'

'Try,' Mr Collins insisted.

'It would have been years ago,' Hal said, the smell of chocolate and hundreds and thousands very strong in the air. 'The Easter she left school,' he said, seeing her face again in the carriage next to him as the Charleston took off. Then in the half-light of the beach hut afterwards.

'And when would that have been?' Sergeant Pearce asked patiently.

'I really don't know. At a guess, four years ago. You'll have to look in the register and get her leaving date,' he said, turning to Mr Collins. 'That's when it would have been.'

Mr Collins glared at him for a few moments, then took another chocolate bar out of the desk, slamming the drawer shut. He ate it ferociously, never taking his eyes off Hal, dipping his head forwards over his desk every now and then so as not to dribble chocolate over his trousers.

'Mandy was sent to me over an incident involving glue sniffing, I seem to remember.'

'Glue sniffing,' Sergeant Pearce repeated incredulously.

'That's right.'

'Did you solve her problem?'

'I'm a careers advisor, not a social worker. Of course I didn't solve her problem. That child', he said, and the word child affected him far more than the word suicide had done earlier, 'came to me damaged beyond repair. She was abused from day one and, as far as I could see, the authorities had done nothing to prevent it.'

Mr Collins twitched uncomfortably in his immaculate trousers, thinking that now would be the time for Sergeant Pearce to ask him exactly why an unqualified careers advisor had been given the responsibility of counselling a glue sniffer. Sergeant Pearce, to be fair, thought about it, but in the end stuck to his original line of interrogation. He tipped his head back slightly and stared up at the ceiling.

'*Never worked out why I'm here. Can't swim anyway,*' he said.

'What?'

'That's what she said.'

'When?'

'To you, in her letter,' Sergeant Pearce chastised him.

Hal pressed it against him.

'Haven't you read it yet?'

'Not yet, no.'

This seemed to implicate him even further, but Hal couldn't work out why.

Sergeant Pearce thought about it.

'Well, Mr Collins,' he said, ignoring Hal. 'I think that's all for now.'

'Very good,' Mr Collins said, getting to his feet and showing the sergeant out.

'I may have to question Mr Price again,' he said putting his hat on at the door.

'Of course, of course.'

'Thank you for being so obliging. A very good day to you.'

The sergeant left, not entirely satisfied. I'll take Shanks's pony back to the station, he thought, gives me time to think.

Harold Price bothered him; this whole business bothered him. He remembered seeing the letter addressed to Harold Price on the floor beneath the girl's swaying feet. His heart really had skipped a beat or two, and from that moment on he didn't just have a job, he had a mission. His mission included not only this girl's suicide, but the strange rumours about Charlie Price and old Delaval, and Perkins at number 16, unmarried, with a kid on the way, not to mention that fortune teller, Irene Trench, in the back garden.

He didn't know how people got away with living their lives like this. Surely they had to be within someone, or something's jurisdiction. And there was him, an honest, law-abiding citizen, living well within the margins of good conduct. Maybe occasionally, very occasionally, he had overstepped the line, but nothing serious ever. All he had wanted out of life was a child with Mrs Pearce, who had been prodded, poked and prayed for until they had reduced her to a pile of rubble. Such a nervous pile of rubble that there wasn't

much she was good for these days. Not even conversation. He
wanted somebody to answer him when he asked why this had
happened to him. Surely, if happiness had been put just out of
his reach, there was time left yet for some compensation.

After Mr Collins had dismissed Hal from his office, with not
quite the feeling of triumph he had anticipated, he pulled open
one of the filing cabinets and took out a mirror and a bottle of
coconut oil. He shook some drops of oil into the palms of his
hands then passed them over his hair. At 1.30 p.m. Jane
Munroe, Head Girl, walked into the office. She shut the door
sheepishly behind her and he took her hand and briefly kissed
it, then told her to take a seat.

The moment he had flung Mandy Watkins's suicide note
into Harold's lap he had let him know, as clearly as if he had
spoken the words, that Harold was no better than him. Harold
Price with all his airs and graces. 'We're the same, you and
me,' he had wanted to say.

'Mr Collins?' Jane Munroe said, crossing her legs then
looking irritated.

He smiled reassuringly at her, but hardly saw her or her legs.
And, suddenly, that line from the letter he had read over and
over again, *you're the only person who'll know I'm gone*, no longer
struck him as pitiful nor the *I forgive you* impossible. He had
been jealous of that letter, more jealous of it than if he had had
a wife who had a lover. He knew that, whatever happened, he
would never receive a letter like that.

He listened to Jane Munroe huffing and uncrossing her legs.
She was irritated with him for being such boring company
when she had risked so much by coming here at this time of
day. He turned round slowly, away from the window.

'Get out,' he said to the girl.

Once Hal shut the door to the beach hut the wind sounded
much further away. Looking around he saw that someone had
lit the kerosene lamp and stood it by the window, but it was
turned down so low it hardly gave off any light. The bottle of

whisky he kept in the hut was also up on the bench with the lid off and the glass next to it half-full. There was somebody crouched in the corner.

'Mandy?' he said, terrified.

'Hal?' the figure said.

'Mandy,' he said again.

'Who's Mandy?'

'Who are you?'

He walked slowly towards the corner, unable to smell anything but the kerosene from the lamp.

'It's me, Stella.'

She was sitting with her back against the side of the hut and her legs wrapped under her because of the size of her belly.

'What are you doing here?'

'Oh dear,' she said, but her voice was tired, beyond caring. 'Is this one of those places I'm not supposed to know about?'

'You're not supposed to know about . . . nobody's supposed to know about. It's mine,' he finished pathetically.

'Perkins knows about it.'

He looked at her, but looked quickly away. He had never seen real sadness in her face before, and the lamplight showed it very plainly. He heard Mandy's letter rustle in his pocket.

'Have you been here before?' he asked.

'Yes.' She let out a slight groan and shifted her weight. 'The night Spanish City opened.'

There it was again, that sudden feeling that he had known her all his life; that they could never know anybody as well as they knew each other. He came and crouched down beside her.

'You make me so tired,' she said, letting her head fall back against the wooden side of the hut.

He sat very still, frightened that if he made the slightest movement she would stop speaking.

'You act like a survivor. The worst sort of survivor, someone who hasn't been through anything. Someone who's barely survived their own life. I bet you wake up every morning and sigh to find yourself alive still.'

'Yes, I do,' he said quietly.

But there was no triumph in her face as she turned to him. The light caught at a chain around her neck; a St Christopher's chain.

'It brings luck to those who travel,' she said, following the direction of his eyes.

'I know.' He leant over her and took hold of it. The back of the charm was very warm from where it had been resting against her skin. He let it drop back against her throat.

'Sometimes I think I'll just walk into the sea,' she said, watching him.

'No you won't,' he said with confidence.

'You sound like Irene Trench.'

They laughed.

'My Aunt Rose walked into the sea.'

'She did?'

Hal nodded. Telling her the story of Aunt Rose made him happy.

'She fell in love with somebody against her will. Couldn't help herself. She thought of it as a curse, but there was nothing she could do about it.'

'Who was the man?'

'A sailor, no, captain. That matters. Norwegian, I think, who docked at Wyley. She died of a broken heart when his ship left.'

'An old story.'

'It was her story. People blame it on the sea. That's why they're worse with their pronouncements here than anywhere else. Just when they think they've kept chaos at bay, the sea washes something or somebody', he said looking at her, 'ashore. You were lucky,' he carried on. 'You were found before being washed ashore.'

'Raymond,' she said, remembering the storm and the Parlour afterwards. 'There was a moment, just a moment, when I was barely conscious. It was after he rescued me, and I was lying on some sort of table in that funeral parlour. I remember feeling him standing over me. I'm convinced he thought about killing me.'

233

He heard Stella breathing deeply to calm herself down. 'It should have been you who found me. Do you remember me saying that to you? I didn't come here because of Spanish City. I came here so that you could find me.'

The next moment her hand was on the back of his neck, raising all the hairs there. He shivered, and when she saw him shiver she dropped her hand.

'Sorry.'

As her touch left him, he felt it. It wasn't a rush, it just fanned out slowly from some central point. Desire. And he knew that whatever happened now between them in this hut, when he opened the door and stepped outside he would be in the world next door where people were brand new. This desire was the desire to live and he had been waiting all his life, since Fitts, to reclaim it. This was what Mandy Watkins had recognised in him because, despite the wreck that was her life, she had been waiting for it as well. Her will to survive for as long as she had done came from the belief that there was something good waiting for her out there, good enough to make this world the next.

Since the closure of Watts, the Clayton Arms had been even more packed than usual. Perkins sat on his own and drank on his own, unless there were strangers passing through who took him for another stranger. He drank a lot sitting at his table watching the darts or whatever else was going on, but was always careful to leave before last orders, careful never to place himself in a compromising situation.

It was still just about light when he left the pub, and it had stopped raining. The sky was getting clearer and higher and he couldn't remember when it had last smelt so fresh outside. He didn't mind the puddles, walking straight through the middle of them, and had just passed the public library and turned left on to Front Street when he heard the car behind him, the wheels making their way slowly through the puddles in the gutter. It would follow him all the way, tailing him until he opened his front gate.

It had started about two months ago. The black car never overtook and it never drew level, it just stayed doggedly at his heels. And he knew that if he turned round, he would see Delaval driving it. He wouldn't be able to see him clearly because of the headlights, but he would see his silhouette well enough.

After he had been followed by the car twice in a row, he had changed his watering hole and gone down to the Seven Stars in South Wyley instead, somewhere he usually only went if he was in a black mood. They had bare-fist boxing in the cellar on Fridays, and it was a good place to go and spill blood. He wasn't always a spectator; people had put money on him before. Two drunken Swedes had bought him drinks all night long, and when he left there was the black car, parked at the end of the quay opposite the Seven Stars, against the hull of a fishing trawler. Waiting for him.

He thought about linking arms with his Swedish drinking companions, but they were already staggering down the quay together. So he started to walk home in the dark, the car bumping behind him over the streets of South Wyley, which were still cobbled. It followed him all the way up on to the headland where his caravan had once stood, past the wall by Watts and along the coastal road into Setton.

But it occurred to him tonight, walking home slowly through the puddles, that Delaval wasn't threatening him, he was just reminding him. He knows everything, Perkins thought. The baby, the poverty . . . the dead weight of poverty. He makes it his business to know. Deep down Perkins had felt a joy very few people could lay claim to; even now, despite how it all looked on the face of things, he knew he had never been, could never be, happier. He also knew, as did Delaval, that he was standing in the ruins; that he had renounced everything in order to experience this joy; had renounced the millions of his heart's desire to be with Stella.

Part of him wanted to run. The other part listened for the quiet splashes of the car to check that it was still there. Every morning he woke up and lay staring at the ceiling, hoping that it would have happened, that he would wake up and find that he was no longer in love with her. But then he would turn, and see her lying there.

The car followed him to the gate of his house where there were still lights on inside, skimming past him and picking up speed as it moved off up King Alfred's Road to where they were converting the old cinema into a night-club.

13

Stella's son, Victor, was, at four, instinctively suspicious of Uncle Hal, who joined him and his mother every Friday. But he had to hide this because Uncle Hal gave very good shoulder-carries, and showed no aversion to being ridden or making the appropriate animal noises, which his dad did. When Victor rode he showed no mercy, and always wore spurs. If Uncle Hal complained, he only ever did so laughingly. In fact Uncle Hal, who wasn't a real uncle, had an ability to become any named beast and loved lying on his back or crawling around on all fours. When he did this, Victor couldn't help laughing, something he didn't really want to do because if he laughed Uncle Hal might think he liked him, and he didn't. These mixed feelings complicated Victor's life no end because Uncle Hal would do anything for his mother, anything at all.

He always took them out, and always had money in his pocket. They went to Moscadini's summer and winter. In summer they walked from the beach hut over the dunes, round by the lighthouse and up the cliff. In the winter, and he liked the winter best, they took the bus to Watts Corner, then they would walk past Camelot caravan site on to the headland.

It was always freezing on the headland in winter because of the wind from the North Sea, cold enough for Victor to pull the hood of the duffel coat he hated up over his head and tuck his hands, already covered in mittens, deep into his pockets.

He would run from side to side, keeping his mother's black shiny boots, which reached as far as her knees, in sight. She wore a duffel coat as well, and sometimes she would turn round and catch him up suddenly because she loved the wind even when it froze them nearly to death. In winter they were the only ones in Moscadini's and they would burst through the doors with steam coming off them, their faces and hands raw red.

He and his mother had a knickerbocker glory even though he never managed more than half of his. 'You've got to finish it, you know,' she would say, half-serious, 'it's important you finish it.'

They would sit at a booth near the juke-box so that he could kneel on the red leather and look over the seat at the Mediterranean Sea on the back wall, a view he preferred a million times to that out of the window. Safe and warm inside, they could hear the wind roaring around the old building and rattling the glass while spray from the waves hitting the base of the lighthouse would splash against the veranda windows. Victor was impressed by these genuine signs of fury. In deep winter all the lights came on at 4.30, and from Moscadini's, you could see the whole of Setton's promenade lighting up, from North Cliff to South where Spanish City was, and the roller-coaster he'd been promised a ride on when he was old enough. The only thing he got to ride on at the moment apart from Uncle Hal was Danny the Deer outside Moscadini's.

When it was dark it was terrifying waiting for the bus at Watts Corner near the machinery at the old pit head. They would sit at the back of the bus if they could, get off halfway down Marine Parade, cross the crazy golf course on to the promenade and walk along beneath the lights towards Spanish City. This was the only part of the outing where Victor wasn't afraid of losing sight of them, afraid of them suddenly disappearing, so he danced around in front and they followed him.

In the summer they would go down on to the beach and paddle, and he would play hide and seek around the old tank traps, avoiding the two vandalised pill-boxes whose smell frightened him. Whatever anyone said, he was convinced there were dead soldiers in there still. But the tank traps he enjoyed, because he was a great believer in defences, and felt, without being able to put it into words exactly, that building barricades against enemies was a necessary part of life on earth.

If the donkey man was there he was allowed a ride on the donkeys. Uncle Hal always asked for Dobbin and the donkey man, who was so bowlegged he could barely walk, thought Hal was asking for his, Victor's, sake, but he wasn't. Dobbin changed size and colour a lot and the donkey man always winked at Uncle Hal as he gave him the reins, but Victor was the only one who seemed to notice Dobbin's chameleon-like tendencies. But then, in Victor's experience, Uncle Hal was easily pleased. He needed real spurs for Dobbin because Dobbin stopped and wouldn't start moving again for ages.

Once Uncle Hal paid the donkey man so much money his eyes boggled. They had the animal for the whole afternoon and Victor rode it all the way over the dunes to the beach hut where he refused to get off, showing a presence of will that pleased his mother no end. He tried lying along the donkey, but there were too many flies and crawling things in the donkey's fur and they kept getting up his nose. Uncle Hal and his mother went into the beach hut and he felt as though he were a sentry on guard duty. But then he at last fell asleep on the back of the donkey. He fell asleep for the whole afternoon, while they stayed in the beach hut.

It was stinking hot inside the hut and there were too many flies. They hadn't noticed before, but they noticed now, afterwards. Stella sat scraping her hair off her face and trying to tie it in a knot. Hal lay back on the blanket watching her, every now and then passing his hand over her back. She sighed and got up, opening the door to the beach hut.

'He's asleep still,' she said, looking at Victor lying along the length of the donkey, one hand on its neck, the other hanging down, the reins loosely strung around his fingers. He scratched his ear in his sleep then muttered something. 'Come and see, Hal,' she said, but he was already standing behind her; she could feel the front of his body pressed against the back of hers.

The sound of children playing and adults shouting came from somewhere in the dunes behind them, but there was nobody on the beach in front of the hut and the sea was empty.

'Take care of the minutes and the hours will take care of themselves.'

'What's that?' He kissed the back of her head.

'This is what people fight wars for, Hal. The details. Life's lived in the details.'

They both carried on staring straight ahead of them, at Victor on the donkey, and the sea beyond. Hal pulled her even more tightly against him, his hands clasped, and rested his chin lightly on the crown of her head.

'This is enough,' he said.

One Friday Victor was allowed to put money in the juke-box at Moscadini's so that Hal and his mother could dance to two of the tunes. That night they waited until it got dark before leaving and ran across the headland to the bus stop to try and keep warm. Waiting at Watts Corner, his mother undid her coat and bundled him inside it despite the huge bump that was the baby inside her, and when the bus arrived it was so bright he couldn't stop blinking. Nearly everybody on the bus was smoking and the smell of the smoke made him feel secure even though the people stared at them and didn't try to talk to him or give him sweets or money like they did the other children.

Joyce, the conductress, with her hard face and tight curls, was always nice to them. She was able to walk down the middle of the bus without holding on to the overhead straps even when it went round corners. And she always let him tear their tickets from the metal ticket box she wore. Today his mother wanted to stay on until they got to the end of their road, because of the cold and because she was always tired at the moment. But Victor insisted on his promised visit to Spanish City. He knelt up on the back seat and stared out of the window. Despite the dirty glass and the darkness, he thought he saw something moving, and it got closer and closer until he made out a man in a cap with a big coat on cycling behind the bus.

He laughed out loud and his mother told him to hush, but they didn't turn to see what he was staring at out of the window. He put his fingers up to the sides of his head making bull's horns, but the man on the bicycle wouldn't wave back. He had seen the man before near Moscadini's when they went there and even occasionally on the dunes near the beach hut. Uncle Hal and his mother never seemed to see him, but he knew it was Raymond Clarke, the bogeyman. When the bus stopped by the cemetery the bicycle went past them. They got off at the crazy golf course on Marine Parade, his mother laughing as Uncle Hal pulled her down the steps, watched sternly by the driver.

The wind was really roughing up the sea, and at one point near the Clock House Café his mother let out a scream as a wave hurled itself right over the railings across the promenade. There was nobody at the entrance to Spanish City in winter, but the gates were kept open on a Friday for the tea dances they still held at The Palace. Victor nodded at the bull's head over the entrance and they walked in. Uncle Hal always gave him money for the wise monkeys in the Penny Arcade. There were other things Victor would rather have spent his penny on, but he knew he had no choice but to put it in the slot for the monkeys. That night the only other person at The Palace was the lady with a moustache who sat in the change kiosk. She nodded curtly at them and carried on with her word-search book.

They stopped in front of the wise monkeys. The heavy red velvet curtains were usually pulled back on Fridays, and Victor was allowed to stand on the top step and look at the miles and miles of chequered dance floor. But tonight the curtains were closed. For once Uncle Hal forgot about the monkeys and slowly pulled the curtains back. There was no chequered dance floor to be seen, no palm trees, no palace, just planks of wood nailed clumsily across the entrance.

'You can't go in there,' the woman from the change kiosk yelled.

Uncle Hal ignored her and pressed his ear against the wood. Victor thought for a moment that he could hear music and that the old folk had been boarded up while in the throes of their tea dance, but Uncle Hal shook his head at him as if he had read his mind. Victor stood back. The woman in the change kiosk got to her feet.

'You can't go in there,' she yelled again.

'Can't get in there more like,' his mother muttered.

'Move away,' the woman ordered.

'What's happened?' Uncle Hal called out to her.

'We're closing down,' the woman said, trying to lower her voice as she played nervously with the locket at her neck.

'The Palace?' Uncle Hal said in disbelief.

The woman didn't say anything she just stood there, waiting.

Victor watched his uncle's fingers start to feel for the gaps between the planks of wood as if he had never laid eyes on the inside of The Palace before.

'It's the council,' the woman said. 'They'll keep the Penny Arcade and Spanish City open in high season.'

'What will happen to The Palace?'

'Don't know; Bingo maybe. It's all the rage these days.' The woman shrugged, then sat down again. But a second later she was back on her feet as, horrified, Victor watched Uncle Hal hurl himself against the wood.

Victor moved slowly away towards the machines he was never allowed to play.

'Just one last look.'

'Hal,' his mother said, her hands on his elbow.

Victor ducked behind the tuppence drop, outraged by Uncle Hal's unpredictable behaviour.

'Just one last look,' he said, turning to his mother and taking both her hands in his.

The woman in the kiosk had decided that enough was enough.

'Trespassers will be prosecuted,' she yelled nearly smashing the glass the kiosk was made of.

Hal listened to her, his forehead pressed against the wood still, then he started to laugh, louder and louder until he was clutching at the red curtains he was laughing so much.

14

It was the dead of winter. Charlie stood in the vestibule of the Spiritualist church and tucked her scarf tightly into her coat. She'd left before the end tonight because there had been too much crying and she couldn't stand that. Bracing herself, she walked out into the night air. The church, when it stopped being a Baptist church and became the Spiritualist church, had been painted white, but most of this was falling off now in large lumps. The words 'Spiritualist Church' had been emblazoned in black across the front of the building. Inside it was red. Charlie, who had gone at first reluctantly and with scepticism, liked it immediately because of the red, which was plush.

She crossed the forecourt, which was gradually being reduced to rubble by the weeds. Even now, with Watts closed down, the air was still heavy with sulphur. She was glad Jamie hadn't lived to see it, he wouldn't have known what to do with himself. 'Would you, Jamie?' she said out loud. Then laughed at herself.

She was so busy laughing to herself that she didn't see the big black car parked beneath a smashed streetlamp near the discount store. It was barely five o'clock, but it was already dark. There was only one car like that in Setton and the moment she recognised it, she knew it was waiting for her.

Her first instinct was to turn on her heels and head straight back for the church, but she knew that, if Delaval had come for her, he would get hold of her sooner or later. So she stood her ground as he emerged awkwardly from the car. He's an old man, she thought, with an unexpected wave of pity for the small child she had nursed.

'Raising the dead, Charlie?'

His voice rang out clear in the cold across the empty forecourt.

'No, just speaking with them, sir.'

He laughed.

'Ah, well.'

'I come to speak to Jamie.'

'And did you speak with Jamie tonight?'

'Not tonight, no.'

She felt none of the hostility towards him she had expected to feel. So that when he said, 'Will you come for a drive, Charlie?' she surprised herself further by saying, 'Yes.'

She ducked into the car, her hand on her head in order to keep her hat on. It was as grand inside as the outside had suggested.

'I thought we might have some tea,' Delaval said, settling himself into the driver's seat beside her.

'It's about time, isn't it?' she responded.

'It is.'

They laughed for a split-second like accomplices, then Delaval started the engine. Charlie lit a cigarette without asking, reaching into her handbag and pulling out the 'Bonnie Scotland' ashtray she carried around with her everywhere. The car soon filled with smoke and she sat back comfortably, enjoying the drive.

After a while they turned through the gates and up the tree-lined avenue towards Ellison Court. Since the building of the bypass it was now much nearer the road. Standing on the gravel, Charlie was amazed to find that she could still hear the sound of traffic. Here it used to feel as if you were in deep country, away from the mines and the rest of the world. She sighed, but not with regret. She liked the modern world and she had a place in it, under its strange orange sky.

Delaval let himself into his own house, holding the door open for her. She hesitated a moment then crossed the threshold. The house was empty, so empty that for a moment she could hear the sounds it used to make, full of people. She followed Delaval across the hallway, close on his heels, then he opened another door and she saw immediately that the room they walked into hadn't changed since the last time she was in it.

What was it, the Drawing Room? Then it came to her, the Red Room. That's what they used to call it, among themselves, because everything in it was red. Whether this was its real name or not, she didn't know. Red curtains, red walls, red rugs, red sofas grouped around the fireplace and an old gramophone against the back wall on a sideboard covered in photographs.

After standing helplessly on the threshold she ignored Delaval's suggestion to sit down and walked slowly around the perimeter of the room instead. There were paintings on the walls of forests and rivers. She had had to keep her eyes down when she used to stand in this room, but she remembered wanting to look at the paintings very badly.

'Nice pictures,' she said in a hard voice.

'My father painted them.'

She stood back quickly and went and sat down on the sofa nearest the fire, which was now lit. She couldn't remember it being lit when she first walked into the room.

'I used to bring you down to this room to see your mother and father. Every afternoon at six o'clock you saw them for half an hour. When they were here in the house, not off somewhere.'

She opened her bag, her hands fishing inside for the cigarettes and ashtray, but not quite having the courage to bring them out. It just didn't feel right to be sitting in this room, the Red Room, a place in which she was never meant to sit down. She kept looking round expecting the door to open, and to be yelled at to stand up. To get out. So that when the door did open, she leapt to her feet, clutching her handbag to her.

But it was only a man she didn't recognise, carrying a tea-tray. She sank slowly back into the sofa, making the most of the diversion to put the cigarette and ashtray on the table in front of her. The man left without her noticing, more shadow than man. She thought she heard the sound of a baby crying somewhere in the house and automatically started forward, alert. Then the crying stopped. 'Ghosts,' she muttered shaking her head. Then, more angrily, 'Bloody ghosts. What?' she said looking across at Delaval who was watching her, an expression of pain on his face.

'Nothing,' he said, dismissively, then added, 'you remind me of somebody.'

He poured out the tea and she took the cup he held out to her, embarrassed. Now she was not only sitting down in the Red Room, but drinking tea in it. What religious people might call sacrilege.

'I was with Harold in France, for a time,' he said, settling himself into the sofa opposite.

'I know, he told me.' She paused. 'You must have seen some things.'

'I have.'

'More things than I've ever seen.'

Delaval shrugged. 'I'm sure you've seen plenty of things. Sugar?'

Charlie couldn't remember if she took sugar in her tea or not so she nodded and stirred it in anyway. She looked down at herself. Her dress was sparkling in the light from the fire.

'Did you look at the photographs over there?' Delaval said suddenly.

'Why?' She felt herself bristling.

Delaval sighed and drained his cup of tea then started gently tapping the cup and saucer together. They looked tiny in his hand, delicate, like something from a doll's china tea set.

'I need you to be kind,' he said at last, with a desperation she had never expected of him.

Charlie stared, 'I can't be kind, it's not in my nature. But I'm warm when I want to be.'

'Then be warm now. Will you?'

She looked away at the fire.

'I should never have gone to America with you all. And I should never have gone to Brussels before that.'

'I don't remember Brussels. What happened in Brussels?'

'We visited a cathedral. Beautiful cathedral. Nothing happened in Brussels,' she said loudly. 'Nothing ever happened anywhere and that's God's honest truth. We never even held hands,' she muttered, brushing some spilt tea from her left breast. 'I should never have gone, that's all.'

'But you did,' he said gently.

'I did. I was sixteen. I was strong, but I wasn't that strong. I'm sorry,' she added, to no one in particular. 'That lake. Great big flat thing it was, and dead as a dodo. Only thing alive on it was them flies wanting to get under your skin.' Her hand went to her throat. 'He wanted to show me the dance hall, but I wouldn't let him. I wanted to see it though,' she added. 'I wanted to see it so badly, but I wouldn't let him show me.'

Delaval had closed his eyes while she was speaking, but he opened them again now.

'The lake rose,' he said softly. 'It rose a little bit more every spring. Nobody knows why, and they couldn't put it all down to meltwater. You remember the pier?'

Charlie remembered her stockinged legs, hung over the side of a boat.

'The lake flooded the Spanish City. You need a boat to make your way round the dance floor now.'

'Well, there's a judgment and a half.'

They sat in silence. She looked at the smudge her lipstick had left on the rim of the teacup.

'Charleston?'

'Stupid name,' she said, brusquely, then considered it for a moment. 'Can't think what possessed them to call me that.'

'Must have been a moment of weakness.'

'Aye, that's it,' Charlie said, 'a moment of weakness. Although, I have to say if you'd met my mother, you wouldn't have thought her capable of such a thing. Weakness, that is.'

She sighed to herself. This was something her grandmother used to do, then her mother. Now it was her turn to grow old. She sighed again, feeling almost pleased with herself that she had got this far. But then she was vigilant about weighing herself every Sunday night. Not a scratch above nine stone. Very good. And she hadn't lost her calves; she'd always had good calves. All that dancing.

'That was a stupid thing your father did. Naming that roller-coaster after me. And even more bloody stupid of you to build it here in Setton. I never wanted it, never wanted any part in it.' Her hands and arms shook as she lit another cigarette.

'I'm selling Spanish City to the council, and I want to give the proceeds of the sale to you. To do with as you choose.'

So this was his mission. Charlie stood up nervously in front of the fire until she could feel her legs begin to prickle from the heat.

'Why?'

'I want you to have the money.'

'What's all this got to do with me?' she said sharply, but didn't sound so convinced. 'You've realised you can't have love and money, is that it? Because you can't, you know, you can't have both, you stupid child.'

She stood perfectly still, staring across the room, to all appearances paralysed. 'I can't do it,' she said, suddenly determined. 'No, I can't.' She sat back down breathing heavily, one hand pressed in her lap, the other dropping ash over the carpet.

'Oh what does it matter any more? Things don't matter any more. The world's changed.'

'Yes, it has. I built Spanish City for a reason, but now . . .'

'I know why you built Spanish City.'

Delaval stared at her.

'Stella didn't come to Setton because of Spanish City,' she said. 'She came because of Hal.'

And as soon as she said it, she heard distinctly the sound of a baby crying again. The hairs on her arms and the back of her

249

neck shot up. She thought about last Friday night and how she had watched Stella, Hal and Victor walk up the road. She had known as soon as Hal held the garden gate open for Stella, in a way words could never have convinced her.

'I want the money. I want the bloody money, can't you see that?' she said, standing up straight again. 'I'm going to have a grandchild.'

William Clarke had drunk more that night than he was wont to and swayed unsteadily at the top of the caravan steps in the garden of 16 King Alfred's Road. Through the open door the heads of Lucille, black and peroxide, and Irene, a strange shade of brown, were bent together over a small baize card table.

'Close the door,' one of them yelled. Lucille had said she was going to have her fortune read, but he hadn't believed her.

He pulled the door closed chuckling to himself, then slipped down the steps and on to the frozen mud of the garden. If Lucille wanted to keep her future private then he would just have to go back home and wait for her there. Whatever Daisy said.

'Pissing weather,' he muttered to himself. Then, as he stumbled his way across the frozen ridges of mud, he started to hum one of his favourite hymns, one he hadn't sung since he was a boy. He banged against one of the metal poles for the washing line, laughing and humming at the same time. A light went on in the back bedroom, illuminating the garden. Mrs Annegan's garden next door was a showcase of fertility and even in this season plants nearly obscured the path. As William was hobbling down the passage, the corrugated iron roof creaking with the cold, the kitchen door in the passage wall opened to reveal Stella standing there in a nightdress and man's jumper. She tried to speak but couldn't, so the small boy in his dressing gown, standing behind her, said, 'It's started, the baby's started.'

It was Bingo night at the Working Men's Club, and this was

where Delaval dropped Charlie off because she had arranged
to meet Tom there. They didn't win anything that night, and
it was freezing cold so they headed straight home. They were
about to turn in at number 18 when her brother, William, of
all people came crashing down the pathway of number 16.

'Charlie.'

'William? What the hell are you doing here?' But she knew
the answer to that; knew that Lucille would be with Irene in
her caravan and that he had come for Lucille.

He stopped in his tracks at the tone.

'You know who you remind me of, Charlie Price? Our
Raymond, that's who. Jesus Christ, if you could hear
yourself.'

She went to open her mouth, but then saw the expression
on his face and knew it didn't have anything to do with what
he had just said.

'It's Stella isn't it? Tonight of all nights.'

'It's started,' William said, automatically repeating Victor's
words without realising it.

'It's started and she's up there alone. You're bloody useless,
the lot of you.'

William chewed on his lip and stuck his hands, which were
clenched in fists, into his coat pockets.

'I used your telephone for the hospital, but they said they
couldn't send a midwife out.'

She stopped at the foot of the stairs to give this piece of
news a few seconds to sink in.

'Victor?'

'In the caravan with Irene.'

'And Perkins?'

William didn't say anything.

'Well, you know where he is so go and fetch him. And
what about Hal?'

'Out.'

Brother and sister exchanged a quick look.

'Oh, for Christ's sake.'

She stamped up the stairs, one hand clutching the banister,

the other pushing down on her knees as she wheezed her way up. 'Stella, love?' she said breathlessly when she reached the top.

Charlie found Stella in the bedroom, kneeling down by the side of the bed. She stood with her hand on her heart, watching her and waiting for her own breathing to calm down. Passing her hand over Stella's brow, which was sweating, she then clasped hold of her hand as tightly as she could without cutting the circulation off, and patted her on the back.

'I'm going to get the midwife. So don't worry. I won't be long,' she whispered.

Stella nodded, her eyes wide with pain and fear. She didn't attempt to speak.

Charlie dragged the old bicycle from the garden shed. Time was of the essence here, and with a last glance up at Stella's window, she pushed the bike through the side passage. She hadn't ridden it for about two decades and got on it with difficulty. It took a lot of near-falls for her to find her balance, but when she did she was away. Despite the freezing north wind. They'll have plenty to think about tonight, she thought as she sped past the houses, almost able to hear the conversations going on inside.

It was only a mile to Setton general hospital and she kept the six chimneys of the aluminium smelting plant in sight all the way there. She didn't realise how laboured her breathing was until she reached the main entrance and let the bike clatter against a wall. The reception desk was deserted so she ended up walking round the wards looking for anyone in a uniform. She was terrified of hospitals, and hurried between the beds not daring to look at the sick, ignoring the cries that rippled up from them at her intrusion.

'Excuse me, excuse me,' a young voice called out behind her as a staff nurse ran up in her squelching white shoes.

'Is there anyone on duty here?' Charlie demanded.

'Sister . . .' she paused, and blushed. 'Visiting hours are over,' she said apologetically. 'Well over. Are you lost? Do you need me to show you the way out?'

The young nurse was worried, but not unkind. Looking at her label, Charlie saw that her name was Margaret.

'No, I don't. I'm looking for the maternity ward.'

'Are you all right?' Margaret said, her hand automatically going out for the other woman's arm.

'I need a midwife.'

Margaret glanced quickly at Charlie's stomach, looked at her eyes then tightened her grip.

'Not for me, you daft cow,' she barked, shaking her arm free.

'Did you telephone?'

'Yes, and they said there were no midwives so I've come to see for myself. It's a friend of mine.' Charlie looked wildly about her. 'I cycled all the way,' she said. 'Look,' she turned to the young woman, 'I'll find it even if you don't tell me where it is.'

'I could call hospital security,' Margaret said, biting her lip.

'What? Because somebody's looking for a midwife?'

Margaret took hold of Charlie's elbow again.

'You could do,' Charlie conceded, 'but that wouldn't be a brave thing to do. The lady I need a midwife for was a nurse. In the war.'

Margaret started to steer her firmly out of the ward, looking furtively from side to side.

'I'll take you to the maternity ward,' she whispered when they were in the corridor. They went up in the service lift, which smelt badly of old food. Level Five was painted the same grey and pink as everywhere else in the hospital. 'Enough to make anyone ill,' Charlie muttered.

'What's that?' Margaret said, glancing down the corridor, but here as elsewhere, there was no sign of life.

'I said,' Charlie lowered her voice, 'please God shoot me before I end up here.'

Margaret relaxed her face and smiled.

'Go to the end of this corridor and turn right. I'm leaving you now. And please,' she put a lot of stress on the word 'please', 'say you found your own way up if anyone asks.'

'Of course I will,' Charlie said, giving her arm a quick squeeze. 'You're a good girl,' she added as the lift doors closed on the young nurse.

She soon found the maternity ward because of the sound of crying. Through the observation window she saw row after row of fish tanks on wheels housing new-born babies. There was a nurse half-asleep in the far corner, and in more than one cot blankets were being shunted into the air by tiny restless feet. For a moment Charlie realised she was looking in the cots for Hal, then laughed herself out of this stupid fancy. A whole new generation lay on the other side of the glass. She was overawed, until she heard the sound of a woman's laughter and followed it to a door with frosted glass and a sign on it reading 'Staff Only'. She opened it.

'Celia?' the woman inside said.

She had her fat feet up on a poufe cushion and was listening to the wireless. There were a couple of vases on the table with bouquets in them that looked as though they belonged to patients, and a small stove in the corner had steam rising from the pan on it.

Charlie sniffed the air. 'Porridge,' she said at last.

'Celia?' the woman said again, turning round this time. 'You're not Celia.'

'Are you a midwife?'

The woman looked about her panic-stricken, dabbing furiously at her mouth and reacting to Charlie Price as if she were Herod himself come to slay the Holy Innocents. Her Innocents, row upon row of them, most of them delivered by her own hands, to save the world. She couldn't help glancing at the other woman's hands for traces of blood.

'Celia?' she screamed.

'For Christ's sake, woman, are you a midwife or aren't you?'

But at that moment Celia herself burst into the room calling out Susan's name with as much panic as Susan had called out hers. Celia wouldn't have looked strange carrying a crowbar and wearing a balaclava. She rushed to Susan's side.

'Why is this woman here?' Celia demanded.

'I don't know,' Susan apologised, bracing herself, ready to die in the attempt. Then a sudden thought crossed her mind. 'You're from King Alfred's Road, aren't you? Somebody from King Alfred's Road called earlier on, a man, and said a midwife was needed.'

'What did you say?' Celia cut in.

'I said there weren't any on duty we could send out.'

'Why did you say that?'

'Because . . . because . . .' Susan twisted this way and that, light flashing off her spectacles, as she tried to find Celia's ear so she could whisper into it.

'No,' the other woman said violently, pushing Susan away. 'That's enough.' She glanced back at Charlie Price, giving her the once-over. 'I must go,' she said.

'But,' Susan protested, starting to clutch at the skirts of Celia's uniform.

'A child's a child,' Celia proclaimed, bent on getting together all necessary equipment. In a few minutes she was ready. After restraining herself from throwing Susan against the wall, she nodded at Charlie Price.

The two left, Charlie triumphant, Celia full of hope that this next child might be the one that would bring salvation.

When the door to the staffroom shut, Susan burst into tears and started to eat her porridge.

William Clarke and Lucille had disappeared hours ago. Hal sat in the caravan with Irene. He didn't know where else to go. He didn't want to be inside or outside and this seemed like a good middle ground. Tom was sitting contentedly at the tiny drop-leaf table, re-threading Irene's chandelier. Irene was standing behind him humming a tune he thought he recognised. Possibly something he had heard at The Palace years ago.

'You're a guardian angel, that's what you are,' Hal whispered so as not to disturb Victor, asleep on the sofa. 'I just haven't worked out whose.

He shivered and put his hand nearer the calor gas stove.

Irene let out another chuckle, but then stopped.

'Oh,' she said. Quietly, distinctly.

Hal was on his feet.

'What?'

'It's done,' she carried on absently.

'What's done?' Hal said, taking hold of her.

'The baby. The baby's born.'

Hal ran out into the freezing night, up the side passage and into the house through the kitchen. There were no lights on downstairs and he stumbled into things as he made for the bottom of the stairs. He had only been in the house once before. He saw his mother standing in the light at the top of the stairs.

'Perkins? Is that you?' she said.

Hal didn't answer, too busy clambering up the stairs two at a time.

'Hal,' she said, recognising him as he came into the light. He stood next to her, trying to get his breath back.

A midwife came out of the bedroom covered in blood and pushed past them both into the bathroom. That's what the air smelt of, blood. She eyed Hal coldly.

'I've come to see the baby,' he said awkwardly, trying to conceal his agitation.

His mother burst out laughing. 'It's only just been born, Hal. How did you know?'

'I was with Irene.'

'Oh.' Charlie went silent.

'How is she?'

'It's a he.'

'No, Stella. How's Stella?'

'Well,' his mother said and disappeared into the bedroom where he could hear nothing but whispering.

Then the door opened and there was Stella, her face impassive. He couldn't see the smile but he could feel it. It filled the whole room and beyond. Then she nodded towards his mother who was holding the child. He had the strangest of all expectations as he peered at it, the expectation of finding himself.

Charlie must have read something of the look, because she instinctively handed him the child even though it had started to scream, and went and stood outside the room.

Hal carried the screaming baby slowly over to Stella, his face making the strange contortions his face did when he experienced a pleasure he had no control over. The next minute Charlie Price was back inside the bedroom.

'Quick. Perkins is back,' she said hoarsely to Hal.

'Quick,' Stella's voice echoed in panic, 'name him.'

Hal stared wildly about him.

'The child. Name the child now.' Her voice was pleading, desperate. He had never heard her sound like that before.

They all heard clearly now the footsteps on the stairs.

'Will,' Hal said frantically.

Stella sat up, her arms outstretched. 'Yes,' she said happily, 'Will.'

Perkins and Hal met on the threshold of the room. The air around Perkins was freezing; he had brought the cold in with him. Hal had to stop himself from saying 'Sorry'. Perkins said nothing. Perkins, who had taught himself French, German and God knows what else, in order to be prepared for all eventualities, now stood helpless and could think of nothing to say.

Hal left, followed downstairs by his mother who opened the front door for him.

'Don't worry,' he said, 'I'll go round the back '

'No, go out the front. It's better that way.'

She held the door open for him.

'Hal,' she said.

He stopped.

'Mind how you go.'

'I have been. I will do.'

She wasn't convinced. He waited until she had shut the door then disappeared up the side passage as quietly as he could, back to Irene's caravan.

15

When Charlie Price shook Mr Dodgson's hand, it was the first time in her life she had ever shaken hands with a bank manager. It was in all probability the first time Mr Dodgson had shaken hands with a customer. The Co-op Bank, which was a small glass and wood construction located behind the linen department on the third floor, had witnessed a lot of broken lives, and few fortunes had been made. But Mr Dodgson knew that, somewhere behind the dusty wood and stale carpet, there was a glory in banking. Just as he knew that somewhere inside him there was another Mr Dodgson, a maverick wearing a bowler hat, waiting.

Charlie Price arrived five minutes after the bank opened, in her wedding suit with matching hat and gloves. She went straight to a young clerk who could barely sit upright on his stool due to heavy drinking the night before. Two minutes into her rehearsed monologue he slipped sideways off the stool and fell under the counter. Mr Dodgson soon arrived on the scene and Charlie watched as the small rotund bank manager dragged the young man across the floor and gave him a few sharp kicks to bring him round. The boy disappeared behind closed doors, but they both heard, distinctly, the sound of copious vomiting.

'His face was green, it was.'

'A disgrace. I apologise,' Mr Dodgson said curtly.

He was about to turn on his heels in order to conduct more vigorous violence on the young man when he realised that there was nobody else but him left to serve. So he stood and listened as Charlie launched into her rehearsed monologue for a second time.

After she had finished, she rummaged in her handbag then passed the letter from Delaval's solicitors across the counter. Mr Dodgson couldn't move. He stared at the envelope on the counter and at the woman on the other side. The sound of her fiddling with the clasp on her handbag was the only thing to break the sudden silence of the banking hall. Mr Dodgson was floored. The man in the bowler hat, waiting inside him, was about to get an airing and he was terrified. Then the fear passed and he rose to the occasion.

Mr Dodgson was no investment banker, and neither was Charlie Price. There was more money on the slip of paper she handed him than either of them had ever seen in their lives before and there were right and wrong ways of handling it. Sending Mrs Price elsewhere for expert advice was the right way, and opening an account at the Setton Co-operative was the wrong way.

When he left Mrs Price in his office in order to go to the bathroom and wash his hands Mr Dodgson took a good look at himself in the mirror. He had always known that he wasn't a bad man, but he had never before suspected that he might not be a good man either.

They spent the entire morning in each other's company and at the end of it shook hands. Once Mrs Price left, Mr Dodgson picked up the telephone and dialled a number he had rarely dialled before, to Head Office. When he came off the telephone he called the desk clerk into his office and gave the boy, who still looked ill, a once-in-a-lifetime talking to. After this he took the main staircase down to the first floor to the men's department, and bought himself a new suit. When he felt ready he would venture into Newcastle for the day and go to a proper tailor. That's what a man in his position should do. He just didn't feel quite ready yet, that was all. After this he went to the shoe department where the assistant, Perkins, fitted him with a pair of shoes he had thought he was going to have to wait until the sales to buy. Then he went back to his office and sat down behind the desk, stretched out his legs and waited to see what his life would become in light of Mrs Price.

Charlie walked out of the main doors and down the steps, holding on to her handbag more tightly than she had done when it contained the cheque from Delaval's solicitors. There was another envelope, also from the solicitors, with 'photograph' scrawled over it, but that was for Hal.

Standing on the Co-op steps on a windy Monday morning, she felt that something lay at her feet, and if it wasn't Setton she couldn't think what it was. She looked about her with satisfaction. The town was dying, and it was a shame, but she wasn't. She brusquely brushed aside a sudden enveloping feeling of loneliness, the sort people who have stood still all their life experience when the ground is slowly pulled from under their feet, and took a deep breath. Life, she thought nearly bursting out of her suit as it came rushing around her, was a marvel.

16

One night just before Victor's fifth birthday and after a bath, the doorbell went. His mother didn't even finish putting the top of his pyjamas on. She went running down the stairs in her bare feet, her wet hands trailing along the wall in a way his never would have been allowed to do. Victor stood at the top of the stairs and watched as Uncle Hal walked in.

After a while she ran back up to Victor, put his dressing gown on and his slippers, then took him downstairs where she finished him off with a sweater and duffel coat. He was told to go and play with his deflating yellow football and went into the dark garden.

Every time he kicked the ball against the back wall of their house the dogs opposite whined as if he were kicking it at them. The harder he kicked the harder they whined until he was no longer afraid of them and began to hate them instead. He carried on kicking, no longer caring whether he slipped off the edge of the path on to the snow, or whether it woke up baby Will. His pyjama bottoms were wet to the knees by the time he heard his father's footsteps in the side passage.

He sent the ball hurling into the wall again and his father came straight over. He didn't say his usual 'Now then, son', he just stared at him, playing outside at this time of night in his dressing gown, pyjamas and slippers. Victor ignored the ball, which had rolled back to his feet, and watched his father raise his head slightly, like a dog. Then his father turned away from him without having spoken a word, and went indoors.

Later that night, when Victor went to bed, he smelt his mother getting herself ready to go out. Irene came to look after him despite the problems she was having with her thyroid these days. He heard his mother asking his father, in her bended-knees voice, if they could take the ferry across the river to Wyley and drink at the pub there. Through his bedroom door he could see small points of light darting across the walls and ceiling as they both made their way downstairs, which meant that his mother was wearing jewellery. This is what they did after their fighting, they went drinking.

Once the front door had shut, he lay in bed in pyjama bottoms that were still wet, and timed his mother and father as they drove out of the estate and through Setton; past Spanish City, along Marine Parade, up the cliff to Watts Corner then down into South Wyley.

Victor imagined himself as Jake, the ferryman, wearing Jake's hat, which would keep slipping down over his eyes as he watched his parents standing in each other's arms at the front of the boat, facing out to sea. He imagined his mother's hair blowing out and half-covering his dad, while her feet shuffled in anticipation across the blue metal deck of the ferry. Every now and then she would turn round and wave at Jake, to ensure that when they got off she could get him to promise to wait for them to come back. No matter how late. Jake would agree, worried that it was the Hope & Anchor they were going to, the only building that threw out light in row after row of derelict housing, stretching down the headland to where the docks used to be. Even without the docks, or the boats, sailors still somehow found their way to the Hope & Anchor at Wyley.

The door shut after them, and they disappeared. Victor fell asleep at this point, and lost sight of them in his mind's eye.

When they came back out of the Hope & Anchor, Perkins fell through the doors laughing, and tried to throw Stella over his shoulder. The cement walls of the harbour were obscured by waves, and every now and then they caught the beam of St Mary's lighthouse several miles down the coast, falling out to sea. Perkins didn't say much, he just kept laughing and catching her in his arms. He didn't slide his hands down inside her coat as he sometimes did.

Stella wasn't wearing sensible shoes, and her feet were cold and wet, but Perkins's arms were warm. The smoke and bad looks in the pub had worn the make-up off her face, making it look eager. She was cold by the time they reached the ferry, and more relieved than she had expected to be at the sight of it moored by the old jetty.

Jake let them ride in the cabin so that they could keep themselves warm and him company. Silent company was still company to Jake. They clustered round the big red wheel, but were thrown about by the waves, so badly that even Perkins had to hold on to something. The crossing between the two headlands never usually took more than ten minutes, but that night it seemed to take twice as long. The sea was rough one minute they were riding high, free of it, and the next they fell, leaving their stomachs behind. Not unlike the sensation of riding a roller-coaster Perkins and Stella thought, but they didn't say anything to each other.

Eventually they saw the light at the end of the South Wyley jetty even though it kept disappearing.

'You shouldn't have made the crossing,' Stella reprimanded Jake, who only shrugged, not taking his eyes off the light, as if everything depended on the safe delivery of this man and woman to the shore.

Stella could smell smoke from the pub caught in her hair.

'Who would have brought you home if I hadn't?' Jake said, looking briefly at her.

'We could have walked.'

'Six miles?'

Nobody said anything. They reached the shore at last, but it took Jake a long time to get the boat steady, and it made a slow wrenching sound as it banged against the jetty even though it was calmer here than it had been out in the middle of the estuary. Jake, suddenly in a hurry, urged them off the boat

'You can't be picking up more people tonight?' Stella said, surprised.

'You never know who might be out there,' Jake replied.

'It's gone eleven,' Perkins said looking at his watch, the one Stella had bought him for Christmas.

Jake didn't say anything, he just stood there waiting for them to leave, not even taking his hand from the wheel. They were safe now and he was no longer interested. He turned the engine back up to full, and was gone within minutes. Not across the estuary again, but straight out to sea.

It took them ages to drive in their old car up through South Wyley and across the headland to Watts Corner because of the wind blowing the snow against them. An hour later they reached the Clayton Arms. They got out of the car, and Perkins walked right up to the window, peering through the gap in the curtains. Inside there were dim lights on, and people he recognised. He started banging at the door. The corner of a curtain was lifted, then dropped. He carried on banging.

'Come on,' Stella said, impatiently, 'you know you can't go in there.'

'I'm thirsty,' he said.

'They're shut.'

'They bloody aren't.'

She came over to where he was standing in front of the door. 'I'm cold.'

'You never feel the cold,' he said, turning round to look at her.

'I'm cold tonight. It's the sea,' she said, putting her arm in his.

He shook it off. When they got home they found Irene asleep in the armchair, where they left her. After going heavily up the stairs, Perkins fell on to the bed fully clothed, and was asleep in seconds. But she could tell, even asleep, that the fury from earlier in the evening was on him again.

Victor was never able to stay in bed once his eyes were open, and the next morning was no exception. He got out of bed and went straight downstairs, past the front room where Irene was asleep in the armchair, and into the cellar. It had been cold enough upstairs for him to see his own breath, and down here he was blowing smoke. There was an old workbench where his father kept an assortment of dangerous and not so dangerous tools, and where Victor spent a lot of his time chipping away at bits of driftwood and sea coal, transforming them into animals' heads. There was a can of Insect Doom on the corner of the bench that his father had given him to exterminate anything that crawled, having led him to believe that the cellar would be overrun most hours of the day and night.

The cellar had a window that looked out on to an overgrown forecourt in front of the house so that he could see the world as far up as most people's knees. He hadn't been in the cellar long that morning when he heard the thudding of his dad's boots on the stairs above, and something else more muffled. He wasn't doing anything in particular, just sitting at his bench on an old packing case, waiting for the day to begin and trying not to dwell on the fact that since his brother Will's birth, he had begun, ever so slightly, to hate his mother. When suddenly he saw her being dragged along in her nightdress, and her feet, as they passed the window, looked as though some animal had been gnawing at them.

She was screaming and when he heard the screams Victor's hand automatically went out for the insect spray. The door of the car, parked on the forecourt, was opened and she was pulled inside. It wasn't until then that he saw his father's boots, and couldn't work out why he had missed them before. They were shuffling in the snow and looked new compared to his mother's bare, bleeding feet. Then her feet disappeared and he heard his father trying to speak while crying at the same time.

'I'm nothing without you. Nothing. You know that.'

Victor couldn't hear whether his mother replied or not. She was shut inside the car.

'I'm nothing without you,' his father said again, but his voice was cracked now, as though these were the words that would bring about the end of the world.

The car started rocking, but his father wouldn't stop saying these words, over and over again, until Victor would have done anything to stop him, even if it meant shooting him.

Then it stopped, and there was the sound of the car engine starting. The next minute the car wheels started turning, slid past the window, and disappeared out of sight.

He had had his finger on the button of the canister of insecticide the whole time, unwittingly spraying it. For a moment he thought of running after them, as much from a growing fear of loneliness as anything, but then started to cry instead.

'Victor. Victor?'

It was Irene, screeching down at him from the top of the cellar steps with Will in her arms.

'Victor,' she carried on, 'are you down there?'

He walked slowly upstairs, keeping tight hold of his dressing-gown cord.

'They've gone,' he said.

Sergeant Pearce detected a certain amount of hysteria in himself that he was having difficulty repressing. He was exhausted but didn't dare sit down because he felt it would undermine the gravity of the situation. Instead, he continued to pace about Irene's caravan, carefully stepping over her feet because she was nursing the baby, Will.

The sergeant had been lying in bed when he heard the bang; an almighty bang. In the old days he would have been up like a shot, but he didn't have the back or the heart for it these days. His hand had gone for the bedside table where he kept a revolver still. Then he had turned over to Mrs Pearce and kissed her on the cheek.

'It's a strange old world,' he had said. But Mrs Pearce said nothing in reply, having slept through the bang, and his kiss.

He had said the same thing to Raymond Clarke when he

met him at the scene of the crime, up on North Cliff. He had seen the column of black smoke from two miles off, but when he got there only the bottom of the car remained. Sergeant Pearce had glimpsed pink among the wreckage, and the steel toecap of a man's workboot. Perkins's, he presumed.

Despite the magnificence of the scene, neither of them stood there for long; it was too cold in the snow. Even in the short time spent there, Sergeant Pearce managed to get covered in ash and his continual pacing was now covering the interior of Irene's caravan in a grey flurry. It was making the chandelier above them tinkle light-heartedly as well, which grated badly against the atmosphere in the caravan. Irene was jogging Will gently on her lap, her lips pressed against his head so that she could sit quite still and never have to take her eyes off Hal. Occasionally Sergeant Pearce would open the door to the caravan and stare up at the house where Victor lay in his bed pretending to sleep, watched over by Charlie Price. Every now and then Charlie would sing a few bars of a song, but didn't have the heart to sing it right through to the end.

Sergeant Pearce closed the caravan door, glanced quickly at Hal's bent head and tried to make a decision. He looked down at his uniform and brushed some ash off the front of it. He felt, for a moment, an intense helplessness. This catastrophe was beyond manipulation; it was far bigger than him.

'Apparently, you were having a liaison with one of the deceased.'

'Apparently?' Hal said.

'The whole town knows, for Christ's sake, and I have reason to believe that your relations with Stella Armstrong . . .'

'My relations?'

'Your relations', Sergeant Pearce continued, 'with the deceased may have led to the incineration of both parties. There will be an enquiry,' he managed to get out shakily. It was intended for Hal, and Hal knew, but didn't look up.

'Where is she?'

Sergeant Pearce stared at his bent head and thought of the

267

remains of the car sitting smouldering in the snow after Emergency Services had finished.

'With your cousin. At the Parlour,' he said.

Will stretched his tiny arms and legs in his sleep, and Hal stood up.

'The children?' Irene said.

'Victor's asleep,' Charlie Price said, stepping quietly into the caravan and pulling her cardigan around her. 'It's going to start snowing again any minute now,' she said, as if some hope lay in this.

'Shut the door,' Sergeant Pearce said pompously. He disliked his pompous voice, but he had no control over it.

'The children?' Irene insisted.

Sergeant Pearce disliked ambiguities, ambiguity in his book was the precursor of chaos. He liked to have the facts of a matter to hand; you could say them loud and clear, without shame. 'Orphans. Unless they have any living relatives?'

Charlie Price was shocked by the violence of this. 'But surely . . .'

'Wards of the State,' the sergeant insisted firmly.

Irene began rocking Will more thoroughly now.

Sergeant Pearce felt the hysteria rising again. These people with their impossible lives were closing rank on him, trying to suffocate him. Charlie's head moved closer to Will, leaning over the sleeping baby to kiss him so that between her and Irene the child almost disappeared from sight until, for a moment, Sergeant Pearce thought it really had vanished.

'Hal?' Charlie said softly at last. 'Did you hear what Sergeant Pearce said?'

'I did.'

'The children are going to be Wards of State.'

'I heard,' he mumbled.

'That means an orphanage.'

'Children's home,' Sergeant Pearce corrected her, paying the facts the attention they deserved.

'Hal,' Charlie Price hissed, not taking her eyes off her son. 'For God's sake, Hal.'

268

Hal looked up slowly at Will and his mother and Irene, standing over him. 'What if there are living relatives?'

Sergeant Pearce watched Hal in growing wonder, trying to stand his ground without fear. 'Such as who?'

'A father,' Charlie said.

This was more than he could bear. He stared at Hal and then at the baby, Will. These people were infinite. He thought about how he had kissed Mrs Pearce as she lay sleeping that morning. How they had always been content with their lot in life: food on the table, a roof over their heads, and how he had the good fortune to walk through life in uniform. How they had never asked for anything their whole lives, apart from one thing that hadn't been granted them. Again he thought of Mrs Pearce and the kiss he had left on her cheek. It was more than a man could bear to see Hal Price walk away from all of this, out of the flames, bearing a child in his arms.

'Do both children have a father still living?'

'Only Will.'

Sergeant Pearce breathed out slowly. 'You don't seem to have a very good track record with children though, do you, Hal? I seem to remember the last time we spoke it was over an incident involving a child.' He turned fully on Hal. 'Children are gifts, blessings. How can you sit there and claim to be that child's father? If you think for a second you'll ever walk away with that child in your arms . . . when Mrs Pearce . . . Mrs Pearce . . .' He grabbed hold of the kitchen surface, and as he started to sway the chandelier was sent swinging and the light from it reflected off the buttons on the front of his uniform, running across the walls and ceiling of the caravan. 'How dare you count yourself among the blessed.'

Delaval was sitting in an armchair in the Red Room at Ellison Court, laughing quietly as the child on his lap stood up and took hold of two handfuls of his hair. The child's mother, Mrs Higgins, who was dusting the mantelpiece behind his armchair, turned round and brushed the feather duster briefly over the child's nose. He squealed and carried on squealing as Delaval proceeded to tickle him.

'There was an accident this morning up at the old tinkers' camp on North Cliff.'

Delaval looked up, but carried on rolling the child backwards and forwards across his knees.

'A car went up in flames. My sister's husband, Bill Pearce, Sergeant Pearce,' Mrs Higgins said, giving a slight pause for pride, 'said it was arson. That's it,' she said, encouragingly to herself, 'and when I looked out of my window there was a column of black smoke rising up out of the top of North Cliff.'

Delaval looked more warily at her now.

'There was a man and woman from King Alfred's Road inside the car when it went up in flames, Bill said. They weren't married,' she added.

'But who was the man, Mrs Higgins?'

Mrs Higgins stared at her employer's unusually wanton appetite for detail.

'Man by the name of Perkins.'

Delaval stood up. 'I see,' he said, squeezing the child so hard it began to cry.

The temperature in the Parlour that morning wasn't dissimilar to that outside, and Raymond looked ill. It had taken a great deal of expertise to hold the stench of burnt flesh at bay. He glanced at the door to the annexe where the remains lay as the sound of someone half-running, half-falling down the stairs filled the Parlour.

'Harold,' Raymond said, looking up as his cousin arrived at the bottom of the stairs.

'Is she still here?' Hal said, picking himself up.

'Of course she is.'

Hal looked at Raymond. There was more ash in his hair than there had been in Sergeant Pearce's. 'Where?'

'The annexe,' Raymond said, watching him.

Hal looked at the door to the annexe. 'I want to see her. I came to see her.'

'There's not . . .' Raymond paused. 'Not much to see, Harold. Nothing. I'm sorry,' he added.

Hal squinted at him as if his eyes were having trouble adjusting to the light in the Parlour, but remained silent.

'I wouldn't go in there,' Raymond said suddenly as Hal's hand went out for the door.

Hal held Raymond's gaze steadily for a few more seconds then withdrew his hand slowly from the door and put it back in his pocket.

Raymond watched the light in Harold's eyes flicker out. People like Harold had it in them to simply drop off the edge of the world one day, and vanish. For a moment Raymond felt envy.

There was silence for a while, then he took hold of Hal's elbow and had gently started steering him towards the stairs when the telephone rang.

'That's right, this morning. Exact time of death unknown as yet. Tonight's issue, yes. Look, I only know what I know,' he said, anger creeping suddenly into his voice. His eyes never left Hal, making now towards the door again. 'There won't be a burial. We're taking them to the crematorium.' Raymond put the phone down. 'That was someone from the *Setton Echo*,' he explained.

'Everyone will know,' Hal said.

'It's procedure, Harold. At times like these you need procedure.'

'Times like these?' Hal repeated, staring at Raymond in horror. 'You bury them,' he said when he was halfway up the stairs, turning and pointing straight at Raymond.

'I will do. Good and proper.'

17

'So there you have it,' Hal finished awkwardly, glancing briefly at Will, then looking away.

The telephone on the counter started ringing, and with a jump Will realised that Hal was still holding his hand. He pulled it sharply away.

With a sigh, audible even above the thumps Victor was giving the pinball machine, the girl got off her stool and picked it up. 'Yeah? Oh.' She took the receiver away from her ear and started swinging it in her right hand, backwards and forwards through a jet of steam from the geyser.

'It's for you,' she said to Victor, trying unsuccessfully to hide the fact that she was impressed.

Victor glared at Hal, as if the unexpected phone call was something he was responsible for.

Will hadn't once taken his eyes off Hal's face since the story finished, and hardly noticed his brother passing.

Victor picked up the receiver, wiped the foundation off it where the girl had pressed it against her cheek, then listened without saying a word.

The girl went back to her stool and sat on the edge of it, staring. When the phone call came to an end he gave her the receiver to hang up.

'Come on,' Victor said, hoisting Hal to his feet.

'Where are we going now?' Will looked up at his brother.

'Come on. She's changed her mind. We're meeting her somewhere else.'

The younger boy silently followed his brother and Hal out of Moscadini's, watched by the girl behind the counter. He could see Hal clutching at Victor's arm mumbling, 'She? She?' And Victor shrugging him off.

At the door, Hal turned. From here, with his poor eyesight, Moscadini's still had the best view in the world of the Mediterranean Sea. He caught Victor's eye; Victor had been looking at the same view.

While they were inside snow had banked around the car and there was still more falling out of the sky.

'We might have to spend the night here,' Hal said.

'You're not spending the night anywhere. Will, get in the car.'

Will slid obediently into the back seat, brushing the snow off his hair.

Hal tried again and again to start the engine. He was blue all over now.

'Get that bloody engine started,' Victor said, raising his voice, livid at the sight of Hal's fingers grasping for the choke. The panic in his voice infected all of them. It was as if, suddenly, something was making its way from out at sea towards them, creeping slowly across the headland.

Hal peered frantically out beyond the windscreen and the falling snow while Will, terrified, was staring out of the back window now covered in condensation so that he could see nothing but shadows.

Hal wanted more than anything to open the window and take a lungful of air, to breathe in something new after all these years. He heard the scuffling sound of Will scratching his legs through his jeans, and remembered him doing this repeatedly in geography lessons.

'Who were we waiting for? Who was meant to come?' he said to Will.

'I want you to drive to Spanish City,' Victor cut in.

★

Raymond picked up the photograph again from Hal's bedside table and tapped his fingers on the glass for a while. Years of painstaking work gone to the dogs in one night. He watched himself in the triptych of mirrors as he put the photograph inside his coat, drew it out, put it back inside, then drew it out again. At last he shook his head, put the photograph back on the bedside table and left the room, forgetting to straighten out the eiderdown from where he had been sitting on the bed.

He heard the stairs creaking before he got to them. Just keep calm, Raymond, he said to himself, it's nothing but your conscience. He took a deep breath, then there was another creak coming from behind this time, from the bedroom. He turned slowly round, able to see clearly by the light of the streetlamp, but there was nobody there. Of course there was nobody there, the house had been empty when he arrived. He stood straining his eyes then shook his head. The next creak came from downstairs where it was much darker. He leant over the banister and peered down into the darkness. Before he could stop himself he called out instinctively, 'Stella?' Then banged the palm of one of his hands against the wall, cursing himself. Why did he have to go and say that? Without waiting a second longer he went downstairs, taking his sheepskin mittens out of his coat pocket and putting them on. He shut the front door behind him and got into the car. Once the engine was running he looked back up at the house.

He took the *Funeral Director on Business* card off the dashboard, opened the glove compartment and put it back in his card box. After hesitating a moment, he got the *Road Atlas of Great Britain* out and sat with it on his lap. He often did this if he had a serious decision to make. He would open the *Road Atlas* at random and study the page in front of him. Only now the coastline and place names were so familiar he quickly shut it, tossing it on to the back seat where it fell open again. He put the car into gear and pulled away from 77 Marine Parade. The car smelt of flowers, fresh flowers, and there was nothing he could do about it. He had to find Hal.

★

274

Several boards had been pulled away from the entrance to Spanish City so that there was enough space for either a child or desperate adult to slip through unnoticed. There was nothing new in this; the council had to replace its barricade at least once a month.

The walls of Spanish City were no longer white, and there was writing all over them. Looking up, Hal saw that the bull's head was still there. Whoever used Spanish City now had decided to keep the bull, and by not defacing it had somehow made it their own trophy. The bull had snow on its head, which made it look as though it was wearing a white mitre. Victor vanished through the hole in the boards, and the next minute Hal was pulled forcefully after him, landing inside Spanish City on all fours.

He was so disorientated that for a moment he was sure he could feel the sun on his back and the brush of skirts against his cheek. Then Victor was hauling him out of the snow back on to his feet where he wavered unsteadily for a few seconds before finding his balance. Victor's gun had made no new appearance since getting out of the car at Moscadini's. They all knew it was no longer necessary, especially here. Spanish City was the point of no return. Even empty as it now was.

None of the fairground rides were left apart from the covered platform the dodgems had once sped their way across. Just near where the waltzer used to stand there was a matador rubbish bin lying on its side half-buried beneath the snow, and the top of a coconut showing beside it. Straight ahead of them, Hal knew, was the Charleston, its huge framework rising up into the sky. It was deathly silent and he heard Will breathing behind him.

'It's all right,' Hal said instinctively to him, for the second time that night.

'Who said it wasn't?' Will responded, defensively.

Raymond drove slowly down King Alfred's Road, but there was no sign of Harold's car there. He paused only briefly outside number 16; it was no longer safe to stop for long in the

275

estates, which had become notorious crime fields. He noticed a disgorged sofa in the front garden and felt glass under the car tyres as he pulled away.

He then drove back along Marine Parade and up to Watts Corner, turning right towards Moscadini's, a route he had studiously avoided for years. When there was no sign of Harold's car there, and no lights on in the building either, he hit the car door several times with his elbow out of sheer frustration. Breathing heavily, he was about to turn round and grab hold of the *Road Atlas of Great Britain* again when he thought suddenly of the photograph on Harold's bedside table. Turning to look over his shoulder he saw in the distance the patchy lights of the promenade, just about stretching as far as Spanish City. He let his head fall back against the car seat. It was just possible.

They traipsed towards The Palace. Looking back over his shoulder Hal saw Will picking his way across the snow, more eager to keep up with them than he would ever let on. He looked like a sparrow, the sort of bird that becomes inconspicuous in a flock, but that on its own looks like a rare breed. He must have been freezing in his T-shirt and denim jacket, dragging his heavy boots along behind him.

'Come on, Nancy,' Victor said as they reached the covered walkway, pushing his brother roughly towards another hole in the boards across the entrance to the Penny Arcade. 'Will doesn't like the dark. I could never get him to come here because of the dark. But tonight he knows he doesn't have a choice,' Victor said.

'Shut up,' Will said, not in the mood to be scared, and preoccupied with wanting to keep Hal in front of him. Hal, who was no longer Pricey, but his father. A father who had the power to raise the dead.

Hal could feel Will's fear as they entered the darkness. Light from holes in the ceiling illuminated the old machines. He could see, dimly, Geordie's cloakroom, the change kiosk and deep darkness to the left where Barry Smallwood's miniature railway used to be. And there was still the sound of money. Everywhere, then much closer as he saw the glint of a coin Victor held in his hand.

'What d'you think, Uncle Hal,' he said, tossing the coin up into the darkness.

He was going to play the wise monkeys.

'Don't,' Hal shouted. 'Please don't. I can't bear to hear them.' He felt Will walk into the back of him.

'Don't, Victor,' Will echoed. The thought of monkeys, alive or stuffed, terrified him and he was the first to push himself through the next hole into The Palace itself, where it was at last light enough to breathe.

After a moment's deliberation that he hoped went unnoticed, Victor gave the machine a kick then followed Hal and Will through the hole.

Some of the glass in the dome was broken and they all made their way instinctively towards the centre of the dance floor, to where snow was falling.

'Built for two thousand people this was. Think about it, Will. Try and see it then,' Hal persisted. 'Glorious it was. Things aren't glorious like that any more. Come dancing . . . anything could happen.'

The sign for the Tropicana was above the bar, and there were plastic palm trees still growing out of the stage.

Hal could definitely hear the sounds of music and dancing now.

'I know you,' Victor shouted at Hal.

His voice echoed strangely, and Will whipped round to see who was speaking. It no longer sounded like Victor.

'And you need to know,' Victor said, shaking Will.

Will turned frantically away then yanked himself out of Victor's grip and fell backwards. He stared up at the sky, which was orange from the snow reflecting thousands of streetlamps, then crawled away and got slowly back to his feet.

'I know. He told me.' He tried to point his finger at Hal, but the air between them was too thick.

'You told him?' Victor turned viciously on Hal.

'Only the beginning,' Hal said.

'Only the beginning?' Will was staring wildly at him.

'Irene's coming soon. She'll tell you.'

'Irene?'

'The old woman, Irene Trench.' He let out a small laugh then grabbed hold of Hal, taking handfuls of his coat. 'She came to see me and told me about Charlie Price; Harold Price. Then it all fell into place: Uncle Hal. All those years I'd lost hold of came back. The beach hut, the bloody donkeys, knickerbocker glories, it all came back. And most of all, Uncle bloody Hal. You're the man. The intruder who wouldn't go away.'

'I couldn't help myself. If you'd known, Victor . . . I couldn't help myself.'

'What about what happened? The car . . . them . . . everything going whoosh,' Victor roared, 'up in flames.'

'Victor,' Hal began, heavily, as if he'd been waiting to speak for many years, 'even if I'd known beforehand . . . the fire, everything, I'd have still done it. I had to be with her. You have to know that.'

'That night, the last night. You came to the house. You.'

Hal could feel the wet from the snow rising up through his legs and thought that if he didn't move soon he would be frozen there for ever.

'I couldn't help myself.'

'And afterwards?'

Hal's hair had gone from grey to white there was so much snow in it.

'You knew something that would have changed everything. That would have saved us. D'you know what happened to us?'

'I've seen . . .'

'You've seen nothing, heard nothing, know nothing. When did you first lay eyes on Will?'

'When he walked into my geography classroom.'

'Eleven years old.'

'He would have been.'

'That wasn't the first time. The first time was much earlier, how big was he? How big?'

Hal made a cramped gesture with his hands.

Victor stared at the space between the hands.

'How new was he?'

'Brand new,' Hal whispered.

'That's it. You've got it. You've got it. Will is the consequence, the consequence of your actions. And who does he look like? Will, come here.'

The boy's boots squeaked as he shuffled over the wet floor.

'Now, take a good look at him.'

Victor kept hold of Hal with one hand as Will came to stand in front of them. 'Look.'

'I know. I saw it when he walked into my classroom.'

'Who?' Victor yelled.

'He looks like his mother. Like Stella.'

'And you. He looks like you.' Victor let go of Will.

The make-up on Hal's face was no longer smudged. The snow steadily falling had turned it into grey stripes of paint running slowly over his nose, cheeks and chin. He tried to wipe it off and the back of his hand went grey. He was neither one thing nor the other, neither Hal Price nor the pantomime cat. He registered the disgust on Victor's face at the sight of him. Not pity, just heartfelt disgust.

'He looks like you,' Victor repeated, stepping away from the old man. Hal didn't have to remain standing where he was, under the broken dome exposed to the elements, but he did.

They all turned round as the sound of someone feeding themselves through the gap in the boards filled The Palace.

'Harold?' a voice called out.

'Raymond?'

Within minutes Raymond Clarke was making his way hesitantly across the dance floor, his hands in their mittens still.

'Harold?' he said again. 'It's Wednesday night.'

Hal stared blankly at him.

'Where were you? What on earth are you doing here?' He made no reference to the two boys, and tried to laugh.

'Why are you here, Raymond?'

'Me?' Raymond said, disbelief in his voice. 'To find you, Harold. I was worried something might have happened.' He glanced quickly at the other two then put on a smile as he turned to Hal again. 'We couldn't have you casting yourself adrift in the world, could we.'

Hal instinctively shook his head, but said nothing.

When he continued to show no sign of intending to speak, Raymond shifted uncomfortably. He had brought in the smell of fresh flowers with him, flowers sculpted into bouquets, wreaths. Even he could smell it, despite the decay here, despite the snow.

'Everything all right, Harold? Not in trouble of any sort, I hope?' he said briskly. Harold didn't answer and Raymond was losing patience. 'We spend every Wednesday evening together,' he explained to Victor.

It occurred to Hal, watching Raymond stand where he used to dance, speaking to him as though he were a child, that he had never really had anything to be afraid of, apart from Raymond. Immaculate cousin Raymond, who had been there from the beginning, throughout the middle and was still here at the end. Raymond who was, in business terms, that strange phenomenon called a success. There were now branches of Clarke & Sons throughout the north of England. In towns better suited to success these days than Setton. God knows, Daisy had put enough effort into persuading him to move. First for her sake, then his, then the children's. Nostalgia was the devil himself, Daisy said, and makes you do nothing but run round in circles like a headless chicken. But that wasn't why Raymond stayed: he had no time for nostalgia, he was an undertaker, and a successful one at that. Raymond put any soul he had into the inscriptions he wrote for the headstones of strangers. No, the reason the Clarkes remained Setton-bound was Hal. Raymond stayed to watch Hal.

'You've gone to a lot of trouble on my behalf,' Hal said to him.

Raymond nodded.

'Been up at the house?'

Raymond nodded again.

'Elsewhere and now here, after all these years. Spanish City, derelict and deserted. And just because I wasn't at home.'

'It's Wednesday night,' Raymond reminded him quietly. Then added, 'God, Harold, look at yourself. You're a mess. Why don't you let me take you home?'

'He's not going anywhere,' Victor said, suddenly kicking into life.

Raymond looked at him with hatred. But Victor had broken the spell, and Hal moved out from underneath the dome, away from the snow and across the dance floor. He sang a few lines from an Al Bowley song and shuffled out the movements of a dance.

'You're senile,' Raymond began to hiss.

'Don't speak to him that way,' Will muttered, stepping out of the shadows.

Hal halted his dance and turned at the sound of Will behind him. His hand went out for the boy.

'I know you,' Will said. 'You're the undertaker, Raymond Clarke. You used to come to the home. I saw you once with Radford in the office. You wanted to know about post, if I'd got post at all. Post or visitors. You'd got Radford wrapped round your little finger.'

Will was standing behind Hal, close to him.

Raymond looked frantically at all three of them.

Suddenly a woman's voice called out from above them, 'Who were you afraid might write to or visit Will? Who, Raymond?'

Victor went running up the steps on to the balcony and disappeared into the corner by the Tropicana. When he re-emerged he was followed by Irene, her hair flying out from her head in all directions it was so brittle from the amount of dye in it. The rest of her looked brittle as well. It wasn't so much that she had aged as simply dried up.

She kept her eyes down as she crept across the wet floor. Nobody helped the old woman because they were afraid of touching her. She stopped in front of Hal, and at last looked up at him. Her eyebrows had been replaced by a thin pencil line, drawn by a very steady hand. There were at least six earrings dangling from each of her earlobes, which made a strange tinkling sound when she moved her head.

'You're an old man, Hal,' she said, giving a quick nod of contentment. 'An old man.'

That was all she had to say to him. She ignored Raymond completely and turned to Will. She slipped but managed to grab hold of Victor's arm because he was standing so close to her. Once she had steadied herself she tried to push him away.

Will watched, terrified, as the rustling old woman made her way towards him, her bright eyes fixed on his.

'So this is the child.'

'Will,' Victor hissed as he started to back away. 'Will.'

'Shush,' Irene said, 'you're scaring him.' She made a sign to Victor to leave them alone, but he stayed where he was.

She tried to find Will's hand, but he tugged it away behind his back.

'I see Charlie in his face. Just a bit of her, don't you, Hal?' she said, shaking her head and smiling kindly at Will's attempts to avoid her touch. 'That's right, that's right, keep away from old age – don't know where it's been, do you?' She laughed approvingly. 'I tried to see the children once,' she carried on, glancing at Hal, 'when they were at the old home, the one above the hostel for the deserving poor on the sea front. Lovely view out to sea you had there,' she added to Will. 'Do you remember?'

Will shook his head.

'Then all the philanthropists died, and there were no more deserving poor, only undeserving, and the home closed down. Usurped by a leisure centre. They moved them to Radford's place on the estate. You didn't try to see the children did you, Hal?'

Victor laughed out of habit at somebody being tormented.

'And where are you now, Hal?'

'Spanish City.'

282

'Charlie's Spanish City. Delaval gave it to Charlie. And she had the sense', Irene went on, her voice rising for the first time, 'to leave it to Will. Is Will sixteen yet, Hal?'

'To the day,' Hal mumbled.

'So now we're standing in Will's Spanish City. Charlie never lost sight of you,' she said, turning back to Will. 'But you, Hal. You . . .' she trailed off, her attention caught by the snow still falling. She watched its progress silently from the sky, through the top of the broken dome.

'You should have been easy, Hal,' Raymond cut in. 'You should have been no trouble at all, but there's something about you, something that makes a man unable to let go . . . like he should be able to.'

'Rest is what you deserve after all these years, isn't it, Raymond?' Irene said, with sympathy.

Raymond looked hopefully at her.

'And peace? Peace is what I want. Always something to be worried about,' he started to mutter rapidly. 'There was never any knowing if she'd try and come back, find out for herself about the children. There I've been every morning for the past God knows how many years of my life thinking today's the day I'll see her walking the streets of Setton bringing disaster in her wake. Or maybe I'll go into work and find her lying awake on the Parlour table.'

'Who, Raymond? Who is it you've been afraid of all these years. It's not just Hal, is it?' Irene said softly.

Raymond was taking small steps backwards glancing nervously about him.

The gun, which had made a re-appearance in Victor's left hand, now started to jerk between Raymond and Hal. Hal pushed Will behind him, unsure who was the least predictable opponent: Victor or Raymond.

'What's he talking about?' Victor started shouting at Irene, but without taking his eyes off Raymond. 'Who?'

'Stella,' Irene said, quietly.

'Stella's dead.' It was the first time Hal had acknowledged this out loud.

Raymond shook his head, spittle flying.

'They were laid out in the annexe that morning.' Hal lowered his voice not wanting to remember.

'Only Perkins was there.'

Raymond's head was flicking from side to side, he no longer had any control over it. 'That morning I woke up and saw a column of smoke rising up from North Cliff. I went running out of the house in the early hours and drove towards it. I knew, instinctively, that everything likely to bring chaos and disorder to our lives, to Setton, had gone up in that cloud of smoke. But when I got there I realised I was wrong. Whatever the column of smoke did take up with it, it didn't take Stella. The only remains in the car were Perkins's. There was no sign of Stella. I don't know what happened, how it happened, but she had gone.'

'But I saw them,' Victor cut in. 'I saw them with my own eyes, and I saw him put first her then himself into the car.'

Raymond looked hopeful for a split-second, then shook his head. 'She wasn't there and nobody had seen her; everybody presumed she had died with Perkins in the blaze. That was the myth. They gave it to me, they believed it. The good people of Setton believed it; Sergeant Pearce believed it.'

'That morning in the Parlour,' Hal said slowly, 'I thought she was on the other side of the annexe door.'

'No. She was gone. If you'd been there, in my position . . . if you'd been me . . .'

'Raymond,' Hal said, beseeching.

But Raymond wasn't listening. 'There'll be no more dancing here. Wasn't I a good dancer, Harold?'

'The best, Ray. The very best.' He paused. 'But you see, I loved her, Ray. I loved her more than anything. Do you understand?'

Raymond stared unblinking at him, then banged his hands together in their sheepskin mittens three times.

'You knew she was alive. All this time. You.'

Raymond stood still for a second as Victor automatically fired off three shots. Then he started to run across the dance floor, sprawling off balance, and Victor ran after him.

The next minute shots started to come back out of the corner, and it was as if Victor could see people, crowds of people, in The Palace and he was firing shots at all of them. Hal pulled Will on to the floor, pressing his face down into it, his hand round the back of the boy's head, and shifting his body so that it was half-covering him.

There were no more shots. Suddenly the air was full of a different sound, and Hal felt once again the brush of skirts against his cheek. Will winced as the snow quickly saturated his clothes, but Hal kept his arm around him and his body over him to protect him from the feet of the dancers he heard all around them, and Will let him.

Epilogue
Great Salt Lake, Utah,
Spring 1981

The exit signs to the State Park beaches along the Interstate had 'closed' written over them. The beaches had been flooded out of existence. It wasn't yet dark but the day was closing in by the time they found the man with his two boats: a red one and a blue one. At first he had no intention of hiring out either of the boats, but in the end agreed to let his son take them out on to the lake in the blue one. They were obviously the first people who had asked after the Spanish City in a long time.

The boy, who was the same age as Will, had a lisp, and Hal didn't catch his name. He spoke non-stop, displaying an energetic local patriotism, but if Hal stopped concentrating for more than a few seconds it sounded as though the boy was speaking in a foreign language.

Hal's clothes were stained with sweat. They had arrived in Utah during the middle of a heat wave and for May it was unbearably hot. His shirt was badly crumpled from having fallen asleep that afternoon on their bed in the Grand Hotel. Where they had left Will, who wanted to see the Spanish City later, alone.

The sound of the boat's motor was momentarily obliterated by a train passing on the Union Pacific railway. Lit carriages hurtled along the lakeside, and were then gone, leaving the motor sounding tiny in comparison. So tiny that Hal almost wished he was on the train rather than out on the lake in a boat with only a lisping boy at the helm.

In the distance now the golden domes of the Spanish City could be clearly seen, the last of the day's sun catching them. The boy turned round.

'There it is,' he said.

Hal nodded and felt Stella's hand, which had crept along the seat, take hold of his.

The boy frowned at the two old folk sat there holding hands in his boat, then his face broke into a smile, and he shook his head in disbelief at life.

'That what you came for?' he said.

Hal nodded.

'D'you wanna get closer? We can get closer.'

Before either of them had time to answer, he pulled suddenly on the motor and sent them speeding off towards the sinking pleasure palace. Sitting upright it was as if he had taken the weight of their intent on to his own shoulders and now, like them, saw nothing but the Spanish City on the horizon.

The pier on which the whole city had once stood was under water, and it was difficult to judge how high the walls had been. There were waves breaking against them.

'Where's the roller-coaster?' Hal said. 'I can't see it.' He tried to keep the panic out of his voice.

'Won't see it from here. We'll have to go inside. Wanna go inside?' the boy said.

He steered the boat with difficulty around to the front of the pier. The main entrance to the Spanish City was now partly submerged, but the boy managed to ease the boat beneath the arch then automatically cut the motor. The room they sailed into was cavernous. The waves bumped them along the length of a cocktail bar, one of five, and a grand staircase rose up out of the water, balustrade intact, to the floor above. The wall at the far end looked miles away.

'Used to be the main dance hall. Biggest one at the City. Black and white floor somewhere under here.'

Stella let her hand trail in the water, but soon brought it out, suddenly afraid of finding that she was touching the heads of dancers.

The boy waited for them to speak, but neither of them did. A sign with a list of prohibited behaviour on the dance floor knocked against the side of the boat as the boy started the motor up again. The sudden sound echoed. The boat made its way across the dance floor, oblivious to the floating debris, and through the window at the other end. They were outside again, in the hollow centre of the old Spanish City, and there were the coaster tracks, a well-engineered tangle, stretching out in all directions across the top of the water.

'There she is.'

The tracks, no longer suspended in air, now dipped down under the water.

'You rode this?' Hal said at last to Stella.

She nodded.

'You've been here before?' the boy lisped, sounding as indignant as if he had just been cheated of something. 'Loading platform was just about here,' he added, nodding his head towards the set of iron stilts that had once supported it. He was suddenly more distrustful of them. A sign on the wall reminded riders to remove their hats before getting into the coaster cars.

Stella laughed when she read it. 'Of course,' she said, 'they would have worn hats.' The last time she had worn one was at Irene's funeral. Irene, who had brought her back to Setton, and back from the dead.

The waves were getting larger and the boy was enjoying steering the boat underneath the tracks where they emerged from the lake. The sun, now virtually gone, cast long shadows of all three of them across the walls. And as Stella turned to watch them move, she caught sight of some writing on the wall. She asked the boy to steer closer, which he did after looking pointedly at the darkening sky. He could only hold the boat steadily against the wall for a while, but it was long enough to see the symbol that had been gouged into the stone then traced over with a black pen: ∞

The boy tilted his head to the side.

'A figure of eight. We made one of those at school with a piece of paper. It's a Möbius strip; a one-sided continuous surface. The only one in our universe.'

Hal, staring at the boy (now flushed), tilted his head sideways as well. 'Or . . .' he said, slowly, 'an aerial view of the Charleston.'

The boy frowned, then grinned indulgently at Hal's light-hearted reading.

Stella traced the symbol with her finger and turned suddenly to Hal. She knew now why they had come, and it wasn't to see the Spanish City or the remains of the coaster whose tracks looked more precarious than ever.

'Years ago, I went to Pompeii, and the thing that moved me most was some writing . . . graffiti . . . that they had found on the walls of one of the houses. I can't remember what it said. It doesn't matter. What does matter is that, after the discovery of this amorous graffiti, the house was referred to as "The House of the Lovers".'

The boy looked away, unable to tell in the failing light whether the elderly woman was crying or not. Without a word he steered them round.

'After all this, we're still here,' Stella said, taking hold of Hal's arms. 'We're still here.'